Tales of
Beatnik Glory

Among the books, tracts and collections written by Ed Sanders:

The Valorium Edition of the Entire Extant Works of Thales the Milesian (With an introduction by Aristotle), The Fuck You Press, New York, 1963.

Poem From Jail, City Lights Books, San Francisco, 1963.

Peace Eye, Frontier Press, Buffalo, 1966

Egyptian Hieroglyphics, Institute of Further Studies, Canton, N.Y., 1973.

20,000 A.D., North Atlantic Books, Plainfield, Vt., 1976.

Hymn to Maple Syrup & Other Poems, P.C.C. Books, Woodstock, N.Y., 1985.

Thirsting for Peace in a Raging Century Selected Poems 1961–1985, Coffee House Press, Minneapolis, Minn., 1987.

Fame & Love in New York, Turtle Island Books, Berkeley, 1980.

Investigative Poetry, City Lights Books, San Francisco, 1976.

The Z-D Generation, Station Hill Press, Barryton, N.Y., 1981.

The Family—The Manson Group and Aftermath, Signet/New American Library, 1990.

Vote (co-author) Warner Paperback, 1972.

DISCOGRAPHY

Sanders Truckstop, Reprise Records, 1970.

Beer Cans on the Moon, Reprise Records, 1972.

Star Peace—a musical drama, New Rose Records & Olufsen Records, 1987.

Songs in Ancient Greek, Olufsen Records, 1990.

CANTATAS & MUSICAL DRAMAS

The Municipal Power Cantata, 1978.

The Karen Silkwood Cantata, 1979.

Tales of Beatnik Glory

Volumes I and II

Ed Sanders

CITADEL UNDERGROUND

Citadel Press
CAROL PUBLISHING GROUP
New York

First Citadel Underground Edition 1990

Copyright © 1975, 1990 by Ed Sanders

A Citadel Press Book
Published by Carol Publishing Group

Editorial Offices
600 Madison Avenue
New York, NY 10022

Sales & Distribution Offices
120 Enterprise Avenue
Secaucus, NJ 07094

In Canada: Musson Book Company
A division of General Publishing Co. Limited
Don Mills, Ontario

Volume I was first published by Stonehill Publishing
Company, New York 1975. A few stories were published
in literary magazines: "Sappho on East Seventh" in
Sulfur, "The Muffins of Sebek" in *Smoke Signals,*
"Auden Buys Some Diapers" in *Credences.* Many thanks
to the editors.

Queries regarding rights and permissions
should be addressed to: Carol Publishing Group,
600 Madison Avenue, New York, NY 10022

Manufactured in the United States of America.
10 9 8 7 6 5 4 3 2 1

Carol Publishing Group books are available at special discounts
for bulk purchases, for sales promotions, fund raising, or
educational purposes. Special editions can also be created to
specifications. For details contact: Special Sales Department,
Carol Publishing Group, 120 Enterprise Ave., Secaucus, NJ 07094

Library of Congress Cataloging-in-Publication Data

Sanders, Ed
    Tales of beatnik glory / by Ed Sanders ; volumes I and II.
        p.   cm.
    ISBN 0-8065-1172-9 :
    I. Title.
PS3569.A49T35   1990   90-2270
813'.54—dc20   CIP

Thanks to Allen Ginsberg and Bob Holman, my pals in perf-po. Thanks to Margaret Wolf, Esther Mitgang, and to Rochelle Kraut, Elinor Nauen and Lorna Smedman for the perf-po data, and to Dan Levy.

And to the memory of Jeffrey Steinberg, Al Fowler, Szabo, Jim Kolb, Phil Ochs, Ted Berrigan, Ellen Bryant and others gone too soon.

Thanks to those who were in the bistros, the cafes, the demonstrations, the sit-ins, the pads, the parks, my brothers and sisters of those years. And thanks also to my friend George Butterick, also taken from us decades too soon, who provided an exemplar of W.H. Auden's handwriting.

Contents

Volume II

Introduction

THESE STORIES are set in the Lower East Side of New York City, where I lived from 1960 to 1970. They are arranged chronologically, and trace the interconnected lives, from the late '50s through the first half of the '60s, of a group of poets, writers, painters, musicians, radicals, Freedom Riders, anti-war activists and partisans of the beat struggle in America.

It was a very intense decade in the Lower East Side, and I was in the middle of it as a publisher of countless mimeographed tracts and literary magazines and as the founder of the Peace Eye Bookstore, a cultural center and scrounge lounge popular in its day. It was at the Peace Eye Bookstore that Tuli Kupferberg and I organized in late '64 the folkrock ensemble of poets known as The Fugs.

I moved out of the Lower East Side at the end of a frenetic ten years. In 1973 I began a study of rebel artists in ancient Egypt, for a cycle of poems called "Egyptian Hieroglyphics." I spent days in the New York Public Library researching the faint traces of rebellion in the ancient Egyptian Imperium. Out of those researches grew the idea for *Tales of Beatnik Glory*.

It was a time of personal turbulence for me, the end of 13 years of nonstop turmoil. The Watergate hearings were underway and the nation was keening beneath the sores of an unjust war. I had just spent two and a half years studying the Manson group, for my book, *The Family*.

I felt healed to return, in my writing, to an era which I genuinely loved and understood, and one I was sure I could limn with a wild candor featuring humor and utmost seriousness.

The American socio-political background of the early '60s suffuses these stories: the execution of Caryl Chessman in '60, the U.S. invasion of Cuba's Bay of Pigs of '61, the Freedom Rides of '61, the Cuban Missile Crisis of '62, the drive against Atmospheric Nuclear Tests, the Birmingham Bombing of '63, the Great March on Washington of '63, the klan and church burners, the censors and those who would have banned eros from the American Imperium, the menace of J. Edgar Hoover and the Secret Police intermixed with decent police forces who ultimately let Freedom grow, and who refused to allow America to become a right wing fortress, the assassination of Kennedy, The Mimeograph Revolution for poetry, the world of the underground film makers, and the rise of the Vietnam War in '64 and '65 as a national nightmare.

The timidity of 1950s American culture was swept aside as it dawned on an entire generation that there was oodles of freedom guaranteed by the United States Constitution that was not being used. Out of that knowledge a generation of Shelleyan eleutherarchs arose, strengthened by the complex and beautiful trends of Beat/Objectivist/Black Mountain poetry, modern painting, left wing politics and jazz.

ii

One of the basic visions that inspired us at the time was the salvation of the American city. In my poetry I called it Goof City, a city of freedom for all to relax, where poverty was banished and wealth truly shared. It was the civilization for which the poet Charles Olson hungered, "an actual earth of value—to construct it."

Kant's *Prolegomenon to Any Future Metaphysics* was a big influence on me at the time, and I thought those entire Civil Rights/Human Liberation years were subsumed beneath a complication of eternal principles, which we could seek out, emulate, and make to rhyme with our lives.

When I first visited the Lower East Side in the late '50s, and throughout the years of these tales, the World War II rent controls were still in place. There were cheap pads, cheap food and a person didn't have to have five part-time jobs to survive. One of America's lasting disgraces—its lack of concern for affordable and dignified housing for all—was not so much in evidence then. That is, the fuel of greed and political corruption had not wrecked the right to affordable habitat for regular people. The Lower East Side was a zone of poverty to be sure, but the late 20th century Rat Race was just a right wing fantasy few ever dreamed they would have to face.

Some of us were sure that we were the ones who had discovered the Lower East Side as a Power Zone, although we soon learned how it had been discovered over and over for two hundred years by the beaten-down, the broken, the rebellious, the radicals, the socialists, the anarcho-syndicalists, the suffragettes and feminists, the Trotskyites, and in our time by the bards and pot-heads, the jazz hips, and those just passing through on the way to the Gold-Paved Streets of the West.

The Lower East Side had been a slum since the population growth following the War of 1812 when "prosperous" residents moved from their houses in the L.E.S. These houses fell into the hands of real estate agents and boarding house keepers. Large rooms in buildings were partitioned into smaller rooms, lightless, without windows. Rear tenement houses were built where once stood Dutch kitchen gardens.

In the '60s one heard an occasional rooster, but we learned that in the 19th century some tenements had hogs in the cellar. In 1867 swine were banned from scavenging at large, and there were protest riots. In 1869 the Board of Health, under the urging of reformers, ordered the cutting of more than 46,000 windows in interior rooms in L.E.S. tenements, for ventilation and health reasons of course, and also as a safeguard against dark bedroom depravity. These strange windows, painted over and usually unable to be opened, we used in the '60s as frames for our posters or mandalas.

I tried to bring some of the flavor of the Lower East Side's history to stories such as "Farbrente Rose" and "A Night at the Cafe Perf-Po." In the center of it all was Tompkins Square Park, named after an early governor who led the fight to ban slavery in New York State. The park has had a long history of social foment. The homeless who live there in the early 1990s are echoes of the poverty riots of 1894 and those "incomprehensible economic collapses" that New York always seems to grant, every few years, to its poor.

It seemed to me that the essence of the moil and toil of my generation was contained in these archetypal streets. Everything that was good and bad about America in the

'60s seemed distilled and boldly drawn in the Lower East Side.

Some locations in this book, such as Stanley's Bar and the Charles Theater, actually existed, but others such as the Total Assault Cantina, the House of Nothingness Café, The Luminous Animal Theater, The Mindscape Gallery, The Café Perf-Po and the Anarchist Coal Collective, should have existed, but never did.

In creating these stories, I came to love many of their characters—Sam Thomas, Claudia Pred, Cynthia Pruitt, Talbot the Great, John Barrett, Past Blast, Rose Snyder, the Mother-in-Law, and even the flawed Llaso, the flawed Andrew Kliver, the flawed Uncle Thrills and Johnny the Foot.

Even though the characters are fictitious, to me it's as if they were actually alive, and even still alive, and I hope to continue to trace their histories in Volume III.

I wanted to bring some sense of the spiritual hunger of the era, so there are stories with ghosts, religious guilt, and spiritual salvation. Among them are the stories, "Cynthia" and "Sappho on East 7th," a sho-sto-gho-po, or short story ghost poem.

It was an era that saw the introduction of LSD and widespread use of marijuana, peyote and other so-called soft drugs. But there were many, many lives wrecked by heroin and speed. Accordingly, it's appropriate to underline that some aspects of some of the lifestyles in some of these stories can be dangerous to your health, if emulated in a relentless, self-destructive way.

Some mention should be made of the word "beatnik." Most of my generation laughed when they were called beats. In fact, Beatnik and Beat were two of the great pejoratives of the era, but how magnetic and alluring it

v

was to rebellious youth when the squares tossed the word "beatnik" around with stupid abandon! It was as good as Turgenev's "nihilist," the centenary of which word occurred just in time for the birth of Beatnik.

The generation might better have been called the Other Generation, in the Rimbaudian sense of "Je est un autre." Poet Ted Berrigan showed us that in 1964 when he came up with the name of one of the better underground newspapers of the time, *The East Village Other*.

I worked steadily on Volume I of *Tales of Beatnik Glory* through 1973 and much of '74. Late that year Jeffrey Steinberg of Stonehill Publishing Company called to ask if I were interested in writing a book about Timothy Leary. I was not, but I mentioned that I had finished *Tales of Beatnik Glory*. He asked to see it, and I sent it to him, he liked it, and he published it, to my lasting gratitude, in the fall of '75.

A few years went by before I began serious work on Volume II. Again, as with Volume I, it came about as a result of prolonged research for some poems. I had begun inventing small electronic musical instruments to accompany my poetry at readings—the Pulse Lyre, the Talking Tie and others.

In '81 I decided to write a poem in imitation of the ancient Greek poet Archilochus, that is, a poem to be part chanted, part sung. The work was to be called "Farbrente Rose." It was to trace the life of a rebel union leader in New York City early in the century, a Yiddish-speaking socialist.

I read all I could about the history of the East Side, and began hanging out there for the first time in over ten years. I decided it was time to write a second volume of *Tales*. I blocked it out in my mind, and realized that it was going to take two more volumes, for a total of three, to take these interlocked lives through the rest of the '60s and into the early '70s, at which time I felt an era would have been traced.

Again it was a time of turbulence in my life. I was busy fighting environmental battles in my new Power Zone, a town in upstate New York. I would work on *Tales of Beatnik Glory* in the mornings and then sally forth to protect the environment.

I completed a draft by 1984, then set it aside as other books, projects and events interceded. In '86 and '87 there was work on my collected poems, *Thirsting for Peace in a Raging Century*, and the composition and recording of a three-act musical drama, *Star Peace*, and an album of musical settings of ancient texts, *Songs in Ancient Greek*.

From July 1988 through the first half of 1989 were months of moil as I chaired the committee to pass an environmentally sensitive zoning ordinace for the Town of Woodstock. During this time, again, as in 1984, I devoted my morning writing periods to adding new stories and polishing those already written, for *Tales*, Volume II.

Dan Levy contacted me about republishing Volume I in the Citadel Underground series. I showed him Volume II, and Citadel offered to publish the two volumes in a single edition, for which I am grateful.

It was sustainedly thrilling to write these tales. I love the milieu, the times, the fun, the fury, the abysms, the truth, the moil, the capers, the games, the goofing, the fulfillment that were the times described in these stories.

The years drift onward, and the *Workers of the World Relax!* beat goof vision still holds strength at the end of a violent century. It stands against conformity and dullness, while it dances in the time-track for spontaneity and experiment, for social justice, for abundance, and for triumph over the hideous forces of warfare and eighty hour Rat Race work weeks.

Ed Sanders
Woodstock, New York
January 1990

viii

Volume I

The Mother-in-Law

WHEN SHE MARRIED the dirty beatnik, the calamity of it spiraled upward and outward through the extant family tree. That a girl of impeccable family, destined to marry well and wealthily, beautiful, conversant in three languages, with nine years of piano study behind her, should stoop to wed a mumbling, shabby, poetry-writing person with an unknown family from an unknown place, perhaps Nebraska, was a profound shock that sent the parents into a numbed period of consulting the police, lawyers, private investigators, and laws involving insane asylums.

As for the beat poet, he didn't care. The parents were just another couple of notches on the stick of squares. This was his attitude: They do not exist. And if they try to exist, I will travel with their daughter, my love, where they do not. And this was the message he once bothered to convey, after which there was no message from the accused beatnik to the parents, only silence.

The bazooka-spews of hostility, however, began years before the wedding. They met in a café on MacDougal Street in late summer of 1959. He was more or less the

3

resident balladeer at the coffee house and was busily occupied that summer organizing a series of Sunday afternoon poetry readings at the café attended by the finest talents of beatdom.

The day they met she was dressed Being & Nothingness ballerina beat. Her long blond tresses were pulled back into a bun, and there were wonderful golden bangs in front. She wore black dancer's stockings and black highheel spikes with those stylish spear-toes. Her brown leather vest, with laces up the sides, was the rage of Bleecker Street, worn over a tight black turtleneck with no brassiere, the ultimate of boldness in 1959.

Her eyes were Nefertiti'd with great Juliette Greco streaks of kohl and lots of green eye shadow. No one would have ever, she was anxiously certain, thought *she* was a tourist from Queens. She *knew* she looked like an authentic Villager.

They sat and talked for eight hours that first mesmerizing day. They agreed to meet after school the next day. And then the next. And the next.

Well, to dress the way she did was one thing, her parents reasoned. After all, it *was* New York and not some whistle stop. But to begin to, to, to hang around with, and god knows what else with, a filthnik in Greenwich Village, well that was unacceptable to parents, grandparents, uncles, aunts, and cousins in the sprawllands of Flushing, New York. They banded together, the family, to ban the nascent love. She was seventeen and her eighteenth birthday was only two months away so they had to move fast.

They wrote, they phoned, they sent telegrams to the beatnik, to his parents, to the school. They hired investigators. But all threats passed right through the young

4

lovers' consciousness into the tunnel of chaos. The parents tried to insist that she transfer to an out-of-town school, a classic technique of parents who dislike the loves of their son or daughter. Fuck you, she countered, I'll just not go to school.

They ran away the Christmas vacation of '59. They tried to check in to the all-male derelict hotel on Bleecker Street and were laughed out of the lobby. They stayed up all night in a Times Square movie house watching *The Blob* and *I Married a Monster From Outer Space*, over and over. The parents called the police on New Year's Eve with a missing-person report but the officer asked them, "How old is she?"—followed by "Does your daughter have a boyfriend?" Since she had just turned eighteen, there was nothing to be done.

They prowled the "beat scene"—frankly starve-eyed, looking for a rational salvation. They wandered the streets, caressing each other in the open day, living that famous final line from Auden's *September 1, 1939* with every lust-spackled muscle. There was no poetry reading, no art show, no film, no concert in an obscure loft, no lecture, no event of sufficiently rebellious nature, that they ever missed.

And the Fourth Avenue bookstores! How many hundreds of afternoons they spent in the twenty or so dusty stores with the worn wood floors; noses whiffing that excellent store-air, a mixture of dust and floating minutiae of antique leather bindings and frayed linen. What a heaven of data, to stand on a rickety ladder at the top of a fourteen-foot wall of out-of-print verse!

Their main problem was no place to plank. His landlord at the 11th Street rooming house would not allow guests of any gender up to his pitiful closet, and he could scarcely afford the rent plus deposit plus deposit for lights, to get his own pad. The parks of New York were their boudoir. They planked in them all. They were the only ones who had ever made love under the streetlight in the midpoint of the arching stone bridge near the Central Park Zoo, according to the policeman who broke up their coupling at a most urgent mutual moment of just-before-groinflash oblivion; ears aware of the approaching footsteps of Eros, but not of gumshoe.

They tried it, lying up against the little jungle-gym park in Washington Square after the park was closed. They planked on the cinder riding track near 72nd Street on the west side of Central Park and were interrupted by police horses—again at a critical moment. They planked sports-car-style on a bench at 72nd on the *east* side of the park (the same night as the cinder track interruption).

They loved to make it in Inwood Park. One New Year's Eve they climbed high in the rocks above the Columbia University boat basin at the north edge of Inwood, and were lean/lying on a steep icy incline between huge boulders—when, right in the middle, they began to slide, were unable to break it, but still kept fucking, and her buttocks were treated to fifteen feet of thrillies down the twiggy glaciation.

That incident was absolutely the last straw. They sold everything they could lay their hands on, and hocked and borrowed, and with the loot rented a small pad on East 3rd Street and Avenue B, which caused a further useless shrill shriek from the parents.

When he dared to drop out of school for a semester, the hatred of her family nearly got him in trouble with the Feds. The father learned of the drop-out and wrote a letter to the FBI sternly complaining that a scurrilous draft-dodging beatnik, who had missed a charge of statutory rape by a mere two months, should be flouting the law by not attending college while still enjoying an exemption from the draft. Why did the FBI hesitate for even one minute—the father raged—to arrest this Communist beatnik churl? Or why was he not forced immediately to join the army?

The letter did stir some attention directed against the beatnik on the part of the FBI. They visited the Lower East Side pad of the young lovers who luckily were not home.

The procedure of the FBI in those days was standard when they found the person not at home. They slid a three-by-five index card under the door, bearing the following thrill-producing message. They wrote at the top the full legal name of the "subject" with whom they deigned to babble; under which they wrote, "please contact Special Agent Edward Barnes, Federal Bureau of Investigation." Under that was the FBI phone number and the agent's extension.

The poet, of course, had not known that the father had sent in the letter. Eerie Police State fears crowded his mind. The pot in the pad was flushed immediately. Was it some sort of crackdown on beat poets? Absurd. He had signed a petition urging clemency for Caryl Chessman—maybe that was the reason for the visit. Whatever the reason, he was haunted by the phantom sound of handcuffs and the sound track of the FBI radio show.

He telephoned the agency and they asked him to bop up to the FBI office on East 67th on a little matter regarding his draft status. Uh-oh. Uh-oh and terror.

He was interviewed in a cavernous room full of desks and agents. They informed him they were not out to "get" him or anything but that, once requested from the chain of command above, the agents were required to file a report. He assured them that he was going to be back in class the very next semester, carefully attempting to paint a picture of his future father-in-law as a trembly-fingered nut.

Because of her father's letter to the Feds, the couple felt it reasonable to assume that the father had written to the New York police also, perhaps a letter about drugs. For the next several years they hid their grass in carefully prepared stashes. They used, for instance, the hang-the-bag-of-pot-out-the-window-on-a-string stash with a razor blade nearby. Another stash was the pot-on-string-hanging-above-the-toilet stash. It was boring to have to take such precautions, but it was very common at that time. The couple knew one fellow who had a dog trained as a living stash-of-grass-gobbler, should the fuzz raid. In fact, during the beat era, one of the considerations when deciding whether or not to take an apartment, was the presence of built-in stashes such as crevices, shaftways, etc.; or how long the door would hold up in a dope raid.

The next crisis occurred when they got married, at which time the family considered putting her, or him, or both, into a nuthatch. An uncle in the family was a doctor. There was a lot of phone pressure on the uncle to look into committing the beatnik, "to save Marie" the mother cried, tears dripping on the receiver. In response to this the beatnik sent the message, "You'll never take us alive," into the family tree, and things grew quieter.

Children eased the hatred. For his part, the poet wrote and was silent. Faced with a total cut-off in seeing their grandchildren, the parents began to soften up. They could all walk down vomit alley was the poet's attitude after the

8

years of warfare. If they got on his back, he decided that he would snarl or glower and say nothing whatsoever. A sneering, glowering beatnik dressed in weird rags was a match for many a middle-class mom visiting the slums for a peep at a grandchild.

So the years of poverty roamed past, roach-ridden, garbage-strewn, happy with rodents. Sometimes they were reduced to using T-shirts for diapers, unable to afford the disposables. Once they seized the T-shirt of a visiting National Book Award poet, right off his back, just days after he received the award, to use as a diaper.

On occasion they gathered their first editions of poetry and novels and sold them to the rare-book dealers. They were always getting writers to sign their books. At poetry readings at the 92nd Street Y, they usually managed to hang out backstage grabbing the 'graphs, man. A *signed* first edition, ahhh that was a pleasure.

In rare desperation, he joined the line of humans at the Third Avenue Blood Bank to get his arm sucked for the ten-dollar pint. Ten dollars: $1.98 for Chux disposables, four packages of spaghetti 70¢, one box spinach egg noodles 35¢, one pound ricotta cheese 69¢, sugar, potatoes, gallon milk, eggs, three marshmallow cookies at Gem Spa, two cans beer, one cola—and they had a bare three dollars remaining. That meant tomorrow was another partial day of schemes—but schemes interspersed with hours of mimeographed treason, learned chit-chat in Tompkins Square Park, four distinct hallucinations, numerous strolls in the direction of the Fourth Avenue bookstores, and f r e e d o m.

As the years went by there began to occur the phenomenon of the shopping bag. That is, when the

9

mother-in-law made her occasional quick Saturday or Sunday afternoon visits to the squalid, enemy pad, she bore shopping bags of largess. Often she would pick stuff from her own pantry, wild "Bohemian" substances like ungobbled tins of palm hearts, Streit's brand chocolate-covered matzohs, pickled watermelon rinds, or partial boxes of kasha. But the shopping bags also contained staples such as diapers and milk and sugar. The mother-in-law apparently never threw anything away. One of her thrills was to present to the grandchildren baby clothes that the mother, her daughter, had worn at the same age. Ditto for toys and dolls that had belonged to the mother twenty years previous.

Occasionally the mother-in-law would show up in the middle of a political meeting, say for the planning of a demonstration, and some of America's most notorious radicals, men and women on whom the government spent millions bugging, harassing, auditing, and burglarizing, all would shift apart in silence as the mother-in-law walked through with the bundles of choff. The father-in-law was the last to soften and remained rather intransigent in his hatred of the "beatnik punk with no excuses." Once he even injected green vegetable dye into an unopened gallon of milk brought to the hovel on a shopping-bag Sunday. They opened the milk later. There is nothing quite like pouring a glass of fresh milk and viewing green fungus juice from Mars coming out of the spout. But gradually even the father began to calm down and to tolerate the marriage.

There was no hovel, no geodesic summer dome in the woods within driving range, no junkie-ridden tenement so foreboding as to prevent the m-i-l, carrying thirty-five pounds of raw produce, clothes, notebook paper, vitamins, magazines, in two or three Care packages as the couple called them, from climbing up however many flights of steps it took.

In the summer of 1964, the couple and children spent several months in the woods off a logging trail in the Catskill hills near Phoenicia, New York. They were living in an old striped party tent from somebody's Long Island estate, above which were second-story sleeping quarters in a clear plastic-roofed tree house. They lived in fond desolation for several weeks until one Sunday afternoon they heard *skwonch! skwonch! skwonch!*—approaching footsteps in the twigs and dry growth, as toward the tent, laden with protein and cheer, walked the mother-in-law.

As the years passed, they were not surprised to learn that the phenomenon of the mother-in-law as the Demeter of Bohemia, was widespread. Wherever writers and artists banded together to struggle, they were present. All hail the mother-in-law.

The Poetry Reading

CUTHBERT'S SISTER, AGATHA, was tepidly torturing him over the phone for the fifth time that day. Why won't she leave me alone? "Look, Agatha, I will never agree to selling the house. My decision is final."

Cuthbert lived in a gloomy room at the Hotel Colburne on Washington Place just off Washington Square, scattered with forty or fifty dried orange peels. "Those orange peels will attract copperheads, you know"—his sister had warned him.

"Here in Greenwich Village?"

"You never can tell. I bet there's at least *one* pet copperhead in your neighborhood, with the kind of queer denizens it attracts."

Cuthbert's hair was white and almost shiny. His eyelids were pink most of the time as were his cheeks which had almost sharply defined ovals of pinkness. His upper lip lifted up and out when he read poetry. He was sixty-one. And he had been writing poetry slowly and quietly for forty years. His room at the hotel was jammed floor to ceiling with memorabilia of the literary life of the Village from the twenties on.

12

"Agatha, I have to click off. I'm going to a poetry reading in a few minutes at the Gaslight Café."

"Are you going to be reading?"

"Yes. Everyone will be about forty-five years younger than I—you see it's an open reading—so it should be quite an evening; either terrifying or terribly exciting. And, please, leave me alone for a few days, all right?"

Cuthbert stood naked in the center of his room, eating a cucumber, trying to remember what pile he had worn yesterday. The poet had devised a clothing system whereby he had thrown everything away except for seven complete sets of attire and had placed a complete clothing bundle every few feet around the perimeter of his room. To select his clothes of the day, he merely spotted the pile he had worn the day before, moved his eyes one pile-notch counterclockwise, and put on the bundle. In this way he found that he only had to do his laundry every forty-nine days.

The Gaslight was packed. Several newspaper cameramen were pushing people aside to get better shots. Someone whispered to the woman selling dollar admission tickets, "Is Ginsberg here?" Cuthbert had scant admiration for the beats but he certainly respected the attention—hostile, friendly, and otherwise—generated for modern poets and poetry by Ginsberg, Burroughs, Corso, Kerouac, and company. Student beat-fever was running high. Poetry readings were suddenly S.R.O. The N.Y. *Daily News* for instance had featured last week's reading in their centerfold. The New York-based newsmagazines had published several articles on the beats which, however, salivated with cynicism and deprecation, such as the article titled "Zen Hur," which appeared in *Time*. Such

13

garbage-jobs by the middle-class/mid-brow publications helped spew energy into the movement. For it was Cuthbert's belief that if you piss off the cultural frontal lobes of *Time Mag*, you must be doing something right. And Cuthbert, who had missed out on the Lost Generation in Paris after World War I, was not about to miss out on another successful literary generation—especially one that seemed to be such an unstoppable and interesting phenomenon. So he decided to join in, to take a shower in the same energy as the beats. What could he lose?

The reading had been advertised as an open reading of "beat poets" but as it turned out, none of the stars of beatdom showed up. About forty other poets did, however, nineteen of whom signed up to read at the sacred table of the list-mistress.

One woman was irate at the fifty-cent minimum. "We should at least get a free cup of coffee for our coming all the way down here to read," she protested.

The manager had an answer all ready. "There is some argument possible that you should pay *us* to let you read."

The poets were requested to read only three poems each, or five minutes, though most managed to eat up at least seven minutes before the nervous poets in the audience began to stare balefully and to twitch with displeasure. The owner of the café announced that there could be no applause because of neighborhood complaints about the noise. By an arrangement worked out with the police, the form of applause would be fingersnaps.

The woman leaned down close to a stenopad and jotted each reader's name upon the list which was supposed to be maintained democratically; first to sign first to read. The man in front of Cuthbert had an imperious voice: "Please place me at the head of the first set"—wearing a

14

fur-trimmed cape, silver-headed walking stick—"for I intend to read a short verse play, *Theseus and The Time Machine* and I seek an advantageous moment for its preparation, for it is a work of genius"—bowing his head, clicking the heels of his spit-shined riding boots.

As for Cuthbert, he found himself scheduled for the second slot in the third set, meaning that his ears would be long assailed with verse blizzards, not that he minded it at all for he loved to listen to poets. But he didn't want to get burned for his slot either, so throughout the reading he monitored the list-table, alert for hanky-panky. Indeed, he occasionally would observe a human approach the table, bend down, maybe smile and whisper at the lister; and lo! she sometimes would scratch out a name here, write in another there. Cuthbert did not care about the others as long as Set 3, Slot 2 remained "Cuthbert Mayerson."

Fingersnaps were somewhat inadequate to satisfy the approval-hungry needs of some poets. For a very few, when they had completed their poems, and the audience was enthused, there was a flurry of snaps like someone crashing through twiggy underbrush. But after a poet who was not well received or not understood (not humorous) there were a pitiful four or five snaps then a dissolving silence. For the fingersnaps to end even before the poet made a move to return to its table, this was painful. And especially painful to Cuthbert, who thought along this line: If the previous reader was given a mere five fingersnaps, what am I to receive, three?

Cuthbert noted that there were several poets present who wrote frantically when anyone was on the podium reciting, stopping only when there was no urging voice, as if the flowing words unleashed their own goat-pen of babble. Other poets came fortified with an honor guard of close friends who sat at the same table protectively and when the poet rose to utter its verse, the entire table would turn their chairs to face the poet directly, would smile appreciatively and laugh heartily, and at the end would snap their fingers calisthenically and with great duration.

Set 1, Reader A: The screamer. This jarred the reading to a start. Carl Rothstein, just released from the madhouse, pointing to his shock burns, with a flat long face and wire-rimmed spectacles, his hair pulled up and back for that Aldous Huxley look, beginning with a deep voice (a feigned deepness it would seem because of the poet's extreme youth): "I have just been disgorged from the alimentary ward of Shreveport Psychiatric." At once he ripped open his shirt, the buttons popping upon the floor, and pointed to his T-shirt upon which was crudely painted: I WAS BUDDHA. Then he read:

> *My mother offered me*
> *a bobsled saying*
> *"There is the Hill."*
>
> *"What Hill?" I replied. "You mean*
> *that Mountain over there*
> *with cliffs and gorges?"*
>
> *"Go on down the Hill*
> *my son!" said she and*
> *gave me a quick,*
> *may I say rude, shove*
> *of her boot.*

This was immediately followed by a piercing scream, apparently to indicate the nature of the down-mountain bobsled ride, which lasted, with pauses for breath, at least five minutes. Man, could he scream.

After his voice gave out, the audience was almost silent as Rothstein walked back to his table, about four fingersnaps punctuating the displeasure.

There was a jazz fingersnapper in the audience in a beret and sun glasses and a black silk scarf knotted on his neck above his Oberlin sweatshirt. He had begun to snap vigorously in abstract patterns about halfway through the scream, nodding and weaving, eyes closed, shaking his wrists like a maracas player, whispering "dig it" and "Groo-oovy!" — "solid" — "existence" — "Dhammapada, man."

After the scream, jazz fingersnapper pulled out a bottle of wine. There were a man and woman and two children, apparently a family of tourists, who sat next to the snapper. He took a swig and passed the wine to the boy of the family who hesitated, looked a his father, shrugged, took a swig, offered it to his mother and father, who said not a word, then handed it back to the snapper. The boy's mother looked like a case of hydrophobia as her eyewhites flared and mouth fell open. She shook her fist at her son, "I'll see you about this later."

Set 1, Reader B: This particular reader looked unlikely to offend, dressed as he was in a business suit with a blue polka-dot bow tie knotted crookedly. The poet began, nervously holding a trembling fist of crinkled white pages. "This is titled *Nocturne Number 467*"—followed by a long pause then a deep hissing sucking of air.

17

Cloistered in the convents of our minds
we pull down our pants
and show our behinds . . .

A titter tattered the silence. The woman from Des Moines grabbed her husband, son, and her daughter and pulled them away, "C'mon, this is filth."

. . . while lemon aardvarks from Jersey City
invade the white
undergarments of fate

Another titter. And the poet continued. The father knocked over his metal-backed ice cream parlor chair. The sight of the family splitting upset the reader so much that he began to stammer. He regained his composure by lighting a cigarette in the middle of his poem with a metallic click-clack of his Zippo lighter followed by a fierce intonation of a doublet of religious sonnets after which he sat down.

Set 1, Reader C: This reader was popular with the throng, for he was the first obvious real-life beat poet. Poverty was written upon his face as was Zen fanaticism and the ravages of compulsive hitchhiking. He insisted on standing on a chair to read, and doing so he bumped his head on the low cellar ceiling, but remained there nevertheless, his head having to lie upon its right side to fit beneath the ceiling. His sandals were homemade, of rope and soles cut from leather luggage. He was funny, at least the packed coffee house thought so. At this point, early in the reading, people were standing in line fifty feet up MacDougal Street waiting to get in. The police were on the scene and the manager of the Gaslight made an announcement that people could not block the exits or the aisles and that the police had threatened to call the fire department. Spectators were forced to squat along the side wall or to sit on the stairway leading up to the toilets, for each table was hopelessly packed. The manager sneaked all the fives and tens out of the cash register into the safety of the thick wad in his pocket, thinking "Money! I'm making money!"—urging his waitress on with an occasional goad, sell more! lean over the table! unbutton a blouse button maybe, touch the customer, anything, sell!

"This poem is called *Ten Thousand Statues of Walt Whitman on Roller Skates Hitchhike Across America.*" The title alone got the biggest laugh of the evening. He read with a moan-drone, the tone dropping at the end of each line like a passing truck.

America!   *we cannot grasp the walnut.*
America!   *robots with shoes made out of living gophers*
              climb from the TV dinner plates to eat your
              teeth!
America!   *you are trying to treat me like a sewer!*
              A new Spartacus is going to grow from the
              mutant garbage dump at the Mum Deodorant
              factory and then you're gonna be in trouble,
              America
                        (the first laugh)
America!   *your hucksters of Madison Avenue with ice-*
              cube armpits. . . .
              (laughter drowned out the rest of the line so
              that Cuthbert could not hear it.)
America!   *your hulahoops form a mandorla above the*
              Final Sausage Factory!

19

> *Porky Pig and Donald Duck have stomachs*
> *full of broken lightbulbs, America*
America! the A-bomb is trying to read us a bedtime
story
(big laugh)

Fuck Fuck Fuck,
America
(bigger laugh)

The poet paused scrupulously at all laughs. Sometimes he'd join in and laugh also. Then he waited not only till the laughter faded but also till the smiles faded, before resuming. He was a great success, the fingersnaps were like a great bonfire.

Set 1, Reader D: The mumbler. The man read in a near whisper so that gradually the audience grew quiet: it became almost like a game as they leaned across their tables positioning their ears for maximum data. But it was impossible to hear; the reader was sitting on a stool and had turned almost away from the listeners. "Louder!" someone rudely yelled, which brought about a temporary rise then a long fade. The poems were like papyrus fragments:

. . . . *love* . . . .
ratchet wrench . . . .
. . . . . *goodbye* . . . . .
. . . . *unguent!*

This was good for those who wrote their own poetry while listening to the readers, for the whisperer's lines were phantom inspirations—and his words, half heard, were permutated wonderfully in their minds.

Was it: "In spite of the late moon"?
Or was it: "Spade of the lagoon"?
Or: "Supplicated tortillas of the bent spoon"?

Set 1, Reader E: The angry witch. This poet possessed a cutting voice with overtones of shrill. By the end of her first poem, her voice had risen maybe half an octave, glasses sliding down her nose because of the way she trembled.

"This poem is dedicated to my husband Roger, who is a skull by now: *Sick Bard in the Lonely Cave.*" The poem opened with notification that a kettle of tapir eyes was slowly simmering and that "even the Sybil" was banned from The Cave of The Bard. The next quatrain asserted the existence of a catacombs beneath Washington Square Park where the "covening minstrels" of Washington Square North were wont to meet.

To appease the "hungry ghost" of her husband Roger, she had buried his (hopefully symbolic) teeth in The Cave of The Bard, the entrance to which was a hidden door at the base of Washington Arch, guarded by a silver baboon and six owls.

This particular poem was causing the jazz fingersnapper to beat on his table with a coffee spoon, he was so excited. The poem mentioned the Gnostic Pleroma where "broomsticks are toothpicks." "Sick Ghosts muttering Neck! Neck!" were to sprout from the teeth. Cuthbert shuddered at this line, and wound his scarf around his neck, reminding himself of his long distaste and distrust regarding the possibility of the reality of vampires, a fact that had caused him to wake up many a morning with a crick of the neck due to having wrapped his head in a protective towel during the night. Cuthbert was quite relieved when the next two poems were translations from Ovid. "Thank

God for Ovid," he muttered to himself.

Set 1, Reader F: An experimental versifier who had flown in from Toronto, he happily announced, just for this august reading. His first poem was entitled *Sixty-nine Drips.* To effect the poem, he brandished a maroon gym sock filled with pea soup into which had been affixed a cocktail straw so that the soup dripped slowly from the sock through the straw into a teacup. As each drip dripped, the reader shouted, "Drip one!" then "Drip two!" and so on until sixty-nine had been reached.

The next and last poem he called 2×2 *Infinity* and slowly began to stagger forward, "Two . . . . . Four . . . . Eight. . . . Sixteen . . . . . . Thirty-two"—varying the time-lengths between numbers. He made it to 2,097,152 before the M.C. hooked him off the stage. This concluded the first set.

Intermission involved a rapid-delivery sell of lukewarm coffee crowned with questionable whipped cream, tea, and cider with cinnamon sticks; and for Cuthbert Mayerson, the rising of the fear.

The second set seemed interminable. Everyone seemed bent upon translating into elegiac couplets their versions of the Babylonian Creation Epic. Cuthbert, nervous, ceased to pay much attention to the tonal blasts. Rather, he concentrated on the all-important final selecting and sequencing of what he was to read.

Cuthbert looked intently at what he proposed to read. All at once, right in front of his eyes, he saw at least four lines that had to be changed immediately. "Neatly, neatly"—he told himself, for he did not want to be unable to read his own stuff. Next he shuffled the order of the poems to achieve that perfect rhapsody.

But angst afflicted him: I have not read for years, for

years! Am I sweating? Are my eyes red? Why is that person reading forever? Maybe I should recite instead some Shelley from memory. I wore the wrong clothes.

Certain readers interrupted his fear. A man who ran a candy store in the Bronx intoned his Image Trouvé Manifesto, based on certain poetic principles learned while stocking his candy jars prior to noontime klepto invasion of schoolchildren. There was a schoolteacher who began a poem: "Carpathian horseman joust inside the rotating triangle"—Cuthbert thought that was the funniest he had heard, and giggled so, and was sneeringly stared at by the teacher's table of henchmen. There was another poet who read at least a three-hundred-line poem called *The Philosophy of Thales the Milesian*, although Cuthbert knew, and snickered accordingly, that Thales had left not *one* extant line of work from which to draw such a fierce and lengthy poem.

There were a couple of diverting sex maniacs, one in particular who read a series of haiku relative to experiments with mayonnaise and the Bayonne, New Jersey, telephone book for 1959. But it did little to allay the fears of Cuthbert Mayerson who, at that moment, would have bet the family mansion that he was to be booed from the reader's chair.

During the second intermission Cuthbert walked over again to check the reading list. Had one or two perchance moved up above him? He scowled appropriately at the list-keeper who assured him, no, no, nothing could ever alter the ordained array for Set 3. Yet, even as she was protesting her innocence, a wan poet with a W. B. Yeats/ Bill Haley haircut strode up, checked the list and uttered an angry wail. "Hey, you moved my name down the list!"

The keeper was really caught this time. "Oh! Well? I

looked for you and I didn't see you—I thought maybe you'd split. Sorry."

"A pitiful excuse"—the man replied, stalking back to his chair.

As the assembly was hushed for the beginning of the set, Cuthbert suddenly became aware of a painful fact. Whereas the Gaslight had been packed for Set 1, the several hours intervening had seen the place become half-empty. And more were oozing toward the door each minute. To make things worse, the first reader had left his table to approach the podium carrying an armload of work that had to consist of at least a thousand pages. "I'll never get to read!" Cuthbert exclaimed.

The man commenced. "The work I shall read tonight is a section from my lifelong endeavor, *Voyage of the Sun God, To Brooklyn*. It is rather lengthy, so I shall read only the final and culminating six hundred lines. The sentences in Gaelic will be numerous and represent the Seventy-eight Commandments from the Sun God to the people of Brooklyn. I shall translate the Seventy-eight Commandments at the end of the poem."

The introduction alone caused about ten patrons to lunge for the exits. A shudder passed among the remaining poets, stomachs churning, fearful, eager, taut fingers on black springbinders.

The man read like a tent revivalist, raising his fist, moaning. Even his frantic performance could not stanch the flow of fleeing feet. Cuthbert was caught, helpless; wanting really to leave, yet tied to his chair with desire to read.

At last it was Set 3, Slot 2. Cuthbert Mayerson read slowly, his coin-shaped pinknesses of cheek aflame. His upper lip jutting out pointedly; sonorous was his voice chanting his short, subdued, and symbolic poems of paidopygophilia. The audience was very appreciative of his work and afforded him the only actual handclapping of the night, a temporary violation of rules that sent the manager rushing to the front door to see if any police were outside.

At last it was over. A woman approached Cuthbert, "Say, I liked your poem."

"You did? Which one do you mean?" Cuthbert was all smiles.

The woman paused, a cheek-muscle twitching. "Uh, the one, uh, about America."

"You mean the last one I read, *The Barefoot Moth?*"

"I guess that was the one. It was the one that received all the applause."

Cuthbert walked happily up MacDougal Street toward his hotel, where, depositing his poetry, he decided to reward himself for bravery; so he proceded to Sheridan Square, grabbing the IRT Uptown to 42nd Street and a refreshing saunter.

Total Assault Cantina

I AM WRITING this from the valley of shrieks and the alleys of despair. The cellar in which I live is damp—brown roaches shine on the wall posts in the candle glare. I am sleeping on a bunch of rags bundled up in buttoned despicable shirts like rag torsos, eight of them, my bed. The food which I consume is garbage. Occasionally I go to the breadline. As I write I look about me and see nothing to which to look for specks of hope. I hook the newspapers, wet with slime and yellowed with egg, from the garbage, cans and when they are dry I lie down on my floor to read them. And I am disgusted. And there is nothingness. No rungs in the ladder of whiteness; for no longer is there any ladder—but only two poles remain, the rungs are shattered—and the poles are used upon the shoulders of mourners to carry the dangling bodies of defeat home to squalor.

My landlord is a verminous crook. He raises the rent on my cellar without mercy. May he die in rush-hour traffic. No, may he live. I don't care. It doesn't care. The Milky Way is nothing to know. The floodlights of the concentration camp have not yet flooded through the windows of my wet cellar, and I don't care. *Grex* is the Latin word for herd. Grex hex sex specks flecks.

I have thought about crawling about or crumbling supine, maybe strapping roller skates to my forearms and shins and scuttling thus, beating the pavement with small boards. But they would put me away. They might. And I remember well what Judith Malina told me so many years ago: Never do it alone, always conspire.

I want to describe for you my cellar. For I have memorized it and the Xerox-like replica of it in my mind is just enough removed from reality that I can bounce fondness-beams upon the page in contemplation of its image. It is dirty, wet, shiny with roaches; the two windows are narrow, located at the top of the front wall; they look like small New York curbside sewer grates. I can hear the feet stomping my metal doors and if I stand on my chair I can watch the legs walk by. To garner warmth I merely open the furnace-room door and a humming breeze lightly cuts the chill. There is nothing to report about the floor other than when the concrete was poured no one bothered to scrape it to a level condition. It is blobby, wavy, stinky with fifty years of coal dust and blotched with the garbage of my forays.

I was once a rising author. The reviewers used to look forward to reading my "next novel." My creations are on my cellar shelves; I had not much to say other than to urge the rebels to stand up in the slice-lines, take it, struggle. And now rotting springbinders hold the cobweb-streaked pages of my youth. What was it? It was a bitter mingling, brothers and sisters. And time is not the guide. Quiet despair. Quiet desperation. Quiet! I screamed till they knelt down to look through the slits into the cellar. Then I lay still. Maybe I shall walk to the New York

27

Public Library to continue my all-important ten-year research into narco-hypno-robo-wash. It doesn't matter. For I am sorting through my files. And as soon as I have them thoroughly ordered, I shall find a university to accept them and maybe then I shall eat grass and live upon the roadsides of America, a plastic container with a moldy spoon of potato salad here, a plastic container with a leftover onion ring, a small untouched ketchup pouch, there. This is what I tell myself. Then we shall roll, brothers and sisters, then we shall hear the trumpeteers and saxophones again.

There is a purple grape shining between the thumb and forefinger of Dionysius. There is an olive in the fist of Demeter. But in the fist of the monster on the front page is the sigil of robot war. I am grunged upon by that monster and sorely affrighted.

There is an ancient bale of hay down here in my cellar, black and greasy with grime. But the baling wire still holds it together. This hay has been here for twelve years, ever since 1961. I laugh whenever I sit upon it to read. For it reminds me of the Total Assault Cantina and of the time twelve years ago we threw a bunch of rifles into the East River that had been smuggled into the U.S. by a gang of right-wing creeps. Ha ha ha. Now that was a caper.

You see, the cantina was located on the floor right above the cellar where I now dwell; that is to say, on Avenue A at 11th Street. Don't bother to look for the remains of Total Assault Cantina now, for the building has been burnt out for years. After the cantina folded, the Mafia used the place for years to store jukeboxes. Then they set fire to the place in an insurance scam.

We were crazed with the strange release granted to us

by the civilization. LSD was years away for us but already we were driven specks of foment. We were walking ergot. But no one was so driven with urgency in those days as the proprietors of Total Assault Cantina. They felt the need. They burned to struggle for the socialist revolution. They beat their fists into their palms considering ways to further the nonviolent struggle. Both were in their early twenties at the time; both had grown up in New York City. John McBride was thin, nervous, with a thick red mustache and short red brown hair. Paul Stillman was more relaxed, meditative, with his hair drawn back and knotted behind him.

Together John and Paul operated the Total Assault, a nonprofit establishment intensely dedicated toward yanking the corpses of J. P. Morgan's neoconfederates through the amphetamine piranha tank. It was just that way— their agitation kept them walking acrobatic along that perilous thin path of roachclips—one side of which lay Gandhian ahimsa, the other side bitter street battles and the violent insurgency of a potential New York Commune. The personalities of the two operators of Total Assault whirled in intellectual combat on the question of tactics. Both wanted to crash that TV tower off the top of the Empire State—but their approaches were somewhat different. It was sort of anarcho-Mao v. anarcho-Tao. The budda-budda-budda of machine gun fire for John became Buddha Buddha pacing rebels for Paul. Both were convinced for the time being, however, that nonviolent direct street action was the correct Way to proceed.

The first café they had operated was a tiny place on 9th Street between B and C. They had called it Cantina de las Revoluciones. They managed to float for about a year before poverty and debt forced it to close. Then they located a much larger space on Avenue A and 11th Street, comprising a whole ground floor with a courtyard. The rent: $100 a month. It was eternity.

It wasn't long before the license inspectors came around, and that meant instant trouble, because John and Paul did not cooperate with the concept of licensing. "Gonna close you down," the inspectors told them. "Can't sell food without a license."

"We are revolutionaries. Taxes don't exist. The Department of Licenses doesn't exist. Why don't you sit down and help us with the twelve-cent soup?" But the licenseers gave them a summons and would not help with the circle of friends peeling vegetables for the Gandhian ambrosia.

Soon they were forced to trek down to the Dept. of Licenses to fill out the forms. They wanted to call the restaurant Café Hashish, a proposal that was immediately banned by the red-tapers. "We're going to the Civil Liberties Union to see about this, you fucking fascists," Paul snorted after a long argument with the officials of the department. But there was nothing to be done.

A few days later they tried again. They were ushered into the office of Mr. William Karkenschul, deputy director of licenses, Liberal Party appointee, a human who was at that time trying to close down coffee houses which offered poetry readings. Mr. Karkenschul read from the notarized business form: "Hmmm, let's see"—mumble mumble, "John Z. McBride and Paul A. Stillman d/b/a Vomit, a Restaurant." Karkenschul stared at the two. "You mean you want to start a restaurant called Vomit!?"—a slight curl of revulsion lifting his lip. "First you come in here last week trying to name your dive with an illegal name, now it's Vomit. Is this some sort of game?"

"Look here, Karko, we *want* to call it Vomit. Now what about it?"

"It cannot be allowed," he replied. "The public won't stand for it."

"How about The Karkenschul House of Puke?"—Paul sneered. That suggestion got them thrown out of the office. "You, Mr. Liberal Party poetry-banner! You show us the regulation that says we can't call our restaurant Café Hashish or Vomit, or anything we want!!"

A few days later they were back at the Dept. of Licenses with a name that sailed through the bureaucratic ocean: Total Assault Cantina. The License Dept. blitzed them repeatedly. They seemed to inspect them once a week. I had a friend that brought the cantina a station-wagonful of hot cigarettes from South Carolina once a month. They were almost caught by the license creeps who certainly would have snitched John and Paul out to the Feds. We carried the taxstampless cigs down into the cellar in the nick of time. As it was, the licensoids required John and Paul to obtain what was called a "License to Act as Retail Dealer in Cigarettes in the City of New York."

When they began to hold poetry readings, Karkenschul picked up the announcements of the readings from the *Village Voice* and sent raiders out to issue summonses, informing the two that they'd have to cringe and beg for a cabaret license if they wanted to continue poetry. There was a law in New York that allowed entertainment in a restaurant by no more than three stringed instruments and a piano: allowing *no* poetry and *no* singing. Otherwise, a cabaret license was necessary, a bureaucratic nightmare involving bribing building inspectors, and requiring employees to register with the fuzz and to carry

31

cabaret identity cards, and so forth.

Another thing that pissed off the authorities was that Total Assault was unable to resist allowing people to sleep on the floor although it drove the landlord nuts. The police would shine flashlights through the front window in the middle of the night and the floor looked like a packed meadow of sleeping bags. Crashers could only cop about six hours sleep however, because John and Paul had to wake everybody up by 10 A.M. in order to sweep and to get the breads in the ovens in time to open for the noon-hour soup rush.

Total Assault was more of a community center than a mere café. A bu-gaze across the room revealed a kitchen containing a quaking Salvation Army icebox, a huge oven, storage cabinets made of packing crates, and a long varnished-pine serving counter. There was a whole wall devoted to collages and bulletins, leaflets and the like, and in the back near the courtyard was a printing-press area marked off by beautiful black Chinese screens, the origin of which Ptah only knows. There was another wall crammed with bookshelves. The Peoples' Library, as John called it, out of which the people steadily drained the books ne'er to return. There were numerous found-in-street divans placed around a large central table for those who liked to dine reclining. The walls were spotted with can-lids nailed over rat holes. The more serious breaches were sealed off with a mixture of Brillo pads and plaster. Near the front window was an old upright piano, stacked atop which was a neat pyramid of sleeping bags for the nighttime mattress meadow.

With regard to the wall devoted to leaflets and collages, by the end of a year there were maybe a thousand leaflets, new overdubbed upon old, from floor to ceiling.

32

In my cellar I have a box containing all the posters and stuff from that wall. Come and get me, New York Graphic Society.

Meetings meetings meetings, they may have held a hundred meetings a month at Total Assault. They held a *New York Times* Sneer-in every night at 7 P.M. where everybody took turns singing and declaiming articles from that day's edition, accompanied by great jeers, chortles, and spits of anger. The ten top stock advances of the day were soundly jeered. And when the market went down a few points, there was a tumult of applause. Sometimes when the market really went bad, Paul would put a sign in the window announcing the good news.

I used to love the Town Meetings on Tuesday nights. They were wonderful shouting matches and many a grandiose scheme was hatched in the air. A free medical and dental clinic was born out of these meetings and still thrives, but much of it was kiosks of ego-babble, though I got to practice my yodeling a lot when the debates grew laborious.

In spite of the good Dharma-Commie karma, the cantina was a fiscal disaster. There was a prophetic sign above the cash register reading: THERE WILL BE NO PROFIT! The biggest money drain was the food-scroungers. There was a porcelain bathtub in the window in which John and Paul created a huge, daily vegetable salad. Next to it was a crock of free tea and another crock of soup. People seemed to drift in the door with glazed eyes like food robots and would serve themselves from the salad tub and soup crock, then there would rise the quick slurps of filling stomachs, after which they vanished without paying. There were so many hungry. But there were a lot of people with plenty of cash lining up for free food also. I must confess that I too, shekels clanking in my pockets, ripped free hunks of rye and bowls of soup from Total Assault Cantina. At first they tried to hand customers chits but these were left damp upon the tables or used to wipe up spills. Each day John and Paul cooked fresh bread. Humans began to steal whole loaves. They would saunter in, order coffee, and whistle out the door with a loaf, and on the way home from work at that.

The cantina was written up in one of the Sunday magazine supplements as being a "groovy place to get delicious free food." That nearly caused a riot. People were driving in from New Jersey to score free beatnik chow. There were hundreds lining the sidewalk and packed inside. That's where John and Paul should have cleaned up, maybe giving a little free soup and charging for everything else. As it was, people were spilling into the printing area where I was working and it pissed me off because we were trying to print some draft cards and fake I.D. for draft resisters at the time. So, to put an ebb to the weekender spew, we printed up a disgusto menu featuring things like eyeballs au gratin and frog-ani skewered on toothpicks and we taped ten or fifteen copies on the cantina windows facing out. Then we filled the salad bathtub with a concoction of Martian cookie-toss that was genuinely disgusting. We cut the heads off a few dozen realistic rubber snakes and plopped them in the gruel, adding doll heads, weeds from the park, a couple of rats, with a sign taped to the tub: FREE.

I ran the print shop, where we specialized in protest posters, poetry mags, draft cards, I.D., & leaflets. I worked hard and they would come in from the streets to babble in my ears for hours as I zombi-stood at the press. Strange people with involved tales. There were those who

34

insisted that immediately I drop everything and print a book of their verse, or a resumé, or six years of diaries depicting their experiments in Zen-Sufi trance-dance in Arabia Petra. I was even supposed to pay for the paper. Then I got into trouble with one of the local street gangs—I forget their name, maybe the Face-Axers, something like that. They really got angry; I wouldn't let them use the printshop tool kit to work on their zip guns. That night the front window was caved in.

There was no money to fix it and certainly no insurance so it was a find-boards-in-the-streets scene. About this time there was some sort of drug panic and the junkies stooped so low as to rob Total Assault. They stole fifteen "tuned" gongs belonging to The Celestial Freakbeam Orchestra. They stole the electric soup-heater from the front window. They stole my electric typewriter, but left the offset; probably it was too heavy for them. When they raided, late at night, they were surprised encountering the zzz-ing mattress meadow so they tied and gagged eleven people and left them zipped up in their sleeping bags. In a further dour overdub, the phone was stomped after a so-called friend made a four-hour call to London and didn't tell anyone about it. Poverty was imminent; John and Paul tallied their main debts:

gas/electric	60
paper bill	80
lumber	160
2 months rent	200
food	200

"Now, how are we going to make seven hundred bucks?"

35

"I hope it's not going to be a Times Square ankle-grab scene"—Sam joked.

They held an emergency hookah-side scheme session. First they contemplated the traditional Brentano's art book rip-off scam. But who could carry seven hundred dollars worth of Skira and New York Graphic Society publications? Next they seriously considered a nonviolent bank robbery. They spent considerable time trying to compose a note to be handed to the teller which a) would reassure the teller, b) would in fact cause the teller to fork over the money, c) would *not* result in their immediate arrest. But there was just no way nonviolently to rob a bank.

One thing they did do right away was to hold a benefit poetry reading, one of those 8 P.M. till 4 A.M. versathons where thirty-seven poets sat nervously waiting to read. That raised a punkly seventy-five dollars, although it was a great thronging social success. Someone left a flute packed to the mouthpiece with amphetamine under a table which they quickly sold and the night's take was upped to a hundred and ten bucks. They thought of selling the printing equipment but why have a revolutionary cantina if you can't print?

The next afternoon John called his aunt in the Bronx. The family had a produce business at the Hunts Point Market where Total Assault had managed to run up a sizable bill. John wanted to hustle a few more weeks of footstuff from his aunt and in the course of the conversation she told him, "Larry's in from Hong Kong. He's been trying to get in touch with you. He wants to talk to you about something."

Larry's in from Hong Kong meant there was dope around, for cousin Larry regularly brought in lots of hash

36

and grass when his ship returned to New York. Aunt Mildred gave him the number and a balking approval for vegetable credit. John called Larry right away, "Got any hamburger?"

"You bet I have," Larry replied. "Listen, I've been trying to get in touch with you for three days. I'm in a desperate situation. Can we meet?"

Larry grabbed a subway to the Lower East Side and conferred at Total Assault, offering a deal that would save it. If John and Paul would store ten hundred-pound bags of compressed grass for one week, Larry and his confederates would pay them a thousand dollars.

"Whoopee!" Paul shouted. "Ra is hip to us!!"

"There was a foul-up," Larry told them, "down in Memphis, and they can't pick it up till next week. I have some other, uh, deliveries, to make and I just can't wait around in New York. Where am I gonna put it, in dad's potato bins at the market?"

The deal was simple. All John and Paul had to do was to hold the dope safe and dry until a certain individual would drive up in a red van and announce himself with the code phrase, "Agnus Dei." With an ahem, Paul asked for a small advance against the thousand dollars and cousin Larry forked over two hundred dollars!!

Late that night, trembling with paranoia, they unloaded the heavy bags down into the cellar beneath the cantina. A few hours later, Paul began to swear that he could smell pot-fumes oozing up through the rather open floorboards. Maybe it was paranoia, but John and Paul both soon thought the pot smell was overpowering. Early the next day they borrowed a truck and drove out to New Jersey where they bought a few bales of hay which they placed in the cantina as "sofas"—hoping the hay fumes

37

would cover for the grass. For double protection they picked up some hundred-pound sacks of flour, pinto beans, and peanuts which they lugged down to the cellar to cover the sacks of dope.

Exactly a week later a man appeared and said, "Hi, I'm Agnus Dei." It was broad daylight.

Paul threw up his hands and said, "You mean we have to load up the hamburger in daylight, in front of a streetful of people!?"

"No"—laughed Agnus Dei, "I'll be back at one A.M."

And so by dark of night they loaded the half ton of grass into the red panel truck. Talk about fear. They scanned the streets again and again. Each passing auto was the Feds. Footsteps were copsteps. They frenzy-finished the job in about two minutes flat.

The man handed them their eight hundred dollars. "See that box?"—the man winked. They looked into the van and saw a packing crate behind a partition. MADE IN HONG KONG was stenciled on the side.

"Yeah, what is it?"

"There are fifty automatic rifles in there for the Operation Thunder people." Operation Thunder was a racist right-wing paramilitary outfit in the Midwest that operated in the early sixties, later branching out into political assassinations.

"They're paying us a hundred bucks apiece."

John and Paul looked at each other. Paul asked, "How are you going to get the weapons to them?"

"I don't know nuttin'. All I know is that I'm supposed to park this van at Twenty-third and Seventh Avenue and leave it overnight. The Thunderbolts, or whatever they call themselves, they'll take care of the rest."

"Let's steal the guns"—Paul whispered as soon as the van had split.

38

"Yeah, let's dump them in the river."

"But, how will we carry them? We can't load fifty machine guns into a cab."

Then they remembered the ancient pushcart outfitted with bicycle wheels that had been in the cellar when they first rented the place. They raised the iron cellar doors and grubbled in the boards and debris in the back of the passageway till they found it. Forthwith, they trotted with the pushcart up to 23rd Street and Seventh where they found the van parked on the west side of the avenue. It was empty, except for the Hong Kong packing case. John smashed the back window and opened the door.

"See if there's a tool kit in the front."

"Yeah, here's one."

"Give me a pry."

They crow-barred the crate-top open enough to see that there were in fact rifles inside, but the box was so heavy they couldn't even move it an inch. John stood on guard duty keeping an eye out for right-wing creeps. Paul removed the lid and started hooking out the greasy weapons. "What'll we do with them?"

John spotted a manhole cover right behind the panel truck. He pried away the cover and said, "Here, in here, we'll dump some in here and cart the rest, whatever we can carry, down to the river."

Paul handed out armloads of the weapons to John who slid them down into the hole. "Make sure they're barrel down. We don't want the workmen to think that any might go off in their faces."

When they had thrown enough away so that they could budge the case, they oof'd it out and onto the cart. They nailed the lid back on and then it was a paranoid sprint to

39

the East Side. They raced to 23rd and Avenue C, then down C to 14th, then to 10th, hanging a left on 10th and they hit Avenue D in a full panic'd gallop. Uh-oh: straight ahead was the East Side Highway. Zzzzt zzzt! the drunken midnighters whipped past. They grabbed the gun box and herenia'd the rifles across the lanes in a sweat-bath scene. They dropped the box on the far side and raced back to the cart, carried it across and heaped the box back on it, frantically looking for an entrance to the park which lay between the highway and the river. They sped south and finally found a path, oops, it dead-ended in a handball court. "We should have brought a flashlight"—Paul groaned, trying to stop the cart before it crashed into the wall.

They spotted a murky opening that seemed to lead through a ballfield with the river just a couple of hundred feet away. Huffily they pushed the cart through center field on the way to second, to home, to the dugout and aha! to a gate at the water's edge. Armload by armload they hurled the rifles into the sewery East River. This done, they collapsed on the ballfield. It was an hour before they could move.

Far, far into the night they celebrated, heaping hookahs of praise upon their lungs, triumphant over the puny smugglers of The Order of Thunder.

It was another year before Total Assault Cantina went bye-bye with the waning desires of the proprietors to face the hassles. Paul left the city and now lives down in Arroyo Aeternitas, New Mexico, whence he has sent back word that he expects to be reincarnated into a pine tree.

John is still +6, but he is caught in the knowledge that they send poets to insane asylums in Russia. "I know I won't be able to live in my own revolution," he wrote me just the other day.

Myself, I began to live in the cellar several years after the Mafia insurance fire. You might say I stumbled upon it. You see, I was working as a part-time research reporter—a stringer they call it—for an uptown newsmag. I was getting a hundred bucks for every report I filed, which was more than adequate at that time, to provide me the leisure to finish that "follow-up novel!" that the critics had assured me in their reviews they were eager to encounter. Anyway, one night I was out researching the post-hippie disaster area of the Lower East Side—you know, for one of those Where Have All the Flowers Gone articles. I was tottery drunk from investigations in Pee Wee's Bar, and I staggered down Avenue A at 2 A.M. past the old Total Assault Cantina. John had told me that some of the hay from the grass-caper was still lying in the cellar, so I lifted the metal flaps, lit a match and stumbled down the steps. Then I passed out. And so it was. I loved the friendly cellar, once I had defeated the rats and water bugs. I approached the landlord who thought I was crazy but gave it up for fifty-five a month.

And I am still living here probably even as you gaze. I am typing this account with my typewriter atop the hay bale from the past. But it is now my dinner time. And I am going to push up the metal flaps and emerge upon the street. Then it's off to the pizzeria on St. Marks Place and a grovel at the source of sources: the white round-topped metal wastebin with the shiny aluminum flap that says PUSH. The wastebin is always crammed with yummy eighths of pizza hunks smashed into those squares of greasy wax paper; not to mention an occasional tablespoon of grape drink hovering in a crushed cup.

41

In fact, I'm usually dining from the pizza trashbin every evening about six o'clock, if any of you who used to hang out at Total Assault should care to drop by and nibble on the past.

Chessman

HE SWITCHED ON the radio. Oops, it was news. It was hard to dial what he wanted, namely some jazz and some horns, in the guts of his smashed sidewalk radio residing in a shoebox.

Caryl Chessman, convicted on May 22, 1948 on seventeen out of eighteen counts of kidnapping with bodily harm, robbery, sex abuse of two women, and auto theft, will die at ten A.M. on Monday in the gas chamber at San Quentin prison in San Rafael, California, a few miles north of San Francisco.

Chessman was known as the Red-Light Bandit, prowling lovers lanes in Los Angeles County using a red spotlight to capture his victims who thought he was a policeman. He has steadfastly maintained his innocence in the twelve years he has lived on San Quentin's death row where he wrote his best-selling book. Governor Brown had granted a sixty-day reprieve to give the California State Legislature a chance to enact laws against capital punishment, but the reprieve is fast running out and the legislature has failed to act.

43

*The odds are very great that Monday, Chessman will get
a lungful of the peach-blossom fumes of potassium
cyanide . . .*

He switched off, a shuddering fantasy of death-gas rising. "Poor Chessman"—he muttered, still slightly zonked
from a late night mesc drop and a morning of fitful
energy spent memorizing the opening verses of *Out of the
Cradle Endlessly Rocking.*

He decided to get some air, so he hit 4th Street for a
stroll to Tompkins Square Park. He spotted his friend
Scoobie and Scoobie talked him into walking over to the
West Side, Sheridan Square, to cop some gage at J.A.'s—a
popular scrounge-lounge of the era located where the Pru-
dential Savings Bank is now. They walked together in the
loping high-speed hipster manner of the time, almost a
run, across the tundra which separated the East Side from
the West.

As they passed the Sheridan Square Bookstore, someone
handed Sam a leaflet announcing a protest march the next
day against Chessman's execution—the march to proceed
from Columbus Circle down to Washington Square to be
followed by a rally at the Judson Memorial Church.

Sam stopped to read the leaflet; Scoobie stood nearby
blowing a complex solo through a tight funnel of rolled
newspaper. "Y'know, Scoob—I think we're going to have
to march for Chessman"—depositing the leaflet in his
jacket.

For years Sam had read about the Chessman case. Even
after tens of articles and broadcasts, it was hard to understand just what Chessman had done to require him to
have to take that final toke. It was like in the '50s trying
to find out, by reading *The Arizona Republic,* just what it

44

was exactly that J. Robert Oppenheimer had done to lose his security clearance.

In Chessman's case, the newspapers were filled with veiled contra naturam babble—of "unnatural acts" the Red-Light Bandit had forced upon his victims. Much was made of one woman who later was sent to an institution, supposedly wrecked in mental health by Chessman's depredations.

The law under which Chessman had been sentenced to death had been removed from the books during the twelve years he had spent on the row, so Sam figured Chessman was being gassed in the name of an hallucination. The State of California was spending hundreds of thousands of dollars to enforce a death because of a forcible act of oral intercourse?

There was a worldwide rise of anger about the impending execution. The Pope was upset. The foreign press railed against it. There were thousands of letters and petitions flooding into the state of California protesting its little metal octagonal death-cone. Sam's brother-in-law's was typical of the attitude of most New York demi-liberals. "Oh, of course capital punishment should be abolished. Certainly it should. However, it should be abundantly clear that Chessman should not be the test case for abolition. He is an atheist. He is a sex fiend."

Hope springs eternal. As a matter of fact, the very afternoon that Sam and Scoobie were walking from the Lower East Side to Sheridan Square to cop, out on the West Coast, Stuart L. Daniels, editor-in-chief of Prentice-Hall, the publisher of Chessman's successful books, was having a conference on death row with the author. After the conference, the editor was asked what the meeting was about. And Mr. Daniels reported, "Believe it or

45

not, he wanted to discuss his writing plans for the future."

Nineteen sixty was an election year, and, as such, certainly not a time of visible pity for any supposed Red-Light Bandit. For instance, in early April 1960, the Union of American Hebrew Congregations sent telegrams to the seven men mentioned prominently as possible candidates for the presidency. Richard Nixon replied that he dug capital punishment for kidnappers: "While we naturally must be concerned about the lives of the criminals that we take, we have a greater concern for the lives of innocent people that might otherwise be taken by criminals if they did not fear this deterrent."

Sam bricked himself out of bed in time to subway up to Columbus Circle for the Chessman march. Sam had never before considered that he would *ever* have taken part in a protest march. As a first experience, it filled Sam with an unutterable urge to march again, to sing again, to protest again. Here was an opportunity to confront the pieces of shit that had ruined it all. The signs were as neat and clear as any Sam would ever encounter, ABOLISH CAPITAL PUNISHMENT, SAVE CHESSMAN, and LEGAL MURDER IS ALSO MURDER. There was a truck bearing a cardboard representation of a death-row cell that went along with the hundred angry and remorseful humans marching at 2 P.M. along 59th Street past the ritzy hotels, waving at the banqueteers at The Plaza tabbing their lips with napkins and gazing down upon the walk. "Come join us!" they yelled. "Join us!"

The march grabbed a right at Fifth Avenue and then it was a slow three-hour trudge down the avenue fifty-one blocks to Washington Square where Norman Thomas and Elaine de Kooning addressed a rally at the Judson

46

Memorial Church. It was young Sammy's first flash of solidarity. His first coordinated anger-flash lined up at the barricades. Little could he guess the thrills the '60s had in store for him, in the matter of sneering and tumbling at the gray barriers.

For Sam, the rest of Saturday was a profligacy of hash, bistros, and yakkety-yak through filters of filth. Sunday, May 1, 1960, was a dry day of listening to the radio. And the Chessman media watch, peppering the airways with snuff bulletins. It wouldn't go away. Sam was nervous, feeling his first twinge of social-protest frustration. He felt like the whole continent was going to the chamber.

Out in California, Chessman gave a press conference and said it was fifty-fifty. If all should fail, Chessman announced, "I intend to walk in and sit down and die."

Also on Sunday, A.C.L.U. lawyer A. L. Wirin visited California's Governor Brown to ask for an additional stay of execution pending a new justice for the California State Supreme Court who would be installed on June 1—maybe the new justice would change the four-three vote on the court that had three times snuffed Chessman's various appeals. Episcopal Bishop James A. Pike also asked Governor Brown for mercy but Brown told them to go jump in the lake.

Steve Allen, Marlon Brando, Shirley MacLaine, Eugene Burdick, and Richard Drinnon all went up to Sacramento to ask Brown to continue the stay until the people could vote in November on the question of capital punishment. Brown said that such a stay would abuse his power and violate his conscience. After the Brown refusal, the lawyers for Chessman had a quick dinner and airmailed a last-minute appeal Sunday night to Washington, D.C. for the U.S. Supreme Court.

47

One hundred college students walked twenty miles from San Francisco to San Rafael Sunday night in order to vigil for Chessman throughout the night.

At 5 P.M. Caryl Chessman was taken from his sixth-floor death-row cell to the elevator in handcuffs clipped to a leather belt. He was taken down to the first-floor "holding cell" to spend his last seventeen hours of oxygen. "I'll see you in the morning"—he told his buddies on the row as he left—a traditional adios given by the condemned as they go down for the final seventeen.

There were two holding cells a few feet away from the eight-sided gas chamber. Chessman was given a new pair of blue trousers, a blue shirt, and cloth slippers. Walking to the holding cell, he was unable to see the gas chamber (so merciful was the architect) located down a small hallway to the right.

Throughout the night, throughout the morn, Caryl Chessman worked on legal papers and wrote his final letters. When they came for him in the morning, he merely put down his pen and prepared to die.

The state supreme court met to consider a petition uttered Saturday morning for a writ of habeas corpus but again voted four-three against it, at 9:10 A.M. of the morn of death.

At 9:25 A.M. an attorney asked the court for a stay to appeal the decision to the U.S. Supreme Court. Again the motion was denied, four-three.

At 9:55 attorneys Gordon T. Davis and Rosalie Asher in the chambers of Federal District Judge Louis Goodwin, requested a brief stay of gas. At the same time, Justice William O. Douglas, having received the airmailed papers in D.C., sent word of denial of stay of execution.

However, Judge Goodwin sent two clerks to tell his

secretary to put a phone call through to the warden at San Quentin to effect a stay. It was approximately 10:03 A.M. The phone number was sent along orally and was misdialed by the secretary. Frantically the number was correctly ascertained and the call made again but the assistant warden at Q told her that the cyanide pellets had just been dropped.

At San Quentin, the place was jammed with spectators. There were sixty witnesses in the witness room, two-thirds of which were radio, TV, and newspaper reporters. Half of the execution capsule jutted into the witness room. There were oblong windows through which to peer into the capsule. There was a sign: POSITIVELY NO SMOKING INSIDE, which was positioned by the entrance door to the green witness room. A handrail was on the outside of the exposed half of the gas chamber, with the sign: KEEP OUTSIDE RAILING AT ALL TIMES.

They all got snuff-pay. The warden as chief lord executioner received one hundred and twenty-five dollars according to the exact ritual. The lieutenant in charge received fifty dollars. The guards, responsible for seeing that the victim proceed orderly without freak-out into his seat, seventy-five each. The chaplain fifty.

On the morning of the gassing they unlocked the front door to the gas chamber. The door was oval shaped, as if the prisoner were stepping aboard a demon airline. The guards checked the chamber for airtightness, for verily not they nor the warden wanted to get washed by cyanide seeping. Inside the chamber were *two* metal chairs, adorned with fabric shackles, so that two by two the state could, in event of mass executions, perform more serviceably.

The "cyanide eggs" were carefully counted and

wrapped in cheesecloth. An officer with rubber gloves hung the cyanide death-balls on mechanical arms beneath the chair above the acid buckets. They measured the acid and poured it into the receptacles that channeled it later into the buckets, so that when the eggs were dropped the prussiate of potash would spew up the peachy fumes. They checked the phone line to the death chamber to see if it worked properly for any possible last-minute reprieve.

Precisely at 9:50 A.M. the warden of San Quentin and the chief medical officer came to Chessman's holding cell. The warden read Chessman's full legal name, and announced the gas hour. The warden shook Chessman's hand and left with the doctor. Chessman's last words to the warden were to deny that he was the Red-Light Bandit.

Prisoners used to be allowed a couple of shots of whiskey in the old days prior to their execution; now they are offered downers and an all-American cigarette and coffee. The guards made one last check of the door to the gas chamber—opening and closing it—to be sure and sure again of a perfect seal. The death-watch guards took a green carpet from the cell adjoining Chessman's and rolled it into place along the ten-foot passageway between his cell and the oval door.

Then it was time to change clothes. The guards walked to the victim's cell to supervise it. The doctor joined them. The victim stripped. The heartbeat was located. A beat-detector was strapped upon Chessman's chest. He then put on a white shirt with the black rubber tube of the detector dangling out. He donned fresh blue denim trousers. No underwear because of shit fit. No shoes, but he was allowed stockings.

50

There was hope all the way. After all, Dostoevsky was given a reprieve even as they lined him up in front of a firing squad. Chessman said goodbye to the prison chaplain, then walked out of his cell, with four guards accompanying him. He turned right and walked along the green carpet to the chamber, stepped up over the lip of the entrance and walked to the right chair and sat down.

The fabric straps were tightened, one across chest, one over his legs, one over forearms. The detecto-tube was hooked to another tube which led into the wall and connected to a stethoscope in the room where the doctor would monitor the beats. They finished the strapping. One guard touched the victim's shoulders and said "Good luck." The legend is carried that a guard usually says, "Take a deep breath as soon as you smell the gas—it will make it easier for you."

The door of steel was closed and screwed tight. The doctor stood poised with his stethoscope headset and clipboard and split-second timer clock. Chessman looked to his right and saw two reporters through the viewing windows and mouthed a final message: "Tell Rosalie I said goodbye. It's all right."

The victim faced the doctor and the prison warden who were stationed in the so-called "Preparation Room." Eye-to-deatheye contact and the spectacle of a coughing, drooling, vomiting victim, could be avoided by lowering venetian blinds placed on the windows of the Preparation Room looking into the death-cone.

At 10:03:15 A.M. the warden nodded to the sergeant who pulled the lever dropping the cyanide pellets into the acid—plop plop. The victim heard the plop and the plop. About ten seconds later Chessman took a breath and slumped into unconsciousness, head nodding, the heartbeat in the headset wild and erratic. At 10:12 he was pronounced dead. The doctor noted the time on the clipboard and took off his headset. The witnesses signed the register and filed outside.

In New York City, Sam was sitting in the library by Washington Square Park, checking out some books, when suddenly he glanced up at the clock. It was 12:59. He gritted his teeth and filled out the library slips. A minute later he began to fantasize about the execution which was occurring right at that moment out in San Rafael. He began to mutter and to curse. The librarian was staring at him.

"Do you know what they're doing *right now!* They're gassing Chessman! Those goddamn killers." The librarian said nothing but turned and saw the light on the book-elevator and trotted over to pull out some tomes.

The Cube of Potato
Soaring Through Vastness

I

THE STEAM CABINET in which he sat was shaped like an old Kenmore washing machine, the gritty quakes of its shakings slightly disturbing the shiny parquet floor-sections beneath it. His secretary was reading Keats to him as he sat in the pure heat: images of dark castle halls and silken bedrooms from *The Eve of St. Agnes* bounced billiardlike within his steam-heated noggin. Emil Cione, the author of the slightly arrogantly titled Pulitzer Prize book of verse, *Am I Goethe or Am I Schiller?*[1], was working on his biology, "my body-tones," preparing for the symposium. His body-tones were of a great concern to him, for certain female graduate students had taken to gazing barfishly at his flaccid ectomorphic body pouched with asthenic bar blubber.

---

[1] Or *Am I Nothing?* as the tome was known in the basement poetry section of the Eighth Street Bookshop.

53

"How much did they say they were paying?" he asked, interrupting the poem just before the lovers 'scaped the castle.

"Two hundred dollars."

II

"How do I look?" asked an anxious voice in another part of the city.

"Like Copernicus, Cheevy, like Einstein," replied a soothing word-stream which once again pointed out his whispered likeness to the great men of science. "Like pale glaciers on bearded mountains . . ." But the word-stream was unable to continue after that particular image, and swirled against the dam.

"How do I sound?" Cheevy asked several minutes later, interrupting the bardic wail he assumed for such occasions, practicing from his triple-spaced all-in-caps opening statement for the Symposium on the Death of the Beat Generation. He was sure he needn't have asked—for not in vain had he slaved those many hours droning into the tape recorder, mutating his public speaking voice, deepening and thickening it. And now, on whim, he could attach a groovy Russian Orthodox choir base line to his normal voice—a voice which usually veered dangerously close to rhinowhine. Voice reworked however, he declaimed with the sort of deep hroat-drone for which, in later decades, NBC would pay a bundle to narrate documentaries on the wild world of jackals. At the same time, Cheevy's detractors viewed these attempts to sing along with Mel Torme as mere ludicrous jiveass wheat-stalk-in-mouth Shakespeak.

He severed his Torme torrent on a sudden. "Actually,

I'm quite glad these bastards are dead—these fried-shoes
boys—these little sniffers after Rimbaud—A figurative
death, of course," he continued, looking up with chin
agrin at his wife's somewhat worried face, to reassure her.

III

Throughout the day of the symposium, editor of fiction
Doris L. Malek was busy in her small cubicle at *Cuff &
Collar, The Magazine for Men* reading through the 275
short stories, and more than elated at not having to spew
an eye on the crinkly, fluffy, seven-and-a-half-inch-high
pile of poems and cover letters, that had piled up during
the week.

Every now and then she uttered a shudder and a tsk tsk
and a sneer sneer. There wasn't, she weened, a decent act
of amatory culmination in the entire collection of veiled
erotic desperation—goddamn fakers!

IV

The rest of the panelists were mulling the muffins of
eternity.

Warner Cleftine went to a party at the Living Theater
in the late afternoon, but couldn't get close enough to
Judith Malina to try to impress her either with his brilliance, or more preferably with a mix of lust/brilliance/
admiration/importance.

John Farraday couldn't find Sy Krim at the San Remo
bar, so scrounged for an hour and a half at the Figaro
reading the French newspapers on the long poles.

V

Now nodding, now shaking their heads, they read the offset announcement, fresh from the morning mail, describing the agenda for the symposium. At the bottom of the flier was a hasty note inviting them to a presymposium cocktail party at the faculty club.

Others would have felt proud to be among the security-cleared few beckoned to the party, but not Al and Ron. Both waxed facially baleful and sore of thought. Jaws of angst pressed molar tooth-roots down into the pained canals.

"They're not serious," one whispered.

"They are," the other replied.

"Stupid fucking punks! They sure are eager to kill it off. The most significant literary event since Pound hitch-hiked into Venice, and they couldn't wait to pull the bell for it!"

His friend was torrid with agreement. "I am certain," he began with a slow, almost chanting voice, "that it is appropriate forthwith to enact a feasibility study relative to Operation Potato Salad." Both broke at once into Hunchback of Notre Dame belfry cackles.

Shortly thereafter, Al and Ron paused at the glass counter in the front of Smiler's Deli on Sheridan Square, bent upon indecision. The dilemma was whether to buy two pounds of oily German potato salad or the other variety creamy with mayonnaise.

They chose the whitish mush-gush for its photogenic qualities, for its great skushiness, and the certainty that it would adhere with smeariness to the skin. Al caressed the white cardboard container with the wire handle, lost in trance-thought. Ron bought the paper plates.

A few minutes later they were practicing hurling plates of salad at the bust of Homer in Ron's apartment.

VI

It was a cold and bitter night. The wind was nearly as exhilarating as the amyl nitrite they were popping in the taxi.

VII

In the lobby of Furie Hall, the Crabhorne Bookstore had set up a small but rather interesting beat generation book booth. There was a painted-over Ace Books metal rack packed with publications like *The Beat Scene*, *Casebook on the Beats*, *Howl*, various City Lights Pocket Poets, *Beatitude*, *Semina*, *Black Mountain Review*, numerous Jargon Press publications, *Kulchur*, *Yugen*, *The Shriek of Revolution*, *Marx-Ra*, *Gone Muh-Fuh Gone*, and other booklets and mimeographics of the day.

Leaning nearly perpendicularly upon an easel was an elegant velvet-covered gold-handled board 'pon which were pinned a history-will-absolve-me collection of twelve letters from publishers stating thanks-no-thanks to the manuscript of *On The Road*—a bit irritating and a bit overpriced at 350 dollars.

Almost like a carnival stall, there was a "manuscripts published in heaven" section—complete with its own little marquee, where one, under close surveillance, could view the original manuscripts of Edward Dahlberg's *Garment of Raw*, Ginsberg's *Sunflower Sutra*, Corso's *Vestal Lady*, the beautiful Reed College calligraphy of some early Phil

Whalen, and the rather out-of-place editors' correspondence and annotations regarding publication of the book, *The Beat Generation and the Angry Young Men*.

The owner of the store was kept adance here and there tidying book piles, flashing his eyeballs back and forth in a closed-circuit-TV goniff-sweep—ever attentive to potential bibliokleptoi, i.e., tome-grabs. A sampler woven of Alka-Seltzer wrappers was sewn upon his soul. For the Crabhorne's rule was this: the very same poet who sells you a signed otherwise unopened *A Lume Spento* may very well lift your mint-condition *Pomes Pennyeach* on the way out.

Business was brisk. Oddly enough, the symposium was held, as if belying its funerary theme, at the beginning of the era of that mysterious rise of library beat-buy. Suddenly there was oozing oodles of money in the budgets of college libraries to buy beat relics and manuscripts. Even on the night of the Symposium on the Death of the Beat Generation, a full run of the magazine *Beatitude* was sold to a representative of the Ohio State University Library for $25. The curator of the Harris Collection of the Brown University Library spent a small fortune that night on early Ginsberg letters. An inscribed first-edition *On the Road* (to Martin Buber) with mint dust jacket brought $17.50. Throughout it all, vectors of Parnassus abounded as several poets stopped by the booth to autograph the piles of their books.

VIII

Emil Cione arrived with an obedient but otherwise cynical bevy of graduate students.

58

IX

The symposium was sponsored by *Foment* magazine,
which for thirty-seven years had lead all periodicals in its
promotion of excellent literature and liberal, almost
demi-socialist thought. *Foment* was so nearly radical, in
fact, that the CIA-Literary-Complex passed it by in offers
of grants and crypto-stipends. There was one period of
years after the war during which few would have cared to
enter the Café Figaro without the latest *Foment* tucked
'neath the axillae of their jackets, protruding enough for
the cover to gain cognizance.

It was impossible for pulse-grabbers at the throat of culture to deny the beats. The information in the minds of
the editorial board of *Foment* magazine, however, was
bedded in the enormous spew of mass attention paid to
Howl and to *On the Road* and to the congeries of poets
who had converged in the mid-'50s in San Francisco. The
living thrill of it, the spirit of it, the birth and sweaty
foment of it, had escaped the ken of the *Foment*ers. And
there was a real hesitance—one might even call it
embarrassment—even among the genuinely sympathetic—to bestow garlands of respect upon a coterie of
"neo-Buddhist roamers who suffer visions." Beatificism
therefore was criticized with a sort of golden worldliness
and quote-clogged mockery—but a wary mockery with
plenty of exit signs, for a critic would want neither to
appear a square, nor would want to be adjudged in later
history to have been a sea-tide of whale dooky, as were
the brusque critics of Keats.

That is, one had to continue to cull the attention of the
querulous young, didn't one? And, if one didn't want to
lose the young's respect, one couldn't very well be in the

position of hurling garbage and leaflets down upon the stage in the middle of a Tristan Tzara poetry reading, could one? For everyone was aware of the frequent fate of literary garbage-hurlers: that later years, even later centuries, find plenty of case-files opened on the garbagers, and plenty of pens poised ready to garbage the garbagers. All considered, the editorial board of the magazine deemed it suitable to hold a gentle wake, as it were, in honor of their recently deceased b. g. comrades.

The format of the Symposium on the Death of the Beat Generation was as follows: The first half was devoted to the origins and social etiology of the generation. The panelists were to have delivered hopefully short opening statements followed by a round robin of comments by the panelists in response to each others' remarks. Then there would be a twenty-minute intermission, certainly the high point of any such event, with opportunities to gossip, relive the past, climb climb climb, and to stare with abandon, face upon face.

After this, there was the second half, devoted with loving tenderness to the roots of demise, that is, to the alleged dissipation and dissolution of the b. g. Then the panelists would receive questions.

It was felt there might occur considerable acrimony from the floor, so within the program for the symposium deposited on the Furie Hall seats was a blank sheet for questions. Just before the event began, editorial scheiss-slaves wandered down the aisles collecting the sheets.

The thick pile lay shortly later upon the moderator's central position, as if it were the thickery of the *Foment* morning mail. He glanced at a few, and winced.

"Is there a sense of God still to be portrayed in modern fictional analysis?" the first sheet asked.

60

"Will the sky-brain survive the supernova?"

"Did the atomic explosion at Hiroshima destroy any human souls?"

"Why was Norman Podhoretz not invited to be on this panel?" And on the same sheet: "Why did Mr. Cione, when he was employed as manuscript reader in 1954, refuse to urge Random House to print the great American novel, *Spine of Ferrous Willow*?"

"Good God," the moderator spake curtly, "it really *is* going to be one of those nights."

We cannot here depict this Intellectual Beatnik Wake in full—for we want, in this tale, for you to have time to attend the party after the symposium. You can, however, obtain the microfilmed transcription for about $2.50 from the Library of Congress, where the CIA Poetry Operations Division, after analysis and inspection, later deposited it.

First of all, it is necessary to know a few details about the panelists and of course about the partisans of Operation Potato Salad. And you must not think it rude of us if we point out certain spastic mis-chips in the facets of their diamond souls.

Panelist A: Doris L. Malek. So-called "acid wit"—scriptwriter, editor, novelist, alky. An atheist by ascience. She is always careful to be publicly bored, because "it's all been done before." Chosen for the panel, and willing to attend, because of vague memories on the part of the choosers of her flaming youth among the poets and radicals of the early '20s. Museum basements were amply supplied with oils of Doris Malek in the Rebel Girl mode from the Greenwich Village cafeterias.

Her secret, alas to report, is that she is a compulsive snitch; has written maybe five hundred letters,

61

particularly to J. Edgar Flabflab, snitching out various "crimes" of her acquaintances. With the growth of drug use, she has enjoyed glorious snitch-years.

Panelist B: Emil Cione. The prizewinning author of books of verse every three years. He has had one successful novel, *The Mountain of Reason,* which missed the prizes, because the central characterization lead to litigation, based as it was on the private life of a leading literary critic who had dared to dribble spittle on Cione's first book of verse, in the *New York Herald Tribune.* But that is a story for another occasion. Cione is a real-estate dealer on the side, an interest picked up in his youth when he had taken a graduate course on the pre-Socratic philosophers, and had learned of the famous olive scam of Thales the Milesian.

For a jive snickerer had approached the eminent mathematician and astronomer, and had regaled him: "How come, if you are so smart, you are poor and hut-bound?" Thales thereupon scanned the winter sky and determined that there was going to be a heavy olive crop. He paid deposits on all the olive presses in Miletos and Chios, and when the crop indeed was superabundant, he rented out the presses at rip-off rates and made the mon. Cione was ready to tattoo this vignette on his forehead.

"My olive presses are all the buildings of upper Broadway. I'll own them all!" Cione told a horrified friend. Some of the finest verses ever to grace a CIA-sponsored magazine were written by Cione standing in county assessors' offices reading old maps of property lines, trying to locate the so-called "litigious few"—i.e., a few feet of borderline controversy o'er which to go to law.

Cione took too much amphetamine to have time to become an alcoholic—that would come later, when he kicked A in terror after his toenails dropped off. His politics, so he bragged, were similar to Pindar's and Simonides'—he was a Cold War poet among C-W poets. His feet were swathed in the russophobic ice. But perhaps we are being unfair, for he did have softness of heart for every one of his students, and cried over the comrades of his youth.

He loathed dirt. He shuddered with disgust at the concept of the "sweaty moil," of brutes mating on mattresses to the pierces of insectual saxophones. Dirtiness was his fear. The dirtiness he *knew* suffused the backroom Communist cell meetings; the dirtiness of North Beach fingernails; and above all the dirtiness of the Dirt Road—as the Bulgarian aperture was known on Times Square. The thought of a membrum entering an anus—an act sometimes lauded in Beatific verse—such a thought, through its repetitious occurrence in full-color dreams, nearly sent him into a nuthatch. In fact, the CIA psychiatric profile on Cione indicated existence of a recurrent dream wherein a stubble-faced beatnik, breathing on Cione's neck with Chianti vomo-fumes, forcibly buggers him while forcing Cione at the same time to hold in his own hands and to read aloud Podhoretz' article, "The Know-Nothing Bohemians," from *Partisan Review.*

Panelist C: Corgere "Cheevy" Samuelson. Alky. Fifteen hundred empty pocket-sized Seagram's 7 bottles are filed in the unused basement furnace hidden from wife. Cheevy was America's great expert, when it cared about such things, on the proletarian novel. His career had begun in such radical splendor that New York Red Squad agents, disguised as poets, followed him from cafeteria to cafeteria in the Greenwich Village nights of the Great Depression. By the era of the symposium, Cheevy had changed. Fear of being found the color pink caused him to shit in terror. After all, where could he store his 27,000 books if he had to go on the lam?

He maintains a secret admiration for Stalin and the Chinese Revolution, but has sublimated his sensitivities so that he no longer writes poems about hobo camps in the Midwest while sitting in the Yale University library. In later years, while waiting patiently for a magenta astral projection above the White House, he has grown rich from a family-operated chain of bookstores in college towns.

We must feel kindly toward Mr. Samuelson, for he nearly cried that night in desperate inner unhappiness because Viking Press had just that day rejected his book of essays—and the snickering word of exultation had not even snickered yet to those on the panel.

Panelist D: Warner Cleftine, the editor-in-chief of *Foment* magazine, and moderator of the symposium. His whitened hair arose in a beautiful Conway Twitty-like puff above his smooth bulging forehead. Compulsively serious. He was fired up with hatred for injustice, and a few years later no one was more effective in arranging the financing of the moratoria against the war. He was adept at getting his friends out of the draft by phone calls to his friends and former college mates at the Agency, till 'Nam soured friend against friend.

Warner could set up for certain writers 730 straight days of financial security and social grace by mystic and unknown means of which they received the great one-two of a Guggenheim Fellowship one year, followed the next by a Rockefeller Fellowship. Ahhh followed by Ahhh.

He was a specialist in invitations to government-sponsored conferences. A packed suitcase lay 'neath his bed at all times.

64

Panelist E: John Farraday—the nearest thing to a beat that could be cajoled upon the panel. Farraday was more of a hipster tough guy than a beat. He attached himself eagerly to the energy of the movement, but was not a believer—sort of like those humans who waited until 1970 to struggle against the Vietnam War.

Farrady felt, for instance, guilt at not being able to write spontaneously. Each paragraph took days; it was not the creative agony of Joseph Conrad, but rather it was "why? why? why?" muttered over and over, head leaning on the Olivetti.

It was strange that Farraday had agreed to appear on the panel. Some ascribed it to the pressures of his literary agent. Others that he had been asked while drunk, forgot, and was horrifyingly reminded by a thank-you letter from *Foment.* He did have a self-defeating urge to insult, which may have supplied the reason—he was to be the spice for a possibly tepid evening.

The two provocateurs of Operation Potato Salad were not from heaven. Al was a notorious rakehell and trouble lover. "When in doubt, riot"—this was his principle apothegm. Above his writing desk, inflaming his mind, was Degas' *Absinthe Drinkers,* a life-style he ever strove to emulate. At the time of the symposium he had a secret wife hidden in rat-cage poverty in the Bronx with four kids. His salvation, he felt, was in the following: Even if I'm a punk, a poor father, a profligate, and a piss ant, if my *Verse* is there, then history will not empty out its offality upon my impish ways. Do you dig how they couldn't destroy Poe, man?

Ron, the second provocateur, was an outstanding

65

translator of Persian verse, and an excellent poet in his own verse-stream. One thing might have hindered his meteoric career in translation and poesy: his fetish requiring the devoration of cockroaches. O, come now! Do not avert your head in disgust! It's not as bad as that. After all, does not Emil Cione lick the cold cream off used broom handles?—which is equally as questionable an act.

The trouble began with traumatic experiences suffered on Wilderness Survival Training for the U.S. Air Force, where, after his secret supply of Milky Ways had run out, and futile searching for small beasties at streams, he ate in the moist crackly cafeterias beneath rocks. And in the wonderful words of William Burroughs, "Wouldn't you?" Any hardshelled bugs will do: preferably the protein-rich June bug. In New York, however, the song is "Cucaracha."

Time and time he is almost caught, by his wife, by his boss. Clandestinity always won, for he knew all too well if fashionable literary circles should hear the merest hint of poet as roach-eater, he would be finished. The Apollinairean Poet as Prophet was at last acceptable, but not *un poête insectiphage*. (The reader will take comfort to know that the urge was yelled out of him in an Esalen encounter session in 1967.)

X

By crowd-noise standards, it was a low roar. The panelists were in place. Water was poured in the glasses. The notepads were placed in front of each chair. The microphones were checked by a number-mumbling attendant. All was of the stone steps leading up the ziggurat of truth. And Warner Cleftine, editor-in-chief of *Foment* magazine, whizzed a "humph" into the microphone, followed by the tinkle-tankle of his watchband against the water pitcher, and the low din subsided and 900 babbling faces pivoted toward the stage and the table and the poised minds there behind it.

Cleftine began. "We are gathered here to discuss and to analyze and hopefully to come away with better understanding of a recent kind of literature strongly mirrored in our cultural soul." He'd advanced just that distance into his statement when John Farraday rose from the table and began to pace in an oblong ellipse on the stage behind the panel. The muttered curses were not picked up by the microphones. Farraday probably had intended to leave the stage getting the hell out of there; yet he was somehow held in orbit—unable to break away. Throughout the symposium he either paced or sat near the wings, swigging a tequila flask with the curtainman whom union rules demanded to be at hand.

"Balzac Balzac Balzac!" Farraday muttered from the pacing. Sprinkled in the audience were ten or fifteen young professional novelists—professional in the sense that they were not poets who as the times grew rough dialed their minds into prose instead, for bread, in dread: brain dead. These properly cool rising novelists, hungry for the black-edged best-seller box in *The New York Times* Sunday literary section—all smirking, look at that pitiful Farraday up there! Look! I am not there! I! I! I! I!

There was an embarrassed group in the audience of Farraday's publishers and editors, the Maxwell Perkinses of his career, who thought he just might be a tube of one-shot lighter fluid. They refused to print his manuscripts in the order of composition. The era of Dickens is over, young man. Instead they urged him to write a quick book on the private lives of the creative poor. "Your experiences, young man, write them up, but with logic, syntax, normal punctuation, and believable characters. Then you'll be rich, son; you can learn to die in every climate in the world, following the sun . . ."

After Warner Cleftine's opening remarks, the evening sputtered forward. The learned comments of the panel were noticeably intertwined and the staff upon which they were twined was this: that the cortege bearing the body of a literary movement—whe'er Futurism, Vorticism, Imagism, or beatery—is a sadly beauteous sight. The audience therefore heard the beats praised as a "bellwether" against "cultural polio" and against "creeping paralysis and tepid conformity."

Cheevy Samuelson had an interesting analysis of the b.g., comparing it to the era of the Dadaists in Zurich and Paris 1916–26. As Mr. Samuelson began to speak, one could view in the front row the famous magazine reporter writing in his legal-sized yellow his sneering notation of Cheevy's "Cuban beard, so fashionable these days among those who admire Dr. Castro."

"Like the Dadaists," Cheevy slowly spoke, "the beats wrote a few interesting books—influenced a few others—inspired a dozen good articles, created scandals and gossip, and had a good ole time. They insulted the public, and perhaps our complacent *res publica* needed it. But they did nothing more. The b. g. diverged from Dada on the metaphysical plane however. . . ." A smile appeared on two panelists' faces at the word *metaphysical*—ole Cheevy and his mysticism, you know. "For it had no known tradition behind it, broken away with finality as it was from the Judeo-Christian tradition. It was visionary, it was a promise of a new American Contemplatio! So

Now, so new, that it hardly existed. Yet, on the literary plane the beat generation can aptly be interpreted as a deliberately effected cultural maneuver on the part of its adherents, to leap into that Art-clogged river of the Cubists, Futurists, Vorticists, Imagists, Expressionists, Constructivists, Dadaists, Surrealists, and Action Painters, and to claim thereby direct descendency! The beats sought to claim such an adornment. O, would that it were so!"

In spite of his energetic presentation, Cheevy sat down to applause as puny as fingersnaps at a coffee-house reading.

Miss Malek announced, to great laughter, that human beings had been jumping off the Bel Air Hotel "waving genitals and manuscripts" for over thirty-five years and she didn't see what all the fuss was about. "I mean," said she, "it's all been done! These people have—rather, had, nothing to give us, nothing." She confessed without a blink to being unable to read for pleasure but rather, or so she implied, for possible borrowing of ideas, techniques, plots, and characterizations. "I read in a business-like way and believe me, there's nothing to (lift from) these books, not even Kerouac's!"

An interesting man arose at this point, his long broomy white hair twined Hasidically into tangled dangles in all directions, and waved aloft the current issue of *Trans-Quake Quarterly*, and announced that, if any should desire, he would repair to the lobby at intermission where issues could be bought, for they contained his recently completed trilogy of novellas, the title of which was lost to us, for an insecurity spasm, or something, caused him almost to whisper the title.

And he continued: "I should like to address Miss Malek

with a question. It is this, in two parts: Don't you think that extreme narcissism helps the growth of the spirit and psyche within the hostile iron clouds of the robot interlude? And, secondly, have you had a chance to read those short stories I sent you?"

The gavel pounded immediately. "We shall have to reserve questions"—Cleftine leaning a little too close to the windscreenless mike—"until the second half of the program, after the intermission. Thank you."

It is fitting to note that the panel, down to a member, agreed that "injustice is unjust." "I *do* hate injustice," Miss Malek said in closing, "and I love life." Several short derision-hoots, even sneers, issued forth from the audience before the applause drowned out the heckling.

One would think there would never be a fistfight at such a sadness scene, yet hostility bounced from the chandeliers when Emil Cione began to talk. To improve his babble-flux, Cione had lowered his head to his lap and quickly had slipped two Benzedrine tablets into his craw. To wash them down, a trusted student had brought him his glass of vodka disguised as water. All this was going down as he was being announced, and he had become confused. He half-arose from his chair as if to walk to a podium, then jerkily checked himself, realizing it was a sit-down scene—nodding at the introductory applause.

Cione had a prepared statement, a rule he never broke—for you could never tell when you might be too drunk or too A'd, and one certainly did not want to appear to rave from the sibylline tripod. His intention was not to be hostile, nor to rave. But something caused him to snap.

Only a small segment of the audience seemed to react to Cione's shrillness, as if he were a gospelist. This portion

70

was crackling with shouted yesses! and short clacks of applause. It was like watching blue-haired snuff buffs—those senior citizens who hang out at murder trials—shift and twitch in excitement as a jury files in to announce a yes-vote for a death penalty.

"The civilization in its mercy, in its democracy of the moment, gave them their say, gave them God-knows-how-many headlines and articles, but the beats mumbled and stuttered and slipped aside.

"I have tried to read these so-called books, but I can't finish them!" Cione barked. "None of these people have anything interesting to say. Type type type, locked in their grimy hobo towers, but what is it? Typata-typata-typata! It was an entire ersatz Byronic nightmare! Bad sex, bad logic, bad breath, bad linguistics! For these little 'personal madmen poets'—to quote Jack Kerouac, who could have been a good writer, if he had only written . . ." Chuckles arose from Cione's faction on the floor.

"But the fact remains that these deadbeat beats are beaten upon their beat feet with the bastinado of indiscipline!"—pausing, though not a throat of laughter was heard to utter, to let the line slide home. "And—beret of inglorious berets—"they are stupid!" pronouncing the *u* at great length as if it were a line of molossic dimeter.

"Booo!" boo'd a large half of the audience, for there were many students of the Big Beat suffering spasms of nausea—kicking themselves first of all for paying two bucks to partake of this jive-o-rama.

"One does *not* admire their chaos!" Cione cooked onward. "But, it *is* a cunning chaos, is't not so?"—voice shrill for a flash, on the *so*. "For if they could get us all into their pads and lairs—that is, break down the

71

structure, then they could overpower us and force our awe!"

"Bullshit!" someone shouted. "Hallucinations!" another. "Bravo!" a third.

"I will never, for the life of me, understand why publishers, and we do not here mean to cast aspersions on the essential worth of publishers—but I cannot understand why, just to fill their annual publishing lists, they should stoop to print such unblinkingly stupid yahoo grime."

He embarked upon a litany of b. g. transgressions, including "their free-associations in poorly remembered languages, their pleonastic verse which seeks to follow the berserk fingers of hop-head jazzmen . . ."

Meanwhile, Al and Ron had edged to the front during the past few sentences. Cione—eyes out of focus near the chandeliers of the ceiling, railed onward about the many indignities suffered because of "these howling Zen freaks" and "these vermin in the cellar of the Communist storefront" (which caused Cheevy Samuelson a certain uneasiness).

Cione next uttered a long sentence which, except for its ending: "next to the offal mattresses the candles drip down upon their demijohns of bad Chianti," was impossible to hear, because it was at that point that Al and John enacted Operation Potato Salad.

"One, two three," Ron counted off; then in tight harmony they sang, "Am I Goethe"—followed by a barber shop quartet "hummmmmm." Then, a Beach Boys soprano sang, "Or Am I Nothing?"—and Ron threw a high arching shot at Cione, the plate following behind the main glob of potato salad beautifully—the glob spreading into a face-covering ovalness.

A precise cube of potato broke away somehow from the

72

main salad glop, and was traveling about six inches in the avant-garde; the cube of potato looking like a mayo-smeared marble sugar cube by Marcel Duchamp.

Cione was unaware. "Livid with shrieks but . . ." The glop still on target, "but lurid in license . . ." Glop still zero'd in on bard-nose. "and lost in laziness . . ."

Someone watching this on slow-motion film would have noticed that the soft edge of the potato cube actually entered Cione's left nostril whereas the rest of the cube broke away and traveled up his cheek, bounced against the upper eye socket and arc'd up o'er the table.

It was a situation with the validity of a microsecond however, as the bulk of the salad was hard behind the sentry cube, and, by an act of Ptah, the plop-smush hit Cione's face almost one-on-one, followed by the crimped-edged plate itself and the bard was fair covered by the oniony wetness.

Yarr. Har. Har. went the audience, forgetting its high purpose for just a moment. Even his grad students, dutifully jotting notes, wiggled and giggled. For verily their mentor, eyes besmirched, could not view their levity.

Immediately the moderator whacked the gavel and announced the intermission.

XI

After the toss Al ran away from the stage. At the wings he slipped on a scattered glob and fell back cracking his noggin. Supine, he spotted Cione's billfold fallen upon the stage beneath the table. He lunged for it and ran to the back of the room, checking the contents as he ran. The thirty-five dollars he added to his own five. After finding a love note to Cione, apparently from one of his students,

73

Al sprinted into the bathroom to read it. It was a long note, speaking in rhymed iambics of trees and leaf-drift and arcane hints at trysts "in the tower"—i.e., the Holiday Inn on Route 22. Al strode to the Crabhorne Bookstore booth where, to his discredit, he attempted to sell it.

Doing so, a smirching olive-quarter fell from Al's sleeve upon the *Garment of Ra* manuscript, perhaps diminishing its value by twenty-five dollars. "Well, we're really not interested," Mr. Crabhorne replied, "but you may leave it here. We'll hold it for him."

XII

Cione sputtered, potato chunks spewing from his lips. "Call the police! Guard! Guard!" He threw a handful of mush back, missed; hit one of his pupils bent down taking notes. "Fool!" he shouted. "Why are you sitting there? Do something!"

Then Cione spotted Ron walking up the aisle getting slapped on the back by chortling friends. Cione leaped off the stage and tackled the young roach-eating translator of Persian poesy. Cione opened an extremely tiny pearl-handled penknife and grabbed Ron's wrist and yanked it down to a rest on Emil's knee, and proceeded to inflict a series of barely skin-piercing stabs into the hand, while leaning down close to Ron's ear whispering, "Death your verse, death your verse, death your verse . . ."

XIII

The intermission was wonderful. Samuel Beckett could have written a sixty-five-page sentence describing the movement of eyes from face to face in the intensity.

Eyeball set EE_1 looked at eyeball set EE_2 who was looking at EE_3. EE_3 glanced at EE_1 who panned slowly across the field of EE_2-EE_3-EE_4-EE_5. . . . EE_{11}, and EE_6 looked wantonly at EE_5 (Emil Cione) while EE_8 etc. . . .

XIV

She was carrying about fifteen books, including all five editions to date of Cione's *The Mountain of Reason*. She paused longingly by the faintly oil-stained jacket of the bard. She clicked her ballpoint into position. Cione waved it away. "I never sign with ballpoints"—as he hooked out his thick Montblanc with a flourish of wrist-flick. He paused to close his lil' pearl knife with the slightly rubicund blade, and wrote his name and the time of the occasion in each of his many books.

XV

The couple was standing at the book booth. The man said, "I don't care what you say. Everybody's entitled to their opinions. Those boys were *not* respectful!"

She was not paying any attention to him. Suddenly she found it: "Aha, I knew it, I knew there was something about throwing potato salad in here!" She was holding a mint-condition inscribed first edition of *Howl & Other Poems*. "Shall I read the section?" she asked.

Sure go ahead."

Who threw potato salad at CCNY lectures on Dadaism
and subsequently presented themselves on the granite
steps of the madhouse with shaven heads and

harlequin speech of suicide, demanding instantaneous lobotomy[1]

"Look," he responded, "I don't care if it was in *The Iliad*. Those young men were disrespectful to a great American author.

XVI

The party was held at one of those shiny-floored fifteen-room New York apartments with the rugs all rolled up for the night and jammed into the children's wing. On the walls were twenty-five expensive paintings, all with melted-snow sections of pure canvas and pencil lines.

The salad tossers had mumbled at the man trying to find their names on the front door list, and pushed their way in. They began their *Absinthe Drinkers* impressions at once. Ron took two senior editors from *Time* and a major newspaper critic into the bathroom with some pot and locked the door, causing a major congestion of the bladderially tense outside.

Al sidestepped into the bedroom and dialed his wife in the Bronx. "How come you never take me to any parties?" she wanted to know when she had pried his whereabouts out of him.

"My career, baby, it's for my career, I don't actually *like* these shindigs"—his hand casually moving from coat pocket to coat pocket in the pile on the bed.

"Well bring some milk home. Have you forgotten that Number Four is sick, Mr. Terrible Father?"

---

[1] Ginsberg. *Howl & Other Poems*, p. 15, City Lights Books, San Francisco. This is an example of an image influencing an image. For Al and Ron certainly did not know that the *Howl* 'tato-toss had actually occurred, performed by Carl Solomon and several friends, who hurled upon Wallace Markfield in the course of a Markfield lecture on Mallarmé.

Indeed he had, as he clicked the receiver in time to grab the hostess down upon the furry pile of garb, attempting a quick act of coat-pile gropery, which failed and nearly got him thrown from the revel.

XVII

Cione's Village Hideaway was known to no one, not even his accountant. Nor did his wife ever discover that he had recovered the thrown-away sheets from the garbage for his lair of license. It was here the novel of novels would be conceived, he told himself, although there were cobwebs in the toilet bowl and curdled six-month-old milk in the refrigerator.

"Do you want some tea?" he asked her.

"Yes. Do you mean grass?"

"Uh no. I have Earl Grey and English Breakfast."

"Oh, no thanks." She stood in the doorway of the bedroom. Cione was already on the bed, his hands behind his head, his belt rakishly half-undone.

She walked into the kitchen and counted the liquor bottles crowded on a wheeled metal cart. There certainly is a lot of alcohol, she thought, gazing at the dusty bottles, many nearly empty, of

Smirnoff Red	Creme de Cacao	Wild Turkey
Smirnoff Blue	Kahlua	Gordon's Gin
Seagram's 7	six-pack of Bud	Old 1889
Stolichnaya	Sloe Gin	Jack Daniels
Cherry Heering	Heaven Hill	Metaxa
Creme de	Four Roses	Banana Cordial
Menthe	Three Feathers	Remy Martin

77

plus four dried and moldly lemons, a mummified quarter of lime, and an old Chelsea Hotel towel stiff and brown from ablutions long completed.

He interrupted her as she was insistently, even amphetaminishly, recalling those recent events of Furie Hall whose witness she was from the front row. He oozed into her word-stream at midsentence, and began to talk himself about the essay over which had been long poised in creation—how he must hurry, for the conference was just two weeks away. The rrrhuht of the zipper sliding open down her back, and the knuckles of his hand feeling the heat of her skin as the fingers zipped downward, triggered off at least a third of a sonnet but he did not dare reach over to the bedstand to make any notes.

Instead, he asked, "Can you type?"—reaching up to grab her; his hand nudging a breast then speeding down the arm and smoothing out over her long wan fingers, the instruments which might, he hoped, whip his rough scrawls into shape.

All at once she sat up and shook her hair loose upon her shoulder. Without a word she stood, put on her dress and walked out of the apartment.

For an hour Cione lay on his side staring at the wall. He bit the lace at the corner and at last drove a fist into the pillow. "Why won't anybody make it with me?"

Johnny the Foot

HE READ THE REPORTS. He accepted the reports. He internalized the reports. What reports? The reports of the dirty beatnik. What a thrill to live in scarabaeic dinginess. America was a bear skull, the poems raged. The morons of Moloch rafted through their sewer of ad-blurbs, censorship, Commie-fear, and wreaked their beaks upon the shiny eyes of the nearly deceased, like vultures of plunder above the mired. And what need, pray tell, was there to wash? To please the delicate nasality of those who only came within sniff-range to put you down anyway?

That is, zones exist. Don't come in our zone. If you do, please love with leg-fling frenzy, or go away. On the other hand, our zone is the future.

And they walked past the Provincetown Playhouse looking for the ghost of John Reed, or waited for e. e. cummings to dart across Sixth Avenue for the daily walk. They sat in the bistros to watch the poets read shriek-songs. They yelled for help in the putrefaction, but settled for kicks and dirt and thrills—or ear-verse in the Jazz Gallery half-light praying for Sonny Rollins to beat away the mucous of soul mal.

79

Yea, Plains of Gold, Nebraska had lost its finest artist when Johnny took a suitcase full of sketches and headed for the Greyhound terminal. And what was it that Washington Square Park gained? It gained a stunned young mammal scribbling with joy, who plugged into a heaven of body-burning solipsism, sex, pot, liquor, and beatific Buddhism. Just to walk unnoticed in the harsh city for months, that alone was Total to Johnny. *"Je est un autre. Je est un autre,"* he whispered to himself sketching on a bench.

And then to make friends with other escapees, ahhh what fulfillment in the park. As weird as you wanted, you were still One with the parklings. And the only people who asked any questions were the police.

The energy came from a desperate search for some indication that the universe was more than a berserk sewer. Johnny scored obscure mimeo'd magazines in the Eighth Street Bookshop and began to memorize the data right on the street as he walked around. The problem was transformation: that principle of mathematics that said there had to be equations of transformation from one system to another. O how sorely Johnny yearned to be transformed, and looked for the symbols of transformation in holy verse; and in the language he heard in the streets and bistros: the words of the "Bop Kaballah"—as one bard phrased it. And he also wanted to feel holy— and, if not holy, like, cooled out, as they said, cooled in the cosmos, at least as much as Siddhartha by the river. As if thinking that the "crowned knot of fire" that Eliot wrote about in *Little Gidding* could be ordered at a coffee house, or summoned as a wraith from a page.

In the First Christian Church of his youth he'd stood up

to sing that tune about the "Beautiful words, wonderful words, wonderful words of Life," just before they passed the collection plate. To Johnny, that was bunk from a punk. But now, as he heard the Words of Life as performed by the anarcho-SkyArt dharma-Commie jazz church of the New York streets and pads, he felt the purest Hieratic Vastness, felt plugged into the Ladder. Greed ceased as a possibility, and the eyeball on the pyramid's apex, back of the dollar bill, rolled out of the park, through the Holland Tunnel, all the way to Minneapolis where it made a blind person see again. That was the sort of possibility that Johnny felt. He was ready for the spaceships to land.

He abandoned soap, abandoned the seasons, lived upon the concrete tracks of lower New York as if they were the props of a stage production. Dirt captured the hill. His socks became a toeless ring of frayed rot. His T-shirt mutated through the gray palette on the way to anthracite. If there was something important to do like trying to score a blue breadline card, he would wash those things that jutted into the air, namely his face and his hands. Winter and summer he wore the same outfit: a black turtleneck sweater, black despicable engineer boots or adios'd tennis shoes, green corduroy jacket and, in a bow to the past, a postage stamp on his forehead.

And his feet. He did not wash his feet from April 4, 1959 till November 15, 1961. His feet were his masterpiece. He felt they were art. After a few months of no-wash, his feet began to mummify. They developed a dry charcoal-black surface similar to the crust in the pocket of a catcher's mitt when it is not oiled properly. Contrary to public opinion, the professionally aged and unwashed mummified foot does not give off any particularly

81

obnoxious toke. It both looked and smelled like burnt toast, and it offered to the bold feeler a texture of great crusty complexity, like a painting.

He tried to enter his feet in an art show in the gallery of the Judson Church in the summer of 1960, but was politely rejected, although he offered to stand quietly in a far corner atop a milk crate where he proposed to lean an empty gilt picture frame against them for proper setting. He even promised to spray them with fixative to prevent untoward vapors of vom vom from offending the delicate gazers.

As vengeance for his rejection, Johnny sprayed his feet with gold spray paint and stood on the gallery porch all through the show with a picket sign of protest on his breast.

Denizens of Washington Square named him Johnny Filth Feet. Johnny had a case file opened on tourists. He didn't know whether to love 'em or to hate them. He settled upon a role as promulgator of revulsion. The scam worked wonderfully in the summer tourist season and netted him a continuous flow of money. The first step was to place the all-important hat by the fountain to catch the shekels. Then he'd launch into a sharp-toned drawl trying to act like a carnival barker. "Beat feet! Beat feet! Come see the despicable beat feet! Never been washed! Put your quarters in the hat! Beat feat! Beat feet!" Somehow, that created tremendous crowds, who circled him thickly, some standing on tiptoes for a better scope, like a golf crowd trying to watch a championship putt.

And it could not be believed how this foot-shill routine kept Johnny Filth Feet rolling in cappuccino and baklava at Rienzi's Coffee House. It even paid the rent. He did other things to bedazzle the tourists that crowded the

82

Village in the beatific era. Growling and slobbering, he often fell at the feet of a passel of map-clutchers. There was one weekend in August of '60 when he fell to his knees, head tumbling forward, and began to lick a Dreamsicle stick upon the ground in its wet, crumpled Dreamsicle wrapper. Tongue-trails wetted the perimetric tar. He groaned, he slithered, a crowd developed. He was arrested. The police dispersed the crowd. The squares put their Brownie Hawkeyes back into their purses.

But what could the fuzz hold him for? Felonious slurping of a Dreamsicle wrapper? They held him in handcuffs in the Parks Department building in front of Judson Church. When he was left alone for a moment, he immediately removed his shoes and socks, brackish tarsals wiggling in the air.

And then the fuzz returned to haul him off to the paddy wagon but stopped in their tracks when they spotted the slime-spackled appendages, and averted their eyes in disgust. After a monotoned conference, they unlocked the cuffs and told him to get out of the park and stay out.

There was another thing Johnny noticed. The tourists loved to get close to the beatniks—some even reached out to cop a touchy-feely. Others were bolder. Never would he forget the razor-nosed woman wearing wing-shaped glasses and her husband, a marvel in bermuda shorts and a baseball cap, who approached him one afternoon as he sat on the ledge of the statue of Alexander Holley. When they were about two feet away from him, the woman leaned forward and almost collapsed to the ground. Johnny thought she had stumbled and reached out to prevent her from crashing her face into Holley's torso. That's when he heard an unmistakable sniffing sound. Her face was only an inch and a half from his mottled jacket's axilla as she filled her questing lungs. With great and severe dignity, the woman straightened up and continued onward with her husband, undoubtedly prepared to regale the relatives at Thanksgiving dinner about the hideous beatnik armpit she nearly crashed into.

After a few feet they quickly turned and hauled out their camera, took a fast snap, executed an about-face and marched out of the park.

Johnny Filth Feet guessed that in the golden era of 1958–61, he had his picture taken about ten thousand times in Washington Square. Countless were the vacation albums in the Midwest containing pictures of him lounging in such a position, as was his pleasure, so that Henry James' old house at the park's north side would be seen in the background.

Filth Feet's greatest moment in the park was the Folk Song Riot of April 9, 1961, an event which turned him for several years into a disciplined, leaflet-crazed rioting maniac. Up to that day, his only protest had been when he sprayed his feet gold outside the art show. April 9 was a Sunday and all that morning Johnny sat surly on the edge of the fountain suffering a brain-throb diagnosed by his friends as a hashover. Added to that was the horrifying rejection of his body the night before relative to the underwear question.

It used to disturb women that he wore no underwear. The time, of course, was 1961. It was all very well that his 3rd Street apartment, a quarter-hour trudge from Washington Square Park, probably set for all time the outer parameters of gunge. One bedroom was known as the "garbage room" and during the course of a year had grown stuffed from floor to ceiling with brown bags of bye-bye. Rats used to commit suicide trying to jump into

84

the garbage room from the ledge of an adjoining building. And it was fine that his beret was glazed with sky grit, that his jeans had obviously been worn for months, that his tennis shoes were a patchwork of tape and wrapped with clothesline cord. When, however, down derry down dropped the jeans and there was no underwear, they were shocked. Added to that, there were other matters, that is, certain genitalic tattoos which quoted Verlaine, the description of which we shall pass over in silence. Let it be only said that when the young woman from Forest Hills the previous evening was confronted, on a sudden, in the pants-drop gloom with an erect member emblazoned in a most rubicund manner with the words, *"Oh! je serai celui là qui créera Dieu!"* she fled.

The Folk Song Riot was occasioned by an arbitrary decree of the New York City parks commissioner, Newbold Morris, who had taken strong exception to what he called the "adverse conditions prevalent on Sundays because of the roving troubadours and their followers." As a result, the police banned Sunday yodeling although for seventeen years the singers had gathered each weekend in the warm breezes.

During the week prior to the riot, folksingers had applied for official permits to sing/yodel/strum, but had been refused. So the ingredients were perfect for a stomp-out. It is rare indeed for conditions to prevail where demonstrators could feel absolute righteousness while surging in blizzardly balefulness across the rough sandy concrete basin for two objectives: 1) the creation of a lawless zone of thrills, and 2) to yodel outside the law. To defy an unjust law, ahhh thou thrill of thrills!

Johnny looked around him and saw that the large circular fountain and the surrounding mall had grown packed

85

with potential yodelers. Tense with discipline and willing-
ness to endure pain engendered by memorized instructions
in the form of secret messages of foment coded into the
mass media by beatnik weirdness-cells, the crowd waited.

The reporters for the New York newspapers, and there
were many present, dutifully noted the "beat" look of the
yodel horde—i.e., a surfeit of sandals, long hair, beards,
and eyes of fornicatorial glaze—into their stenopads. *The
New York Mirror,* for instance, bannered the riot on its
front page: 5000 BEATNIKS RIOT IN VILLAGE. When Johnny
Filth Feet saw that headline later, he nearly swooned
with riot-gasm.

And then it began. Within a half-hour Johnny the Foot
learned a key principal of agitation. The rule was not, as
he had before felt certain, "When in doubt, riot"—but
rather it was "It only takes a few." For an electric
unification seemed to pass into the crowd when the
trigger-pack, "a group of 50, many in beatnik clothes and
beards"—as *The New York Times* haughtily reported—
began to march from the southwest of the park (Mac-
Dougall and West 4th) in close-order yodel-formation
toward the waiting-for-inspiration yodel mob, goaded all
the while by trained left-leaning folklorists and known
novelists.

The congeries of bearded banjo boys and "girls with
long hair and guitars" *(The New York Times)* at the fountain, went nuts. Otherwise stable humans with patches of
the Bronx Folk Singers Guild proudly sewn on their field
jackets, railed with defiance. Carried by the trigger-pack
were signs which carefully presented the righteousness of
the riot. Among them were MUSIC TAMES THE SAVAGE BEAST,
and WE WANT TO DO WHAT WE HAVE ALWAYS DONE.

Filth Feet's spirit soared! Long-suppressed abilities to

hallucinate were unleashed and the visions began at once. Before his mind-screen a glassy-eyed endless plateau of beats chanting Zen koans in unison were marching, marching, devouring every barricade, stone wall and stanchion, toward its goal: a beard on every other face, a poem on every lip, money for all.

The trigger-pack reached the fountain and began to strum, yodel, pluck, hoot, and to thicken their voices with subversive Appalachian accents. A woman autoharpist with insolently lengthy tresses, stood then upon a hasty platform of guitar cases and began to sing "We Shall Overcome." And that was it—the police walked forward to break up the music. She was just pushing the A-Seventh bar on her harp when whonk! they shoved her and the cases went askitter, one of them hitting Johnny in his hashover.

The woman was hauled away, her harp falling to the pavement where it gave forth an atonal confusion of reverberations. Drool began to wet Johnny's lips.

After the autoharpist was hauled away, the leadership vacuum was filled by a thin young man from the Bronx Folk Singers Guild who strode forth and began to plunk his banjo contemptuously. "Stop that banjo! Tweet!"— barked out a police captain to Sergeant Mokler of the elite folk squad. And the gendarmes charged the lone banjo. Johnny began to hallucinate with vengeance, especially since the banjo plucker was only three feet away from him and he could see the raised clubs advancing. This little scuffle resulted in the ultimate prize of the Folk Song Riot, the capture of a billy club. The club was raised aloft to whack, and the banjoist was quick enough to duck, not missing even a beat of "Down by the Riverside" it will be noted, whereupon the billy club crashed into the fountain buttress instead, causing a painful punishment of vibrations upon the officer's hand. The club bounced loose across the front basin and the Bronx Folk Singers Guildperson popped the booty into his banjo case and ran away tinkling.

When this occurred, Johnny's mind went temporarily bye-bye. Flash: Halloween '55. State police cars arrive at the tense farm community to restore order. Flashing lights on car tops punctuate an intersection. The fires in the looted country store glare. Two tall metal windmill towers are circled by a tight ring of stolen outhouses. Above the towers is lashed the bicycle rack from the elementary school. Six overturned Buicks and Oldsmobiles stand in a perfect set of three-car parallel lines on each side of the outhouse/windmill construction in front of Gomell's Feed Store and the Farmers State Bank. It was the purest form of environmental art, Johnny told himself as he stood upon the roof of a nearby lumberyard, panting for breath, gazing with love at his masterpiece, which had taken him and his friends six hours to complete.

Unable to resist pissing off the state police, he jumped from the lumberyard roof and sprinted toward the railroad tracks. "There he is!" the coppers shouted. Then two sharp barks. They shot at me! He ran a quarter-mile up the dark railings, and hid in Samson's orchard, gleeful happy muttering, while far below in the valley the policemen cleared away the towers and the privy-henge, using the moon-shaped ventilators as hand-holds to lift them upon the hay wagon on the way to the town dump.

Johnny's happy fantasy was interrupted abruptly by the harsh reality of Washington Square when several of New York's Finest grabbed him and attempted to treat him like a sponge mop. They dragged him along by the feet so that

88

his face was on the concrete brooming the popsicle wrappers. "Hey! Ouch! I'm leaving! I'm leaving!" he yelled up. They let him go and he scrambled to his feet. He spotted the tourists staring in a thick baffled silent ring like mushrooms.

"Good. Get them!" one of them yelled. "Hurt the beatniks" another chub-chub from the outlands slowly drawled, giving his sentence a robotic hollowness. Johnny was finally angry.

And he quickly learned another principle of rioting. That is, in a riot one can find oneself in the so-called leadership cadre, propelled there as if entranced.

Johnny Filth Feet found himself jostling forward to address the throng. He tipped over a metal wastebasket to stand upon. "We have the right!"—he screamed, "the need, and the duty! to yodel!" And then he let loose from all his lungs and throat, a drastic tarzanic high-low yodel/warble. About halfway through the prolonged yodel, someone set fire to the rubbish in the basket and the flames began to rise up, pain-tongues curling upon his feet. His mummified condition probably prevented him from suffering intense pain, for, as if nothing were trying to char-broil his extremities, Johnny yodeled onward. The sight of his feet enveloped in flames as he orated to the thronging pissoff, created genuine mania in the crowd.

Nothing in the ensuing years would ever match it. Lunch-counter sit-ins in southern bus depots, voter-registration drives in Mississippi, peace walks, ruining war-research computers with maple syrup—nothing would be so intensely sparging of insight-thrills for Johnny Filth Feet as the Folk Song Riot of '61.

Finally, Johnny was carried from his perch into a police van. "Police Brutality!" people began to scream, a phrase

89

Johnny had never heard. "Fascists!" others yelled. The beat-mob surrounded the van and started rocking it back and forth. It almost went over, poised in that either/or moment of car tilt when you have to jump out of the way as it comes crashing back or you can surge in jubilance as it tilts over. The van crashed back down and Johnny face-punched his way out the back and the screaming crowd demanded him again atop the charred metal. The police dragged him back into the van but for two hours the people surrounded it and kept it from leaving the park. And what was Johnny charged with later in night court? Making a speech without a permit.

And out of the thousands only ten people were arrested! Another ace principle learned: You can riot and everyone can escape! Johnny laughed in a convulsion of inner peace all the way to the Tombs. By midnight a total stranger had bailed Johnny out and he and the stranger were soon drinking orzatas at the Café Figaro.

It wasn't for another fifteen years that the arrest in the park would cause certain problems relative to Johnny's post-beat career. This was solved by pulling some political strings and having the records of the arrest forever sealed. For "everything oozes"—as Sam Beckett so dutifully annotated; and it was no less so for the happy roaming beatniks of yore. Within a year of his arrest in Washington Square, Johnny Filth Feet fled the set without a whisper.

What happened to Mr. Dirt Foot? Did he rise to lead the ten thousands in marches of anger? Well, he did travel south on some voter-registration drives. Did he then go back to run for the Nebraska State Assembly? Did he take over a New York publishing company? Did he fade guzzling cheapo down among the Bowery replicas? Well, I did locate him several years ago and I must say that it was startling to note how remarkably he had altered the channel of his life. He showed me his feet after I had taunted him a bit during our dinner. They were as white and polished as Carrara marble.

But I do not want to anger him by revealing his name, for he is a prime source of money for many of my projects. For instance, he supplied the money for the LSD in the Chicago water supply. So you will understand when I say that we do not want his name floating around police intelligence files. But I can say that he is currently a vice-president in the trust department of a prominent New York bank, and is moving up.

Mindscape Gallery

HER NAME WAS Louise Adams. She was twenty-two years old, a student at Cooper Union where she specialized in wood sculpture. She also worked in hand-painted pottery. More than anything, she was a painter of canvas, and a good one. Her greatest difficulty had been her parents who dearly wanted her to marry Murray of the real-estate empire. To drop some asterisks around this desire, they threw away some of her paintings. "You have broken our heart. After all we've done." Get married was the message. "You can never handle it alone. It's a man's world"—her mother told her. "Get what you can."

They were wrong and their nastiness in tossing away the paintings cost them her presence out there in Patchogue. She threw her possessions out by the trashcans except for a bed, record player, books and art supplies and moved to the Lower East Side to paint. She told them to leave her alone. She refused to communicate with them and refused all offers of financial assistance. She obtained an unlisted telephone number and ripped the listing label off the dial.

They tried to come to the apartment only once. When they announced themselves at the door, she just took off her clothes and opened up, "Hi Dad, hi Mom, come on in. I want you to meet my friend Big Brown. He'll be over in a few minutes. You'll love him." Her mother's only reply was a shudder. She took a chance that they wouldn't have her arrested and immediately rolled a joint, which she lit with an enormous suction of smoke and held it in her lungs. "Would you like some?"—pot-puffs escaping her mouth with each word as she offered the j to her father, leaning across so that her bare breasts slid down the front of her mother's overcoat which remained on throughout the short visit.

Louise Adams soon had to give up Cooper Union. But that was fine with her—tired of being a schoolgirl and unable adequately to worship the pitiful abilities of her instructors when she knew she was a better artist than any of them.

She was tall, about six-foot-one, and rather slender. Skinny with energy. And as soon as she spewed in from Patchogue, she was an immediately sought-after, almost worshipped, friend on the East Side art scene. She just loooooved to explore the pleasures of the body, and loved to hang out at Stanley's Bar at 12th and B almost as much. She never had any trouble with any of her new friends becoming possessive or jealous because she constantly and pointedly scoffed, scowled, jeered, at the possibility. Furthermore, she quickly established a complex of rules regarding her friends so that there was a great privacy and at the same time a great diversity.

She *believed* in the East Side. In the frenzy of her rebellion, she would not have considered for even a minute being humiliated by a man with whom she had grown infatuated. Nor by a brother artist operating at the very same barricades as she.

Louise had lived on the East Side for less than a year when she met Barton Macintyre, a painter also, who was soon professing his fiery love for her, joining a rather substantial list of humans so professing.

At first she was attracted by his energy and his apparent dedication. Barton Macintyre worked at making it ten or eleven hours a day—churning out the paintings. Jesus, he hungered for success. Macintyre was twenty-six and chub-chubbed upon the scales at about 225. As for hair, his chest and arms looked like an exploded eyelash factory. His face skin was almost flour-white and possessed a wide full-nostriled nose plus a long but carefully attended beard. His mane, however, was beginning to go bye-bye.

Barton's daily garb consisted of baggy brown Sweet-Orr corduroy trousers and a sports jacket. He always carried a tie with him in the jacket pocket. You could never tell when you were going to be called uptown for a meeting regarding a sale or a show, man.

He was very careful about his attire. He had a closet full of seventeen blue workshirts, five or six jackets in grays and tans—all in denim/corduroy, and a floor full of various types of shoes and moccasins from Abercrombie & Fitch and the Bean catalogue. He was loath to stray from the current artist fashions.

Louise liked to wear long-sleeved blouses with drawstrings at the sleeves and at the neck. Discovering Ukrainian clothing, as made by craftspeople of the Lower East Side, was a joy. She must have ordered ten of these blouses, many of them sewn with flowered patterns, from Madame Braznick, a manufacturer of dancing boots and Ukrainian attire on East 7th Street.

At Christmas, the first year they knew one another, she ordered for Barton from Madame Braznick a long black Cossack coat with cloth bullet-holders designed into each side of the upper chest. The bullet-pouches were stuffed with hand-sewn flower patterned cylinders. Barton flatly refused to wear the coat. He did carry it with him, in the gift box, down to Stanley's that night where he showed it, guffawing and snorting, to all his friends.

Barton was addicted to art openings. He made sure he was on the mailing lists of virtually all uptown galleries and museums. In the early sixties, he would dash from gallery to gallery in order to attend four or five openings the same night. It was inspirational. He needed it. The out-of-sight lofts with broken windows, the half-finished art on the walls, the irrational rages, this he could endure if the leprechaun in the paint-stained beret at the end of the rainbow would only hand him a fist of MONEY!!

Whatever his secret concern for lucre was, Barton was ever concerned to project an image of controlled wildness—exposing just the "correct" amount of nuttiness, drug-abuse, alcoholism, and feigned flip-out. And his ego surged. Wild energy—that was what attracted Louise Adams.

Barton viewed everything he created as something major. He labored according to The Theory of The Frame. Anything created was enshrined in a frame. If he wanted to make a sketch of something, first he made a sketch of various ideas for the sketch. The sketch of the sketch was framed, signed, dated, as was the sketch itself. Doodles, telephone lists, everything, framed. He soon had his mother's apartment in Riverdale filled up storing his frames.

There was one series of works he did throw away—i.e.,

his notes perfecting his signature. His first problem was his secret belief that no one whose name was Macintyre could really make it big on the New York art scene. He had long considered changing his name to another, say more successful type of name; he hungered for one whose last syllable was a vowel. But he finally decided not to change his name for the following reason: Hell, I'm on the verge of making it anyway. I'm just about the most well-known painter on the set already, why not therefore just ride it all the way with Macintyre?

So, for about a year he worked on his signature. He wanted it to look as cool and individual as Picasso, Braque, Dali, Miró. Barton Macintyre II was the signature he had used since high school. He hated the way it looked, having stayed static since his junior year. First he dropped the II. No good. Next the Barton. If only he could make the word Macintyre itself a work of art he would be happy. To this end he scrawled and painted his last name at least fifty times a day for weeks. He consulted popular books dealing with handwriting analysis and personality. He was horrified reading the personality traits revealed by his then-current method of signature. So he changed it drastically. Finally he settled on a swooping flourishing signature which he could repeat blindfolded. "More stylish than Braque, more substantial than Picasso"—he told himself.

He rented what he considered a dream pad, a four-room so-called "box" apartment where the rooms opened off in several directions from the entranceway. This was in distinction to the railroad flats which offered much less privacy since one traipsed through all rooms in order to get to the farthest one. He was happy. The apartment was his when the previous tenant, a senior citizen from

Latvia, was hauled away by his relatives to Beautiful South Shore Leisure-Retirement Colony.

Barton decided that it would be "out there" to leave the apartment just as it was. The man had been a tile-freak. The entire bathroom, floor and walls and ceiling, was covered with two-inch pastel ceramics. Not only that, but the entire living room and bedroom were also covered ceiling and floor. Barton left the old man's furniture just as it was, although he did clear out the room overlooking Tompkins Square Park. Many a painting of Barton's was inspired by gazing down into the park fantasizing drooling brontosaurs mating in the mist.

Barton considered his Tompkins Square pad just a temporary hassle to endure on the way to the aforementioned leprechaun with the paint-smeared beret and the slight scratching-sounds of bankers writing checks and cocaine honked through ivory straws on yachts. A house in P-town, a house in East Hampton, a house outside Paris. "Houses"—he cried, stumbling drunk down Avenue C, "Houses."

When Barton Macintyre felt he was in love with the painter Louise Adams, his first move was to zap his rivals. He crowded in on Louise. He answered the phone a lot when he was at her apartment and did his best to discourage incoming male calls. He used up as much of her time as he could get away with. He spread the word among the denizens of Stanley's Bar and local cafés. To her own surprise she found herself tolerating this sweating brute who was driving away all her lovers. She believed his love and was even tentatively beginning to become dependent on it, and gave him in turn her tenderness and plans and cares.

Poverty was Louise's main problem at the time. She

had her potter's wheel set up in her apartment and was able to use the kiln at Cooper Union. Her vases, jugs and pots were placed on consignment at several West Village stores and they sold pretty well. They were very skillfully painted with ornate forest scenes and elf-satires bearing the faces of renowned artists of the day.

An opportunity arose for her to rent a storefront on East 9th Street between First and A, for fifty-five dollars a month. Her plan was to live in the back and sell her work in the front. According to law, she had to make use of the storefront as an actual store. She built a high loftbed in the back near the ceiling. She cleaned the paint off the brick walls and polished them. She installed with her own sweat a Sears & Roebuck shower stall. She built racks of shelves to hold the pottery and a partition to separate store from living quarters. In the back was her castle of happiness: at last she had enough room for her painting, her woodworking and her claywork.

She had no idea how good her painted ceramics were, just the word of her friends, so she undervalued them, selling for five or ten dollars vases and jars she'd spent weeks painting. They were soon gone and she was not about to glop out more in a spew of crudity. She needed money badly however, so she reluctantly placed some of her paintings on view in the store section, again at modest prices. She sold two paintings within the first week and was overjoyed. She bought rounds for her friends at Stanley's. She bought an armload of canvas and extra supplies and a pair of red dancing boots from Madame Braznick.

For his part, Barton Macintyre was slightly upset at all this. He was all for the pottery bit, the groovy storefront, but her sale of paintings, well, that was unfair. He therefore encouraged the pottery. He would pick up a pot and announce, "Say, this looks really good, almost beautiful"—while his eyes passed over in silence the rows of her new paintings.

There was a half-flight of black metal steps leading down to the store entrance. He carried the complimented pot to the front window; "Why don't you hang this on thongs in the window?" he asked as she was attaching a circle of sandpaper on the floor sander.

"Damn you! This is going to be a gallery of paintings! Paintings! not a ceramics studio!" Then she dropped the sander, and snatched her pot from his hands.

On another occasion he was holding one of her wood-carved panels, part of a series of long walnut planks intricately worked in human figures and slum scenery. "You ought to go practical with this stuff, " he advised, holding it horizontally in front of her face. "This would be ideal material for a rich man's rare-bookshelves." For this, after she had seized it away from him, she shoved him out the door and banished him up the steps.

Her small successes inspired her to undertake a series of paintings she called Mindscapes. The series was numbered chronologically and when she was finished she had completed ten Mindscapes.

Her method was this. She banned her friends from visiting. She got plenty of sleep and made sure she had no hangover, methplummet or distress. She placed the phone in the closet with cushions on top of it. Then, in a frenzy she described what was happening in her brain, as she viewed her mind-screen. Faces, images from the past, quotes, hallucinations, desires, with usually one single image dominating the pictures. Feverishly she took notes, made sketches, modeled shapes in clay, literally exhausting herself after several hours roughly blocking out the painting on a five-by-seven canvas. Afterward she spent several days finishing the painting. She began a new Mindscape each day so that at the end of ten days she was working on completing ten Mindscapes at once, moving from canvas to canvas. The Mindscapes astounded her friends. Many of them were so impressed that they brought their friends around to see the works. About that time, Louise decided to call her store The Mindscape Gallery and furthermore to hold a formal exhibition and party celebrating the Mindscapes. She gave herself a month to get it ready.

For the outside of the gallery she carved a wood frame inside which she inserted small canvases in a row, each canvas a painting of a letter of the words, Mindscape Gallery. For the next month it was all work.

There were pressures unforetold. The rabbit at the lab kakked, so she had to endure a nightmare of buses and fear traveling up to get an abortion from a human known on the East Side as The Butcher of 86th Street. Barton, of course, was strapped for moolah at the time and could not share the expense. As a result she waxed behind in the store rent. She could always like sell the place for maybe three hundred dollars because she had done so much work fixing it up. But she hated to sell Mindscape even before it really got rolling. She could have gotten some assistance from her parents, and they offered to help, but she turned them down, although her heart had softened a bit and she had invited them to the exhibition.

There were so many things to do. There was a misprint on the invitations. The printer dared to want an additional partial payment to do a corrected version. She blew up at this, and decided to silkscreen her own, a project which took her days to finish.

There were further matters of repainting the gallery, aligning the lighting, purchasing wine and food for the party, and dealing with Barton.

Macintyre was eager, on the other hand, for her to accompany him on the usual rounds of dinners, strolls, hours-long grope sessions, bars, parties, galleries and cafés. One of their favorite places was a café called The House of Nothingness, located on 10th Street near the Tompkins Square public library. Nothingness had a garden section for the warm months which contained a really outstanding miniature Zen rock garden of raked white sand around which patrons could sit and meditate.

They were sitting by the rock garden when he asked her if she would prepare a dinner party for him, his cousin (a salesman for a book company due in New York for a market conference), and a banker he'd just met at the Cedar Bar. And, of course, she could sit in herself at the proposed feast. She was surprised at his request since she had just been telling him of her frantic preparations for the gallery opening. "When is the dinner to be?"—she asked.

"Next Tuesday."—he replied. The opening was Wednesday.

"You must be joking. You know I have to work on the show."

'Yes, I understand. It's just that you're such a good cook. And I wanted to get the fellow from the bank interested in purchasing some pieces."

The day of the opening of the Mindscapes exhibition arrived after an all-night spurt of work. The gallery was at last prepared for the jostling, excessively cigarette-hungry, shrill party of the art-flock. The Mindscapes were hanging beneath skillfully placed lights—they were beautiful to behold. Louise was happy. The phone was ringing about every five minutes with inquiries about time, how to get to the gallery, and so forth. To shield the paintings until the party should begin, she had draped a large sheet of cloth across the entire front of the gallery.

It was 3 P.M. Louise had gone down to Houston Street to get a couple of cases of wine and some ice-blocks to chip down for the shower-stall coolery. Barton Macintyre had agreed to remain at the gallery to answer the phone or to receive any deliveries while Louise was away.

A human tapped at the front door. "Hello, my name is Victor Richardson. I am with the Creever gallery. Is Miss Adams here?"

Barton was dumbfounded. Victor Richardson of dollarland? Victor Richardson the millionaire?! "She's not here. She went somewhere hours ago." Barton did not take the collector behind the sheets but talked with him in the foyer where the paintings were out of view.

"This is Louise's first exhibition—of paintings, that is. You ought to see her earthenware pots! Boy, is she a skilled pottress, if you know what I mean"—smiling at the collector.

"The show has been late in getting on the walls. She may not have it quite ready by the time listed on the invitation." Barton was still smiling. "Say"—looking at his watch, "it's going to be three or four hours before she can get things ready; why don't you come over to Stanley's? We'll have a beer and then why don't you stop by my place? As long as you've come all the way over here. I've been working for months on a series myself. I'd like you to look at them, to get your opinion. I'm exhausted from the project—but elated. You'll see what I mean. If I could only . . ."

Barton could hear the phone ringing as he locked the front door of the gallery. The two men walked down the street toward the beer and maybe—Please, God, please! prayed Barton Macintyre—a sale.

Vulture Egg Matzoh Brei

I

SHORTLY AFTER DAWN they collected all the Popsicle sticks they could find from the wire mesh baskets on the periphery of the fountain plaza. They made a sticky, sooty pile of several hundred, then lined them in a neat straight row, whereupon Avram Maniac, as he was affectionately known, uncapped a giant tube of library paste and squished a dot of white on the end of each, dancing oddly foot to foot, and hooting imitation trumpet riffs through the side of his pressed lips. Maniac was a genius at the lip-horn, but a few hours of it was unnerving to the listener, especially in a hot summer tenement with nothing to eat for four days but buckwheat pancakes, calf eyes stolen from the butcher, and ripped pigeon crumbs. But they were out of the pad now, and it was a beautiful morn and no one yet felt compelled to yell at Maniac. Stomp your lips, Maniac baby!

They fashioned a tall rectangular central stick-tower rising in the grapejuice-stained dawn upon a foundation utilizing the inside top step of the circular stone fountain/

wading pool in the center of Washington Square Park. It was a work of major importance, they assured themselves. The date: July 1, 1959.

There were three of them working on the stick-work: John Barrett, Avram Maniac, and Newt. Maniac, it must be noted, expected to hear the sirens at any moment, for only a few hours ago he'd oozed away from the I Am Jesus ward at Bellevue Hospital. In fact, he was wearing hospital attire stenciled "Property of Bellevue Hospital" on the back. But that was like money in the bank. Weekend beatniks from Queens would pay a pretty penny for genuine flip-out garb.

The night before, Avram had traded his maroon Bellevue bathrobe to Mary Meth for twenty-seven little white methedrine tabs, so dawn found him twitchy-jittery and wide awake, all the better he thought, for it made his pajamas appropriately soiled and sweaty with insanity, as he smeared himself with glue and shriekily hooted making the sculpture of sticks. He figured that there was someone out there right at that very moment strapping on their sandals, who would soon get on a subway headed for the Village little aware that he or she would get the honor of paying ten bucks for Maniac's nuthouse finery. The glue was also flying into Avram's hair which was normally curly and matted and strangely bebumped as if numerous small cocoons were waiting there for some future spring. But now it was like a flattened opossum on a highway—a pitiful squashed elevation of hairy-boned grime.

The boy named Newt was a twenty-year-old dancer two years out of the Bronx High School of Science. This tense specimen of indecision could never enter a conversation for more than two minutes before blurting out that he had been scientifically measured a genius. He was short, not over five-foot-four, and extremely skinny—his rib cage could have been used as a rhythm instrument in a jug band. In fact it was, many years later when he was sacrificed by a Kali-worshipping rock band in San Francisco.

"I am a sunflower surrounded by gleaming careers!" he shouted again and again as he leaped voraciously from fad to fad—first sketcher, then poet, composer, weaver, singer, woodworker, and finally his true vocation of the year, as dancer. And Newt danced around the clock, specializing in wild tourist-attracting herpitudinous shudders on his "stage"—i.e., the plaza near the Washington Square fountain.

Sometimes Newt would strap a roller skate to the top of his head and perform a headstand under Washington Arch, twirling and flailing his arms to draw attention. The crowds of tourists couldn't take enough pictures as Newt somehow caused the skate to move toward the fountain and the headstanding young dance would yogambulate in a large circle around the spurting waters. Newt's disciples, and there were many, devoured that data as if it were a theophany.

Newt was ambitious; he considered himself only a year or two away from the big league of Beauty-Motion, meaning his own recitals, large halls, tours, quarter-page ads in the *Village Voice*, airplane tickets. "Newt has found the node, man, Newt has found the node!" he shouted from his rollerskate headstand, his arms gyrating like someone shaking sparklers.

John Barrett was twenty-one at the time and attempted to subsume himself beneath a supernal frenzy. He was a poet who pronounced his vocation with gritted teeth and his every waking moment was spent patrolling "the set,"

106

which in the parlance of the park was anywhere in the slums of the Lower East Side or the orderly well-preserved Bohemia of the West Village, as long as you stayed below 14th Street. John Barrett was a bit over-dressed for the weather, but felt more ready for Blake-flash when attired in a turtleneck and his year-around jacket. Beneath an exterior of scheme-filled awkwardness, Barrett thought he was at *least* as talented as Keats. Especially Keats, for somewhere he'd read about the hateful garbage the critics had dumped upon poor Keats after the publication of *Endymion.*

"Critics will never get away with that shit with me!"—Barrett muttered, smashing a fist into a palm. Barrett was the type who listened intently with reddened eyes spewing tears through a Beethoven concerto and then rasped hoarsely, "I can do it! I can do it! I *can.*" By this meaning the composition of perhaps another *Iliad,* or at least an immortal sequence of tough lyrics of slumopathic lust. Or something.

"God, I'm a good poet!"—was his permanent judgment of himself as he scribbled his eyeball-data into his note-books, smoothing and polishing the ripped images, every-thing holy, everything notable. "Shriek! Shriek!"—oh how he loved that word *Shriek,* "Shriek, I'm up to number forty-seven!" This meant the series of notebooks begun on 6-15-1957 and running relentlessly till that beauteous morn in the summer of '59. The sequence did not exhaust itself until 1963 with number 128. The entire exquisite ir-ruption being subsequently purchased by the Harris Col-lection at the Brown University Library where it may be inspected to the heart's content.

Oh and ahhh how he felt the Muses—particularly Erato, Terpsichore, and eu-yodeling Melpomene—all properly attired in black leather skirts and Allan Block sandals laced knee high; and all yelling Fire! Fire! Keats-shriek! Blake-flesh! Moans of Byron! in the fierce egoist lightning of his soul. "Keep working arrogant Self"—he commanded. "My notes are mere prolegomenon scrawls, man, for the FINAL POEM. I am on fire to birth the last American poem! I am Pindar!"

To this end, he became an anecdote-junkie, constantly urging his friends to hyperextend themselves, to leap freaky into arcane weirdness. It couldn't be weird enough. So he stirred up people like Newt and Avram Maniac to dance before his eyeballs, his notebook filling up with verse froth.

Meanwhile, the stick-tower kept falling over in the breeze so they glued a perpendicular bracing at the top and leaned the whole apparatus against one of the thick concrete buttress posts which stood every few feet around the fount's edge. Newt produced some Tarot cards from his musette bag, a strange sight in those prepsychedelic days, which they glued to the outside of the Popsicle ziggurat. "I wish we had a camera," Newt complained, bending back to observe the art, shrugging his shoulders in abstract patterns to Maniac's squeaking lips.

By the time it was finished it was 6:30 A.M., and the Parks Department sweepers were pushing their wheeled garbage carts and brooms toward the fountain to clean up the papery gunge from the night.

"You want this?" one of the sweepers asked, pointing to the tower.

"Nah, take it. It's all yours." Whereupon the sweeper picked it up and a card fell away, delivering a prophecy upon Barrett's foot. Barrett stared at the card.

"Hey, Barrett," Avram laughed, "according to that card

you're in trouble man. You're gonna be talkin' to the worms, baby. That's death there on your toe. Ha ha ha."

Barrett reached down and picked up the card, still wet with glue, and jammed it back on the stick-tower. The sweeper stuffed the whole thing with crunches and stick-snaps into the garbage can.

II

Sun-Ra poured its shafts of grooviness down upon the set and the park began to fill up. A dozen ears perked up when a high-pitched gargling sound was heard from the direction of Fifth Avenue, more like a Persian warble, which signaled the arrival of a human being known as Uncle Thrills, who was appropriately attired in gray bibbed Alpine shorts, a wide-brimmed straw hat, and a perfectly square black beard which collapsed on the inside into total white.

"Here I am from the God-tower!" Uncle Thrills shouted, "Thrill Freak ex Machina! ImGrat! ImGrat!" ImGrat, acronym for Immediate Gratification. "Rapple dapple dally doh!" he continued. "Glupple Globble Gloffle Gluffle! Gloppe Glope har har! Har!"

Barrett was scrawling as rapidly as his poor fingers could flail, trying to copy every syllable. He really wished Uncle Thrills would slow down, because his notes were so awfully chicken-scratchy. And what university library would ever want to purchase such an unruly notebook?

"Hey Thrills, baby," Avram yelled, "Tune us in to the Thrill Flow, man!"

Uncle Thrills obeyed at once, sprinting upon his babble trail, and young John Barrett, Avram Maniac, Newt and all the others listened with all-suck. For Uncle Thrills was important—he had stuff printed in *Partisan Review*, in *Beatitude*, and if you knew where to look, you could find him in *On The Road*.

Barrett had Uncle Thrills' speech patterns down like someone who'd memorized phrasing off an early Jonathan Winters tape. But he couldn't very well duplicate Thrills right on Thrills' own turf, so he restrained his imitations until he was in calculus class or among his friends down at the *Catholic Worker* for a little Theos vs. Thrills theology battle.

How poetically Uncle Thrills' face muscles twitched on the steps of the fountain, Barrett thought! "What else is there in this universe if it ain't kicks, baby?" Thrills demanded to know. "You got to feel good so the Gods can dig it. This set is zero!"—pointing to the haze above the park. His disciples dutifully followed his hand to the top of Washington Arch. "What holds this, this mush . . ."—his face twisting awry in disgust at the word, "together unless it's kicks, some fierce sky-punk's kicks, man? Kicks!"—shuddering with some unknown urging; perhaps it was self-approval. "Those old trees over there, see them?"—pointing to the tall oaks to the west. "They grew up on corpse sweat, yeah! You know what's under this fountain? Poor dead shreds of pissed-on motherfuckers of a hundred years ago, that's what. This was Potter's Field, baby, and a public hanging ground. There used to be mandrake roots growing all over the park."

"I ain't gonna be no chump! I want thrills. Not yesterday, you dig, not tomorrow, you dig . . . but now! ImGrat! ImGrat!" He began to stamp his foot. "That's what I want, Lord. Thrills Now! Thrills Now! Thrills Now!" He began to chant it, and a circle of his friends joined him. The din of thrill shouts aroused the police

110

from their post on MacDougal and they came running over to quell the spew.

Suddenly, Uncle Thrills broke away from the chanters and trotted toward some early-morning tourists. "Say man, you got a cigarette?" he asked, making puffing sounds with his lips, holding two fingers up to his mouth. "Lay a cig on Uncle Thrills, huh, muh fuh?"

With an ashen face of near heart attack the tourist forked over a Pall Mall to The Thrills, who walked away toward the pissoir, already having unzipped his Alpine shorts, violating various exposure laws, singing, to the tune of "I Love the Lord Jesus," "I lick the Lord Jesus upon his bland bod. . . ."

He had a way of forcing the place alive, and the fountaineers were cackling with laughter as Unc' Thrills walked away. Barrett looked at his fingernails, and took a painful nip of one. Several hurt badly from peeled and infected strips of edging. He consoled himself by counting the fingers *not* chomped, sort of a negative confession, and noticed today that fully six or ten were pure and chewless.

Thrills began his shouted lecture even as he returned from the john to the circle. "The Superior SQUISH! plugs into your every movement! You had *better* know it! Let them have their thrillies, the Gods. Aiee! the Gods definitely go nuts on your body, young lady!"—flashing a quick grab in the direction of the buttock of a stroller. "You *can* lick and chew the silver threads from Sky to Earth! Wow!"

That was Uncle Thrills when he was happy. More often he'd moan like a dog pack. His favorite shriek was a line from *Waiting for Godot:*

111

> *I've puked my puke of a life away here,*
> *I tell you . . .*

Quoting that drove Thrills into a foaming frenzy. *"Waiting for Godot!"* he shouted so hysterically that his voice went up about half an octave. "God the Idiot! God-ot! Bah! Oh how I've peeeeeuked my peeeeeuuuuuke of a life AWAY!!!"

Disciples of Unc' Thrills used to practice that line to catch those great sneering inflections. Barrett remembered his high-school classmates doing the same thing, swaggering out of *The Wild One* to practice sneering like a Brando biker in the bathroom mirror.

Uncle Thrills loved the attention. His scheme of life involved the careful construction of a legend of himself as a genius. To this end he had contrived three careers: as novelist, as inventor, and as artist.

For eight years he had been working on a long multilanguage novel, bragged to be over 10,000 pages in length, entitled *Cryptozoic Aeon,* the epic story of the genealogy of a human genius (Uncle Thrills) which began in the warm germic algae soup of the cryptozoic aeon and passed through some 14,023 sequential life forms until somehow arriving in his current life form, U.S. Genius 1959. Now that was egotism. It must be said, however, that all anyone had ever seen of this monumental endeavor was a musty springbinder of untyped pagination.

As an inventor Uncle T. held several patents. One was for the so-called battery-powered Thrill Beeper® —which was really more of a tiny cattle prod and was supposedly able to activate wonderful pleasure nodes within the brain when applied to certain areas of the scalp. (A scalp-map

112

depicting proper zap spots was supplied to the purchaser.)
Uncle Thrills loved to chase young beatlings around the
fountain waving the Thrill Beeper.

Another invention involved a bathtub meditation system. This grew out of Thrill's habit of submerging himself
in a hot tub every morning for spiritual communications
with Poseidon. He stayed beneath the water for over a
half-hour, breathing through a copper tube which
extended up and over the porcelain lip of the tub. To
facilitate his visions, he sewed a black wool canopy which
fit tightly over the top of the bathtub. He also created
quite exquisite stained-glass tub-covers enabling the medi-
tator to look up during submersion for vision-inducing
Gothic colors.

As for his painting, one is afraid that, without Uncle
Thrill's complex mythological explanations, which he
gladly supplied to each purchaser, the works sagged sadly
in merit. His long interpretations of his paintings seemed
to fool many collectors, who would buy a canvas titled,
say, *Chaos Charted on a Hesiodic Map*, or, *The Angry
Spirit of Protein Spits Verbs at Deus*, when the paintings
in question were constructed of platefuls of spaghetti
thrown on the cloth and sprayed with fixative, the
spaghetti blobs encircled by ink-sketched coronels of
organic molecules.

Which brings us to the checks. Man, could he grab the
checks. In a dazzling blitz of hype, Thrills would learn of
the address or phone number of a collector or rich patron,
preferably patroness, of Art, and within a day would gobble a check, sometimes even a blank check, out of them.

You scoff? It was strange, especially since it would not
seem to be so easy to acquire an instant check, but those
who wouldn't normally think they would *ever* fork over

money to some mumbling nut waving a manuscript, would, as if in a trance, find themselves scratching away at an elegant French writing desk. "You just write Uncle Thrills a check—I'll cash it over at the Eighth Street Bookshop—I'll be finishing my translations from Ibsen soon. This will make it possible."

Thrills liked to use the innocent-faced John Barrett in some of the check capers—which meant that Barrett might find himself guarding the door of a bedroom at a party—Thrills inside droning hypnotically at a trapped countess, shoulder straps sliding helplessly down a spa-smoothed back, "write a check, O beauteous Imperatrice, write a check, write a check . . ."

Thrills would do anything—his favorite gimmick was a peyote-methedrine mickey in the champagne, followed by a seance wherein the spirit of Walt Whitman would urge all to write, write, write! out that generous check to this great man of our times.

Accordingly, it was with regard to copping a check that Uncle Thrills began to huddle with Newt and Avram Maniac by the fountain. "You see," he said, "I know some European royalty, married to American money. She just *adores* novelists, can not resist that urge to help. And I just happened to have brought my manuscript—bloof!"—as he blew dust off the springbinder, "with me. She lives up at the Dakota Apartments. Let's go."

He waved over at Barrett. "Hey Barrett, you coming with us? We'll cut you in." Barrett demurred and off strode the trio in quest of the Holy Check.

III

Barrett watched his friends depart—and soon his mood sank down into that negative trough, to face his three-headed enemy: boredom, confusion, fear. Hi!, Barrett greeted the hallucination. He filled the holes with filled holes, so to speak, for a while by doodling on his hands and arms with fountain pen. "RA Is Hip to It All" he mock-tattooed 'pon his forearm—then rolled up his sleeve, so all could see, and stood up and strolled around the park. This is a thrill-stroll; this-is a thrill stroll; this is-a thrill stroll, he told himself. Maybe someone will be blowing some gage; nothing like a fear puff to tighten up the day, he thought.

It must be remembered that Washington Square Park was steeped in the Eisenhower era—i.e., squaresville, baby. The beats, the derelicts, the surrounding campus of New York University, the parents of young children, all vied for the use of the turf. No music was allowed (except Sundays), nor poetry readings, nor drummers. Only recently, villagers had acted to close the park to dangerous auto traffic that once swarmed through the park's center. But the rules for the park's use remained strict and robotic. The police were always instant breaking up a crowd listening to a poet, or bumping lovers from the grass. And speaking of grass, which was what Barrett was keeping an eye out for; smoking a reefer in Washington Square in those '59 days was an exercise in total fear that was forever burned in the memory. With sneers of derision spittling upon the concept of the taxation of hemp, the dharma-commies lingered upon a remote bench sucking the pale clouds upon the alveoli of the lungs, while the senses were on Anslinger Alert: eyes left, fear-scan, eyes right, fear-scan, eyes even scanning the sky—and ears: ears attuned to the farthest footstep, mouths ever ready to swallow the smoldering kernels of aphrodisia, should fuzz pounce.

115

But there was not a puff of pot in the entire park, which was just as well, for he heard the gong inside him, a gong that sounded the poesy hour, the high point of his day. He found a bench beneath N.Y.U.'s Main building, opened his knapsack, removed a small stack of books, and spread them side by side upon the slats. "Ah holy books," he whispered, stroking them like those secret painting-patters whose greatest thrill is to jack the leg of *Oedipus and The Sphinx* at the Metropolitan Museum.

There were *The Cantos* of Ezra Pound, *Howl & Other Poems*, Allen Ginsberg, the *Collected Poems* of Dylan Thomas, *Wasteland & Other Poems*, Eliot, *Echo's Bones*, Sam Beckett, *Buddhist Texts Through the Ages*, the new issue of Roi Jones' *Yugen* (with Ginsberg's *Kaddish* IV & V), plus *Beatitude*, issue #2.

He read with a tension that made him breathe heavily. He became so excited he had to pace back and forth in front of the bench, pausing to lean down now and then to pick up a fresh book. He read them aloud, alternating stanzas from different books. At first it was Pound's Canto 45, with its beautiful litany 'gainst Usura, which began to make the young man tremble; and then a few lines, right after the *Canto*, from Ginsberg's *Kaddish*, Part V—the Caw Caw cows shriek in the white sun over gravestones in Long Island section—followed right away by the first sixteen lines of *Wasteland*, cut back to *Kaddish*, Part IV (oh Mother what have I left out, O Mother what have I forgotten), and Barrett by that time was literally jumping up and down.

Finally, risking the reproach of cops and park attendants, he vaulted the bench and ran into the forbidden grass, threw himself down and began to reap the slender golden-headed wheat flash into his notebooks, his

116

fingernails jammed with wax from candled poverty.

He could *see* the Verse Flood! a river of lines from various bards—O it thrilled him to see his own lines mixed in his mind with the verse flash flotsam of his heroes. It was as if he were unconscious, as he wrote. An hour, posing as a minute, passed. Now, these *are* the thrills, he thought, as the pure jolts poured back and forth, pen to brain, brain to pen. "Melpomene! Baby!" he shouted with glee. Μελπομε'νη—that is, God-dance.

IV

If Melpomene in fact was watching Barrett's scriptive convulsion, she saw how pitiably attired he was in a coat caked with candle wax from his hovel of no electricity, with buckwheat noodles crusting his lapel like melted Secret Service pins. Every day he seemed to knock a candle over, bespewing himself with the tallow. How like a seized bard, he thought. And the coat, which had suffered duty as his winter coat also, had acquired by its ceaseless service, an olfactorial hint of zebra anus, offending nearly everyone it came near.

That morning he had lost the heel of one of his shoes and the exposed nails were slowly drilling into his foot. The New York spring rains had rendered the shoe leather swollen and brittle. Both shoelaces had broken a long time ago and the halves had been realigned as laces, ends slowly frazzling. The halves themselves snapped next and with only a quarter of each remaining, he could barely tie two holes together per shoe. On wet days he wrapped tinfoil around his socks to keep the seeping moisture from sourly souping the griseous inner foot-soot.

It's time to go to the *Catholic Worker*, he thought. I'll

visit the breadline and maybe I can con some clothes. He packed his books and walked over to the Bowery, and on east to Chrystie Street, to shed his sark. He still felt a nag of guilt that said, "Barrett, thou dost not deserve a new coat"—his preferences for socialism, or rather anarcho-peoplesrepublicanism not being sufficiently developed for years to come. He also knew he'd have to bullshit with the woman who staffed the second-floor clothing cage for maybe hours before he could summon nerve to ask for a coat, and maybe some shoes, if he had enough energy left.

He raved a bit with the *Catholic Worker* staff, mutter-ing nolo credere at the possibility of the Christ Lamb. He aped Uncle Thrills right down to ImGrat! ImGrat! Where Barrett had been born, atheism was the coolest stance, in that you could cause, say, a locker room of football players after practice to become a frothing mob of poten-tial killers by insisting on discussing the virtues of atheism. Even as he softly whispered "ImGrat, ImGrat, ImGrat," the lady who ran the clothes box coaxed him into a prayer circle, and Barrett found himself reading aloud from the Bible when his turn came up. He forced back what he kept telling himself was a mote-caused tear. He reproached himself severely for the lachrymosity later. "Toughen up, Barrett, toughen up!"

Nor could he allow himself to deny the free *Catholic Worker* lunch, which he gobbled aplenty. He conned a few extra slices of that good C.W. whole wheat home-baked, for his pocket; later he'd buy a can of sardines, some halvah, and suffer an evening banquet by the heal-ing waters of Washington fountain. He was the healthiest human in the room full of the sanguine hispid-faced hungry men and women trembling with age and alcohol. "Yum yum!" he blurted out, trying to catch a thirds on

118

the pea soup by flirting with the ladler. Not that he ever later on gave a penny to the *Catholic Worker* when he was out there on the poetry circuit pulling in fifty a year.

After lunch, Barrett waded into the clothes cage which was overstuffed with groovy winter attire. He found a wonderful brown riding jacket, sewn on which was a great draping rust-hued cape, with copious pockets suitable for pounds of notebooks and the apparatus of scrounge.

For his feet he found a pair of rubbished bowling shoes, each of a slightly differing size. They must have been discarded rentals from an alley—since the left shoe, red and green in color, was painted with a 9 on the heel back, whereas the other, plain brown in hue, bore the number 14. They were extremely comfortable, free of rot scent, and worthy of the stroll of Apollinaire past the riverine book booths. Donning his new attire, Barrett felt a spew of raw genius.

V

He was full, he was happy—the angst of an empty stomach emptied away—for e'en a nascent Keats is de'ego'd and deprived of depravity by the talons of the Food Hawk. He was in the mood for a stare scene at Rienzi's Coffee House where his antlered eyes might be assuaged by eyeball data, pulchritudinous and groovy, sandals on taut tanned calf muscles, muscles under flamboyant attire waving and bulging, existential stares from the window as he passed the San Remo Bar. He dazzled the Bowery, he was sure, as he oozed along in his new bowling shoes and apollonian/apollinaire jacket, to Bleecker, up Bleecker to MacDougal, right on MacD, to Reinzi's.

He chose a white marble table with inlaid chessboard at the front window. For what good was a long sit in Rienzi's without a full view of the MacDougal Street parade? During Barrett's years in the Village, he developed methods of gazing that would have been useful fifteen years later had he decided to form a psychedelic cult of eye-trained followers, instead of becoming an English professor/bard.

He lit up a little Henri Winterman Café Crème and sat, just sat, drinking espresso tinted with lemon rind, followed by a cappuccino, then another strong espresso, raising his energy to the level of, say, a Wash Park pot puff fear-scan, as he impaled the passing grooviness, haughtiness overdubbed above unselfconfidence, pausing to jot down in notebook the fleeting flashes.

He would not have called it boredom, but after a few minutes the window-stare caused an inner confusion or mild desperation like that of a cultist trying not to fall asleep in front of his guru during a meditation session. Therefore, he was happy to switch his attention to the observations of face muscles, for he found a sad lack in English verse of the description of the activities of the human face during moments of love, tragedy and heavy action. For instance, what were the face muscles doing during the seduction scene in Keats' *The Eve of St. Agnes?* And was not Ezra Pound in book after book telling everybody to "Make It NEW"?

To Barrett, such concerns provided possibilities to enter literary history with a bang, as opposed to that other odious possibility of entrance, e.g., whimpersville. So he turned from face to face in the coffee shop, jotting down face-muscle data. He paused at a boy and girl sitting at the table next to his, and decided to time-track, so to

speak, their activities in his notebook, perhaps as a vignette for a short story—for he certainly did not want to
get lost in a career as a poet without having acquired the
ability to spin up a story for a magazine in a time of
poverty.

He could not pick up a copy of the *New Directions
Annual* in the Eighth Street Bookshop without feeling sore
remorse that a story of his was not contained within. A
story, not a poem, for he felt his lyrics much too completely unpublishably unundestandably totally garbage-
ably brilliant to risk printing, yet again possessed with a
stubborn belief that critics were going to vampire his
career.

The girl was attired in a tightly fitting blue suit with a
white lace blouse beneath the vestlike suit top. Barrett's
notebooks are unclear as to the color of her hair, but it
was cut just above the shoulders, was parted in the
center, and there were bangs upon her brows. Beneath
the bangs were wide brown suffering but sensual eyes
sadly encircled with the apple bruises of tiredness—or
maybe the languor of summer-school final exams. With
her was Levine, a poet whom Barrett had met at a
Ginsberg-O'Hara reading at the Living Theater.

The girl reached into her briefcase and drew forth with
hand atremble a clutch of typed verse, maybe fifteen
pages in all—and handed it to Levine who read them
most attentively for at least ten minutes, his jaw muscles
munching a phantom cud of Old Mule chewing tobacco.
Levine turned back to several poems for a reread, nodding and humming through his nose in apparent approval. Then it was chopsville.

Slowly Levine unscrewed the fountain-pen cap, his
head bent down, his eyes staring slightly upward in a

baleful Ivan the Terrible glance into her returning stare. Barrett watched this unaware. The girl certainly did not ask the guy to edit or to emend her work.

"I hope you don't mind," was all Levine said as, in a quick slashing of x's, rubouts of phrases and sentences, and even, horror of verse horrors, rewrites of entire lines, he chaos'd her poems.

She watched this quiet and white-faced. "You see this line?" he asked, twisting the page so she could view. "'I have learned nothing,'" he read. "Well, instead of nothing, I usually write 'naught' or 'aught'—you dig! Because 'nothing' is so, uh, unnoticeable, but 'naught' is, sounds more, like, what a poet would say."

She was not so sure. Her lower lip jutted and trembled. And you could tell watching Levine hold her poems crunchingly, he did not consider her a poet. "'I have learned naught'" he read, then he scribbled the change.

At the same instant as Levine read that sentence, a human in a frayed purple top hat just beyond them leaned down toward his companion's face, holding a lightbulb up next to her nose, and shouted, "You prove this lightbulb exists! Prove it!"

Barrett was overjoyed, heading for his notebook to jot those twain of pearls.

> I have learned naught.
> you prove this light
> bulb exists.   Rienzi's 7–1–59

You can check it out at the Manuscript Collection, Brown University Library.

It was after his second espresso and second hour at Rienzi's that John Barrett headed toward the restroom.

There was a thick post located near the stairs down to the john, with a table on the other side obscured from sight. As he started down the steps, he noticed a spade cat at the table, in a beret, sun glasses, and smoking a cigarillo in an ivory holder. Barrett nodded hello.

The man gave a quick look to his side, like a basketball player before a back-pass, then, in the manner of dope dealers of the time, blurted a mumbling rapid sentence softly, "Would mumble mumble buy mumble grass, man?"

At first Barrett wasn't sure what the man said. Then it clicked. "Maybe a nickel bag," he replied, and walked down the steps. It was really stupid to buy pot on Mac-Dougal Street. Barrett knew it. But somehow he felt he had to go along with the offer, like someone who can't leave a bookstore without a purchase to please the cashier.

First of all there was the problem of quality, because notorious burner-hustlers worked the Village coffee houses, and it was sure injurious to the beat image as tourist pot-seekers from Indiana University were sold a pitiful mixture of catnip, oregano, a faint dusting of real cannabis, and maybe a sprinkle of de-doped canary seeds.

"May I see it?" Barrett asked. There was a flash of disgust on the guy's face as he slid a hand into his pocket and palmed a thin foil of crinkly substance into Barrett's fingers, all the while fear-scanning over the shoulder and up the steps for the narks.

"Hurry up, man," he said. "There's fuzz everywhere." It was in the Rienzi's urine parlor that the first beatnik narkos flourished—becostumed in berets, beards, sandals, black turtles, and shoulder holsters. It was supposed to be humorous to watch a beatnik policeman head for the john every five minutes to try for a collar.

Barrett unfolded a corner, peeked at the green, and sniffed. The grass was mysteriously almost as verdant as a pool table and it smelled like the spice shaker over at the pizzeria.

Barrett loved any real opportunity to get righteously indignant. And now was the time. He only had twelve dollars as his entire worldly hoard. If he spent five for the bu, that left him on the poverty line with seven to last through a week's spaghetti, day-old bread, and whatever he could grab off free and pungent in the sun at the Fulton Fish Market. It also meant he couldn't pick up the book he'd ordered at the far-famed Orientalia Book Store on the techniques of Japanese Nōh Drama—another area of scholarship the wily writing of Ezra Pound had inspired him to consider.

Therefore, Barrett was relieved and the Nōh book was as good as bought when the odor of the grass indicated it was a Zippo-lighter scene. "Why're you trying to sell me spice, man!" Barrett demanded in a loud whisper. "Fuck, I can go across the street and shake this shit free out of the pizza shaker." And he left the bu upon the washstand, walked up righteous to his table, paid the chit for the overpriced beatsville coffee, and headed out into the glare of MacDougal, such a narrow and overarched street that it was almost like walking room to room.

Barrett headed up MacDougal for the park. Suddenly the burner passed him, nudging him with a shoulder. The burner turned back upon him, adjusting his beret to the back of his head. His words were a hiss. "I don't want you telling anybody you *think* I tried to burn you, or you and me are going to go through some changes."

"Leave me alone, burner," Barrett almost moaned in reply. The burner vanished left at West 3rd Street toward

124

Sixth Avenue, dancing at the heels of a pack of tourists, then was swallowed into their midst.

VI

"Man, you shouldn't *ever* buy grass in Rienzi's!" They laughed. "Hey, Barrett just got burned in Rienzi's! Ha Ha Ha!" A circle of loungers at Alex Holley's statue as Barrett took a slurp from a Thunderbird bottle someone passed him.

"Check that motherfucker!" one of them exclaimed.

"Yayah! Here comes J.S.D.!"

The sucking circle of T-birders at the statue's ledge were excited. You were always excited whenever a friend would stroll, saunter, cringe, or crawl, into the park. Barrett looked up and there he was, loping into the plaza, stilt-legged J.S.D. J.S.D. was maybe twenty, and extremely tall—the type coaches start taking out to dinner by the time they're thirteen. J.S.D. was wearing a pair of tan Levi's about six inches too short, and a fishnet T-shirt which was very popular at the time. J.S.D. had a habit of pointing his finger and shaking it while tilting his head to the side—according to Barrett's notebooks—before he began to speak. The barman at the Jazz Gallery gave him his name from the first letters of jazz/sex/dope, which triad comprised the substance of J.S.D's worldly interests. He was a Wurlitzer of saxophone solos—all you had to do was give him the name of the record, and the instrument you wanted, and he was ready to give you an oral recital. Obscure alto recorder parts, for instance, that you could barely hear on early records, J.S.D. knew them all. He was the Mozart of the Jazz Gallery. If Sonny Rollins came out of retirement to play the Gallery, J.S.D. would sit all night, head in hands, at one of those one-dollar side booths at the club, and memorize the entire gig. The next day he was at the park ready to perform it all. As for the other initials in his name; id est: sex and dope, those occurred hourly daily nightly.

"What's happening, J.S.D. baby!" Barrett exclaimed, holding a palm out for five. J.S.D. whacked palms, sat down next to John Barrett on the shady side of Holley, drained the Thunderbird, cadged a cigarette, and asked the immortal question, "Anybody got any pills?"

Twenty minutes died in the mirth. Barrett looked over at J.S.D. whose head was tilted aside, attracting Barrett's attention, and his finger was pointing wildly. One would have thought J.S.D.'s eyes were going to liquefy, he was so torridly impaling the advent of a girl known when she was not around as Racy Tracy—portions of her body in various orbits of wiggly jiggly—all of which drove J.S.D. into a brickbat down-scope with respect to his middle initial.

Tracy looked just like the red-haired woman staring out from Edouard Manet's *Le Déjeuner sur l'Herbe*. And that was her scene, the picnic of the senses. There was one slight difference, she was not yet quite as chubby as the picnicker sur l'Herbe, but the face was one-on-one. Barrett tried to bring this fact up, but Tracy was already aware. She said that she was mad at Edouard M. for not having at least *one* of the guys nude also at that famous creekside foursome.

Tracy was a watercolorist, specializing in portraits of the denizens of W. Sq.—particularly the spade cats. She was good at it—she worked hard—although her name has

126

never appeared in subsequent years in *ARTNews* or *The Voice*, or on SoHo posters, so it is difficult to know if she kept it up. Each early morning she grabbed the D Train from the Bronx, with a pad of paper and her case of colors, and headed for the park. There was, of course, the sensual side of it too, she being addictively an adept, in the votive sense, of the "onyx lollipops"—as she spoke of it, as of FLASH! Man, was she popular.

J.S.D.'s favorite summer pastime was tar-beach sex, and the arrival of Tracy triggered off such a possibility of paradise that he brought it up immediately. "'Ey Trac'! What's happening. Let's go over to East 9th and roof it! My friend's got a sun tent set up over there, and we can use the shower in his pad." Tracy and J.S.D. were famous on the set for the number of roofs they had made it on. They even once broke the lock on the door, and went up the spiral staircase to the roof of Wash. Sq. Arch where they celebrated the birth of Himeros, God of Loin lunge, out of Chaos.

J.S.D. and the others did not pay much attention to her paintings and that pissed her off. They were always trying to set up house with her—having in mind more of a wash-the-dishes scene than her being a painter. Barrett was somewhat upset that whenever Tracy was around she seemed to look through him as if he were gauze. He didn't exist. "Look at me," he spoke breath-level, "please."

Tracy laughed, and showed J.S.D. her latest portrait, but sensed at once that his mind was dialed into a mono-channel. "Not today, J.S.D. Maybe tomorrow. I'll be down here about noon. Okay?"

"Okay, baby, see you then." J.S.D. turned to Barrett, "Hey, let's go over to Dom's and cop some stuff."

127

VII

Dom's pad was above an outdoor fruit market on First Avenue and the arising air always had that scent of potato buds and acrid cantaloupe. When they arrived Dom was standing at the stove cooking a pan bread of beat-up matzoh crackers mixed with corn meal in a large iron skillet. He was sweating and his oleaginous muscles were bulging as he shook the skillet, his laced sandals occasionally slapping the linoleum. Dom's voice was almost a caricature of a Deep South accent—mayan for man, squayah for square, Zin for Zen.

Dom lived with June, a nurse at Bellevue Hospital until very recently when a ward nurse had found her grabbing fingers in the hospital dope cooler. June wore her yellow hair in a near crewcut; she was thin, with hips elegantly sliding perpendicularly from her thin stomach for about an inch before angling downward. She was a bit of an A-head and was a familiar figure at the fountain in her uniform after work. She liked her white nurse's stockings and wore them that day beneath a Mexican wedding dress embroidered with briar roses across the bosom. J.S.D.'s head tilted to the side and his finger began to point, and Barrett copped at once the real purpose of the visit, watching the pants-down stare passing back and forth between June and J.S.D. out of Dom's sight in the living room.

In the kitchen Barrett belched with nervousness looking through the cupboard doors upon an Old Mother Hubbard barrenness. The only things to eat in the pad were a box of matzoh meal, a box of matzoh farfel, a box of corn meal, and a pint of cooking oil and that would all be gone soon as Dom heaved the pan bread out of the skillet onto the plate, a gray curl of corn-oil smoke arising from the hot iron.

He and June were totally broke in a New York summer—hardly a time to be down and out in the beat apple, although wintertime on the Bowery by the burning barrels had to be infinitely worse. Besides, Dom had his dope business to keep him going. He was rumored to be able to supply virtually every substance mentioned in Robert S. De Ropp's book *Drugs and the Mind,* and his living room attested to that claim with many shelves stacked with pharmacist's jars of semilegal substances such as *Lophophora williamsii,* wild lettuce from Mexico, belladonna, yohimbine bark, Indian tobacco, ginseng root, and even some sort of dried worm from Sumatra that purportedly placed the user into the Land of the Warm Fog. Illegal drugs such as coke, meth, bennies, pot, skag, yellowjackets, goofballs, mescaline and opium were kept ingeniously stashed in the ceiling light fixture of his neighbor on the floor below. Dom had drilled a hand-sized hole in his floor just above the fixture. Dom said that you had to be very careful in retrieving pharmaceuticals from the bowl-shaped light because it was easy for the arm to miss the fixture and find itself waving in empty air. The residents in the apartment were very religious and Dom was afraid that if they ever looked up and saw a hand descending from the ceiling they might consider it some sort of epiphany and start screaming.

Dom had just flown back from Tangier where someone had dropped a total burn on him in a hash deal. He tried to make the story humorous but his words were crispéd and sere. "There I was, man, pushing a cart out of this marketplace; my eyes were seeing dollar bills and the

129

lease on that summer place in Vermont. When I loaded the stuff into my trunk it turned out to be, I guess, a bunch of camel dung bricks mixed up with pieces of clove. I lost everything but my plane ticket. All I got out of the whole trip was a sack of vul. . . ." He paused, suddenly snapped his fingers, turned and walked through the curtain of beads into the living room.

Dom came back holding a lumpy bundle tied up in a bandanna. He undid the kerchief and placed six brown-speckled oval objects on the table. He lifted one of them up to his ear and shook it.

He explained that he had bought them last week in Morocco and he'd been solemnly assured by the purveyor that they were fresh vulture eggs from nests in high mountain crags. He had meant to give them out as gifts but now, with the Food Hawk screaming 'gainst his eyes, began to meditate aloud on the possibility of frying up a bit of omeletic vulture. "Lordy, I hope they're fresh enough to eat," he said.

He closed his eyes and broke one into the sizzling skillet, wrinkling his nose at the same time as if expecting a miasma of rotting buzzard to issue upward. But the egg looked great. He broke the other eggs and mushed them up with a fork, sprinkling matzoh farfel into them and a splash of oil. Right away the orange-yellow plexus began to spew forth soft odors of yumminess so that all four of them crowded around the skillet, freshets of salivation forcing them to swallow.

"Man, I don't know, they look fertilized," Barrett cautioned.

"Fuck it, man," Dom growled in reply. "We need protein. They can always pump it out of us up at Bellevue if we get sick. You got a dime to call the ambulance?"

Barrett nodded.

The V.E.M.B. looked like a flat circle of yellow modeling clay upon the serving plate, but boy was it delicious—the only known instance in the beatific era of vulture egg matzoh brei. And it may have been also the only instance in the same era of vulture-egg protein stoking the fires of fornication. For June and J.S.D. began to send little ships out of each other's eyes to meet and negotiate a body brei. And the meal was barely ended when J.S.D. took June's hand and guided her to the fire escape, whence he spat a glance over at Dom as if to say, cool out your wrath South boy—and then in a slow turn of his head he focused his attention on June, smile spreading. They giggled and bent over to crawl out the window and climbed upon the metal slats.

Dom and June had a tar-beach roof cabana reachable by a ladder from the fire escape. There was a mattress out of sight behind the water tower, which was shaded by a couple of those large umbrellas borrowed from hotdog carts. June and J.S.D. went up to fuck almost every day that summer—not exactly groping in front of Dom but it was a silent rule that Dom would keep away while they were up on the tar.

Barrett thought he saw a quick bite of the lip, but Dom turned his head before John could be sure. Dom kicked the floor with his sandal, and muttered. "I don't know. I'll just never get used to them."

"What do you mean?" Barrett asked, "Them making it on the roof?"

"Nah, man, I guess I mean spade cats."

Barrett wanted to change the subject. He also wanted some fresh data. "May, uh, I go up and watch?"

Dom looked startled, but said, "Suruh, go on ahead."

131

John B. reached the top of the ladder and paused, his head and most important, his eyes, just clearing the rim of the roof; he could feel a very pleasant breeze float up the back of his riding jacket. He looked down the six flights to the trashy alley. Shudder. Then he lifted his eyes unto the action.

June and J.S.D. had just about reached the mattress, their arms tight around each other's back, June's long fingers sliding under J.S.D.'s belt, under tan jeans, over the darkling buttock—a little insistence of pain perhaps, as she scritch-scratched her way.

"Ow! Watch it," J.S.D. laughed.

John Barrett himself laughed as J.S.D. slid down his Levi's, folded them carefully, then laid them across a TV aerial. June couldn't wait—she knelt down as if to worship the Afro-herm, rubbing her hands down both sides of him—and then took as much as possible into her mouth. For a few seconds, from Barrett's vantage point, her head looked like someone nodding frenetically listening to an anecdote at a party.

Then J.S.D. pushed her away and June sank slowly down to the hot, slightly dour-smelling Sealy Posturepedic, rolling her white stockings off most efficiently—it reminded Barrett of a baker rolling dough for pretzels, and he nearly fell off the metal ladder trying to put that comparison 'pon his notepad. After that, she lay back coyly in her briefs and J.S.D. was on her and she was barely able to remove them before shyly but adeptly she glided the dark guitar-neck within her. "Come on come on come on," she said, "come on."

Barrett fought away a curling of drool from his lips—and found himself aroused against his gabardine trousers. Another long stare and then he forced himself to look

132

away, more specifically to look fearfully downward as he attempted a thumpless silent creep back down the fire escape.

VIII

John found Dom jacking off lotus-posture on a prayer rug, looking at a wall map of East St. Louis. Is that what he really saw? It sure looked like it—although Dom quickly removed any indication of manstupration when Barrett lunged through the beaded curtain. "I've got to get out of here before things get weird," Barrett spoke deadpan, "but first can you deal me some bennies?"

They were a bit overpriced at six for one dollar, but Dom had already wrapped them up in an empty Rolaids package before he could complain. When Dom found him browsing in the other room by the dope crocks, he suggested he try a speedball, which was a "steal" at fifty cents. Barrett wasn't sure exactly what was contained in a speedball and was far too cooled-out to pull a Q & A scene to relieve his ignorance. He thought it was a mixture of cocaine and either morphine or Nembutal—like, a ride up ride down same ride. He knew he'd probably never take it, or leave it around collecting dust in the paperclip bowl, try to offer it to a shocked graduate student ten years later, so he bought it.

Barrett was pretty tired so he blew fifteen cents for the crosstown bus back to Washington Square. During the ride he noticed a mother with young child sitting on her knees. She was teaching it various words, and after running the child through the obligatory "mama" and "dada" and "gonkit" (blanket) she pointed over at Barrett and said, "See the beatnik, Tommy!"

133

"Come on, honey, say beatnik, beat-nik!"—breaking the word in two. And the child rolled a drooling face toward Barrett, smiled, and said, "jeep jik!"

That made Barrett's day, and he spent the next hour and a half in the musty silence of his favorite bookstores, The Eighth Street and The Phoenix. He was still able, at that early point in his career, to experience mysterious bookstore flashes or energy transferences by, say, standing very near the New Directions rack in the basement of the Eighth Street, or reading the mimeo'd *Ezra Pound Newsletter* at The Phoenix. Ahhh sweet bookstores of New York.

He finished the latest issues of *Semina* and *Kulchur* and caught the time off the wrist of a clerk, and sped back to the square to log some time working on the sequence for his first book of poetry. He sat down again by the statue of Alex Holley, but far enough away from Uncle Thrills, who was holding court at the fountain, that he could barely hear Thrills' shrill wail, and escaped into the sentences.

Siobhan McKenna Group-Grope

THE TAN FOG of particulate dooky lay low 'tween the high clouds and the barren skyline cenotaphs of New York City. Within the closure of lower Manhattan, in tenement slums of the poor, a poetry reading was held in late September of 1961 at The House of Nothingness on Tompkins Square North. It was an open reading—one where any and all were allowed to read their works.

In warm weather the readings were held out back in the court where there was a beautiful rectangular garden of raked white sand with a triad of small boulders bunched in the sand at one end. The garden was molded after a similar garden in a Zen temple in Kyoto.

There were seven humans—three women, four men, who were walking through the streets after the reading toward an apartment at 704 East 5th Street just off Avenue C. Each of them had read their poetry. That is, when they arrived at Nothingness, each had approached the person running the readings and had placed his/her name on the reading list. There were twenty-three readers that September night, divided into three approximately

135

one-hour sets. Readers were requested to limit themselves to ten minutes each but occasionally someone droned through a 115-quatrain translation of the Pyramid Texts of King Unas so that after, say, fifteen minutes, people began to shift impatiently at their tables. In all truth the majority of those attending had come clutching spring-binders of their own verse to read and viewed time-hogs with disapproval.

Of the seven walking through the midnight East Side, three were editors of their own poetry magazines. They knew each other's work intimately and discussed it whenever they met, which was just about every day. Their life was the world of poetry and poetry publications and the recounting of the anecdotes of poet-life. They lifted a common nose of disdain upon the rest of the world, especially television and newspapers with their ceaseless spew of right-wing death.

In spite of the horror, terror and vileness of the *res publica*—the ennui, the mental spasms that sent them down plateaus of nothingness constrained to watch the blobs convulse and mull and melt—in spite of it, they met that fall after the readings to listen to poetry records, and, while lyrics softly babbled from the speaker, did lie down toward the Galaxy to pluck the vast lyre of grass-grope. For no right-wing government can prevent the sneers and derision of the people smoking pot in private.

Compared with the bunch-punches of the psychedelic years to come, it was tenderly innocent—but it was thought to comprise an historical first, the premiere instance in Western Civilization of such activities.

They specialized in Caedmon/Spoken Arts records—committing skin-clings to the best minds of three generations, including Dylan Thomas, e.e. cummings, Marianne

Moore, Delmore Schwartz, William Carlos Williams, Edith Sitwell, and even T.S. Eliot, although it is to be admitted that Eliot reading *Murder in the Cathedral* made it somewhat difficult to keep up the stoked fires of fornication. (A complete list of poets, to whose verse were held the parties, is appended.)

It was actress Siobhan McKenna's reading of Irish poetry that the group played again and again in their fuckings. God, it turned them on. They exhausted their love-surge listening to Siobhan McKenna. They talked about writing her a letter inviting her to attend one of their midnight specials the next time she should visit New York. They were especially excited to find out that McKenna had performed as Lady Macbeth in Gaelic at a theatre in Galway.

"Let's find out if she had made a recording of the play in Gaelic!" someone exclaimed, bright-eyed with eagerness.

There was no theory behind the group-gropes—unless the theory of the heated bottom. "Who loves himself loves me who love myself"—the bard sang; and that was the gropers' theory. They didn't discuss it really—but fell down regardless into the furrows of the avoidance of coma. If anyone asked, "Why do you think we do this?"—someone carried the hookah-tip over to the person or toppled them onto the mattress with a grope-tackle.

Some were hesitant, waxing bold later. Others the reverse. It was like that Ezra Pound poem, *E. P. Ode Pour L'Election de Son Sépulchre*, Part IV, only as applied to phonographic fornication. Ava, for instance, wrote long-line poems of religious nature and wore extremely demure attire, but once the police lock was poked into place, became a torrid participant. Brash-

137

mouthed Bill however, who was a veritable Tourette's disease of obscene expletives, became almost unparticipatingly shy, although he was eager to hop around the mattresses with an ancient box camera. For the most part, the seven relaxed into a common soul and grew to know each others' bodies and desires and energies to a labyrinthine degree.

When the sex-hungry poets arrived at the pad: Ava, Bill, Rosebud, Nelson, Rick, Trudy, and a human named Obtak who considered himself to be the reincarnation of Shelley, they drank a round of yohimbine-bark tea that Rick had made during the day after a street-scrounge for mirrors. Right away they stacked the poetry records atop the turntable. Rick had a gentle thing about mirrors and that afternoon he'd collected as many as he could find in the Bowery area from thrown-away dressers. He hauled up five cracked, pitiful specimens which he lined around the mattresses. That was his chief thrill, to watch others reflected fucking in mirrors, at the same time listening, say, to Edith Sitwell, while Ava massaged his pornic area with a banana skin.

There was a small offset press in the back room on which Ava printed a monthly verse-paper. Ava and Obtak had to work awhile in the room fixing the inking mechanism which had become maladjusted so that only the left side of the page was being printed. When it was fixed, they fell fucking beneath the machine on a blue air mattress, unable to wait for the poesy. Someone in the bedroom put on an e. e. cummings/Luciano Berio composition. After a few minutes, Ava and Obtak came out of the press room, Ava laughing, "I guess it's time to go to bed." She leaned against the bathtub and whipped off her blue velour pullover, dropped her jeans skirt, flaming over to

138

turn on the water. She took a bath with the assistance of Nelson, and then appeared at the mattress, dabbing at her hair-ends with a towel.

There were two mattresses side by side, one double-sized, one single. Before anything they smoked a lot of grass, via the toilet roll dope blow. They took the cardboard inner cylinder and Rick punched a small hole into the top of it, inserting a thick burning bomber in the aperture. At both ends mouths were positioned. One end sucked his/her lungs full of dope. Then, on signal, he/she blew the lungful through the tube into the sucking mouth-lungs of the other, in a fast whoosh. Then it was off to the zone.

There were variations of this, for instance when Bill inserted his cock through the roll when there was a lit roach burning perpendicularly and several of them took a toke.

For serious bedside smoking, however, there was a five-tube hookah made out of a jug from an office water-cooler. The toke-tubes were long lengths of rubber lab tubing wrapped in velvet ribbons. The carved burl was kept packed with grass and throughout the festivities any-one could lean over from the mattress and snerk.

They started with an arpeggio of e. e. cummings, Mari-anne Moore, Dylan Thomas, and a flash of *Howl*. Then it was the McKenna hour. Siobhan McKenna's voice, soft, full, beautiful, triggered off a cross-mattress grope spasm that turned the arms and legs of the lovers into a quick frenzy of motion like a dropped fistful of jackstraws. When she read Yeat's *The Stolen Child*, with the chorus in Gaelic, three suffered orgasm immediately. "Siobhan! Siobhan!"—Bill moaned, as he was engaged in E3- with Obtak, Ava, Rick, and Nelson. E3- was a term used by them to denote concomitant double-handed beatoff plus fellatio by Ava, with simultaneous impletion of Ava from the back.

There were numerous combinations but usually they paired and trio'd off by the end of the records. Ava and Nelson slept together. They always seemed to pair off and indeed, of them all, were the only ones to live together. Ava pushed her slight frame against him. Soon she was atop and seesaw bumping. She was able to come that way, rocking, rubbing forward, sliding into the happiness. Next to the frenzying Ava/Nelson, Rick and Rosebud lay side by side, Rick bringing her to a moaning cliff-leap by means of an extraordinary device fashioned from a furry pipe cleaner.

Obtak and Trudy, she side, he at her back, eyes shut tight, making it on the single mattress. Trudy was able to lift her leg and move it back and forth across the partner's chest during conjunction.

As for Bill, he usually fell asleep after a single act of love culminating in a long warbling scream they called the "yohimbine yodel." Bill had read a poem that night at The House of Nothingness titled *Homage to the Buttock*. Later on, Bill and Ava were seeing how hard they could whack themselves together and the pops filled the air from the pubic cymbals. Perhaps thinking of his poem, Ava whisper-urged him to climb upon, nay, to impinge himself within, her buttocks. He became confused and soon had to stop, thinking she had bidden buttockal pain upon herself because of his poem—for verily there are few who trod the paths of Mt. Bulgar.

He continued to think so except that he gradually learned that she genuinely was an adept of buttockery. Forever he remembered her lying topless upon her stomach on the sleeping bag on the air mattress in blue tights and Rick pushed his hand upon her behind and into the inward-curving, rotating the muscles circularly. "Don't stop, don't stop"—she whispered. "That arouses me more than anything all night."

Bill and Trudy loved Dylan Thomas, especially when he read *Fern Hill*. It drove them crazy. That night they played it over and over, seven times, until Bill was constrained to utter his famed yohimbine yodel after which he was soon asleep.

Hours oozed. They talked. They smoked. They wrote. They ate. Some departed. Some slept. Some kissed till dawn. And the gatherings went on each Monday for ten weeks before their Galaxy spiraled into dissolution. One went one way, one another.

During the ensuing decade, the seven ran into each other occasionally—at Orly Airport, in domes of meditation Colorado mountains, and so forth. "Remember those nights of Siobhan McKenna?"

"I sure do."

And always the friendship. bloomed. to renew again. the pleasures. of former. commingling.

Recorded poets grope-list:

1. *Yeats (Siobhan McKenna reading)*
2. *e. e. cummings*
3. *Ezra Pound*
4. *T. S. Eliot*
5. *Dylan Thomas*
6. *Edith Sitwell*
7. *A. Ginsberg*
8. *Marianne Moore*

9. *W. C. Williams*
10. *Delmore Schwartz*
11. *Arthur Rimbaud (Germaine Bree reading)*
12. *E. A. Poe*
13. *Lawrence Ferlinghetti*
14. *Edna St. Vincent Millay*
15. *W. H. Auden.*

Lophophora Roller Rink

    HE DECIDED TO forego the reading of any more novels after he had tallied his future reading list in the languages he was studying, in the poetry of the languages, and in certain religious studies relating to Coptic sects, Buddhism, the Vedas, and the beat poets. He did not have time for many years to read novels, he felt. *On the Road* often lured him into its lonesome pages, but he was able to resist consuming much time therein. Joyce, however, was a poet in everything and the young man felt it was okay to linger within.

His refusal to study contemporary fiction was a disaster that surfaced fifteen years later when he tried his hand at a couple of novels. Even the critics who were his best friends had to turn down assignments to review them for *The New York Times* Sunday book section.

He was living on five dollars per week consumed in spaghetti, day-old bread, chicken parts (hearts/necks/wings/ani—like, twenty-five cents a pound on Avenue A), and what could be borrowed from markets by stealth just after predawn outdoor deliveries. His pad on East 4th Street was a three-room citadel of verminous grime. He

143

loved it. He had rented it furnished from a policeman, who was acting somehow as the agent for the prior occupant who had recently been placed in an asylum. The legal rent for the pad was eighteen dollars a month, though the policeman charged him forty-eight.

The method of acquiring an apartment in those days was this. The *Village Voice* was published on Wednesday, but advance copies were delivered to Sheridan Square around noon on Tuesday. One waited in role as nervous pad-junkie for the delivery truck and when it arrived, grabbed a copy and ran rudely, without even opening it, to the cigar store, where there were phone booths. Once inside the booth and the door was closed, one read the pad ads, and made immediate phone calls. Less than one minute after the *Voice* was delivered, he had made an appointment to see the famous pad on East 4th, and less than thirty minutes after the phone call, he rented it, not knowing the renter was a cop.

The prior occupant of the apartment had left numerous letters around the place signed "Nancy the Lion Heart" which were long love letters from her to "King Richard the Lion Heart." The policeman had apparently been involved in carting her away to the institution. One day a letter arrived from the rent control board, addressed to Officer Smekolsk—which the young man could not resist opening—announcing that the legal rent was being raised from sixteen to eighteen dollars per month. That meant the cop was skimming thirty illegal bucks! A quick contemplation of his dope-hoard, however, made him decide not to make any trouble for the officer.

He kept the pad furnished exactly as he had found it, and filed Nancy the Lion Heart's letters away carefully, in event she should escape the asylum. It was a roach farm, and the only thing he could find time or inclination to keep clean, besides his bed and desk, was the middle drawer of the kitchen table. He threw the knives and forks from the drawer into the bathtub—an act which necessitated scooting the utensils out of the way when taking a bath. The emptied top drawer was used for the dope: pot, skag, amphetamine, papers and needles.

His only interests were books, dope, thrills, and his friends. He had not seen a TV for three years or had he listened to the radio except for the midnight jazz shows. Newspapers were pillows for copping z's on the subway or on a park bench. The world of *Time* mag was absent, man. For instance, the advent of the twist caught him unaware. He was stumbling home wrecked one afternoon when he encountered a group of Puerto Rican kids on the stoop doing the twist to a blaring portable radio. In his apartment he turned on the radio and tried to locate it. Finally on WMCA they played a weird record called "The Lone Twister," sung by a gravelly voiced male crooner. "I'm de lone twista"—the voice sang.

"Hey, that's what I am, man, too, the lone twister!"— his roommate Wilfred yelled from the other room as he twisted the tie on his arm before the blood clouded into the dropper and Wilf pushed the rubber bulb and the skag zombied the vein. Wilfred was working his way through De Ropp's book, *Drugs and the Mind,* the beat bible of dope gobble, trying whatever he could get his hands on.

For instance, in a few minutes they both planned to take peyote. It apparently wasn't illegal to receive *Lophophora williamsii,* the peyote cactus, from mail-order "cactus ranches" in Texas and the Southwest, so there was a flood of buttons that year for the mouths of the Lower

145

East Side, and only yesterday Sam had trudged up to Stuyvesant Station to pick up their packet from the thrill farm.

When at last it was time to chew, Sam was alone. Wilfred had gone out somewhere stealing or scoring or scrounging and had told him to sail ahead. The poet lay upon his back, after swallowing five dark spansules packed with flakes of peyote, waiting to experience the period of nausea that was supposed sometimes to occur just after ingestion. He felt no sickness-waves, however, and within a few minutes the gods switched on the lights of peyote. He looked around the room and saw colors and gradations of colors in objects that he had never before noticed. He began to stare up at the copper-colored lining on the inside of the socket of the ceiling light fixture. The copper normally would have been a mere dim blur up there in the cracked plaster but under the grace of *Lophophora* it gleamed with new fire. Minutes he stared at the flaming copper.

He had been advised to close his eyes for peyote flash-patterns which would maybe present themselves as great whirling Ezekielian religion-wheels. This he did and waited for the colors. Instead of Ezekiel, he immediately experienced a time jump and there lit up upon his mind-screen a full-color reverie of Mr. Roddle's '49 Plymouth packed with his seventh-grade schoolmates in 1952 driving to a rollerskating party in Bluff River, Colorado. Why was he thinking about the roller rink? He didn't care—he felt like someone in some small futuristic movie house watching his own biotape. He even murmured, "Roll it, O Zeus, roll it!"

Mr. Roddle's blue Plymouth came with those fuzzy brown seatcovers that caused hideous spine shivers

146

whenever one's fingernail accidentally scratched across it. Sam could see the inside of the car, the kids clutching the skates in their laps. He saw himself with his arm around his girlfriend Annie Thornton!—whom he hadn't seen for many years.

Annie's father was driving the other car of skaters. The last thing Sam wanted was to be spotted by Annie's father in the rearview mirror necking with Annie, so Sam remembered having talked her into riding with Mr. Roddle. Every time he saw Annie's visionary face, his stomach felt that empty ache and it was no less so eight years later as a derelict beatnik. She was a dark blonde with long delicate hair on her forearms. Even in the seventh grade she had already acquired her wanton beauty, and to see her again, as if it were real, was sad indeed. Ache, beatnik, ache.

Annie and Sam had taken piano lessons together with the same teacher for about five years. That's where he had first seen her, sitting with derrière-length tresses at age seven at the keyboard during one of those torturous recitals the students periodically had to give for their parents.

Then Sam remembered the movies he and Annie Thornton used to go to on Saturday afternoons. Her father would sit way in the back while she and he sat in the third-row front. Her white jeans, the starch of her white shirt knotted at the waist. Her hair. The popcorn. The secret cigarette smokers snerking Lucky Strikes bent low in their seats. The sweat of the palms of nervous hand-holders. What a smell-mix.

He remembered putting his arms around her, fearful of rejection. And then she leaned her head on his shoulder, purest of thrills. And her hand as it held his, what could

147

match this? Could it have been that a beatnik trio writhing nude on mescaline upon a mattress could not duplicate in any way the thrill of a hand held in a matinee of a Durango Kid movie?

The seventh-graders had begun to hold parties for one another. Some went together to dancing school: organized sanctioned body contact—an hour and a half of fox trot, box step, the jitterbug, two Cokes, then home by 10 P.M. The parents wanted to control it, to prevent any pants-down scenes. When a "weak" parent was discovered fronting parties where there were necking games, they were immediately halted. Sam remembered one party there was a game devised on the spot called "pick-a-leg" where, divided in halves, one group would sit on a high ledge and hang their legs down. The others would "pick a leg" and then there were five minutes of rubs and smooches in the dark followed by another round, new pick-legs, and new smooches. When the snitcher snitched, these parties were banned.

The solution to this "problem" was the institution of bi-weekly skating parties. Let the little punks skate their fires away.

Clommer's Roller Rink was located right on the Kansas/Colorado state line. It was owned by Walt Clommer, a local sports hero just in the zenith of his career as a major-league catcher, preparing to spend his remaining forty years operating a roller rink, a Dairy Queen, and a used-car dealership. His daughter Sophie was Miss Colorado in 1957 or '8.

There was great excitement when Mr. Roddle pulled into the parking lot. Sam could never remember anything of the interval between arrival and putting on his skates inside. He leaped from the car and zombi-ran to the front

148

door. The next two hours would be total fun: no politics, no hidden meanings, no parents, no visions, no hassles.

Clommer's Roller Rink was a bit run down, sorely in need of paint, and rather weatherworn. The cost: fifty cents to get in, thirty-five to rent skates, if needed. The interior was high ceiling'd and heated by a vibrating furnace in the far corner. The rink itself was edged by a rickety railing of two-by-fours behind which were wooden benches skaters could rest upon. There was a side room with a sacred snack bar full of Milky Ways, popcorn, hotdogs, Cokes and bubbly orange.

The music was provided by sempiternal records of organ music. At the far end there was a cylindrical device which indicated the type of skating to be done on the floor. This oilcloth roll had a handle which could be turned to change the notice. Occasionally the music would stop and the manager, who skated around and around the floor cooling out daredevils and keeping the flow unidirectional, would utter a tweet on the whistle he wore around his neck. Then he would skate over to the cylinder roll and turn the handle till it indicated the skating he desired, such as COUPLES, TRIOS, LADIES CHOICE, WALTZ, etc.

Sam was a punkly skater. Skrunk! Skrunk! Skrunk! he practiced, lifting his feet uncertainly rather than gliding. Curves were hard to negotiate at first and sometimes he would carom centripetally and crash into the bare wood guardrail—oof!—his torso doubling over the board in sudden pain. The skate floor was ground down by the ceaseless skrunks, so that there was always a fine dust upon it. When he fell, he begrunged himself. Humiliated, he headed toward the restroom to wash, for he hated to look creepy in front of tender Annie Thornton.

149

Each time they went to the roller rink, he always spent time working on learning how to leap and twirl. Annie Thornton, just as she was a better pianist, was a much more skillful skater than he. With a sigh Sam saw himself skating with her, gliding, twirling together, crossing arms across each other's back, holding hands.

The really skilled teenage couples sometimes dressed alike, with matching pompons on the fronts of their skates; the boy, say, wearing a red and white sweater, and the girl in red and white skater's skirt. In those seventh-grade days, Sam had dreamt of the year when he and Annie would skate in matching outfits too, her arm wrapped on his shoulders, he his finger hooked into her back belt loop, his senior ring bouncing on her chest.

Toward the end of the evening, Mr. Roddle left the rink and went out to his Plymouth where he sat inside with his head on the steering wheel. Sam could not remember eight years previous going outside and seeing Mr. Roddle get into his car. It was eerie. Then he saw Mr. Roddle sobbing. He certainly didn't remember seeing that. A woman came out of the rink and walked over to the car window. "Something's got to be done!"—she yelled. She reached in and began to shake Roddle's arm. "Stop it!"— he shouted. And abruptly the peyote vision fell apart, just as the car door opened and Roddle's leg appeared.

A knock at the front door poofed the roller rink and drew him back to East 4th and 1960. He found the door. It was Wilfred his roommate with an armload of mimeographed pages. Wilfred had begun to write down his dreams in shorthand. He mimeo'd his shorthand notes and used to give them out on MacDougal Street while hitting on the tourists for change.

Wilfred walked to the kitchen table, removed his works

150

from the silverware drawer, cooked up some skag, tied up, shot up, and then walked back to the bedroom, turned on the radio for horn-shrieks, horn-mania, horn-defiance.

Sam returned to his cot and tried to retrieve the bio-tape of the skating party but the vision was like a tenth-generation photocopy. No roller rink. No teen-skate '52. What he saw stretching before him was a checkered plateau clear unto the horizon and, in the distance, saw wavy blobs rise up, coalesce, melt, then rise again. "I am a nuclear potato. I am a green bat in a purple cave." He began to laugh. "I am a handprint on a burnt wall." He rolled over on his lumpy cot to face the wall, and still the convulsing blobs kept rising and sinking.

"Hey Wilf!" he yelled, "Come here and look at the blobs!" And he roared with laughter. "Roll it! Roll it!"

Luminous Animal Theatre

THERE WERE THREE of them at once, the tripod, as she thought of them. The three, who were in love with Claudia Pred, founder of the Luminous Animal Theatre: The first was a playwright, the second was a tax examiner, the third a critic. There was a possible fourth, a rich New York stockbroker and book publisher who had invested heavily in *Newsreel-'84*, the new Luminous Animal production.

There were numerous others who had fallen down in groveling obeisance, even in the past half-year, whimpering near her hemline, salivating and swallowing, nervous for reciprocity. Claudia, as a matter of moneysaving practicality, fashioned as many of these salivating lovers as would endure it into Laborers of the Abyss, that is, into production assistants, artists, scene-swabs, janitors, and ticket-takers for the always-busy Luminous Animal

Claudia Pred
Cantatrice and Carpenter of
Beauty-motion

152

the headline of her first big review in *Dance Magazine* had flashed, when she was just twenty-two years old, five years before the occasions described in this tale of gloria mundi. A carpenter of beauty-motion, that's what she was indeed, and she had a tremendous impact on dance in the early 1960s.

1. She had begun her career very early. Right from high school she had enrolled in the New York School of Dance and Drama, where she studied for three years, by the end of which she was already putting on weekly performances at a loft on 22nd Street. And even at that early point in her career, the *Village Voice* was monitoring her art with semiannual reviews. Fred McDarrah, for instance, who chronicled the 1960s for the *Voice* with maybe a million peripatetic shutter-clicks, already had a file-cabinet drawer packed with glossy proofsheets of Claudia by the time she was twenty-four.

2. She loved dancing; dancing she felt the fluxions of Eternity. Her energy was legendary but her legs were weak. Try as she might, she did not seem to strengthen them. Not that her tries were very forceful, for she seemed, in such attempts, to tire quite easily. And she was not about to become an A-head in behest of "dance, deva-datta, dance!" But, in front of an audience, when it counted, she was all energy, all performance, all creatrix. She was Of Beauty; let us say it, for many a night we sat in Luminous Animal staring at her ceremonials of beauty-way, muscleway, danceway.

3. She had a strong and oaken physique and full cheek-bones able to cast shadows from upper light down upon the face flesh. Her hair, long waves which crested every two inches or so, was combed back out of the way, or worn in braids, or woven into a cunning knot at the back.

153

On the night of a performance, she placed a goodluck hair pin in the back knot made from a brass penstalk that had once belonged to Herman Melville. Often there were pendulous hair bunches she fashioned on each side, to hang down to the middle of the eyes—another item of thrill for dance stare-freaks watching the hair grow glistening wet with perspiration in the course of a performance.

4.   She was radiant. But it was not the pale lux of pity, buddy, it was the harsh light of Apollonia. Severe. Strict. Melted peanut butter sandwiches in the sun. But such strictness of bearing merely turned on the stare-freaks, that is, her followers, men and women of various reasons and wishes. And she cultivated them. She focus'd a substantial portion of her rarified artistic taste on her costumes and her personal attire. Every part of her had *THE* aspect; and she was ever a subtle contortionist, presenting the bone, the visage, the palm of the hand, the portion of the foot, to the beholder in its most moving view, offstage, onstage, and under the stage.

5.   She was a magnet. She had the most necessary trait of leaders, the ability to engender intense dedication to the most miniscule of projects. Her disciples were ever eager to entangle their lives with hers, and there wasn't a drama department in any New England college which didn't have a few rebel students, especially women, who wanted to emulate Claudia Pred's life in the New York theater scene. They were astonished that she held so many projects together at the same time.

6.   That is, she was resolute and domineering while appearing indecisive. It was a classic theatrical management technique, a least as old as Richard Sheridan managing the Drury Lane Theatre. Her apparent

indecision was really a total resistance to compromise; and since her schemes were usually well underway at any point, she could appear as indecisive as she wanted. And, to be sure, highly literate and articulate vagueness which at the same time evinces reassurance is of inestimable value in warding off the scent-tizzy hounds of banks and creditors.

7. And she was stoic. She rarely shrieked. And never thought herself to be in the wrong; and probably wouldn't have been able to function at all if she had felt in any way she were marching under any other banner than that of Truth, Justice and Socialism. She was generous—she paid many a paper bill for various groups printing protest leaflets on her mimeograph machine, or for poster boards and ink for her silkscreen equipment. She ran what she would want to have called a community—but she was always aloof from her associates. Part of it was a natural coldness that is a curse to so many creative people.

8. She was a lister. She kept one-hundred- or two-hundred-unit lists for each project, and her clipboard bulged with them. Hot projects, or projects needing repair, were placed at the top. The bottom of the clipboard bulge was reserved for those that functioned smoothly, and for projects still in the visionary or spectral stage.

9. She was a diarist. She kept it all—the march of the mosquitos of manners. And she spared nothing, no one, no memory, under her theory of TROUBLE. She LOVED TROUBLE, as long as there was no violence involved. There was something in her that rode against convention with shiny-eyed glee; without that boring periodic occurrence of religious fervor that such brave individuals

155

often endure, those who trample out the fresh surfaces of ne'er-been-done-before. In her diaries, she constructed her own language to describe her complex life and loves, which is going to be a pain in the ass for her future biographers—unless she codes her hapax legomena to the English language. And her writing resembled amphetamine calligraphy on a napkin at 3 A.M. in the Café Figaro, a fact which prevented lovers and unlovers from sneaking by stealth into the pages for some quick thrillies.

She also encouraged filmmakers to record her productions. And she tape-recorded everything she could afford, and there were thousands of still photos of rehearsals and personnel carefully annotated and saved for the aeons. The posters for Luminous Animal productions were made by the best artists, and a full signed set of them today will bring about ten thousand dollars at auction.

10.   In the matter of men and morals, she had to evince an exaggerated toughness. One may remember that it was 1961. For one thing, the males kept cringing in adoration, or if not cringing, they came on whippy tough-guy. They tried to tell her what to do—always making crummy unwanted suggestions, especially on artistic matters, like, "Say, I know exactly how to improve the plot in your current production. Here is my critique . . ." Others wanted to sow confusion, to weaken her, and to overpower her. Scorn, derision and toughness; these were her weapons.

11.   She was known to torment her lovers. Lord forbid they should fail in the bristlings of Eros. Subtle hisses and boos met that sort of failure. But she liked the nuances of reconciliation and to be forgiven her temporary cruelties. When she broke up with someone, she always felt herself to be the wronged party, but it was she who usually had to endure them tacking up a list of grievances on her doorstep.

156

12. On occasion she felt herself falling in love with a Sister of the Abyss, as she called her dancer friends. She loved that two-month period of total tenderness the affairs more often presented; after which, she felt herself enormously more sane, and would then leap back into the theater with pure devotion. Former lovers later would see her photo in the drama section or dance section of a magazine and shake their heads like someone waking up from dream zzzzz, eyes opening, seeing the face of a radio by the bed, seeing an actual face! which slowly dissolves into the radio, knobs, dial and speaker.

13. In spite of her archivist attitude, she had a habit, which she grew to despise, of Moving On. Burning Bridges. Leaving behind begrieved humans shaking their heads. Th' earth-blob orb'd sun-blob not too many times before Claudia began to feel guilt for things gone awry— especially certain events in the remoteness of her early career. Such guilt allowed her to be bushwhacked at any moment, like an acid flashback. Sometimes her face filled up with tears right in the middle of a performance—but her friends chalked it up to her Art. And after a decade in Bohemia, the plexus of remorses for addled projects, sour affairs, ruined friendships, was sometimes unbearable. One man gave up poetry to become a nut, losing his toenails and teeth age thirty-one in the amphetamine death trap—she blamed herself. Another leaped—she blamed herself. Another, whom she rejected, banned herself from the theater, for which she had been a designer without compare.

14. She had a superstitious magic-believing side. She blew a horde of fear-stuffed nights inside old books by A. E. Waite and Dion Fortune. She had a glass-enclosed case

157

of old basement-of-Weiser's-Bookshop occult tomes from which even her closest friends were banned. She felt that the United States was soon going to go up in a big "hydrogen jukebox" boom boom—and that she and the other chosen would totentanz through the city ruins, collecting the paintings and artifacts of their choice from crushed museums.

She had a vague interest also in astrology, which concerns were centered on a zodiacal analysis of her career. That is, she felt the stars all lined up with this message: Claudia Pred will dance inside a whirling rainbow across a vast meadowy theater filled with a billion eye-bodies silenced in amazement.

15. She attracted a broad spectrum of critics—for her political actions, for dance, for drama, for her singing, for her costumes. The same work of art would produce great praise and great hostility, both of which she could easily endure, but not derision or mockery, which when she read it, drove her into a foaming rage. Some would rail and mewl against the political statements she chose to make in her beauty-motions—mewling that she was "politically naïve"—i.e., an apparent socialist, or, worse, in the rightist Cold War babble of the time, a com-symp, which was strictly naughty-naughty-mustn't-do in a dance-and-drama scene heavily financed by the warbucks crowd.

The *New York Post* pointed a finger at her as a sufferer of "Joan of Arc complex"—which criticism twisted her into a fury. It didn't take very long to learn a useful rule: never to read any criticism whatsoever, while remaining silent in the squinting faces of critics. Even as she did so, a small temple of belief was set up in the back of her mind emblazoned upon the portals of which was a rewrite

158

of a certain sentence from Voltaire: "the last critic stran-
gled with the guts of the last theatrical moneyman."

The critics she hooked to her art, however, stayed
hooked. The words, such as "genius" and "protean
energy" and "beauteous frenzy like no other," spewed
from their typewriters.

There was one lamentable situation relative to certain
critics trying to take advantage of their power. That is,
they would flock to her side, listen sympathetically, try to
drunk-fuck her, then totter back to the cab or the train.
She had several characteristics of body which the critics
loved to analyze manually; most far-famed of which were
her buttocks which were as legendary as those of Clau-
dette Colbert, and were discussed most attentively by her
critical fans. Critics just couldn't stop themselves from
lunging, fingers fluttering grabbingly, toward this living
statue of Aphrodite Kallipygos, in the course of an interview.

Enough of this description, O Rapidograph scratching
in the night, for we must moil ahead with our story,
though we could easily tarry for many a chapter describing the remarkable Claudia Pred, cantatrice and carpenter of beauty-motion.

Ever since she began to produce dance dramas, Claudia
had dreamt of finding a playwright/composer who would
write a dance-opera-drama which used maybe a small
jazz ensemble—which she could stage, and star in, at
Luminous Animal Theater. She thought for quite a while
she had discovered such a genius in Roy Shields of East
3rd Street. Shields was known by the nickname Dirty Roy

on the Cedar Bar-White Horse-Stanley's-and-Bowery tavern circuit, for his squalid apartment, and for certain
indiscretions relative to his ambi-subaxillary musk farms
which evinced themselves in profusion whenever, say, he
decided to try out his jitterbugging techniques at the face
of a jukebox. Claudia cleared up that problem when they
became intimate by banning him to the shower amidst
sharp rebukes which became Pavlovian later in their affair
when he automatically took a shower whenever she yelled
at him.

That was okay with him, because part of Dirty Roy was
all desire to become Tuxedo Roy—although he would
have punched you out if you had told him that in early
'61. He can come and punch us out today, but it's true
that his gameplan called on him, for a few years at least,
to become Scandal Roy, then Calm-down Roy, then
Come-to-terms-with-life Roy, then Tuxedo Roy. As
Tuxedo Roy (becoming what he once despised, a liberal
dispensing a check here for a worthy cause, a check there
for a worthy cause) there would be those winters in rich-
land, summers in villaland, and falls on Shubert Alley.

But we are being unfair to Roy Shields, for at the time
of this tale he was the most powerful writer on the off-
Broadway stage. And he was enough of a composer to be
able to write melodies and lead sheets for the jazz quintet
that backed some of his plays.

Roy Shields considered himself the greatest playwright
since George Bernard Shaw. (A few years later, in the
acid era, he took a few trips up at Millbrook and came to
believe that he *was* G. B. Shaw, but, by that time a good
businessman, kept this startling reincarnational belief to
himself.) In fact, he considered himself vastly superior to
Shaw. Aeschylus, that was Shield's league. For, was it not

160

true, he asked, that only in Aeschylus could one find the appropriate comparable abilities in combining dance, music, beauteous verse, drama and social foment within the same sempiternal concretions, that I have?

"They will tremble, or more probably, like, weep, reading my folios in 2200 A.D.," he told Claudia, "trying to figure out why the civilization treated me so shabbily; nay, why it took such an obvious delight in performing a flamenco dance on my face!"

Shields loved the danger-thrills of insurrection. For instance, it thrilled him immensely reading how Aeschylus inserted secrets from the Eleusinian mysteries into some of his plays (such as *Iphigenia* and *The Archers*), for which the Athenian populace brayed for his death. To Roy, the modern equivalent of the mysteries were state secrets. Oh how he hungered that someday he would get hold of advance information about some immoral government scam, such as the CIA invasion of Cuba, and put it on right away as a stage production, exposing it to the world, before the actual invasion.

In the Shavian manner, Shields wrote extensive, and I mean extensive, introductions to his plays, the intros often being as long as the plays themselves. He published his plays under his own press, Triumph Publications. They now fetch a goodly sum from rare-book catalogues, which probably makes him regret all the boxes of them he left behind unsold at the Luminous Animal Theater. He was a poor businessman—thinking for instance that all you had to do to collect from bookstores was to send an invoice with the shipment of books.

Especially for Claudia, Roy had written a long skit-skein which he titled *Newsreel-'84*. The play was based on George Orwell's *1984*, and Franz Kafka's *The Trial*, and

161

the extensive series of books published in the 1950s, inspired by the Korean War, which analyzed brainwashing as a political tool. The time of the play was April 4, 1984, and consisted of acted-out news stories for that day from *The New York Times*. Heavily featured in the work were political trials in the form of nightmarish dance-rituals put on in public.

Roy parted from Orwell's vision of permanent war, by positing a world-wide condition of a different form of hostility. In the civilization of *Newsreel-'84* everyone belonged to exlusive, angry sects. All obedience was pyramidically spewed to the top of each sect. Friendly communications between humans of different sects was prohibited. Through an intricate set of rules, leaders alone of sects were allowed to meet, behaving and talking monotonically, like zombies. Claudia played a dancing (dancing was forbidden) neo-Zombicult nun who secretly falls in love with a six-foot-six-inch black neo-Catholic priest played by a poet known on the set as Big Brown.

The production presented numerous problems. Claudia felt that the play, with its several incidents of flag-burning and partial interracial nudity (this sent shock waves clear into the closet of the district attorney's office in the fake-sex days o' '61) was quickly going to get her into TROUBLE. Besides that, she didn't really think very much of the play's quality, especially when measured against, say, Roy's beloved Aeschylus. Roy, on the other hand, was upset over certain adjustments he was required to make in the play which resulted in more dancing and in bringing Claudia's role more into prominence.

Claudia thought the work too suffused with, well, (*boring* was the word in her mind), heavy-hounding political analysis. She mistrusted the theatricality of a standing chorus chanting for fifteen minutes at a time, in trochees, backed by a jazz ensemble wailing in trochees, the words being a lengthy socialist analysis of social conditions in a far-off era. These danceless, actionless portions of *Newsreel-'84* were what Claudia felt might produce a counterpoint of snores from beyond the footlights. But Roy had trapped her on that one. For, in agreeing to give her a bigger role, Claudia had promised in return that the choruses would remain uncut.

Nevertheless, the play had a sudden-at-every-point powerful energy into which she injected her remarkable dancing and singing. As for her singing, she had that octave of basic notes, the Broadway (and off-Broadway) eight, which she could sing well in different styles, from softsad plaintiveness, to high emotion, to screeching anger, which was a rare ability in such an expert dancer. She could have signed with a folk label later on in the decade, and she'd probably be deposited right now in a stone-and-redwood mansion in the Santa Monica Mountains, strumming and fretting at injustice.

There was a long ketchup-soaked sequence featuring a character known as the Lord High Chopper who was made up to look almost exactly like the then-current mayor of New York City. This had already been mentioned several times in the gossip columns as the show opened for previews, and the Democratic district leader was reported to be very upset over the "insult against our dedicated hard-working mayor."

This party official had prompted a blitz of fire inspectors, building inspectors, health inspectors, tax inspectors, to besiege the theater as it struggled to prepare *N-'84* for its opening just two weeks away.

There was nothing that Claudia could do short of self-censorship. Too much had been spent on the production. Too many were dependent on it for salaries. Besides, Claudia could not afford to get the reputation for stuttering or backing down from the pulings of political hacks. So, she pushed the performers very hard, held many practice sessions, and slowly mutated the vignettes so that the play grew eerily smooth.

She woke up when a warm hand slid beneath her gown. She quiver-startled at the touch, then rolled over, legs lifting apart for a more intimate tangency. She did not seem to mind, yet who can ever know? They held out their arms in a most un-Shavian pattern of Eros, for the usual morning clingings. Gown and pajamas wound up under the covers at the foot of the bed. They fucked for a while, but both were freaky for hot shower slurps so they adjourned to the bathroom shower stall, where she blew him under the torrent, and then he knelt down in the hot wet and brought her to a semblance of bliss with a drive-crazy quicklick, from which he pulled away at least two crucial minutes too soon, but she rebuked him only in her head, how sad that such a didactic person as Roy Shields should lack such erotic information.

Therefore the vibes, as they say, or the vectors, were misdelivered somewhere other than a paradise pro tempore, so in the dance of her preparation of breakfast for two, the conversation tensed with bad art as well as the golden cage and the silken nets Blake sang love traps all soaring souls.

He thought he brought up the subject of the play in an oblique, constructive way. He mentioned the "tension" in

164

the first trial scene in the third act, finding fault with her "outbound twirling"—i.e., her dance notations, a nomenclature which peeved her right away, which he felt should be "more centripetal, so as to give the cultic uniqueness its necessary implosive quality, don't you agree?"

That one sentence triggered off an argument that proceeded in the gibberish mode toward a schism in their affair. "Do you think anything *could* be done with that concatenation of casual behavior?" she wanted to know.

And so it went. His art, she shouted, wobbled prolixly between the poles, boring boring boring! and didactic! didactic! didactic!

At the finale of the argument, Dirty Roy was banned from her pad, and his pitiful suitcase of manuscripts and peestains was hurled toward the door as a prelude to him returning to live at his East 3rd apartment.

"Boring!" she shouted from her door as he walked down the linoleum of the tenement steps.

"You are made of lignum vitae mallets!" he shouted back, crashing his fist into the mailboxes.

"My God, he's wearing a cravat," she thought. Not only that, but Mr. Twerthel, the tax examiner, had recombed his hair Julius Caesar-style to cover a bit of the baldness. And he was *not* wearing his usual muddy brown three-button suit with the linebackerlike shoulder pads; rather, he was wearing a White Horse Tavern tweed with matching charcoal trousers and, by all that is holy, a pair of Mexican sandals with car-tire soles.

Mr. Twerthel was bent over a small wire wastebasket into which, upon Twerthel's urging, Claudia had agreed

165

to deposit all receipts, check stubs, phone bills, and the like. The basket was heaped nearly to the brim and Twerthel was retrieving the fiscal data piece by piece, and noting each down in his ledgerbook. "Would you like a cup of coffee, Al?" she asked, leaning by accident ever so slightly with a heavy breast in Ukrainian blouse against his shoulder, which act erased all tax data in his mind for a second and substituted certain sensations of seldom-felt happiness.

Mr. Twerthel had been assigned to her case some six months previous in order to facilitate collection of past-due federal employee withholding taxes and to audit her books.

Somehow, after a few visits with Claudia, the tax collector found himself working on her taxes so that, rather than owing any back taxes, the government would be required to refund money to Claudia and to the theater! "I could get in a lot of trouble for this." That was a sentence he repeated many times.

His psyche, however, was locked into a pattern of obedience. He was convinced he was doing his share for the salvation of civilization while at the same time he could be near his damozel in tax distress. "I don't intend ever to pay any taxes." That was her position and it made the tax man sweat with nervousness.

Soon Twerthel had taken over the bookkeeping for the entire theater; he was forced to begin to dream up strange excuses to cover his time spent there, and he began keeping a separate wardrobe in his car, his Bronxville beat garb which he wore at Luminous Animal; stashing his tax-man suit and tie in the back seat.

Claudia saved maybe ten hours a week, not having to worry about computing taxes, keeping records, making notes of expenses. Twerthel did it all. He even took to verse, and carried his freshly typed sequence of love lyrics inside plastic sheets in a leather ledgerbook. Some day he hoped to show them to Claudia.

She had seen him around—he couldn't have been more than seventeen or eighteen. He came up to her as she was entering the theater for rehearsal. He was not quite her height, and what was immediately noticeable: his thick black eyebrows and beautiful face. What a face. He was carrying a basketball wedged 'gainst his body and his arm angled out and down over it, and in the same arm's hand he carried a rather frazzled hardbound edition of Nijinsky's diaries.

It began so simply. He asked her if he could watch rehearsals. She paused, almost breaking her rule of closed rehearsals before openings; then told him no, not before the opening, but to come around later, in a few days maybe. As she walked into the darkness of Luminous Animal, she thought of asking him something, turned, but heard the sound of a basketball dribbling half a block away.

After rehearsal she walked down the Bowery for dinner at Ping Ching Restaurant in Chinatown, passing a small park where she spotted the boy shooting baskets. She yelled at him, and he leaped high for a rebound and globetrotted the ball over with quick intricate dribbles.

"Would you like a job?" she asked.

"Doing what?"

"We need somebody to act as usher and to help clean up after performances, sweeping and aligning the seats,

167

and so forth. We've an opening in ten days, so there's lots to do."

She told him they could only afford twenty-five dollars a week, for six nights of work, but of course he could learn a lot, watch practices, help with the props. "Do you go to school?" she asked.

"No. No school," he replied, a bit of a fib.

"What's your name?" "Paolo." "My name is Claudia." She shook his hand. "Can you start tonight?" Yes yes—and he turned and sunk one from the top of the circle—yes yes.

Claudia decided to show a week of previews, and to becloud the desks of local media editors with press releases. She personally called up the Democratic district leader who had been so upset over the mayor's role as Lord High Chopper. And she sent a formal invitation to the mayor and the district attorney to attend the opening. The first preview of Newsreel-'84 played to half a house, but with each succeeding evening there were more and more people. And the response, standing applause at the end of the second preview, gave Roy, at least, those fabled rays of hope. But Claudia was still very skeptical about the show's chances. She saw it still too much a rough-hemp rhapsody, that is, a coarse weave. "This production is still too jerking, too abrupt; it's more like an old World War Two documentary film than . . ."

"Then it's your fault, Cl . . . [he almost said Clotho] Claudia!" Roy Shields snapped right back. "You're the three Fates wrapped up in one in this whole damned production. If you hadn't forced all those changes . . ."

"The reviews will finish us, no matter how many come to previews." And that was her final opinion, although she certainly could never babble it aloud. Never babble defeat to your cast, or Lord forbid, to the backers: that was tattooed on her soul.

At 2 A.M. after the first preview, Claudia was alone in the theater, except for Paolo who was making an occasional skwitcha sound with the broom among the seats. She was in her office listening to a tape of a work submitted for production by the Celestial Freakbeam Orchestra, a Lower East Side ensemble operating out of the Total Assault Cantina on Avenue A.

It was a tremendous piece of music, with orchestration by Joshua Gortz, and words by Sam Thomas, the editor of a poetry magazine, *The Shriek of Revolution*. The work was described as a Ghost Dance, and its personae were two dance/singers, personifications of Hiroshima and Nagasaki, who would perform on a stage which was wrapped entirely around with diaphanous gauze or angel hair forming a mushroom. Claudia was so excited by the tape and text that she wanted to hear it on the larger stage-speaker system.

She glided noiseless up the steps to the stage. In the back of the theater she could see strange leaps. Paolo was lunging around in the demi-gloom, apparently using the inverted T of the large janitor's broom to give him support for pole-vaultlike leaps, like an ice-skater sliding with a lawn chair across a frozen lake as if practicing with a partner.

She had kidded him earlier in the week about his basketball, which he brought to the theater every day. He grew quite angry, and asked her to come down to the Bowery court with him. She stalled a couple of days, but finally went with him, and watched him dunk it a few times, quite a feat for someone five-foot-nine. He could do it with a half or full spin also—that's when she noticed his legs, and his marvelous chest, which curved up abruptly from the top of musclely stomach to the nipples, then curved gradually back toward his wide thin shoulders. She learned that he had been coming to Luminous Animal for the past two years; that's why he had looked so familiar. In all her years in the theater, she never really learned who came to the performance, for she never mingled with the audience before or after a show. She had a closed passageway constructed from backstage to the rear of the ticket booth so she could monitor the money, and avoid the faces in the lobby.

Paolo, she soon learned, had a fixation, a fascination, a compulsion, for dancing. His father had studied dancing, or had been involved in a dance company in some way— and had died in Korea. Paolo was about as intense as they come—everything he gripped, he gripped so that his taut hands turned white: sitting in Washington Square reading Nijinsky, fingers gripping faded cloth.

Claudia walked to the lightboard and turned on the stage. The leaps stopped. She put the Celestial Freakbeam Orchestra tape on the Wollensak and attached the Wollensak to the large stage speaker used in *Newsreel-'84*. "Paolo, would you come here please?" she asked.

"Would you like to listen to a new tape?" she asked when he had vaulted upon the stage. He sat at a judge's bench and read a few pages of the text. She watched his legs begin to move slightly with the music, and then. . . .

"Let's explore it," was all she said, then worked the rheostat so that the stage contracted into a very soft orange oval with darkness surrounding. She walked into

170

the orange and waited for Paolo to enter. He wasn't sure
what she meant. "Would you like to dance"—lifting her
arms, "with," half-turn, "me?"—she asked, making it
clear.

By that time he was in the orange oval. "Can you pick
me up?" she asked, and put her arm around him; and
with his surprising strength, he lifted her, and twisted her
overhead. They whirled in the dark, then in the oval; he
knew, from long stageside gazing, how she danced, and
fitted himself into her Way.

Throughout she wore golden slippers—one of those
things which strongly woodburned themselves into a
memory. Years later, Paolo, long after he had become an
editor at Random House, could close his eyes on a hash-oil
weekend, and see in long leisure reverie, those convoluted
swirlings of Claudia's golden slippers on the dark dusty
stage.

Claudia would always regret their finale when Paolo
was left without a guide as Luminous Animal went on its
first European tour with *Newsreel-'84*, and he dart-
boarded Nijinsky's diaries and headed for the foul line and
a career with the Princeton five. For a while anyway, it
was all sipping joyjuice through a straw for both. They
danced without a stop that first night till 4 A.M., achieving
an ironic ecstasy through the tragic music called
Hiroshima and Nagasaki.

She was amazed. He could memorize at once any rou-
tines she might suggest, and could repeat them in any
order. And he accepted her leadership, and the Celestial
Freakbeam Orchestra wailed onward.

The day she watched him dunk the basketball she had
made her decision, and she moved fast. Three nights
later, that is, the night after their primal dance, the

171

dancing resembled an elegant touch-football game. Paolo was glistening with the sweat of contact, as if oiled up for a muscle-mag photo, resplendent in gym shorts and a St. Agnes Boys Club T-shirt which Claudia soon removed. Claudia was attired in a cutaway portion of her nun's habit costume for *Newsreel-'84*. This became hot indeed, she said, and so she removed it and was down to a purple bodystocking.

The music tonight was still the Celestial Freakbeam tape, but Claudia chose to interpret its often insistent rhythms in a more conjunctive manner. Her hands caressed his rib cage—and he locked his hands around the back of her shoulders. After this they moved close together for several minutes.

"Take them off," she whispered, leaning upon his ear. He did so, and sank to his knees, half-covering his erection. She slid toward him, her bodystocking flung aside and lying half-in, half-out, of the oval of light; knees at the edges of a beauteous V, feet underneath herself, and right away she slid upon his knees and up his muscles of thigh, and he was inside her.

She pulled his arms under her thighs; then she locked her arms around his neck. "Stand up," she whispered.

He got to his feet, and stood rather uncertainly, in such a new position of the ballet of Eros. "Turn up the music," she whispered again, and he carried them over to the tape recorder, still inside, and she reached down to turn the volume knob.

"Dance," was her next whisper, and then they were silent for several minutes, until there was a burst in the music; and she undertook a particularly twig-ripping series of leg flailings, legs outstretched behind his back, Paolo having difficulty holding himself inside. Then his

172

heart began really to tom-tom his rib cage, and he couldn't keep his eyes open, and he sank slowly to his knees, still inside her, she on top, into their original position.

She could sense that he was just about to come; she pulled off him, and reached down, cuddled his balls with a soothing cool palm—urging him to his feet with the other.

They then began to dance again—she paying just enough attention to his crotch to keep it erect. And the Celestial Freakbeam Orchestra played on.

Then, in what may have been a first in American Dance, she leaped up, using his shoulders as a vaulting horse, and jack-knifed her body, while at the same time spreading her legs. Paolo knew somehow he'd better brace himself quickly and did so, stamping his foot down slightly behind himself in a couple of short back-steps. And then Claudia, in a move that revealed her extraordinary strength, somehow lowered herself down so slowly, slowly, and without any stuttering of the motion's fluidity, flattened her body against him, and the frightened cock, which expected perhaps a mash-job, was brought back into the warmth. Paolo evinced a few undancelike contortions, that is, he just about collapsed to the floor, rolling himself over and on top, and let loose, burying his face upon her mouth and her neck, unable to stop.

But the Celestial Freakbeam Orchestra tape was but half-completed. And just a few seconds later Claudia 'rose to dance some more. And it was all beauty. The come, or aphros, or foam, dropped down from her legs, or fell in smooth beautiful gobs here and there, her legs soon aglistening with it. And she brought Paolo onward.

173

She lifted him, pressing him against the rear wall of the stage, out of the oval of light, into the darkness, and just for a second, licked the tip of him, springing it to hardness right away, then let him slide down the cool thrilly wall. And so it went.

During the next several nights, they tried a lot of variations on dance-sex, including pas de deux oral intercourse on roller skates, and various worshippings upon the pink altar while the subject stood in accommodatingly modified fourth position, not to mention a few engagements upon the couch of the dressing room.

When the initial several days were over, and they began to calm down, as of Eros, they started seriously to work on the Celestial Freakbeam tape. An idea began to develop inside her. She could be seen bent over her clipboard writing rapidly. Its possibilities meant she had to coax him into singing. He had rather a hoarse voice, she found, but it possessed that all-important characteristic, so rare on the stage (or on records); he could catch a note and hold it! After that determination, it was merely a matter of mutating his voice into an aurally pleasing contraction/constriction/construction of larynx.

It appeared to be love, or whatever it was, for she had long ago banned that word from intimate discourse. She found herself thinking of him all the time, kindling within her a distracting triplet of shyness, tenderness and passion. She became distracted, and with her obvious fatigue from dancing all night every night, she eased up on the practice schedule for *Newsreel-'84*, for which the cast was grateful—and the show relaxed into a finer mode as a result.

174

She was worried about Paolo's intensity, which might have found an outlet in jealousy. But she could not stop thinking of a tripod. A tripod: with intense dance-genius Paolo, the anarcho-Hegelian writer Roy, and the Croesus of off-B'way, Ron Lawler, as legs—and she, Claudia, chewing the sacred bay leaves, drinking the spring Cassotis which was channeled into the Luminous Animal temple; she taking seat adangle in the center of the tripod out o'er the Delphic crevasse whence drifted the intoxicating mist of "mephitic" dope-vapors, triggering off not the voice of a seeress, but the action to which she was destined, god-dance. And it was with Paolo something told her it could be done. His force-field, the curves of his aura, fit in with hers. She could "feel" the curving aura. God-dance, god-dance.

Roy was less than enthused, because, banned to his pad, he'd not been alone with Claudia for over a week. If he was jealous, he assured himself that his concerns were strictly limited to *Ars Gratia Cursus Honorum (sui)*, that is, getting the pole position in the chase after the white stag of fame.

"I suppose," Roy snorted, after he had Q and A'd some data about the new project from Claudia, "you'll call your show"—*show* delivered with a sneer—"Sex Dance with Cybele?" This was the morning after Roy, cool as a fool, had come to Luminous Animal, it must have been 3 A.M., beating, drunk, kicking, drunk, swearing, drunk. But Claudia had bolted the night latch and the Celestial Freakbeam Orchestra played on.

"Don't insult *me*, Mr. Fourth-rate Brecht!"

Opening night for *Newsreel-'84* finally arrived. Roy was in emotional traction with angst. The toilet tank in his hall was filling and unfilling with neighbor-disturbing frequency. Claudia had never felt such boredom on the day of a first night. She actually overslept, whereas normally on such a day she was up like a child on Christmas morn. It was a busy day: at least fifty phone calls to be made, the enduring of last-minute squalls of Genius and Art, a final practice. The lists piled up on her clipboard thick and black.

The espresso coffeemaker in the lobby broke down. The pastries didn't arrive. Paolo forgot to mop the bathrooms. Someone had stuck gum into the phone. Several of the spotlights on the outside had to be replaced. The ticket-beggers were a pain. All someone had to have done was to have attended high school with anyone faintly connected with the production, and they called up for freebies.

Claudia insisted on total cleanliness of the entire building before an opening, a position adopted for arcane reasons of preritual purification, which her mystic nature demanded. Therefore, the theater was given ablutions as if it were a ziggurat awaiting dawn.

Luminous Animal was located in a cavernous dank cinderblock former garage on the Bowery near 3rd Street, down the hill from Cooper Union. Oh what a pit of grease it had been when she had first rented it. A team of the most dedicated Laborers of the Abyss had slaved two weeks to foam away the grunge, and another two weeks to tar the roof and to paint it, blue on the outside, black inside.

Most of the available money had gone into a fine resilient stage which ran some eighty feet across the back of the garage. There were a few plywood dressing rooms, a

176

lobby, and a large area enclosed by black burlap curtains to serve as the art department, which lay cluttered with silkscreen equipment, an old A. B. Dick mimeo, carpenters' benches, storage bins for scenes and costumes, the Luminous Animal Archives, and even a small darkroom.

For the audience there was a hodgepodge of backless funeral parlor chairs, street sofas, cushions and lawn furniture. On the outside of the buildings, situated just above the entrance, was a ten-foot-tall reproduction of a paleolithic painting from Les Trois Frères cave in the Pyrenees, the reindeer-headed human figure which Claudia used as a symbol for Luminous Animal. Abbé Breuil, who had first published a drawing of the figure, had named it the Sorcerer, an appellation scorned by Claudia. She saw the figure as a deer-dancer, or rather, as a primal configuration of drama, that is, of god-dance.

Surrounding the Luminous Animal sign was an enormous bank of lights a friend of Claudia had borrowed from a military installation in Brooklyn.

The landlord chose this day of frenzy for gouge maneuvers. The landlord was known in the neighborhood as Louie the Criminal. (Today however, he is no longer a criminal. He is SoHo Lou, respected art dealer and speculator in Peruvian powders.) Louie got into trouble right after the lease was signed and had to disappear for a while, so Claudia dealt with Louie's brother, Tony.

At first the conversation was pleasant chitchat. "Hey," Tony said, "I see you've got big crowds at your new show."

"We'll know tonight," she replied. "The reviews could drive away the uptown crowd, or they might not even review us at all, which could be worse."

"I was talking it over with my wife. We both felt that if

177

the play does real well that we, as owners of the building, should share in a small percentage of the action—in addition to the rent."

"Are you serious?" Claudia's voice dialed to shrill in the middle of the sentence.

"Well, I've read the newspaper articles. The play certainly is getting controversial; and it could get me into trouble, like bring heat on my other businesses. Do you understand what I mean?"

Claudia was angry. "Look here, Tony! You can't expect me to cooperate with robbery. We negotiated a fair lease. I put three thousand dollars into fixing up a decayed, incredibly filthy building. I just can't go along with you. I'm sorry."

"Well, let me put it to you another way, sweetheart. Louie's back in town and he wants his garage back. He wants to get into the auto-repair business again—"

"You mean vehicle-disguise business!" she interjected scornfully. "You can't threaten me."

"Yeah? Who you gonna go to, the mayor?" He laughed. "If anything happens to your Taj Mahal over there, I'm not going to be responsible. I trust you are insured."

She clicked the receiver on him, and sat there trembling. But the blessed flow of gibberish swept her up right away, and she was called to the stage to oversee some repairs to the Lord High Chopper's throne, and she forgot all about Tony the Creep.

That evening Claudia strayed from her custom of always remaining at the theater the day of an opening, dining uptown with her chief financial backer, Ronald

Lawler. She figured an elegant restaurant was the proper setting to pull off the delicate caper of securing a commitment to provide money for a new production before the fate of *Newsreel* could be determined.

This was difficult to accomplish, since Lawler, a stockbroker who also owned a big New York publishing company, believed in the Eleventh Commandment: Thou Shalt, O Lawler, Not Fail to Get a Return on Thine Investment, a belief unshakably maintained although he had become involved in the theater in order to come into contact with beautiful women. That is, in the mode of gangsters who used to sponsor burlesque performers and torch singers, Lawler tried to specialize in off-Broadway actresses. But he was always attentive to the shekels. He was ruthless, manipulative, lecherous (on the mental plane, since not even daily cocktails of vodka mixed with a half-cup of Vitamin E oil could aid his dongal impuissance), but, to himself, he was a positive, if not revolutionary, force in the American theater. He thought of himself as the Divine Liberal, in the nineteenth-century English tradition. He served as treasurer for several cultural foundations (thereby avoiding himself having to contribute).

Lawler's current problem was that he had fallen in love, and worse, the love had jelled into obsession. Whining obsession, the mode of adoratio which Claudia most easily could handle.

Her response could have been to proffer a cracker of derision for the puppy in a shoebox on her doorstep. But she seemed to like Ron Lawler. It wasn't just the checks—but in spite of the checks. And they'd never fucked, or even lain down on his yacht in sunny carezza. But they seemed to get along well. He was completely

179

undemanding—and would never, she judged, do anything so frantic, in his obsession with Claudia, so as to injure his family relationships—a wife and children up in Mays Landing.

During the meal Lawler sought to shake into the air two questions: a) what are the chances on *N-84* making some mon? and b) when can we spend some time together?

It was difficult, just minutes before its opening, to speak of a theatrical production as a floparoo, especially to a nervous backer, but that's just what she did, gambling that his affection coupled with her persuasiveness, would enable him to envision glorious crowds of success flocking to a new production starring her and Paolo. "Who?" he asked. She tried to describe Paolo's extraordinary abilities. She mentioned his power of leg, and it was like mentioning the secret word in the old Groucho Marx quiz show on TV, so excited became Lawler—it was all he could do to keep his hands above the table.

"He's the finest dancer I've ever worked with," she told him at the end of a long paragraph of praise. "Have you heard," she continued, "of the Celestial Freakbeam Orchestra?" He hadn't, but tried to give a vague motion of his head to indicate, of course!—Do you think I'm stupid?

She continued, "They've written a wonderful, uh, morality drama, which they've submitted for production. They call it a Ghost Dance. It would be marvelous. The stage is wrapped in gauze, in the shape of a mushroom. The specters of Hiroshima and Nagasaki appear . . ."

Lawler shuddered, and broke in to change the subject. Like the bazooka shell his ancestors, their millions made in the New England codfish-oil trade, had trained him to

180

be, he repeatedly steered the conversation back to his two concerns, mon and time-with-Claudia.

She responded. "I think *Newsreel* may well be very successful. But it more likely may be too many years beyond its time. The critics will be too stupid to understand it. It's got a lot of boring choruses. Of course, nothing is certain here, and the previews have picked up. But if it fails . . ." She paused.

Ron gave a wince at the word *fail*. But Claudia dared not notice such things and continued to present her best babble, best stare, best angles, best smile, best nudging foot. "If it fails, I want to start immediately on a production of *Ghost Dance*. The costs will be greatly reduced, since Paolo and myself will be the only ones on stage. The biggest expense will be paying the Celestial Freakbeam Orchestra. There must be fifteen of them; and some will have to quit their outside jobs. They have performed a lot at the Total Assault Cantina, where we went for that poetry benefit, you remember?" Lawler nodded, yes yes he remembered.

"And I'm counting on you, Ron"—reaching for his hand. "Also, we may want to film it, if the money can be raised. That too might supply a return for investors."

Ron tried hard not to imply an affirmative answer but he found himself fluttering his hands and nodding his head in agreement.

He turned his attention again to question B. "You never seem to have time to do things. We could fly anywhere you want, any weekend you name. Or," he continued, "we could take out the boat. I have it down in Florida."

She wanted to see him, and he saw it in her smile, and the stockbroker was almost happy. Just as they left the restaurant she kissed him, "I'll see you often, I promise.

181

We might even be able to spend some weekends together. It depends on how long *Newsreel* runs, of course."

Waiting patiently in the lobby was Assistant District Attorney Arthur Mynah, a former classmate of John Mitchell at Fordham Law, belching nervously. Mr. Mynah's suit was tight and was the color of phlegm-tinged split-pea soup. His stomach was taxing the ability of the Arrow shirt company to cover it, a blubbery dingle-dangle brought about by daily visits to smoke-filled greasies near the Criminal Courts Building. The assistant district attorney still tried to button his suit coat, a mistake of crimping and wrinkles that should have sent him over to his Delancy Street tailor, but didn't, for five years had not passed, and therefore it was not yet time to obtain a new suit. Mynah's assignment: to prepare himself for possible criminal indictments growing out of *Newsreel-'84*. There was the shameful matter of ridiculing His Honor, the Mayor. There was also possible criminal interracial lascivious (*lashivus* was the way Mynah pronounced it) carriage in one torrid dance between Claudia-the-nun and the Priest, a dance which had caused flocks of A.D.A.s to visit the theater for a look-see. And finally there was the matter of the burnt flags. This arose out of a vignette where competing sects burned each other's flags in public ceremonies. The flags which were burned appeared to be the actual flags of major world powers, including England, France, the U.S.S.R., and the U.S.A. Burning a Russian flag, that was fine. But burn an American flag, and you were in trouble.

Throughout the play, A.D.A. Mynah kept a glazed

182

stare upon the proceedings. The theater was packed. Every last weird divan and packing crate was filled. The play was interrupted several times with loud applause not to mention numerous gasps of surprise as when the flags were burned or during the torrid intimacies.

As soon as the curtain closed, Asst. Dist. Att. Mynah raced backstage where, like an umpire, he removed a whisk broom from his back pocket and brushed the flag-shreds into a paper bag. "If this is a certified American flag, you are in deep trouble," he said with a smile, leaving his card with Claudia as she prepared to open the curtain for a bow.

The audience stood and applauded for four minutes and thirty-six seconds according to Roy who was monitoring his wrist. The reviewers were ecstatic. Claudia spotted Roy waiting in the wings. She ran over and hugged him, "My goodness, it's going to be a hit!"

"I told you, I told you!" Roy was hopping with joy, a spewing champagne bottle in his hand. Roy was attired in a tuxedo and a polka dot bow tie. Roy was still employed as his building super so when he had left his apartment that evening he had paused, donning his garbage-spackled work gloves, to haul the garbage cans from the cellar to the curb, then absentmindedly had stuck the gloves into the tuxedo pockets, and now, as he glub-glubbed the champagne, he noticed the incongruous fingers poking from his pockets and quickly stuffed them deeper out of sight. "It's going to be the big time! the big time!" he shrieked to himself.

Claudia finally make it through the throng to her dressing room where she collapsed, but not before pulling her clipboard off the wall and moving the lists for *Newsreel-'84* to the top. "Dance, Aeschylus, Dance!" she sang. Then there was a knock.

It was the most prestigious drama critic in Western Civilization—a notorious womanizer, drunk, coke-fiend, plagiarist, writer of pseudonymous Ace Books murder mysteries on the side, and manic-depressive. But one favorable line from him containing three powerful adjectives was worth a hundred grand.

"Miss Pred, I'm Milton Clark. I believe we met at the Stanislav opening. I can't tell you how much I enjoyed your performance in this marvelous theater. I was wondering if you could spare some time for an interview about Luminous Animal and the production. I have rather an urgent deadline. But I've brought my typewriter with me, it's up at the Plaza. They have a private booth reserved at Bertolucci's where we could talk without interruption. So, if you could accompany me to a late supper, then I could . . ."

"Of course!" Claudia was beaming. "But I will take a shower first. And see that everything is in order."

Paolo stood near when she came out of the dressing room, amidst a crowd of friends whom she proceeded to greet. He saw her coat. "Aren't we going to dance?" he asked.

"Not tonight, honey." She hugged him. "You have the keys. Wait for me here. I'll be back in a couple of hours."

Claudia turned away abruptly and walked out the front door, the arm of the critic cuddling her shoulder. Paolo went inside and threw a gold slipper against the dressing-room door.

After everyone had left and he had swept the gritty floors, Paolo turned on the stage lights. He began to pace back and forth, in obvious anger, dribbling his basketball. With a growl, he suddenly threw it out into the sea of divans. He danced alone, jumping and twisting. He kicked off his tennis shoes. Then his shirt, his jeans. He twirled. His legs were very long, very thin—except for his upper legs which were over-muscled. His black hair was falling over his face. He practiced rebounding, leaping high to grab imaginary basketballs; then rolled upon the sooty stage, gray streaks across his back and buttocks.

Later he walked to Claudia's dressing room to wait.

An Editorial Conference

HE RENTED THE two-room apartment at 521 East 11th Street in December of 1961 for fifty-six dollars a month. It was on the third floor. One room was a combined kitchen and living room. The other was supposed to be a bedroom. There were no closets, only a five-pronged clothes rack nailed to the wall in the bedroom. The rooms were tiny and both had lumpy metal ceilings stamped with leaflike patterns in six-inch squares.

The two living-room windows opened onto a fire escape which protruded rustily upon a back courtyard crisscrossed with clotheslines and wet clothes getting gritty from the anus of Satan, otherwise known as the Consolidated Edison smokestacks belching a few blocks away. Some mornings he would awaken with the inside of his nose black-caked with fallout.

Spanish music floated in from the courtyard by day by night by dawn. Someone close by had a rooster and occasionally he heard a faint baaaa. On the roof of the building directly opposite his fire escape there was a five-tiered pigeon warren which was used ostensibly to supply food for a family in the building. The super, however, swore up and down that the birds were shipped downtown to a Chinese restaurant for squab gobble.

The backroom or bedroom had a single window to the outside which was sealed shut, its panes painted lightless with many coats. When he pried the window open he saw why. The vista was of a gray-streaked solid brick wall about five feet away and a sheer drop to the rubble of the alley dotted with dropped garbage bags, a common disposal method on the East Side.

Like many dinky New York apartments, there was a window between the kitchen and the so-called bedroom. This too was completely covered with years of paint, the newest being avocado green. The icebox was strictly early American and rattled as the motor struggled to propel the refrigerant. The door was almost as cold as the interior and a piece of rubber insulation hung down from the top and prevented it from closing properly. Next to the icebox was a large, low sink which apparently had been originally intended also for use as a washtub. Next to the sink was the bathtub with a removable porcelain-glazed metal covering. Above the bathtub were the kitchen cabinets— whose crooked doors could never quite be shut and whose interiors were a sour-smelling barrenness of decayed oilcloths, cockroach egg cases, kernels of roach-chewed rice, coffee grounds, and greasy dust.

The watercloset was jammed into a small booth in the hallway. There was something wrong with the light fixture so he placed a candle on the ledge. Either the user left the hall door open, or lit the candle, or voided in darkness. The toilet gurgled with spilling water twenty-four hours a day. Roaches loved the watercloset. There were hundreds of them. He gave up at once trying to maintain the watercloset with the result that his friends, even the funkiest among them, were loath to lower any exposed skin upon the seat.

About forty-five minutes after he had paid the rent and deposit, he moved into the apartment. His possessions were scant: consisting of a small silver waterpipe—very hip in 1961, sixteen cardboard boxes of books, a typewriter, a suitcase of clothing, a small open-drum Speed-O-Print mimeograph machine, a milk crate full of mimeo ink and art supplies plus numerous copies of issues of his poetry magazine, *The Shriek of Revolution*.

There were eight layers of linoleum on the floor. These he chopped up and carted away by the armload. The bare floor itself had never been painted or varnished. It was raw wood. He wondered if he should leave it the way it was. Enough paint splashed on it when he was working on the ceiling and walls, however, that he decided to make it black also.

He wound up painting the entire apartment, floor, ceiling, walls, door, black except for one wall which he painted white intending to cover it with murals. The living room was red orange when he rented the place. There were many buckles, cracks and ridges in the plaster. When painting, he left the cracks and ridges red orange so that there were these groovy abstract red lines and patterns running through the black expanses, man. As for the long white wall, he spent the next few months carefully painting it with multi-colored cuneiform stanzas of Sumerian poetry which he had studied in college.

In those days the Lower East Side on Wednesday nights was a free department store. For it was then that residents would place upon the pavement old furniture, kitchen cabinets, smashed TVs, mattresses tied up with cord, etc., for the refuse department to cart away. Sometimes, as

188

when an elderly person without family would die, the sidewalk outside an apartment would be jammed with trunks full of old clothes, boxes of books, lamps, utensils, and the debris of fifty years. This produced a grab scene almost as if someone had thrown money on the ground. Citizens were thrilled to seize from an old trunk a sport shirt from Honolulu or a photo album dated 1923.

The very first Wednesday he forayed and found a large, lidded packing crate from Japan which he lugged home, painted black, and added to the pad as a table. Some things he had to purchase. One such item was a ten-foot-by-ten-foot bamboo mat edged with black cloth. This was the living room fun-rug. Floor pillows he obtained from old sofas found on the streets. He hung another smaller bamboo mat in the doorway between the two rooms. He rigged a string from the bottom up over a nail at the top of the doorjamb so that the bamboo curtain could be raised or lowered by a tug on the string.

He walked the side streets looking for a throwaway mattress. It was a poor day for freebies. Finally he spotted an old mattress tied up into the shape of a jelly roll with rope and leaning against garbage cans at 9th and Avenue C.

The first thing to ascertain, when checking out a free street mattress, was why it was that the owner had discarded it. He regarded the mattress. Even as a throwaway, it was rather a pitiful specimen. In the first place, the prior owners had not been the most continent of humans as evinced by several widespread spills, so to speak, all over the middle of it. But, when given the firmness and bounce tests, it seemed very substantial. To the nose it was not particularly offensive and he could find no indication thereon and therein of cootie, tick, crab

189

or roach. Therefore, all considered, he grabbed the mattress upon his back and staggered toward 11th Street to his apartment.

His kitchen utensils consisted of two large wooden bowls, two Chinese soup spoons, two glasses, a can opener, a knife, and several pots. Within a few days of moving in, the power company turned off the lights and gas, sending him a letter that he would be required to put up a cash deposit for the big Con Ed turn-on. He decided to tough it. He bought candles instead and was happy for a year.

For lunch the day Con Ed turned out the lights, he had boiled a pot of broccoli and had fixed a peanut butter and broccoli sandwich on a long Italian roll. The unused broccoli was stored in the quaking refrigerator where it remained decomposing for eleven months. When anyone opened by accident the refrigerator door, it was curtains for the nose. No smell ever devised quite matched the wafts of Tales From the Crypt putridity corpsing forth when someone opened the door. Even the memory of it sickens the brain cells.

Since he had no working stove, he ate raw food and the cold contents of cans. From urges unknown, he started eating a strange concoction he called Yum. Yum and vitamin C, except for an occasional pirogen and sour cream feast at the nearby Odessa Restaurant, was his exclusive diet for months and months. What was Yum? Well, first he made a thick dry two-inch bed of oats in the wooden bowl. On this he spooned two globs of Hellmann's mayonnaise. Next generous drip-drops of soy sauce. Atop this mound of pure delight, he broke two fresh eggs and mixed the feast into a beige and yellow rippled blob. This was Yum. Want some?

190

He ate Yum every day from the time he put the broccoli into the useless icebox until the end of 1962, eleven happy months. He was very willing to share his meals of Yum with any visitor arriving at dinner time. There was often shyness or hesitance on the part of the visitor who watched the editor prepare the wet, yellow, yum-mush to share it with him.

The spirit of Yum pervaded his life. Once just after the lights went off, his blonde love was due to arrive at night to sleep over. He went down to Houston Street to a wholesaler and purchased a twenty-five pound bag of raw oats.

That night they poured the entire sack of oats into the bathtub and added generous amounts of corn oil and hot milk she had brought in a thermos. Then they celebrated their first stay together in months by an immediate act of love in the hot bath of oat-mush. They rubbed each other with fistfuls of oily oats and playfully poked the milky grain here and there, mound and entrance. Her breasts shone with swabbings of shiny oat-lint. They emerged from the tub looking like The Bark People and rolled upon the bamboo mat kissing and licking away the kernels of Demeter.

As soon as the apartment was painted and furnished, he turned his energies to the new issue of *The Shriek of Revolution*. Through extensive correspondence, he had received enough good poetry from the peripatetic writers of his generation to print the fourth issue.

He typed the mimeograph stencils, always a tedious chore requiring slow correction of mistakes with an erasing device and rubbery correction fluid which was brushed on the typo, blown dry with a breath-huff, and then the word was retyped. Sometimes he typed far past midnight by candlelight until the man next door began to pound the wall with a broom.

He wrote several editorials, one calling for everybody in the Lower East Side to mail the sooty contents of their noses every day to the Con Ed company in protest against their volcanic smokestacks. He wrote another editorial in which he described a mythical meeting of the "editorial board" of *The Shriek of Revolution*, using the real names of five or six of his friends.

As he described it, the editorial board meeting quickly abandoned crucial judgments regarding the business of publishing *The Shriek of Revolution* and assumed the form of a bunch-punch. Prominently mentioned in the description was a poet named Cynthia Pruitt, known as Cynito to her friends at Stanley's Bar. Cynthia was a wonderful person who roamed the halls of the peace movement and the pads of the Lower East Side for several years in the early sixties. She was an outstanding poet. He had printed some of her work in *The Shriek*. He wrote the "editorial" never thinking for a minute that any of his friends, including love-loving Cynthia, would take exception to his very detailed description of uncompunctious conjugation.

After the stencils were typed he ordered a few boxes of blue mimeo paper. When it was delivered he began to print the new issue. He placed the small mimeograph upon the white metal bathtub-covering and brushed the ink upon the inside of the printing drum. He placed a stencil on the outside of the drum, smoothed it out, checked the inking, put paper in the feeding-tray, and began to turn the handle to print with a feeling of elation that was just about religious. Everything was deity. Galaxy was. Star-robes trailed the void. He adored his

192

mimeograph machine. He kept it sparkling clean. He sometimes would sit meditating upon the bamboo mat looking for hours at the Speed-O-Print sitting up on top of his bathtub.

After all the pages had been printed, there remained the grim job of collating them. Since the magazine was usually around thirty pages in length, he could collate one whole issue at a time by the following method. He would sit cross-legged on the floor in the Bodhisattva position, man, and nearly surround himself with three concentric semicircular rows of page piles. He proceeded to lean out and to collate, working left to right through the outer circle and then through the second half-circle and finishing with the last page by sweeping across the innermost row that surrounded much of his cross-legged body. He tamped each completed issue on the floor along the top and side edges to align the pages for later stapling. Slowly the pile of completed issues grew until he finally finished all five hundred.

The next and last tiresome task was when clunk! clunk! clunk! he stapled each copy three times along the left edge. Whew. Then he addressed, stamped and mailed out as many magazines as he could afford postage for, to his poet friends, to other editors, to his former literature professors, to his easily shocked aunts and uncles.

It was 12:30 A.M. and he was reading by candlelight when there was a knock at the door and the high whines and growls and huffs of what sounded like a dog pack out in the hall. He opened the door and in trotted two unleashed German Shepherds who ran about the bedroom-kitchen-workroom sniffing and salivating. With them was a person whom the editor had met only once, a very nervous man named John Carlin, slight and five-foot-ten, with carefully combed hair that was almost crewcut short at the nape of his neck, but was long on the top, whence it was brushed forward down over his forehead obscuring his eyebrows, just below which the remaining hair veered sharply toward his right temple. His beard was short and most precisely trimmed. He was a speech instructor at N.Y.U. who lived in a small three-story house on East 7th, near Tompkins Square.

He announced that he was very very disturbed about the description of the editorial board meeting in the new issue of *The Shriek of Revolution*—especially the portion depicting Cynthia Pruitt uttering suction with respect to the editor and the editorial board. He was so mad, in fact, that he had come to beat and to pummel. A quick glance at the person's face and at the large canines, who knows—perhaps trained to eat larynxes, convinced the editor of his certain plight.

The passage of the editorial in question was this: "And Cynthia rolled upon the floor filling her mouth with the carnal cob of Nelson Saite, drama editor, as he lined her ravening buttocks up against the steam-valve of the radiator and completed the metal node within her."

Now, the editor knew that Cynthia had been staying down at John Carlin's house for a few weeks but he had not heard from anyone—and such gossip spread quickly on the East Side, any indication that Cynthia and John were setting up an exclusive relationship—that is, a pact of mono-grope relative to groin-clink. He had also to consider whether or not Cynthia herself may have urged Carlin to come over to confront him. He decided she had not done so. First of all, if the editor had actually wanted to describe a *real* event, he certainly had observed Cynthia, Charlotte, Nelson, Claudia Pred, and other friends of his

194

participating in strenuous intergroin group-grapples, so that what he had reported in his editorial board meeting had not been so far removed from fact.

On the other hand, he did feel upset that someone was unhappy over what he had printed with the intention of creating pleasure. And he well understood the possible jealousy that could be involved. So he apologized and said that most of the magazine had already been mailed out but had he known of John's concern he certainly would have not printed the description.

After a few more minutes the man with the dogs left, with a parting statement to the effect that if the editor had not at least expressed some sort of apology, he would have beat him up. The episode caused the editor to retire to Stanley's Bar where he handed out a few copies of the new issue to his friends. He drank till four and returned home slouchy drunk, singing and stumbling against the sides of the narrow halls climbing to his third-floor bamboo lair.

The Filmmaker

IN LATE WINTER of 1961–62, just before spring, the Jonas Mekas columns in the *Village Voice* on underground films and filmmakers stirred Sam Thomas to make the leap into the 16-mm universe. Week after week the information swept him forward until that wintery night, fraught with brrrr, in a year when it still snowed deeply in New York City, he was sitting in the Total Assault Cantina on Avenue A.

A bunch of them had been popping cylinders of amyl nitrite into their innocent noses in the bathroom for that instant heart attack rush-flood. He was afterward clearing his senses with tea from the big Total Assault crock by the window when he decided. Not that he considered it a moment of history or anything. It was just that at that moment all obstacles melted.

He walked over to his friend Nelson, who was lying upon a bench in a far corner of the cantina. "Hey, Nelson, I just decided to make a film, but I don't exactly know where to start."

"You have to remember the three A's, man: action, arrogance and aggression!"—was Nelson's advice. "If you

196

want to make a film, don't wait around the lobby of the Bleecker Street Cinema looking for ideas. Buy a camera and commence!"

And that was the way it was. For about two years, he had worked steadily at two part-time jobs—one in the afternoon for a messenger service on 47th Street near the Gotham Book Mart, running the toothpaste slogans back and forth among the midtown ad agencies. The other job was on the weekends when he swept and washed glasses at the Jazz Gallery on St. Marks Place. Slowly the moolah had accrued. And now his brain was moiling like wax paper afire to jump into the abyss of Absolute Joy he felt making a film would be.

His mind flipped through an assortment of problems: film cost, development, his lack of knowledge regarding lenses and lighting and lens-settings, what kind of camera to get, shooting techniques. To solve the problem of the camera, the next day he called Harry Jarvis, a brilliant filmmaker whom he had met one memorable night at Stanley's Bar during a time Harry was quickly cognac-ing his way through a seventy-five-thousand-dollar Rockefeller grant to make a film version of Maspero's translation of the Egyptian *Tale of Two Brothers*. Harry urged him to purchase a so-called "battle camera, like, the kind they used filming the war." He specifically recommended a used Bell & Howell model 70-DE, which would be sturdy enough to withstand a few drops and bangs.

Sam lived near Stanley's Bar at 12th and Avenue B. Stanley's place was *the* bar of the time; as through its doors passed a steady stream of artists, poets, filmmakers, musicians, and every type of radical publisher and nuclear-disarmament peaceworker.

Avenue B between 10th and 12th, in those days, was a

sacred road. In addition to Stanley's, there were several other artists' bars, and above the bars the cheap pads, and there was the Charles Theater where there were regular showings of underground films. The filmmakers met at Stanley's after the screenings and there was a great sense of energy and excitement.

Sam had met a number of the filmmakers in Stanley's, including the legendary Ron Rice walking around in green shoes with his sad Chaplin face; and Taylor Mead, the poet and star of Rice's seminal film, *The Flower Thief*.

There was Tuli Kupferberg, standing outside the Charles Theater selling his inimitable magazines. There was Harry Jarvis urinating on rare magic texts in the porcelain egressatory in Stanley's, novelists raving about form, poets looking for Shelley in a crowd waiting to get into the Charles for the Mekas brothers' movie *Guns of the Trees*. It was a thrilling era. And Sam Thomas hungered to leap into its frenzy.

As he sat in the Total Assault Cantina, vowing to become a filmmaker, the two main influences in his life were Mekas and Samuel Beckett. The Mekas influence was this: that the obstacles standing in front of making a film were hallucinations. There were no obstacles. Or rather, piss on obstacles.

That was where Beckett came in. He thought, I'll treat them like walls at whose foundation I will fall and scrape, looking for chinks through which to chew and to chip till completion at the other side.

He was greatly moved by such Beckett characters as Molloy and Watt, often modeling his speech and mannerisms after "Beckett-folk"—as he called them, as if they were a colony of the living. Scrape scrape, chew chew,

198

persist persist; to the neophyte filmer, this was tough Sam B.'s message to the citizens of earth.

He searched and priced equipment throughout the city. At Willoughby's on 32nd Street he finally located what he wanted at a reasonable price. The 16-mm "battle camera" had a rotating lens stage with three lenses: telescopic, wide-angle, and so-called normal. He called up Bell & Howell after the purchase and obtained an operating manual for that model. He sat up all night slurping tea at Total Assault memorizing the data.

Sam met a filmmaker from Colorado at a reading and received from him a wonderful lecture on the "Yoga of the lens." He friend told him to take the camera with him wherever he went, to forget about loading it with film for awhile, and to practice ten hours a day for a few weeks "filming" things he observed, especially heavy action, like fights, crowds forming in the park, angry truck drivers, police raids. The point was to be able to stay cool. His friend advised Sam to undertake a rigorous program of physical exercise. "A moviemaker should be in as good a shape as any other athlete," he said.

He should be able to twist, contort, lean slowly forward while sinking to the knees, bend backward, all while keeping the camera exactly on the imaginary line smoothly filming the action. A cameraperson should be able to walk through a scene of grisly riot, chaos, or site of snuff, the camera running, following the action in a smooth flowing riverine motion: you dig, muh fuh?

He also recommended that Sam purchase a device shaped like a large seven, called a Stedi-rest, which greatly aided handheld camerawork. The Stedi-rest enabled the filmmaker to avoid spastic jerks and quakes during filming. The camera was screwed into the top of the "seven" and the arms of the Stedi-rest pushed against the stomach and upon the shoulder by means of curved cushioned supports which were built on the ends of the large seven, perpendicular to the ends. With the torso supporting the camera's weight, the hands were relatively free to move about, the camera was much less likely to be dropped and it was always more or less in position ready to be used.

He rigged his apartment with film equipment and photo-flood lighting. The photo-flood equipment was positioned to beam full Ra-glare on the top surface of his madras-covered mattress on the bedroom floor. He draped the walls with colorful cloths purchased on Orchard Street. And he began to make short sample films to make certain he had fully memorized all necessary information about lighting and lens-settings. He corralled his friends for epic sessions of fornication after poetry readings and concerts. Some of the outstanding humans of the beatific era were filmed for posterity, all engaging in various desperate frothings of skin. Sam looked forward to that day in 1983, when he could show up at the good junior senator from Tennessee's office down in D.C. with a wonderful film shot when the senator was just a wee young experimenting lad on Avenue A.

After a month of constant practice and experiment, he was ready. By stroke of luck, he located a cheap film source, a Mr. Joive who had an office on Ninth Avenue near 46th Street. The rumor was that Mr. Joive had borrowed about a million feet of film from the U.S. Air Force on huge reels each containing thousands of feet of film. The same rumor stated that the film had been destined, prior to Mr. Joive's interception, for use in high-altitude aerial surveillance of the Chi-coms. Mr. Joive had a lab

200

out in Brooklyn where a blind employee sat, in total darkness, peeling off hundred-foot rolls from the big reels. Mr. Joive sold the rolls at a wonderfully low price, in black unmarked cans—and was really responsible for a lot of the underground films being made in New York. For instance, Sam Thomas was able to purchase one hundred cans of Mr. Joive's Chi-com film, and to begin at once his first movie.

For a long time, the filmmaker had been aware of the A-heads. If you lived on the East Side, and spent much time mixing with the street culture, the A-heads were unavoidable. They roamed the streets, bistros and pads compulsively shooting, snorting or gobbling unearthly amounts of amphetamine, methedrine, dysoxin, bennies, cocaine, procaine—all of them burning for the flash that would lead to FLASH! It was almost neo-Platonic, as beneath the galactic FLASH! were subsumed the demi-flashes all urging toward FLASH!

Everybody from Washington Square to Tompkins Square called the streets "the set"—as "I've been looking for you all over the set, man. Where's my amphetamine?" With a generation readily present who viewed their life as on a set, there was no need to hunt afar for actors and actresses. What a cast of characters was roaming the village streets of 1962!

There was plenty of gossip at the time that the President used amphetamine and that his doctors injected him every morning. There were further speculations that the generals who met in the Pentagon War Room every day planning atomic snuffs were a bit A-bombed themselves.

In New York, the filmmaker was amazed observing the violence of the amphetamine-heads and the raw power-grabs that occurred in their glassy-eyed universe after a few months of sleeping just twice a week. If generals, corporation executives, presidents, premiers and others were users of A, what were the implications? Shudders were the usual response to speculation that A-heads had taken over the governments of the world. As noted A-head artist Zack Thayer put it, "I *know* the President of the United States uses amphetamine. He *has* to. Otherwise how could the muh fuh play all the tunes, you dig?"

It was also commonly accepted on the set that the Germans had invented amphetamine and that the Nazis had shot up amphetamine during campaigns in North Africa in W.W. II, inspiring tales on the East Side of futuristic battles involving fierce-breathed amphetamine humanoids, babbling shrilly like rewinding tapes, in frays of total blood.

Another commonly accepted thesis was that amphetamine temporarily raised the intelligence of the user—"I am the genius of A! I am Rimbaud!"—yelled Zack Thayer, squirting purple ink from a hypodermic needle upon a canvas. They also seemed proud that A-use destroys brain cells. "I lose trillions of cells every day, man, grooo-VY!"

Amphetamine altered sex. Some under A's spell waxed unable in Eros or sublimated their desire beneath the frenzy of endless conversation or art projects. Others with strong natural sensual urges experienced this: that the erogenous areas became extended under A to include every inch of bodily skin. "No piece of skin where you can't cop a riff of flash, man."

Men could not easily spew and women loved it forever. The image of amphetamine-driven Paolos and Francescas writhing twelve hours on a tattered mattress was humorous but true.

Gradually the filmmaker became aware of their actual art as opposed to their life-style. Some of them were extremely talented artists. One of the problems was the high snuff-ratio of their art. Most of it was abandoned or lost in the endless succession of evictions from apartments. When they first occupied a new pad they immediately proceeded to turn every surface and every room into an "environment" of murals, painting, sculptured piles of furniture and debris brought in from the street. A landlord, once observing that the entire pad had been turned into Art, so to speak, would throw up his arms in alarm and head for eviction court or the local police precinct.

The filmmaker decided to make a film about power, using the world of the A-heads as Archetype. He taped a presidential press conference, intending to intermix sections of the conference with the river of tapes he was making of East Side A-babble. For a couple of weeks, he scouted the scene, lugging along his Wollensak tape recorder into the apartments, and taped shoot-ups, fights, conversations, and room noise. He decided to title the film, *Amphetamine Head*.

For a while, he considered holding a mock A-head cabinet meeting with Zack Thayer in the role of president. He soon abandoned the idea because he could not afford the props, tables, chairs, and so forth, to make it real. During his research for the film, he had located a schoolteacher on the West Side who had been collecting the A-head drawings and paintings for a number of years. His house was packed with canvases and sheets of drawings—literally thousands of works. The teacher submitted to a filmed interview and a number of works by Zack Thayer, Manfred the Nut, Bill Klinger and others were filmed. Inspired by the quality of this art collection,

203

the filmmaker decided to make the film a straight documentary of the A-heads at work and play, and to forget about the President.

He began work on the sound track. For the film's introduction he woke up one morning with a flash. He covered himself completely with the blanket to make a sort of deadening sound chamber, reached over to switch on the Wollensak recorder, pulled the microphone under the covers and then, in the best zombi voice he could muster, started bellowing: "Am, am, am, am [very slowly]—phet, phet, phet, phet [slightly faster]—ta, ta, ta, ta [faster]—mine, mine, mine, mine [fast]—Head, head, head, head"—and over again, "Am, am, am, am, phet, phet, phet, phet, ta, ta, ta, ta, mine, mine, mine, mine, Head, head head head." And so on, till it grew so quick his voice tripped on the syllables.

Later, when he was actually filming, groups of ten to fifteen A-heads huddled on street corners would join the chorus of "Am, am, am, am, phet, phet, phet, phet, ta, ta, ta," et cetera.

As a film set, Sam decided to rent an apartment and stock it with choice crystals of amphetamine; and to allow A-heads to live and work there upon the condition that he be allowed to film freely and to tape everything said. He located an apartment at 28 Allen Street, a few blocks south of Houston. It was a typical two-room tub-in-the-kitchen slum apartment painted dogtongue green. The human who had previously lived there had somehow caused the walls to become streaked with long lines of gray brown grease furry to the touch because of the trapped soot. The plaster was tumbling from the ceiling and the front window, opening on Allen Street, had been bashed in and replaced with the door of a cigarette vending machine. What a crummy apartment. But a Moorish palace for the purposes of the filmmaker.

He enlisted the assistance of his friend Llazo, a poet and "space cadet" who had written various poems about the A-heads, coffee-house classics such as *Flutemaker's Hymn* and a long sonnet sequence titled, *Two-Week Flash*. Llazo was dispatched to wander all over the set telling people about the apartment lurking with free amphetamine down on Allen Street. The result gave insight into the finding of gold in Sutter's creek. Within fifteen minutes, the A-heads began to flock, and the sound of the trilling flute was heard in the hallway of 28 Allen Street, 'phet-freaks banging most urgently upon the door.

The onslaught caught him off-guard, and when he refused to let them in the pad right away, he could hear them muttering, "Oh man!" as they clumped down the stairs. He wanted to film the pad in its "natural state," and then to film the metamorphosis as the artists enacted their painterly transformations. He knew he hadn't much time, so he rushed around; he swept the floors, washed the bathroom, dusted the windows, made up the floor-mattress with clean sheets and a cover. He even placed around the pad some paper towels, soap, tissue, and a bit of food.

He had brought with him about ten clip-on light fixtures and twenty three-hundred-watt photo-flood lamps, which he clipped all over the apartment so that any area could be lit up for filming. He quickly checked the illumination on the walls, feeling them to be most important for filming the construction of wall murals and collages. He surrounded the mattress with lights. And the bathroom. He switched on the lights and filmed the clean, neatly arranged apartment.

205

Llazo had returned by this time, and Sam left him in charge while he rushed out to cop a few ounces of amphetamine, trotting up the avenue to score in a hurry, lest Llazo be faced with a riotous congeries of pissed-off A-heads.

He located a dealer who traded exclusively in the finest crushed crystals of amphetamine sulphate. When the dealer became aware of the movie project he was excited. "Wow, a movie called *Amphetamine Head!* Here, let me give you some extra. I can groove with a movie 'bout A, man. Be sure and invite me to the opening!"

The dealer at once began to regale the filmmaker with lengthy anecdotes about his life story, but the filmmaker had to leave in the midst of the torrent, which continued unabated even after the door had been shut. Sam felt the weight of the brown sack. The dealer must have given him about four ounces for the thirty dollars, an unbelievably good buy.

Returning to Allen Street, the filmmaker discovered seven humans inside: a girl named Diane sitting in the bedroom drawing in a notebook, Zack Thayer and Claudia: artists; Tom Four-a-day—a famed dopefreak; Sheilah the micro-swirl muralist; Llazo the poet, and, god knows how, a Norwegian sailor.

Diane was seventeen—and six months removed from the Bronx, sitting with the others on the mattress and floor of the bedroom, yakkety-yakking. Amphetamine had possessed her. She wore her long black tresses swept back into a vague tangled knot behind her. Her eyes were huge and dark—capable of fixing a baleful glazed gaze upon a partner of shoot-up, art or grope. She wore a black short-sleeved scoop-neck bodystocking. Her shoes and other clothes were in a brown bag on the window ledge between the rooms. There was a hole in the stocking's toe. "See that abscess?"wiggling her white toe which bore a pink sore on the outer tarsal—"Zack shot me up with methedrine. A foot flash!"—breaking into giggles.

Diane drew eyelashes with ink and brush above her lips so that her mouth babbling torrentially had the look of a convulsing cyclops. Next, her twitching Rapidograph pen began to work on her toe. She drew flower petals around her shoot-up sore. Then she ripped at the toe-hole and peeled the stocking up to her thigh and spent the next hour drawing a maze of stick-figures all over the leg. Soon, she had cut a jagged circle out of the stomach of the bodystocking with a razor blade. She studied her stomach, craning her head down, and then began to shave each pale stomach hair with the blade. Sometimes a meth mini-spasm would occur and the steel would nick the skin, leaving a thin red slice. Ouch. She drew an ink-sun in the Mayan style rising from the top of her pubic hair. This done, she stood up and said, "Hey, somebody said you were going to bring some amphetamine."

This startled the filmmaker who had been watching her, not thinking to switch on the lights and to film it. He pointed to the paper bag he had brought, "There're four ounces in there."

"There is!?"—she almost shouted, and jumped along with the others toward the flash-source. She cooked a solution and shot herself up. "Flash! flash! flash!"—she shout/laughed, pirouetting upon her leg fair-covered with stick-figures. Then Diane sat back upon the mattress and grabbed a notebook, "I'm going to jot some thoughts."

She wrote for several minutes then picked up the single-edged razor blade again and started scraping her lips with it. The filmmaker was busy at this time filming other peoples' shoot-ups. He glanced into the bedroom and winced involuntarily, seeing Diane scraping her mouth with a razor. When little edges of lip-skin would be hooked up, she would pick the skin with pinching fingers and tear it off. Soon, long blood-pink strips had been peeled from her lips. The filmmaker stood on a chair and adjusted the photo-floods. He found it hard to photograph the event, so unnerving was it to see and to hear the scritch-scratching of the razor.

He had been worried about the moment when he would first switch on the floodlights and begin to film, that people would get uptight. But nothing happened, the group just accepted the extra light and the camera as another tidbit of grooviness. That is, the babblers kept babbling, the painters kept painting, and the flautists kept fluting. In fact, the walls were so fully lit that Sheilah was happy: "Hey man, that light is groovy on my wall"—as she stood drawing on it with extremely small swirls, dots, triangles and faces, as was her style, "I'm going to paint the light-blobs."

For the next several hours, the filmmaker scurried from room to room, shutting lights on and off, shooting the shoots, changing the location of the microphone, changing tapes, changing film. For film-changes, he had sewn together two dark clothes into a large sack, inside which he could crouch in darkness to change film. He didn't want to take any chances with the "government-surplus" film with respect to accidental exposure of the photosensitive surfaces.

Sam was eager to catch Tom Four-a-day on film because Tom was very famous on the set as the dope-fiends' dope-fiend. To Four-a-day, drugs were God. He got his name from his ability to forge or cash at least four hot checks a day. No one was certain of his real name.

"I am the Gauguin of dope"—he would brag, always careful to mention that he had once been a wealthy insurance executive who had abandoned it all, boring job and family, to worship the teeming cornucopious saxophone spilling dope-tabs down upon the table.

All Four-a-day would talk about was drugs. Like, the first thing he said when the filmmaker entered the room, "Man, yesterday I smoked a whole dime of Acapulco gold, today I took a grain of morphine, man I'm still nodding, then some procaine for a tough edge, also two yellowjackets. An hour ago I bought some bennies over at Lou's. Just took six in the bathroom of Rienzi's. Man, the high is out there, out there!"—looking up toward the ceiling, eyes closed, skin wrinkling on the back of his neck, shaking his head. All this was filmed, and many minutes more—capturing forever the sad-voiced dope-fiend.

There was a knock at the door. "Who's there?"

"It's Manfred. Let me in."—the knocker adding a toodle-doodle-doop on his flute. The human at the door was known as Manfred the Nut, a far-famed A-head just possibly certifiably crazy. There was the matter of Manfred's Phantom, a nonexistent "spirit" which accompanied Manfred day and night and was his constant companion in conversation. The listener, of course, could only hear one side of the dialogue.

Sometimes Manfred and his Phantom held heated arguments. He discussed everything with Phantom and often asked its advice regarding a painting or sketch then being undertaken.

Sheilah opened up and there he was, Manfred, flute in his belt, an old blue tie with a horse painted on the front. Stacked on his head, perpendicular to his physique, were about fifteen large pieces of tan cardboard and a brown bag of pencils, his art supplies for the next several days. "Hello there everybody"—Manfred greeted them, his voice strained and loud.

He turned back upon the hallway and yelled, "Come on in with me, Phantom!" And then, "Hey, I hear there's some amphetamine here and that Sammy is making a movie about us. Oh, hello Sammy!"—walking toward the mound of amph' lying on a suitcase, rolling up his sleeve.

When freshly shot up, Manfred the Nut became a vortex of activity. And it was as if his Phantom had shot up also. Both of them talked back and forth squeakily. Manfred decided to make a metal flute but he had no pipe. He left the pad and returned minutes later with some wrenches, drills and a crowbar. After a sweating hour of groans and clanks, Manfred unscrewed and removed the radiator. "It's not winter yet. They don't need this."

The purpose of removing the radiator was to secure a short piece of pipe with which to make a flute. He dropped the radiator with a thud! in the middle of the room and loosened off a length of pipe. Aha! He lifted it like a prize then fell to his knees cackling and blowing hoots through the un-holed piping. Next was the task of marking the holes and the tiresome drilling and the fashioning of a wooden mouthpiece. This project took all night—with numerous pauses for additional amphetamine and for a few heated exchanges with his Phantom. The filmmaker followed the radiator-flute construction with a fifteen-second shot every hour or so.

He also filmed a great sequence of Sheilah shooting up the Norwegian sailor, who was in uniform. Everyone laughed as she told of the language problem when she had first picked him up at The House of Nothingness, but the sentence, "want beatnik girls?" was very understandable to the sailor. Sheilah conned five out of him for groceries which they brought to the pad.

Around midnight Zeb arrived. "Hey man, help me up with this!"—he shouted up at the window, huffing. He was bearing a large metal-edged cardboard drum which was packed with long triangular scraps in the shape of school pennants, in violet, red, and orange cloth shot through with gold and silver threads. Zeb had lugged the barrel ten blocks tilting it on its edge and rolling it, driven by the A-bomb.

"Hey, wow, dig this!"—Zack exclaimed when they had hauled it up the steps, "This'll make a groovy tapestry." Zeb and Zack were known as "The Two Zs" in the A crowd. More specifically, Zeb was known as Bad Z and Zack as Badder Z, because of his crueler reputation. They were always getting into fights; their faces were scarred from slapping each other with razor-blade fragments wedged between their fingers.

Zeb was wearing a grimy patch over his right eye. There was a greasy lock of hair lodged behind it. "What happened to your eye?"—Manfred asked.

Zeb lifted his eye-patch to show the assembly. "Disgusting!" Claudia turned her face away.

"Your eye looks like a hemorrhaging clam, man; what happened?"

"Well, I stopped by Ace's the other day to deal some art books I'd offed from Marlboro. Ace tried to give me an eye-pop. He had a real special spike he said some nurse at Bellevue gave him for draining swollen eye veins. Well, man, I figured if this fucking spike can suck it out, why not use it to pop some A in my eye? I wanted to shoot it

211

into my brain, dig, through the optic nerve. Can you *dig* those changes! A direct brain-flash! Wow, something else!!"

"What happened?"

"Well, dig it, he found a lot of raised veins in my eye; I hadn't been to bed in four days. So he got ready to hit and, of all the times to turn spastic—the fucker lunged into my eye! Man, it was a dartboard scene."

"You're a lucky mother, man, you could be blind."

There followed next a long discussion of various arcane methods and places, of shoot-up. Someone dragged out the ancient tale of nut-shoot. How flashy it was, supposedly, to shoot up genital veins. "But you got to watch tying up your balls, man, because like you can become a tenor with the Mormon Tabernacle Choir if you keep the tie on too long. The best thing is to use a rubber band, you can get it off quick."

Zack, Zeb, Claudia, and Llazo began the tapestry. They took the bedspread and nailed it tightly to the kitchen wall to serve as the base of the work. Then they started gluing the triangular bright strips upon the spread until it was covered in a weird quiltlike manner. Claudia made plaster of Paris in the bathtub and they all hurled globs of it upon the "tapestry." On top of each glop, which was more or less round in shape, Sheilah drew an indented circle with her finger.

When the glops had dried she painted the dented circles with oil paints.

Zack filled three salad bowls with red, purple and orange. He dipped his hand entirely in the purple bowl and advanced toward the tapestry, smearing a neat purple borderline around the entire work. Then Manfred, who claimed the idea was from his Phantom, suggested that Zack "smear handprints on the tapestry like those caves in France where the Cro-Magnons slapped five on the ceilings."

"Good idea, good idea"—Zack muttered and proceeded to place about fifty handprints on the tapestry in between the globs of plaster. This whole act of creation was immortalized on film.

To finish the tapestry, Sheilah wandered bug-eyed into the bedroom waving a thick silver spinal tap from her great-uncle Mitchell's medical kit. "Does anybody want the final flash?" she asked, jabbing the mattress with the thick two-inch silver needle.

Diane thought Sheilah was serious and offered her buttock for a zap. Sheilah laughed, "I can't shoot you with this; this is filled up with paint."

Sheilah walked into the kitchen and spurted several arabesque swirls of orange paint upon the tapestry. Next, in a surge of formalism, she squirted two rows of four large contiguous orange circles, for a total of eight, upon the cloth. This done, she stood back studying the work and announced, "Total beauty! This should be in the Louvre."

All through the night and through the next day the events oozed past. Some he filmed, others he missed. He did catch for history the construction and destruction of the Miniature Garden of Amphetamine Sand. They apparently got the idea from the white sand Zen garden in the courtyard of The House of Nothingness café, on 10th Street and Tompkins Square North.

Zeb grabbed a double fist of amphetamine and made the suggestion, "Let's make a Clear Crystal Garden of Perfect Thought-Form!"

"What do you mean?"

213

"Here, I'll show you." Zeb turned over the barrel that had contained the cloth scraps and placed an inverted rectangular baking tin on top. He mashed the dope crystals into fine grit with a spoon and evenly dispersed the granules, like sand, over the metal surface. For the rocks necessary to such a garden, he broke up a Baby Ruth candy bar into three pieces and placed them at the end of the metal plate. Zack took a fork and, with the tines, raked even lines in the A-strand, like the raked patterns in sand gardens.

"Now we can be like the Gods, man. Let's lick up the Zen plate!" The four artists stood on all sides of the white rectangle with the triad of Baby Ruth hunks, and lowered their faces upon it, slurping, licking and slobbering as they devoured the granules. This was destined to become one of the most famous vignettes in amphetamine filmmaking.

At 3 A.M., two musicians, Bob Krowe and Stu Elgin, tap-tapped a the chamber door. "Hey, man, we heard there was a party here and that some cat had laid five pounds of methedrine on you."

"Nah, only four ounces, come on in."

Krowe was a well-known jazz bass player who pushed his stand-up bass around the East Side by means of a half-roller skate tied to the bottom. Stu Elgin was carrying a battered saxophone wrapped in a pillowcase and a guitar adorned with glued bits of glass, nuts, decals, stamps and feathers. In years past, Stu and Krowe had organized a jazz quartet that had toured the East Coast club circuit, like Buffalo to Baltimore, but had given it up for the East Side dope circuit. They were good musicians and the whole pad joined them for a 3 A.M. jam.

Manfred was on flute, Elgin on sax and guitar, Krowe

214

leading on bass, Four-a-day was percussive with some short sticks with bells nailed on them—and then there were the Astral Wallbeaters: Llazo, Zack, Claudia, Diane and Zeb, not to mention Sheilah, who was jumping up and down in rhythm inside the ice compartment of the overturned refrigerator. The sailor was left in the bedroom giggling and babbling to himself in Norwegian.

The music arose with an enormous din of sax, bells, flute, bass and scat-along yowls. The wallbeaters bashed and whacked till the plaster began to drop. "Hey man, you recording this!?"—Krowe yelled over at Sam.

"Yeah."

"Groovy. We'll just call this piece, *Suite A: White Jam on Allen Street,*"—Krowe laughed, as he slowly pushed the roller-skate bass around the room, pausing at the trunk on which the mound of A was dumped, to reach down for a pinch which he honked into his nose, and then resumed his contorted bent-over fingering.

There was a thud thud at the door. Everyone stopped. Zeb walked over and put his head against the panel. "Who is it?"

"It's the police."

At just that moment there was a tug-of-war in the other room as Zack and Llazo were jostling for control of a black necktie used to tie the arm. Each was the owner, although it was difficult to se why anyone would want possession of such a greasy, skin-smirched specimen. "C'mon motherfucker, it's mine, I'll cut your ass!"

"Hey man, I was *wearing* it this afternoon. Gimme!"—giving a mighty tug.

"Shit, you never did nothing with this but tie your arm, man; it's mine!"—and gave a yank so that Zack fell across the table of ink, glasses of water with hypos resting in them, paint, towels—all which cracked to the floor.

"Shhhht! Will you shut the fuck up. The fuzz are here."

"Pssst,"—he motioned at Llazo to stash the A, and whispered, "Don't spill any." The pad was totally still. Only Diane hissed and whistled now and then as she scribbled onward in her yellow-paper spiral notebook, "I want to write about my first ice-cream cone. Let me tell you about it. It was at Glower's Drug Store twelve years ago. . . ."

They turned out all the lights so that the police couldn't see a thing inside the pad, a timeless beat maneuver. Zeb opened the door, with the chain still attached. He saw that it was really the fuzz, so he shut the door, zipped off the chain, and opened wide. "Good evening, officers. We were just having a party. Sorry, if we were disturbing anyone."

The officer: "There's someone lying on the sidewalk outside by the garbage cans who claims to have arrived on a spaceship. We heard the noise up here and we thought maybe he belonged to you."

"Gee, I wonder who it is. He's not one of us."

"It's not *me*"—Manfred the Nut piped up from the dark bedroom.

"However"—the officer continued, "it's three-fifteen in the morning and the neighbors are beginning to call in about the noise up here. We heard it all the way to Canal Street."

"Sure officer, the band was just playing some dance music for us. I'll tell them to stop." Whew. As the officers turned and clumped down the stairs.

Zack Thayer became very sadistic under 'phets. That's how he'd met his wife Claudia, when he was crashing into a bank of amphetamine runway lights, and he pulled

216

a caveman scene, cutting up the face of Claudia's boyfriend, and forced her to come away with him. Claudia wasn't exactly a masochist but there was plenty of violence in their relationship. Zack and Claudia were the premiere A-head husband-and-wife team, almost a caricature of that violent puppet act that children dig.

After the police split, Diane looked up at Zack and opened her stripped lips, "Hey, why don't *you* shoot me up. I could dig it. Make me go to heaven, Zack!"

Zack was all too eager to accommodate her, and leaped for the glass of needles. He filtered a solution of dope and filled an eyedropper with needle affixed, to the brim. With a flourish he stuck the needle into a blue gray vein on the underside of Diane's forearm. Jabbed would have been a better word. He slid the needle long inside the vein much farther than necessary. Then, as he injected the dope within it, he shoved the needle to the hilt inside her and began to twist slightly so that the needle tip pushed up against the top of the vein from inside. The viewers could see the skin rise from the jabbing needle, like a mole burrowing across a putting green. It had to be painful. Then Zack began to twist the needle in all directions. The girl was expressionless. Her eyes were closed and she was gasping and breathing heavily. "Go on, man go on!"—she whispered, eyes still closed.

The filmmaker switched off the camera and even the lights, because he wasn't certain that she and Zack were not going through a sadomasochist riff for the sake of the camera. After what Zack did to her arm, the filmmaker stopped filming altogether for about an hour, though Diane, once shot up, did not seem to feel much pain from the gouging, but continued filling up her notebook.

Sam began to film again during a fight which would

217

later comprise a vignette dubbed "The Glue-Bottle Violence Scene." It started calmly enough while both Zeb and Zack were operating on a large piece of plywood with a mixed media of paint, plaster, hypo-ink and raisins. Zeb was gluing abstract patterns of raisins upon the wood. Zack had just discovered under the kitchen sink an old jar of nuts and bolts which he proposed to begin gluing to the panel. The problem was that there was just one glue bottle and the bottle was just about empty. It was 4:50 A.M., hardly an hour for such a purchase. Surly waxed the two glue-needers as each tried to hook out some glue at the same time.

"Watch it, motherfucker!"—Zack growled.

At that, Zeb grabbed the glue bottle and smeared the entire contents upon the portion of the plywood on which he was laboring. This caused the freak-scene immortalized in the film.

Zeb wound up getting stabbed in the top of his head with a hypodermic needle. He fell down to the floor, holding his head, the spike dangling from the skin, and Zack stomped him in the stomach. It was sickening to hear, sort of like a stomped paper cup. "Zack!"—Zeb threatened from the floor, "I'm gonna peel a slice off your nose! Like Diane did to her lips!"

It could have gotten worse but Manfred and Claudia intervened and a cut-up was averted. Zack was always getting cut, and more particularly, always cutting. The following year, after the film had been finished, the filmmaker was scrounging early one morning in Washington Square Park—when word was flashed along the benches that Zack had been stabbed in the chest that very morning during an altercation arising from a methedrine burn.

Zack had been delivered, according to the tale, d.o.a. to the hospital. Just as he had been declared dead by the doctor in the emergency room and the sheet was ready for his face, a miracle had occurred. Zack's "body" suffered an amphetamine twitch-spasm and his life-line, like, was revived in his body. When the doctor noticed the dope-twitch, Zack was rushed into surgery and saved. This story was told and retold like some sort of religious parable.

"Amphetamine saved Zack's life, baby, you better believe it."

When the sun had just risen, Sam turned out the floodlights. His film supply had run low and he wanted to save enough to film the comedown, certain to occur in a day or so, when he knew there would be strife aplenty.

He decided to sleep since he was very tired and he had abstained himself from sucking the white. He was the only one copping z's in the entire pad as the others raved and painted onward. As he drifted toward sleep he overheard a conversation between Llazo and Diane. Llazo wanted to borrow her blade so he could cut a hatchway into her bodystocking in order for them to make it. "I'll sew it back in place myself after we're done, I promise."

"Okay"—the girl with the coal-dark eyes assented.

He apparently cut a successful passageway for soon the groans and sighs were floating above the babble in the dark room. Others joined them writhing in insatiable A-sex. At one point Zack walked up to Sam and woke him up with a rude nudge. Sam squinted his eyes, trying to focus in on Zack whose bent fighter's nose was smeared with a streak of red, maybe paint.

"Hey, man, you got a rubber band?"—Zack asked. Sam had none. Zack was naked except for a gray ink-stained

T-shirt with the arms cut off. Zack removed the sealing strips from one of the film cans and proceeded to wrap it around the base of his erection, then strode back into the other room, apparently to pull a sodomy scene on the reluctant Claudia.

"Zack! Zack! No, No! Zack!"—followed by guttural gowls from the dark, as Sam drifted back to sleep.

It was late in the afternoon when Sam woke up. Things had pretty well quieted down. It wasn't long after he awakened that the last of the four ounces was used up. After this it was all comedown. Forays were made into the streets looking for the white gold. They began to hit on the filmmaker for some more dope, "C'mon, man! Buy some more A!"

"Or else get out!"—Zack snarled, giving Sam a shove.

In terms of power, Zack Thayer began to take over the pad. He ruled with the irrationality and violence of a textbook on dictatorship. He beat up Claudia so much that she had to move over to Mary Meth's pad. And the police started raiding the place though no arrests were made.

Police visits were made easier by the fact that someone had removed the front door of the pad—"I want to make a table with it, dig?"—and, in place of the door, had nailed up a shower curtain. As for ownership of the place, Llazo had actually signed the lease originally, but Zack forced him to sign a statement relinquishing the entire scene to Zack. Zack nicked Llazo's finger with a spike and coerced a red fingerprint on the document.

To make things worse, for reasons unknown there was a dope-panic in lower New York. The sudden amphetamine drought made the East Side a Sahara of violence. They held meetings to discuss raising funds, with occasional

220

hock-shop glances at Sam's camera equipment.

Finally the filmmaker left, having used up all his film, and uneasy for his own well-being under the circumstances. He carried with him all the light fixtures, films, and, with fearful clutch, the camera.

Several days later he returned to the Allen Street pad to take some shots of the pad's "final state" since he had heard the landlord had thrown everybody out. The condition of the pad, as Sam encountered it in doorless dereliction, was that of bombed-out chaos. A large mound of debris had accumulated in the middle of the kitchen, including the refrigerator which lay on its back, the door open, its trays and grates removed.

The refrigerator was stuffed with old clothes, drawings, bags of garbage, and pieces of the bright triangular cloth used for the tapestry. There was an old TV set, guts dangling to the floor, sitting next to the refrigerator, with a headless mannequin protruding from the picture-tube hole and painted with ornate configurations.

The sink was completely clogged and filled to the brim with dried plaster. The tapestry with the huge orange circles on it was intact on the wall. Sam was tempted to take it with him except the landlord showed up and threatened a violence scene if Sam didn't stop filming and split.

He managed to film the final state of Sheilah's microswirl wall mural before he had to leave. The mural was in three sections, covering the upper half of the kitchen wall plus the entire ceiling and the bathroom floor. She had poked holes in the plaster of the kitchen wall and inserted some of Manfred's abandoned flutes which gave the artwork a stubbled effect.

The bedroom was a tangle of wet clothing, shoes and notebook pages featuring ornate eyeballs and melted

221

faces. Someone had ripped the mattress completely apart, apparently to secure a piece of stuffing to use as a dope filter.

The panes of all the windows were each neatly x'd with crisscrosses of the black tape Sam used to seal the film cans.

"Why?"—Sam asked Zack.

"The Out doesn't exist"—he replied. "You dig, it's all *In.*"

Sam spent the next few months shooting the A-heads, when he could afford it, in outdoor settings, mainly in Washington Square. He finally finished the sound track and edited the film. The credits were shot in the form of a moving hypodermic needle squirting letters upon a raw canvas.

In the succeeding years, the filmmaker turned his attention away from film and became a schoolteacher and poet in a Washington State mountain valley.

But his fifty-five minute, black-and-white movie *Amphetamine Head—A Study of Power in America,* remains. A print may be ordered from the Total Assault Film Archives, Battle Creek, Michigan.

The AEC Sit-in

RUSSIA DROPPED A 100-megaton nuke-puke in November of '61 causing a spew of strontium 90, cesium 137 and other carcinogenic spores to float upon the wild winds. The Russian tests wreaked despair within the nuclear disarmament movement in New York City. To oppose the blast, a few pacifists decided to picket the Russian Mission to the United Nations located on Park Avenue at 67th. They were arrested outside the mission because of a New York City ordinance prohibiting picketing there, a law spawned of the fear of right-wing violence during the Cold War.

Then, tooth for tooth, rumors began to float throughout the later winter of '61–'62 that the U.S. government itself might set off high-megaton nuke-puke. In New York, various nonviolence peace groups held meetings, including the Total Assault Ahimsa Squadron (the action arm of the Total Assault Cantina), Maniac Artists of The Abyss (MATA, a group of artists and painters 'gainst the nukes), and the two main peace-action groups of the era, the Catholic Workers and the Committee for Nonviolent Action.

223

After a lengthy stomp-dance upon the ahimsa threshing floor, the decision was made that immediately after any announcement of atmospheric testing by the U.S., the peace groups would sponsor a nonviolent sit-in at the front entrance of the New York office of the Atomic Energy Commission in order to prevent the entry of AEC employees.

On Friday, March 3, President Kennedy announced that if the Russians did not sign a permanent cheat-proof test-ban treaty before the end of April, he would resume testing of nuclear weapons in the air.

The sit-in was scheduled for Monday. The weekend was spent preparing and printing the leaflets and notifying demonstrators. Two leaflets were written—one as a fact sheet for those committing civil disobedience which recommended serving jail sentences rather than posting bail or paying fines. The other leaflet was to be handed out at the sit-in explaining the purpose, decrying atmospheric tests, urging the workers to quit their jobs at the AEC and not to pay taxes for nuke-puke. The peace groups pursued the doctrine of "openness and truth"— that is, of informing the police and AEC officials exactly what was going to take place. They sent out announcements to the press.

Monday morning was a bitter wind-swept day of foul septic blasts from the direction of New Jersey oil refineries. The New York Atomic Energy Commission was located at 376 Hudson Street on the lower west side of Greenwich Village near the piers. Before the demonstration, the police had erected a ring of gray barricades around the entrances.

That morning the poet awoke nervous. He washed himself slowly and did not eat, meditating about the impending confrontation. He washed with meticulous detail because he remembered all too well the shabby treatment afforded by a sheriff in Ohio who had once arrested him and had scoffed at the condition of his body with respect to grunge. Ever thereafter, the poet had always spic-and-span'd himself prior to any demonstration.

As he left his apartment, he was scared in the pit of his stomach and walked down the street, often with his eyes closed, as imaginary clubs bashed his face. That very weekend there had been demonstrations in Times Square where club-wielding police on horses had ridden up on the curb into a large crowd packed upon Father Duffy's traffic island—and the blood had dripped from the whacked skulls.

When he arrived at the AEC, there was that strange electric aura which always seemed to occur just prior to civil disobedience. The bitter cold, the throngs of police, the pickets, the barricades, the weird intelligence agents with movie cameras, the traffic oozing extra-slowly by, the reporters, the nervous protest leaders—all combined both to thrill and to terrify. He spotted a few of his friends already sitting behind the barricades outside the front door. They waved and soon he too had slipped through the blocking legs of the police and under the gray boards, silently nodding to those already sitting.

He sat with his knees bunched up and his arms locked around them. He could see the supporting picket line move slowly in a large oval, their signs hoisted against Kennedy's nukes. They were warned by a police captain to move from the door or they'd be arrested. Then it began.

There was a quick engine roar as a paddy wagon

backed up to the sit-in. Two detectives with food-bloated faces in thick dark blue overcoats and narrow-brimmed felt hats, double-nabbed the poet, one to a shoulder, sucking him out of the close hem-in of the barricades and hauled him toward the police van, half drag, half carry. Then it was a heave-ho scene and the poet plopped aboard.

Not all of the nineteen arrested "went limp"—as they termed a totally relaxed arrest posture, but some walked to the paddy wagon. The argument was that going limp created violence in that it tended to anger the gruff, huffing police haulers.

When the van was full, the back door was locked and it drove away to the New York Criminal Courts Building at 100 Centre Street. Those jammed aboard sang Numbers 1, 2, and 3 on the arrested-pacifist Hit Parade: "We Shall Overcome," "Down By the Riverside," with a little satiric "God Bless America," thrown in.

For the next five hours they were treated to the criminal justice stockyards, herded along with the hordes of sullen unfortunates arrested that day in New York City. Finally they were placed in a small "holding tank" packed with the accused, located just outside the courtroom. There was a parade back and forth of legal defense aides with scribbled clipboards trying to assist the poor.

After a seemingly endless chain of mumbling confrontations with the judge, many of which seemed to be drug related—the pacifists' docket numbers and names were moan-droned by the bailiff and they were herded into the room and the arresting officers lined them up in front of the judge, a dour scowler with curtains of chin blubber dangling.

The first thing to be noted in standing before de judge

was that the big brown N in the motto, IN GOD WE TRUST, high on the wall behind him, had fallen off. The judge flashed some red onto his face when defendant Randy McDermott, lining up with the others in front of the bench, refused to face the judge, but rather insisted on facing the spectators. "I refuse to recognize the existence of these proceedings," he announced.

There were titters in the courtroom at this and the gavel-whacking judge admonished the supporters in the front row to shut up. The judge then launched into a Cold War lecture which culminated in the old "You'd never get to do this in Russia—you'd be sent to Siberia." Then he gave Randy, because of his noncooperation, notice of bail of five hundred dollars but the others he released on their own recognizance. All defendants were charged with discon, disorderly conduct. Those who had gone limp were given additional charges of resisting arrest. The august red-face set a date for pleading of March 23, 1962, 10 A.M. "And be on time!" the judge admonished.

On March 23, most of them pleaded guilty to disorderly conduct in exchange for the dropping of resisting-arrest charges. The poet and the others were sentenced to ten days at the Hart Island Workhouse. Thank you, Judge Wallach. Next they were escorted back into the colons of the Tombs to be fingerprinted.

The poet was opposed to the FBI fingerprint storage system and he knew that the New York City fuzz were going to flash his prints right down to D.C. for the big file. He notified the guards that he was not going to cooperate with fingerprinting, and was astounded at the commotion this seemed to cause.

His refusal convinced the jail officials that they might

have some sort of Pretty Boy Floyd on their hands. Aha, they rubbed their hands, smiling knowingly, aha, a criminal! They told him they were going to take the prints by force and still he refused.

Then they sent him to see a prison psychologist, the purpose presumably to determine if the poet would pull a wolverine scene while resisting the printing. He assured the officer that he would be totally nonviolent but that they'd have to carry him to the print room.

When he was dragged into the room, the officer seemed to assume that he was going to cooperate, even when the poet fell several times from the chair into a limp heap upon the floor. The officer picked up the poet's limp right hand, the fingers dangling in desuetude. The officer rolled a smush of ink across the smooth desktop with a roller. Then he blacked the poet's fingers and placed them upon a fingerprint card. "Roll your fingers," he ordered.

"I'm sorry, I can't cooperate. I don't believe in fingerprinting."

The cop cursed. He grabbed a finger, and pressed it onto the card, trying to roll it himself. But it was too smudged to use. "C'mon, cooperate!" he hissed. The poet contemplated deliberately twitching his fingers with each attempt, but he didn't really want to get beaten up by a bunch of guards. He ruined four fingerprint cards before the set was finally complete, by which time a superior officer was waiting in the room, his carotid pulsing rapidly on a florid neck above a tight white collar bearing golden adornments. Mr. Florid Neck grabbed the finger card and raced away to run the print. "Aha! Now we'll check *you* out right away!"

A few minutes later a gray school bus with barred windows drove the fresh prisoners up through the Bronx No

Thonx and then to a ferry which slowly threshed into Long Island Sound to Hart Island. He told prison officials he was a journalist and poet and hinted that he was going to write an article about jail conditions. Apparently the prison staff assigned someone to check this out, because he was approached three times while on Hart Island and was asked things like, "How's the article coming along?" and "How are they treating you? Be sure and send us a copy of the article."

They were processed into the citadel after which there was a nude stroll through a milky-hued footbath and a check for cooties. At the clothes bin, they were given some bent black shoes, loose jeans, blue shirt, towels, and a thick brown green overcoat. Never in his life had such a negative rush of immediate boredom stormed his soul.

They were assigned bunk-space in a large dormitory where there was a TV they were allowed to watch, staring from their double-tiered beds, in the evening. Newspapers were not allowed; something about people stuffing them down the toilets. In the cavernous chow halls the food was served on metal trays with workers glopping the slop into the compartments with defeated splats from griseous ladles. The bread was of punk quality, exuding uncooked flour and could have been used to make sod houses. They called them "rocks from The Rock," since they were baked at another jail out on Rikers Island, otherwise known as The Rock.

Everyone worked. The poet was herded to the clothes department (known as the "clothes bin") where he was assigned the job of keeper of the shoelaces. In later years, usually while drunk, he would rattle off exactly how many black, how many green, and then how many green long, how many green short, shoelaces there had been in

March '62 in the Hart Island Prison. Ditto for the number of long and short black shoestrings. Each day it took him about thirty minutes to see that the jail shoes were all properly laced, after which there was nothing to do. He sorted the laces over and over. Whenever the guards were away he would stare out the back window upon the bay shore, and the listless waters, the gulls upon them, and in the distance the junkies burying bodies.

The prison assigned the heroin addicts, after they had gone cold-turkey of course, to dig the graves of all the New York City derelicts and unclaimed bodies. It was a grim scene, to see them march out each morn, shovels on shoulders, to the pits. The bodies apparently were buried in four layers, one atop another, with identity tags tied to their toes, so that later, should relatives want them, they could be claimed. After a couple of years, so the rumor went, the skeletons were dug up and thrown upon the crumbly beach, a bony roost for the gulls, and the same ground used for new burials.

The junkies who dug the graves were known as the "Garbage Squad," because of the voracious appetites of the freshly detoxified men. Late in the afternoon after the rest of the prison had eaten, the Garbage Squad was marched in from snuff-bury, to the chow hall where they proceeded to eat every drip of protein remaining in the kitchen.

He felt such despair in the cold mornings lined up in a bent row on the sidewalk waiting for the first gobble-shift to eat their sausage and cornflakes and weak coffee. It was bitterly cold in the smelly island dawn breeze; their rough green brown coats were buttoned all the way. Where they lined up, the morning sun shone through the bushes on the left. The sidewalk lay several feet indented into the

230

ground and the shrubs were planted at the top of a waist-high ledge so that the sun was only seen by gazing through the branches.

He heard the countless spits, like punctuations, of alcoholic men with colds. He fantasized a cloud of commas swarming across the sky. The alkies loved to spit into the shrubs, a thing once seen and never to be forgotten, the shiny hockers dangling from the branches, resplendent in the sun.

The single saving event in his stay at the island was encountering a dormitory full of poets, most of whom were there on long terms on drug offenses. Their quarters were in a small room reachable from his own dorm by a small corridor. To visit the poets was forbidden but he managed to sneak there about once a day.

The poets never wrote down their works, and they were unpublished. In the jailhouse evenings it was quite a thrill to hear them chant-sing literally for hours their memorized rhymed epics. The themes were the big-city tensions—the drugs, the arrests, the cops, the FBI, jazz, loves down the furtive gullet of no reproach. They memorized each other's poems, and there were numerous authorless rhymed tales passed down from the years. Readers may well have heard some of these poets reciting in Washington Square on Sunday afternoons.

When he told them he too was a poet, they invited him to recite some of his work, but he was very embarrassed to have to say that he had very little memorized, just a few flashes here and there. "Hey man," they said, "you should be like that cat Pushkin. That cat had *all* his poetry right in his head, you dig. That's where it belongs. He could close his eyes and recite for hours."

The night of his second day on Hart Island, 3-24-62,

there was a televised fight for the welterweight world championship between Bennie "Kid" Paret and Emile Griffith. It was a grudge battle. Kid Paret, a former Cuban sugar-field worker brought to temporary riches via face-punch, had been the champion. Emile Griffith took away the crown in early 1961 by a knockout. Paret then recaptured the crown on July 30, 1961, in a hotly disputed decision. An angry feud developed. Rather than to retire, Paret was pressed from all sides to continue his career and a further face-punch was arranged.

The jail dorm was totally silent and dark save for the tube. The dorm guard sat with his feet on the desk, watching the fight. The convicts sat upon their bunks and stared.

During the early rounds Griffith seemed the casual winner. In the twelfth round Paret was snuffed.

Griffith backed Paret into the corner ropes. Bash. Paret fell against the padded corner brace, his head and upper body jutting at an angle outside the ring. Then there were twenty quick bashes upon Paret's face and head: baf, baf, baf, baf, baf, baf, baf, baf, baf, baf, baf, baf, baf, baf, baf, baf, baf, baf. The referee stood staring. The dormitory was staring. Everybody staring. In Miami the fighter's wife watching the battle on TV screamed, "Stop it! Stop it!"

The final scene for the TV-starers showed Paret bent back, eyes closed, loose light-colored trunks with wide stripes down the side, his kidneys pressed against the corner padding, his left arm hanging defenseless at his side, the right arm still cocked but skewered to the side. Griffith still bashing.

Finally, at 2:09 of the twelfth, the referee, Ruby Goldstein, yelled "Hold it!" and threw his arms around Griffith

232

to prevent further hits. Griffith was loath to stop and made a lunge or so to continue—then subsided. And Paret slid down to a crouch, his knees askew. The lowest of the three parallel ring ropes was hooked under his right shoulder, his arm still jutting upward in a fighting posture.

He was in a coma. They removed his mouthpiece—and carried him away. In a few minutes the TV announcer mentioned that Paret had been given last rites. He was taken to Roosevelt Hospital where a doctor gave him "chances of recovery one in ten thousand."

Shortly thereafter the guard switched off the TV. Lights out. No conversation. The poet lay stunned. He spat out the side of his bunk, as if a ptooey! could exorcise what he had just seen. He didn't know whether to pray for Paret or to fall into a frothing rage at the so-called art of boxing. He made a personal vow that if there ever were an actual revolution and if he were ever in an orb of power over the People's Bureau of Athletics, then he'd try to ban boxing.

On his bunk he tried to pray for the injured boxer. A few days later the poor man died. But he couldn't get the fight out of his mind. It echoed with the baf baf baf baf baf baf and the blood-lust roar, and the tense blood-stare silence of the dormitory.

The morning after the fight there was a radio news report announcing impending high-altitude nuke blasts out in the Pacific on Christmas Island. He immediately began to map plans for "indiscriminate sit-ins" against the tests. God, was he eager to hit the streets. He paced around the dormitory muttering and cursing. He was visited by fantasies of escaping, though he had heard no one *ever* escaped the island—something about marksmen who stand on shore and aim for the head, if swimming, and for the back, if rowing. "Two tried last year—got 'em right in the back."

He gnashed his teeth and thirsted to join his comrades roaming the streets. Instant! Instant! Though he knew that he had fifty more years to beat his head against the death machine.

Peace Walk

I

THE LIGHT BLUE GREEN Ford was at the top of the hill two miles from town and started downgrade when it came upon a straight line of walkers carrying some sort of signs.

"Melvin, why are you slowing down?"—his wife wanted to know. He didn't answer but pointed to the right at the sign-bearing hikers.

"Melvin, why are you leaning down like that?" she queried further.

Melvin was bent over the steering wheel, with his neck craned up, trying to see. He read her a sign: "NATIONAL DEFENSE THROUGH NONVIOLENT RESISTANCE—now what does that mean?" The auto was now traveling about five miles per hour. He could not see the pickup truck barreling up to the hill crest behind them. There was a screech!/ whomp!/smash!, the wife-head punching a neat shattered concavity in the safety glass. With the screech, the walkers scattered into the ditch, signs plopping to the ground, leaflets fluttering upon the tarvia.

Mindful of cars careening snuffishly into the ditch, several walkers sprinted up the embarkment not stopping till arrival at the edge of a cow pasture.

The woman was not seriously hurt; maybe it was the malletlike shape of her head which enabled her to punch out the windshield with impunity. An ambulance and several state police cars arrived and detained the walkers for questioning. They showed the troopers their cover letter provided by the American Civil Liberties Union outlining their rights.

"You all got anyplace to stay tonight?" a trooper asked them, as he cleared a pile of reports from the back seat of his patrol car, perhaps preparing to offer them the hospitality of the county jail.

"Yes, officer, we're staying tonight at the Shiloh Baptist Church." The marchers spoke in their most pleasant tones, seeking to nip at the earliest moment any thought of arrest for vagrancy.

After the fuzz departed, the walkers held a short meeting about their signs. The signs were large rectangular oilcloth envelopes fitted over light metal tubular frames which were affixed to lightweight aluminum poles with handles. The slogans were printed as large as possible on both sides of the oilcloth envelopes, and since they were so lightweight, they could easily be borne nearly perpendicularly by the marchers. After a discussion it was decided that not much more could be done by the walkers to ensure highway safety other than to hold the signs upright and not to engage drivers in conversations and to talk well away from the edge of the road. The marchers then picked up their fallen bundles of leaflets and their signs and walked on into the town.

II

For love of Peace, for a civilization of Ahimsa (non-violence), for the end of nuclear fear, for guilt, for glory, for love of God, for sun-fun, for worship of Manes the Persian, for sensuality: a congeries of men and women, many from the Lower East Side of New York City, began a one-thousand-mile walk through Tennessee and Virginia to Washington, Dictrict of Columbia, in the spring of '62. They called themselves the Memphis to Washington Walk for Peace, and the project was sponsored by the New York-based National Committee for a Nonviolent Civilization.

The organizer of the walk was a brilliant Gandhian named Thomas Bartley, the architect of a series of peace marches in America, Europe, and the Soviet Union in the early part of the decade of napalm. Bartley was tremendously charismatic, the author of a book, *National Defense Through Nonviolent Resistance,* and had spent a number of years in India studying the Gandhian movement. Bartley did not accompany the Memphis walk but remained in New York helping maintain the all-important home office.

Bart was an expert at raising money, mainly through phone pleas and fund-appeal letters mailed to money-bursting citizens opposed to the arms race and to nuclear testing, a hot issue in the spring of 1962 when the United States H-bombed a couple of islands in the Pacific.

A lot of the money for the peace walks came from religious donors—from wealthy Quaker dairy farmers and supporters of the Fellowship of Reconciliation. And let us not forget the sudden largess of rich people in crisis, not to mention the secret checks of guilty liberals.

"Oh, another item that should be included in the main first-aid kit is a hemostat," Bartley added.

This created a couple of frowns around the room. "A hemostat?" someone asked.

A friend leaned to the questioner's ear. "It's that thing that looks like a jeweler's grip—Nelson uses one for a roachclip. It's for spurt-stop in case the Klan operates on our arteries."

There was an atmosphere of fear which tinged the meetings held to plan the peace walk at the National Committee for a Nonviolent Civilization offices. For instance, there were reports that there were counties in the mountainous middle sections of Tennessee where the sunset-necks boasted that no black had ever slept for even a night. And everyone fully remembered the TV footage of that burning Greyhound bus. Still, the time seemed propitious for such a walk, and the danger seemed attractive, even thrillsome. An integrated peace-stroll through the rural South urging citizens not to pay taxes for war, to quit jobs at defense installations, and to renounce all forms of violence—such a project was a toke of paradise to the editorial board of *The Shriek of Revolution* magazine, most of whom signed up for the ahimsa saunter.

It was decided at the planning sessions that the walk would consist of a "core team" of ten to twenty members. Supporters would be invited to join for a few days, a natural phenomenon which occurred when the march passed through, say, a college town and netted the local dissidents and civil rights activists.

There was no problem, in those innocent years, of violent provocateurs, shovers, jostlers, or FBI Cointelpro dissensionists who might have caused trouble. That was a situation which developed years later during the Vietnam War. There was, however, a sort of Ahimsa Security Clearance wherein potential walkers were required to submit short biographies and to explain their reasons for wishing to join.

After a hot debate, it was decided that although the march was to be fully integrated, there would be no interracial couples in the core group. A compromise was pushed through enabling such couples, "responsibly married," to join for a few days as supporters.

The walk was small enough not to have voting—it was talk talk talk, till there was consensus; and the next day, if someone wanted to reconsider, the meeting was rebegun. In the event of impasse or trouble, there was a stratified decision-making system. When the so-called "core group" of marchers was unable to reach a decision, there was a smaller steering committee who could decide. If the steering committee was itself unable to agree in consensus, there were two walk coordinators who could finally decide. In the event of an emergency, there was a single project director. The Memphis-to-Washington director was William Storm, an outstanding black activist, poet, and French scholar who had moved in to the peace movement after years of Freedom Rides, voter-registration projects, and delicate flutter-tongued lectures on Symbolist verse at a Quaker college.

Many of the march preparations were a last-minute frenzy. Copies of the A.C.L.U. legal-rights letter and brochures describing the purpose and itinerary of the walk were sent to the police chiefs in every town along the walk route. Newspapers, TV and radio stations were sent press kits. Ministers of churches along the route were sent

239

extensive packets of literature, for it was extremely important to collect the sympathy of ministers. Indeed, without church basement floors for copping z's and without the use of church kitchens for communal meals, there would not have been the peace-walk movement of the early 1960s.

A team of advance workers drove along the entire walk route two weeks prior to commencement of the project, arranging hospitality at churches and setting up public meetings. They sketched maps of defense plants and military installations along the way to determine the best locations for picket lines and leafleting.

Just before departure, the executive committee presented each walker with a mimeographed document entitled "'Memphis Walk Discipline," an item still interesting for its revelations regarding the mores of the era. Copies of the walk discipline were carried in abundance by the walk in order, for instance, to flash it to hesitant church wardens concerned that naked leftists might practice Tantrik Yoga on the sacristy carpet at 2 A.M. in a respectable one-hundred-year-old Methodist church. In the hallowed memory of Herodotus, the discipline is printed below:

MEMPHIS WALK DISCIPLINE

*All participants in and supporters of
the Memphis to Washington Walk for Peace
are expected to accept the following discipline:*

1. Our attitude towards officials and others who may oppose us will be one of sympathetic understanding of the burdens and responsibilities they carry.

2. No matter what the circumstances or provocation, we will not respond with physical violence to acts directed against us.
3. We will not call names or make hostile remarks.
4. We will adhere as closely as we are able to the letter and spirit of truth in our spoken and written statements.
5. We will always try to speak to the best in all men, rather than seeking to exploit their weaknesses to what we may believe in our advantage.
6. All members of the Walk team will be sexually continent while members of the project.
7. Whether or not men and women sleep in the same or separate quarters will be up to the discretion of the Walk Steering Committee in consultation with hosts.
8. Any person using or under the influence of narcotics (taken for nonmedicinal purposes) will be asked to leave the Walk.
9. No alcoholic beverages will be taken on the Walk. No bars will be frequented. In other situations, the Steering Committee will decide on the appropriateness of taking alcoholic beverages.
10. All walkers will be as clean and neat as possible.
11. All women walkers are strongly recommended to wear skirts.
12. Hair and beards will be trimmed and neat.
13. Every member of the Walk team must be willing to perform any task necessary to the function of the project as long as it lies within his capabilities and does not violate his conscience.

Particularly difficult for bristling libidos to funnel down

the gullet was Rule Number 6, humorously referred to by walkers at the Celibacy Oath.

Rule Number 9, no vodka and beer, was accepted by the editorial board of *The Shriek of Revolution* as an opportunity to dry out damaged kidneys and livers. As for Number 8, no dope, it was decided that cannabis was not actually a narcotic but more of a headache remedy and that therefore it was not within the purview of the regulation.

When the executive committee of the National Committee for a Nonviolent Civilization gained cognizance that key members of the editorial board of *The Shriek of Revolution* magazine were planning to join the march, the committee banned copies of *The Shriek* from being carried or, God forbid, distributed on the march. It was understandable, since *The Shriek of Revolution* advocated via editorial, story, song, cartoon and poem many things opprobrious to Southern sensibilities such as immediate legalization of cannabis (a bold position in 1962). *The Shriek* also had once issued a rather famous manifesto urging civil rights parades through Klanland featuring interracial fornication on flatbed trucks with accompanying loudspeakers blaring the lyrics to "Shenandoah."

The committee therefore dispatched walk coordinator Bill Storm to *Shriek of Revolution* headquarters, that is, to Sam Thomas' pad on East 11th where he slipped the following note under the door:

> *Chicken Little:*
> *The Sky has fallen in !!*
> *Do not REPEAT Do not*
> *bring any copies of*
> *The Shriek of Revolution*
> *with you . . . I*

242

assume you didn't plan
to anyhow.
Explanations forthcoming
Storm.

That note was the lead poem in the next issue of *The Shriek.*

In the days prior to their departure, the Congress of Racial Equality provided the walkers with several training sessions on how to deal with the violent, canine, often cattle-proddish extremes of Southern justice. This done, the backpacks, leaflets, sleeping bags, first-aid kits, and bags of powdered milk and food were packed up and the marchers converged on Memphis by bus, by thumb, and in the two walk-support vehicles. In Memphis they held a rally, picketed a local missile base, and headed east.

IV

An advance crew went out each morning in the station wagon to purchase food supplies, to do laundry for the march, to check on general-delivery mail at the next town, to deliver press kits to the local newspapers and radio stations, to call up the New York committee office, and to check in with church or campground or house where marchers would sleep. Often housing was found at the last minute. Anywhere within a ten-mile circle of the final march-point of the day was suitable. On occasion a church would cancel out when an official would drive out to cop a visual on the arcane-looking peregrination and grow nervous. When this happened, the advance crew headed for the church section of the Yellow Pages or looked up the nearest state park on the map.

243

There was an old blue Chevrolet panel truck called the peacemobile bearing on its top a huge plywood food-storage box. The peacemobile always hovered close by the walk, for you could never know when you might need water, rain gear, first aid, extra leaflets or safety. A decision was made not to decorate the peacemobile with any radical messages, or even with the peace symbol, because of the possibility that it might be pressed into service to escape marauding cattle-prodders or Klan types.

As the walk progressed, the number of core walkers hovered around twelve, half men, half women. They sang a lot. Several carried guitars and harmonicas and as the walk picked up local civil rights activists and religious leaders along the way, the singing became a spirited combination of Gospel, Labor Struggle songs, and Bomb-ban. Like other intense peace projects (such as the San Francisco to Moscow March for Peace of 1960–61), the Memphis march developed it own special slang language, its own in-jokes, its own inner intimacies. When alone, they danced together and certain walkers resurrected twangs and Midwest accents suppressed for years. There was a bit of escapist guilt in some of them, almost a hedonist-Jansenist mix of fun and self-mortification.

But it was healthy. Who could deny the sudden body-rush of happiness each morning in belief that the day would have its sanctity. Today I shall give out five thousand leaflets! Today I shall enter the minds of the unaware with messages of peace! I will sleep upon your floors tonight, scary dark church, beneath a grand piano in your basement!

Some of the walkers cynically mimicked the Southern speech patterns they were hearing, especially the different types of Tennessee laughter. They noted the men waiting

244

early in the morning by the roadside for their rides to work, attired in work shirts and overalls, thumbs often hooked through those tool loops at the side, standing in a slight slouch, one foot slightly forward, a striped billed cap usually associated with railroad employees; and the universal black lunch box with the curved thermos-bearing lid. They noted the worker-farmers, that is, families who ran a small farm and also worked at outside jobs. One failing of the Memphis march was that it couldn't sow the seeds of alternate life-style, couldn't urge people to live, farm, share together, or to open up and dance dance dance. All they could offer was positions on peace and war and racism. Land-distribution and money-distribution issues were carefully avoided. The feeling was this: Who really wants to die in Tennessee?

Sam had not known Becky Levy prior to the Memphis to Washington Walk, though both were from New York and both were partisans of Lower East Side culture. Both had spent numerous evenings at the Total Assault Cantina on Avenue A, and both knew the proprietors fairly well. Sam and Becky found themselves walking side by side much of the time. They sang well together, and could lift up a two-part harmony version of "We Shall Overcome" that could make you cry. Every night they called up the Total Assault Cantina and exchanged information. There was a map of Tennessee and Virginia on the cantina wall whereupon the progress of the march was being followed with map-flags.

Sam was the walk marshal, with responsibilities covering the overall onwardness of the march, to see that the correct highways were followed, to mark where they had ended the preceding day and to direct the march to the same spot the next day, to make sure that no one was left behind sleeping in a Unitarian Church closet, and to ensure that all premises were abandoned in a clean and pristine condition.

Becky was the treasurer—collecting the donations from meetings and forwarding the money to committee headquarters in New York. She kept records of all walk expenditures and provided the walkers with their five-dollars-per-week expense money.

Both Beck and Sam loved the universe of the roadsides—filled as they were with the detritus of America: strange oblong slabs of tire, bolts, flattened tins, squashed turtles, and an atomic amount of bottles and caps. Sam collected 1,763 Hav·a·Tampa cigar wrappers in Tennessee alone, not to mention Virginia where King Edward Imperial cigar packs seemed to prevail. The roadsides had their individual odors also, a sort of sweet putridity that varied slightly mile by mile. At first the walkers were tempted to serve as janitors on the roads of degeneration—stuffing debris into bags—but it was futile; who had the spaceships needed to clear the American ways?

Becky was an ace bottle collector, dragging a brown gunnysack which she filled with muddy returnable bottles to sell to less-than-eager country stores in exchange for aspirin, foot salve, and Bull Durham tobacco.

About the time their romance was aureate and roseate, Sam was embarrassed by the hot Tennessee sun which barbecued him in tender parts necessitating the immediate purchase of underwear. Sex was out of the question, so punished was he by the cruel focus of Ra-rays. His arms also became severely burned and he was forced to treat the lesions with wrappings of gauze and bandages.

Sam slept one night inside a huge kitchen cabinet at a

Methodist church. He shut the door upon himself and lay upon his sleeping bag. All night long on the cabinet shelf he dreamt of Becky and her campfire eyes. When he awoke he knew it was love. He looked for her and found her by the powdered milk and vat of oatmeal in the recreation room of the fane. He stayed by her side through the day, stomach shivering with love-angst. The walk was proceeding through a particularly racist series of counties and every day local yokels shouted hatefully from passing autos; the sheriffs stopped the march for lame reasons; even school buses putting past were a source of thrown sandwiches and fruity missiles.

The fear from such events intensified Sam's and Becky's friendship, although it took a week of walking together before they summoned nerve enough to hold hands on the way to a nighttime rally.

After the meeting, Becky suggested, "Let's take a drive in the station wagon," but Sam was far too uptight to accept the possibilities. Instead he became irate and demanded that they return immediately to the church.

One thing he didn't like about Becky was her extreme knowledge of the details of peace-movement gossip. She knew everything. Another was her frequent allusions to the extraordinary sexual abilities of her former boyfriend. She was reduced, she hinted, because of the austere walk discipline, to kicking sex at the age of twenty-two after four years of making love three times a day three hundred and sixty days a year.

As for Becky, she did not admire Sam's seeming inability to bathe. Sam was weird, with his shouted Greek poetry, his arms wrapped like a mummy, his shyness combined with the filthiest language she had every heard. But she liked his intensity and also his writing, a fact which,

247

when stated by her, flipped him into a temporary Nirvana.

Certain frozen moments were glyph'd in his mind: Becky in a corona of brilliance: Becky of Eternity dancing like a backbending Egyptian sistrum-shaker painted on a potsherd: Becky the Rebel, who declared she was going to organize for liberation even in heaven.

She often wore a brown and tan striped dress with ruffles of the same material upon the bodice. Around her neck, stagecoach-robber style, she wore a triangl'd red kerchief tucked down into her bosom. Sam trembled to look at her.

They told each other how the thrills coursed through their soul, how happy they were to be together. Both, however, were inclined to scoff at a "peace-project love affair," a common phenomenon inflamed by project intensities, and which usually failed miserably. Accordingly, they tried to stay aloof, with rare public shows of affection, and in private they were only caresses and half-hour kissing sessions.

V

There wasn't much chatter after the accident. Trudge trudge, then a pause to talk with a local neophyte newsman from the radio station, then trudge trudge trudge. Becky was specially ablaze that afternoon, running this way and that in a gray skirt and heavy brown clodhoppers, leafleting distant farmers and children in yards. She was the finest leafleter. An obscure plowing machine moving on a distant hill would send her into a sprint; she had a strange custom of holding a clutch of leaflets at arm's length in front of her as she trotted across

248

a field to hand a leaf of peace to a startled farmer. Every mailbox passed by the march received a Becky leaflet.

At the end of the long day the walkers were very tired. In the words of Sam, they were "skincovered onto-burgers trudging through dust." For the editor of *The Shriek of Revolution* suffered sorely from foot chop-up. Why he should have chosen to walk Tennessee hills wearing tight, frictional-to-calf-muscle, knee-high riding boots had its origin perhaps in his well-known lickerish foot worship and hangups regarding toe bondage. The riding-boot heels had quickly worn down so that as he walked toward the Shiloh Baptist Church, the nails ground hamburgerly into his feet. Later he limped into the only cobbler's stall in the town where he ordered new heels covered with horseshoe-shaped metal taps, to be ready by trudge-time in the morn.

She carried several items in his baggage he figured would aid any unforeseen boredom. One was a clandestine packet of plans for the forthcoming issue of *The Shriek of Revolution*. He also carried a book on birdwatching, a small telescope (gaze, oh voyeur, gaze), and a copy of Hesiod's *Theogony* which he was in the process of translating into a pornolaliac epic of New York slang. Sam loved Hesiod—and would drive fellow walkers nuts with his howling renditions of the "Hymn to Hecate" section of *The Theogony*. He scoured the poem for clues to the course of Western civilization, shouting "aha! aha!" as he sang the clue-ridden dactyls of god-birth.

Like most of the walkers, Sam kept a journal in a notebook. He called his entries "Tennessee ecloques" as if the South were Boeotia. It was during this period that Sam began translating Sam Beckett's poetry (especially the poem *Enueg I*) into Attic Greek, endeavors rejected by every modern periodical from *Atlantic Monthly* to the *Kenyon Review*. Upon his trapezoidal-faced backpack were painted the wonderful words from *Oedipus at Colonus*, Τὸν ἅπαντα νικᾷ λόγον —i.e., better and groovier ne'er to have been born.

In his heart the strains of compulsive hedonism mixed with the bitter Manichean Nicht Nicht Nicht. He suffered from the malady of coldness. His demeanor was often a tundra of dryness, and never had he allowed anyone to look beneath the locks of his sullen heart where the grief coursed oceanic. And in the back of it all was this personal belief: I am going to flip out. A chattering filthy mouth and weird intense scholarship were means he used to cushion his belief. "I am a depressed Buddhist," he told himself, "and this will save me from being flapjacked into a hell of *mens insana in corpore delendo*."

His position on the manic-depressive scale depended— not necessarily on the quality of, but rather on the quantity of, his breakfast. Throughout the walk, he continued his Lower East Side practice of compiling a gorging morning shovelful of Yum to gobble. Yum, you will remember, was Sam's steady diet during those months, and consisted of a foundation of about a pound of uncooked oatmeal poured into his brown wood Zen Yum Bowl, as he called it. Into the oats were folded several raw eggs, a glop of Hellmann's mayonnaise, soy sauce, and very occasionally a splash of vodka. Sam attacked the Yum Bowl like a starved canine, filling the air with expressions of joy, slurps, slurgles and urgings for his sisters and brothers to share the delight. He revered his mode of breakfast, and rightly so—for sleepless drunken nights, ennui, fear, pain, metaphysical distress; all were conquered by morning Yum.

On the other hand, a shiny ovalness of Yum, garishly lit in the often fluorescent light of a church-basement morning congeries of sleepy peace walkers, was a less-than-mouth-watering, even repugnant, sight to the circle of eyeballs. It was the taste of Yum which was its thrill, however, and my mouth as I write these words, waters more lustfully for a Chinese porcelain spoon packed with Yum, than does my Faber-Castell pen ooze blackness. Ahh those days of Yum, eh Nelson?

At one time Sam had been a careless methedrine-shooting A-head. He had lived for the Flash, but threw his spike and dropper away during a demonstration outside the Bacteriological Warfare Center at Fort Detrick, Maryland—and ever since had been an enemy of the messengers of meth.

The Shiloh Baptist Church was located on the far outskirts of the village. It was a one-room wooden structure built up off the ground on posts. There was enough room under the church to crawl freely. The posts looked like legs and gave the church the appearance of a large walking box. There was farmland on one side of the church, a steep hill to the rear, and in front, between it and the roadway, the Crazy Bend River, actually more of a rivulet, sniveled through rocks on down past the gas station and the creamery.

That night there was a pot-luck supper sponsored by the local NAACP chapter, after which there was a fiery pacifist gospel meeting at the Shiloh Church. The meeting was more of a unity rally on the subject of civil rights than a debate on the nuances of unilateral disarmament. The minister was a woman with a great booming voice that could scare you into looking for ghosts and she could sing with such fervor that the dim-lit church pulsed with

251

Jesus-vectors. Even the atheists among the walkers were swaying and clapping, pretending for a few minutes that there could be such a thing as a graceful eternity.

Walk leader Bill Storm rose to address the crowd, delivering his "Fool for the Lord, Fool for Peace, Fool for Liberty" speech he had developed for such occasions, with an immense intensity. Who would have known that the suave French scholar could have moved even his fellow marchers so much, exposed as they had been to various versions of the speech in church after church.

There was an hour of singing, with everybody, walkers and congregationists, standing in a swaying circle holding hands while singing that Civil Rights/Gospel mixture that was so compelling. Spines shivered when they all hummed together while the minister sang "Were you there when they crucified my Lord," to a fantastic floating jazz piano background. Some order of Transcendence was achieved when the swaying circle sang "We Shall Overcome," especially the verse beginning "Hands around the world." At the meeting's end the circle hummed again, continuing the melody of "We Shall Overcome" while the minister uttered a searing prayer-chant-threnody to Jaweh God. "Deeper down than hell, wider than all heaven," was the Lord of whom she sang-spoke. It was the sort of experience the walkers would never cease to summon.

After the meeting was two hours over, Carole, Nelson, Sam and Becky walked out of the church, prior to bed, holding in mind a possible violation of Rules Number 6 and 8 of the walk discipline. They strolled down to the creek and along its bank until they found a spot downstream completely hidden by thick tree-growth and concealing boulders. They sat at the water edge and unstashed a super-secret pouch of cannabis which Sam

252

quickly rolled by flashlight. They were talking and quietly peace-puffing when "splomp!" the water splashed up over the foursome.

"Jesus, what kind of frog could make a splash like that?" Becky wanted to know. The splashes continued, then Sam got bonked by a loam-hunk on his sunburned arm. "Someone's throwing at us," he said, and scrambled to his feet, swallowing the roach.

"Yeah, let's get back inside. I believe we are being given a lecture by the rubicund necks."

Back in the church, they dismissed the event as just another item of weirdness. Soon the entire march was zipped up in its array of army-surplus sleeping bag cocoons. Sam and Becky lay near each other, each on top of a cushioned open-back pew. They were holding hands in the darkness, pew to pew, until one of them fell asleep and the arms droped away.

Suddenly it was as if Santa Claus and the reindeer were making an emergency landing on the metal church roof. Everyone awakened with a start. Several windows were smashed. The clod-ballers were at it again. They were throwing from the steep hill in back of the church so most clods were raining on the roof. After a whispered conference it was decided that a volunteer squad would take flashlights and approach the throwers for a nonviolent confrontation.

"Hey! Why are you throwing things at us? We are coming up to talk to you. We are completely unarmed! Do you hear us? We are a peace march on the way to Washington! Do you . . ."

Thunk, thunk, thunk, thunk, the hard clods fell. One marcher, a famous accident-prone organizer, felt his forehead split open as he advanced toward the barn whence the hurlers were hurling. Finally their flashlights located the culprits: a farmer and his two sons whose property was contiguous to the church's land.

The essence of the farmer's complaint, pried from him after a few minutes of hostile shouting, was this: "We don' mind you walking for peace and stuff lawk thet; whut we don' like to see is white girls and neegras sleeping in the same church."

The walkers explained as soothingly as possible that what they were doing was protected by the U.S. Constitution. The sons brandished their clods in reply. Besides, the walkers continued, they were leaving almost at sunrise, for they had a tough twenty-five-mile day ahead. Actually coming into contact with his enemy seemed to quell the farmer's anger. When they saw the farmer place a hand over a yawn, the walk realized the worst was over. Sensing a lull in the violence, Becky did not want to lose an opportunity to leaflet the farmer and sons, so she raced back into the church and brought back leaflets and a copy of a pamphlet recounting Danish resistance to the Nazis called *Tyranny Could Not Quell Them*.

They invited the farmer inside to check on sleeping arrangements and were rather surprised when magenta-neck and his loamy sons accepted and toured the church. As he paused at the door, his sons already returning up the pasture to their farmhouse, the farmer delivered rather chilly parting remarks. "You folks are gonna have trouble tomorrow. They had a Klan rally over in Toupou tonight. Ain' no neegras ever slept over that way ever. You in trouble. They gon' git ya, hyuf hyuf!"—the farmer breaking into cackles.

Sam was worried that Farmer John and company might try to set fire to the church so he resolved to sleep out in

254

back upon the woody hill as a sentry. He thought he had lodged a hint to Becky that she might join him there in the paradise of a shared sleeping bag—but his hint, so-called, was so vague as not to be a hint at all. What he had said to her was, "I'm going out back to sleep on the hill. See you in the morning." That was a hint?

VI

Early the next day the walk passed the dreaded line into Toupou County, Tennessee, where blacks weren't and asskick was. The advance crew quickly reported back that the church where they were supposed to crash that night had canceled. A public meeting at the town library had been nixon'd also when several gruff voices phoned in threatening a big book-burn. A search among religious institutions revealed a lack of Christ-like charity, and the walk was faced with a camp-out among the yahoos or perhaps a forced march throughout the night to reach another county.

There were dust-off attempts by the dozens—old road-sters swerving into the walk path. By the end of the day they were walking almost in the ditch. All along they were dogged by a reporter from the local radio station phoning in hostility reports every hour. The walk-support vehicle monitored the broadcasts on the radio. "Hello everybody, this is Vince Martinson, your Hound of Hillbilly Heaven, on Station JQLX, the Voice of the South, with a bulletin from our roving reporter out on Route Twenty-seven with the integrated Memphis to Washington Peace Walk. Come in, Wade Scurdy!"

Hi, Vince, the group has just passed Gorder's Dairy

255

Queen and is proceeding up the mountain. Sheriff's depu-
ties arrested Clint Murt, the nephew of Mayor Jack Murt
of Ellis City, for breaking the front window of one of the
vehicles which accompany the walkers. One of the girls
assures me that they walk every step of the way and that
the vehicles are only used to carry their leaflets and other
equipment. One of the walk leaders returned a few
minutes ago from town with the news that they were
turned down by the high-school athletic department for
permission to sleep in the school gym. The Veterans of the
Korean War offered to allow the marchers to camp out in
their skeet-shoot range providing the lights are left on
overnight; this was refused after a vote by the peace
marchers.
And so, Vince, at this moment the pacifists have no place
to stay tonight.

"Thanks Wade Scurdy; now let's hear Lettie Hunt and
her new cry-cry-cry sensation, *Tears on My Six-Pack. . . .*"

The march reached the top of Toupou Mountain by tortuous road and began the long steep twist down into the
town of Plinthane, Tennessee, the home of the State
Champion Plinthane Bulldogs and the county seat of
Toupou County. Cars of the curious were parked on both
shoulders, teenagers lounging and snickering on the
fenders and hoods. Some wonderful person rolled a sss-ing
cherry bomb toward the walk line but Nelson sacrificed
his tam-o'-shanter to the gods by dropping it on top of the
deadly firecracker, with the result that it was shredded.
Ha ha ha, went the scoffers. "Where's the niggers?" someone yelled, squinting at the line of sunburned peacelings.

By the time the walk had at wearily last reached the
gas-station edge of the town, they were singing defiantly

at top lung. This could have proved foolish for, in addition to "We Shall Overcome," the editorial board of *The Shriek of Revolution* found itself in a splinter group singing "When Is the U.S.A. Gonna Have a Left-Wing Government?"—a tune of no commercial potential from the liquid pen of Sam and Becky.

Standing directly in front of the city-limits sign the sheriff was waiting. He had one question: "You people have a place to stay?"—flashing an incarcerational smile. He hitched up his trousers as if it were possible for the thick brass-buckled belt to rise over the rotundity of his laundry-bag-shaped tum tum, and received the A.C.L.U. cover letter.

"A.C.L.U. huh! That's a Communist front organization, isn't it. Don't mean a thing to me. You haven't got a place to stay, that's what's important. I guess you ought to walk straight through to the county line. . . ." He chuckled. "Ole Bill Wintzer, he's the sheriff in the next county; I bet he'll take you out to breakfast, you all wander into town about dawn. It's only sixteen miles."

Just about the time the sheriff was orating, Bill Storm arrived in the station wagon with the extremely helpful news that he'd found shelter for them in the only Unitarian Church for fifty miles. Overjoyed, the walkers piled into the vehicles and put kilometers between themselves and the hostile Tennies.

The minister was waiting for them outside his brand new brick church. His face was smooth and the color of flan. He wore clear plastic-framed glasses, and looked a bit like McGeorge Bundy. He was obviously nervous about the whole matter; his hand trembled clutching a copy of the walk discipline as he faced the tired end-of-the-day peacelings unloading their gear with a you-will-obey! stare.

257

He turned to Bill Storm. "We want to make certain, Mr. Storm, that no one uses the phone, that no one enters my office, that no one removes any foodstuffs, that no one enters the church proper, that men and women sleep in separate rooms."

"Certainly, Reverend Miller, certainly."

The good minister must have been moonlighting for some sort of intelligence agency because he was wearing a weighty photo shop of equipment around his neck, including a small Minox camera with the measuring chain for photographing documents.

It was a laugh. "What's he gonna photograph with that," Nelson wanted to know, "our grocery list?"

"Nah, our secret hoard of Polish money orders."

Whatever his purpose, the good Reverend Miller began to take pictures from all angles. He must have taken 250 snaps, with particular care to get front and side zaps of each walker.

Since it was Saturday night there was a virtual train of automobiles of the bored slowly circling the county courthouse bumper to bumper. Some of the walkers went to the courthouse to leaflet the old-timers sitting on the benches. At the church the walk steering committee was trying to hold an internal meeting to plan forthcoming demonstrations at defense plants. Beer cans were clunking regularly against the fane's front door as cars peeled by.

Soon there was the rrrrrrr of a siren and the sheriff screeched to a halt outside. He was flustered as he broke into the meeting room surrounded by a passel of his associates. "They gon' burn this church down if we don't get you out of here. You'll have to come with us."

The pacifists protested most vigorously, but the sheriff

was firm. "Please, please, I don' want to hear anything about the A.C.L.U. We have the obligation to protect you. And the only place we know for sure where you'll be safe is in the armory."

"Oh, no!" four walkers groaned at once.

Just before their incarceration, Sam and Becky managed to sneak a phone call to New York to the Total Assault Cantina. "John! John!" Becky shouted. "They're going to lock us up in some sort of National Guard armory. They say—that is the sheriff says—that the Klan is out to do us in. Can you call the wire services and *The New York Times* for us? Ask them to call down here to inquire about our safety. It may keep us from getting hurt. We're really shaking in our shoes!"

They were transported in squad cars to the Toupou National Guard installation which, with its turrets, battlements, and long, thin vertical windows built of greasy, charred-looking brick, seemed more suitable for crossbow warfare than modern militaristics.

The walkers were herded rather roughly into a large basement classroom in the armory, and the door was locked behind them. They cleared away the chairs and lecture charts and the women rolled out their sleeping bags at one end, the men at the other. In the center of the room was a brass catafalque upon which was mounted a machine gun in cross-section, which apparently the Guard used for training purposes. No one seemed eager to sleep near the catafalque. There was a large mirror on the wall between two blackboards which reflected the weapon. There was a sign printed on the mirror's upper frame: DRESS NEAT! "This is hell," Becky announced, and scrawled a red lipstick message on the glass above the reflected machine gun and beneath DRESS NEAT!

Welcome to Styx
Population 12

They had made no agreement to meet, but it was less than an hour after the lights were turned out that they crawled toward one another in the gloom and found each other's mouths at the base of the sawed-away machine gun. It was a suitable occasion for their first loving. Becky lifted up a leg and rested it upon the machine gun and they padded a sleeping bag beneath them. There were the sounds of zippers unzipping and then the game of silence, as others listened, but could not see, to the silent caresses and stifled breathing of a peace-walk floor-fuck.

VII

The next morning was a beautiful Sunday in Tennessee. They were ordered to leave the armory's premises as crudely as they had been ordered to enter. After breakfast back at the Unitarian Church, the walk decided to hold a short demonstration outside a church where it had been learned many of the town's outstanding citizens attended services.

The church was a beautiful specimen. It was built of large gray stones with rough convex faces. There were tall white fluted columns across the front of the church and upon the frieze above the architrave was a stained-glass window depicting a crook-bearing Jesus and a woolly lamb. There were fifteen white steps spreading like a fan from the columns down to the pot-holed boulevard. There the peace marchers slowly circled, holding their signs, handing out leaflets, waiting for church services to be ended so they could lay some peace data on the congregation.

From within the church they could hear an impassioned plea by the minister for sinners and I-see-the-Lighters to come forth to "be reborn again in the name of Jesus." The minister led his flock in a perfervid rendition of "Just as I am, O Lamb of God"—during which singing the sinners were supposed to come forward.

There was a final prayer and when the deacon opened the white perfect doors and the black robes of the minister swooshed upon the doorsteps to shake hands. Out moiled a Sears & Roebuck catalogue of spiffiness—seventy-five or so neat people gossiping on the steps, no one paying any attention at all to the leafleting pacifists.

There was one couple that lingered in conversation with the minister on the steps. The man wore a brown flannel suit and a flat-top haircut with just a hint of the ducktails he might have worn back in high school. The woman was attired in a very plain sacrifice-everything-for-the-children dress and winter coat. Daughter A was dressed in white socks, white shoes, white bonnet, white sweater, white crinoline. Daughter B was dressed the same but all in yellow.

While Mom and Dad were encountering the minister, Daughter B wandered down the steps toward the marchers. Once within arm range, Becky handed her a leaflet and bent down to talk with her. "Hi! Do you know why we're here?"

"No."

"We're passing through town on the way to Washington. We're going to walk all the way to tell people never to fight with one another, to throw away their guns, never to drop bombs. . . ."

Meanwhile Daddy Flat-top had spotted his daughter

talking to Becky and trotted down the steps, removing his coat, his face tone becoming borscht-like. The first thing he did was utter a strange sound, "Kwoakh!" which was a mouth action to garner saliva followed by a quick spit into Becky's face.

He grabbed the leaflet from his stunned daughter and tore it up. And only minutes after reception of the wine and bread of Jesus, Flat-top went crazy. "I fought for my country, you little bitch!"—pointing to his Marine Corps tattoo (he had removed his shirt also) on his shoulder near where oft he rolled his Lucky Strike pack up into his T-shirt sleeve.

"We're sorry you're upset, sir," Sam butted in while Becky mopped away the Eucharist-tinged spittle.

The man raised his fist at Sam. "The sheriff ought to round you all up and kill you in the town square. Machine-gun you. That's what happens to scum! You bums!" All around the raver the churchgoers were silent. Several approached marchers and took leaflets, asking questions, one or two apologizing.

But the man foamed onward. Soon the sheriff arrived and the deputies dispersed the crowd, enabling the march to saunter away. Sam and Becky paused to kiss, leaning up against the sheriff's vehicle. Becky handed the officer a copy of Bartley's book, *National Defense Through Nonviolent Resistance*. "I hope you read it, Sheriff. We'll be seeing you"—waving goodbye and turning to stroll.

"Fuck him," Sam muttered, walking hand in hand with Becky out of the Sunday village.

Raked Sand

"THOMAS JEFFERSON, George Washington, Aristotle, Plotinus—all dead, all down on Uncle J's worm-farm, but we, we're *alive!*"—beating his chest, "We're alive!"

"Millard! Another round of 'arf and 'arf for Nelson and myself"—feeling in his pocket to make sure he had the fifty cents to pay for it. They were sitting in Stanley's Bar waiting for Kennedy's speech on the Cuban situation, for there was not only no TV set in their apartment, there was no electricity.

"If Kennedy zip-guns the Russians we *all* may be down at Uncle J's."

The Soviet build-up had first been publicized in September. Sam heard of it by word of bar-babble, since he had not read a newspaper in five years. "No time to dig everybody dying man. I have books to read." Jesus, he thought all this war puke had gone away. "So you say Cuba's got the big ones now?"—he asked, nervously writing

                    Lost lost
                        lost
                            lost
            lost
                lost
                    lost
in beer-ooze upon the oaken bar top.

Nelson tried to explain it to Sam: "Well, mu'f', because 'sixty-two is a congressional election year—you do know that, don't you, Sammy?"

Sammy did not know.

"The rocket-breaths in the Republican party—that is, the candidates and their ilk, were out there waving the flag whispering the Democrats are weak punks wanting the people in Kansas to hurry up and learn Russian, before the Big Parade.

"Russia began to ship bombers and rockets into Cuba. I'd be willing to bet it's shit for shat for U.S. rocket emplacements in Turkey. Anyway, Kennedy was out there last week campaigning for the Dems, when all of a sudden the CIA began to flash him some data about nuclear missile bunkers down in C. So he was called back to Washington. They said he had a head cold."

According to Nelson, the Kennedy brothers remained in the war room all the weekend of October 20 and 21. The code-scramblers were churning with messages back and forth between Kennedy and Khrushchev. The president announced he would address the nation on Monday night, October 22, 1962.

Wave after wave of fear spewed from the media. There was an extraordinary amount of Cuba-hate already present in the country. Fear: Russians force U.S. out of naval base in Guantánamo. Fear: Russians zap access to Panama. Fear: Russians brick out space and missle facilities at Cape Canaveral. Fear: Cuban-type governments in other Latin countries. Fear: Mafia never to get back its Havana casinos.

The Joint Chiefs of Staff were instructed to stick around D.C. Vice-President Johnson was called back early from a trip to Hawaii. Twenty-five Commie ships were supposedly on the way to Cuba with chop-up parts. Soviet *Ilyushin-28* bombers capable of carrying nukes were being uncrated and assembled in Cuba.

Grovel, beatnik, grovel.

In response, the U.S. Navy and Marine Corps were beginning to stage a hostility scene in the Caribbean, with forty U.S. ships hanging out off the isle of Vieques near Puerto Rico. Twenty thousand servicemen, including six thousand marines, were ready to hit the bricks. The way Nelson was telling it to Sam, somewhat in the manner of someone telling a midnight ghost story in a graveyard, was making Sam twitch.

The Strategic Air Command was placed on alert world wide, meaning flight patterns with doom-nukes in the direction of Russian cities at all times. Even the American troops garrisoned in Berlin were alerted for imminent chop-up. God knows, Nelson said, what sort of instructions were given to the fleet of Polaris submarines with their rockets each coded to destroy a specific Russian city, sliding in the Russian seas.

Evacuation was ordered for dependents at Guantánamo Naval Base. *The New York Times*—Nelson handing him a clip—had printed high-altitude CIA photos of intermediate-range ballistic missile facilities being gouged into the Cuban mountains, with a kill range of .two thousand nautical miles.

Shit in fear, beatnik punk.

That Saturday, the right-wing Cuban exile group Alpha-66, vowed publicly that its "naval units" would sink-snuff any British merchant vessels it discovered in Cuban territorial waters. When Sam heard that, he broke out into the song,

Cuba Si, Yankee No
Get the hell out of Guantánamo

lifting high his brown-black 'arf and 'arf.

"Shut up!" someone shouted. "The speech is about to begin."

Nelson adjusted his chair for total tube. He was wearing his kilt, a tam-o'-shanter, his Scottish colors, silver-buckled shoes, and rabbitskin sporran or waist pouch. "If we go, I want to go in my colors," he said.

Kennedy spoke for eighteen minutes. The tone, the somber convoluted doom-tinged eloquence, something gave the president's speech a fearful Poe-like quality. He announced that a total blockade of Cuba would begin at 10 A.M. on Wednesday morning, just thirty-some hours away. Not a slurp was slurped along the bar counter.

Kennedy banned all surface-to-air missiles, bomber aircraft, bombs, air-to-surface rockets, warheads, guided missiles, and rocket-support matériels. All ships entering Cuban waters would be inspected. He announced that the missiles in Cuba could strike as far north as the Hudson Bay and as far south as Lima, Peru.

"We're in trouble, Sam." Sam was sweating. The consensus in the bar was that there was going to be a war.

266

"We'll all die of leuk, that is, if our eyes don't melt"—Nelson shuddered.

"Shhh!"—they shouted along the bar.

"Seventh, and finally, I call upon Chairman Khrushchev to halt and eliminate the clandestine, reckless and provocative threat to world peace and to stable relations between our two nations.

"I call upon him further to abandon this course of world domination and to join in an historic effort to end the perilous arms race and to transform the history of man.

"He has an opportunity now to move the world back from the abyss of destruction. We have no wish to war with the Soviet Union, for we are a peaceful people who desire to live in peace with all other people. . . ." Nelson began to hiss at this point, but the barkeep reached over and jostled his arm to silence.

"Any hostile move anywhere in the world against the safety and freedom of peoples to whom we are committed including in particular the brave people of West Berlin will be met by whatever action is needed."

After the speech, Nelson looked at his friend Sam and in his deepest voice said, "I'm going to get fuuuuuuuuucked up!"

As of frig-up, they sat drinking tequila with clam juice till 4 A.M., closing time when the wet, staggering, skin-covered meat phantoms walked home.

All during the next day the tension grew, mostly in silence. There were no street riots, no shouts from any outraged opposition. There were a lot of sullen humans herding sullenly. The Liberal Party of New York busted its chops to send off a telegram of support to the president. Only a sliver of the population shook its fist. In office buildings, it was like the World Series all over again as the typing pool sneaked quick listens to radios in desks.

The stock market was unhappy. A day or so later when Premier Khrushchev wrote Bertrand Russell to state that he would not go nuke-batty or take rash action in the crisis, the stock prices rose in a brisk rally, thus enabling Soviet NKVD stock-market operatives, disguised as Wallstreeters, to reap a wheaty bundle.

There was another night before the impending doomsday blockade which Nelson and Sam again spent mugging their livers with tequila and clam juice.

The morning of the imposition of the blockade was awful. A dilapidated airplane hangar full of old shoes blew up in his stomach every time Sam tried to move. He dragged his crushed-turtle-on-highway body to work an hour late. Mr. Ironheart, the head of the purchasing department, was upset.

"Piss on you"—Sam muttered, pulling his neck low into his old Navy highneck sweater so that his boss could not cop a visual on the grease-gray shirt Sam'd been wearing a week straight.

"What did you say?"

"I said, 'misty clue.' It's the last day of Pompeii, Mr. Ironheart."

"That's not what it sounded like."

During lunch Sam watched people on the street flag down passing cabs to get the latest on the blockade from the radio. There was a lot of Goodbye Cruel World chatter at the water cooler. Then it dawned on him that on today, of all days, he should probably be able to summon up courage to do something so outrageous as to get himself fired, that he might suck up at last those sacred twenty-six weeks of unemployment checks.

When he should have been writing letters to expedite furniture deliveries, Sam typed idly. In a cloud of boredom, he typed "Don't Care Don't Care Don't Care" for fifteen pages, and mailed the "work"—at office expense—to *Fuck You/A Magazine of the Arts,* which protested it would print anything.

He opened up his desk drawer to fondle his trusty ashtray full of morning glory seeds. He gnashed several between his incisors, swallowed, and waited fifteen minutes for that stomach-wall thickness-flash. His hangover blended marvelously with the morning glory effect: i.e., of having stomach walls six inches thick filled with unspeakable fermented micturitions. But the colors flashing before him as he typed, they were pleasant.

His problem: how to confront the despicable wolverine of the purchasing department. Sam, he told himself, it's the end of the world maybe, and you can't even climb on some puke-suck in order to get fired! Come on!

But he couldn't do it. His blesséd early life had endowed him with a single overriding principle: when in trouble, fawn. He wouldn't have seriously hassled his boss if the ashes from the volcano were raining in the window.

He was contemplating puking, his stomach walls feeling like some sort of three-ply wineskin, when Ironheart buzzed for him. Now is my chance! He shoved open Ironheart's door and pushed the papers askew grabbing open the ritzy box of H. Upmann cigars which had payola'd its way there on Christmas.

"Hey!"

"Hey what, Mr. Ironheart? These are Cuban cigars. It cannot be that you will continue to smoke these when our country prepares to destroy Fidel! Shame on you!" Sam picked one out, bit off the tip, and tongue-flicked it upon the carpet, also a Christmas gift for granting the university carpeting contract to the correct company.

"Yes, Sam, you seem to be upset. And certainly, I believe you are right. I *will* throw these cigars away. They were not very legal to begin with." Sam could not believe it, watching those unemployment checks vanish.

"Mrs. Hutchinson, please show Sam out of the office. He is apparently not feeling well."—into his intercom. Sam walked out, forgetting to scrunch down to hide his filthy collar.

"I am a coward!"—Sam spoke out loud, chewing morning glory seeds back at his desk, the office faces lifting toward the sentence. One of the Sipletto sisters was sneaking a listen to her radio. "Are there any battles?"—Sam yelled over, much too loudly for Miss Sipletto who frowned at him.

"They ought to blow up the whole island"—she replied.

Anger pushed him. "Cuba Si, Yankee No!"—he bellowed in the startled office. He waved the *Times* at them. "This is a fear scene, all of it. All these circles of destruction, bah! The Democrats just want to get reelected! And the Republicans are death breaths!"—hoping to get Ironheart's attention. "What about *our* Polaris subs with H-bomb missiles right at the mouth of the Volga, man!"

"I am not man. I am Lois Sipletto. Now lower your voice or I'll go right in to see Mr. Ironheart!"

"Please do,"—he replied, almost with a tone of supplication. "Maybe you can get me on unemployment."

After work, he treated himself to dinner at Total Assault Cantina. Nelson joined him. "Hey, Sam, this may be our last meal on earth, baby. Next stop, Saint Peter's pizzeria."

"Well, last day or not, I'm never going back to my job. I'm never going to work again for the rest of my life."

"Did you hear that Louise Adams is throwing an End-of-the-World party tonight over at Mindscape Gallery?"

"She is!?"—Sam was excited. "Uh, is Barton the Bonfire back in town?"

"Yes he is. Why don't you give up, Sam? They're in love."

"Bullshit! Bah! Barton just wants to make sure her paintings and superior skills never leave the Lower East Side. That guy is a ghoul. Who's paying for the party?"

"Louise. I talked with her on the phone. She said, 'I sold a painting so tonight we celebrate the death of the West.'"

"You see? What did I tell you! That fucker will be standing at the door like it was his scene, praying for an art collector to come."

They went back to the apartment to get ready for the party. Sam underwent his fortnightly prefornication ablutions in the kitchen tub. Tonight is the night, he told himself. Tonight I shall declare my, my, my. . . . What I'll do is get drunk and high, and ride in on her mind in a Byronic hurricane. To hell with Barton!

Prior to departure, they assembled their meager hoard of dope upon the kitchen table: two capsules of yohimbine (a vaunted aphrodisiac then in vogue among the poets and artists), three roaches salvaged from the ashtrays, one Asthmadoro cigarette ("Forget that!" Nelson exclaimed, remembering his friend who had eaten a teaspoon of one and was found standing on her head in the corner carrying on an imaginary conversation with Samuel Beckett; her heart stopped beating three times in the emergency room), six buttons of peyote, four capsules of amyl nitrite, twenty-seven morning glory seeds, two caps of mescaline, one quart of vodka.

Nelson surveyed the pitiful thrill-pile. "What a poor inventory of pleasure with which to usher in The Fall." Nevertheless, in a fast flurry of indulgence they smoked the roaches, ate the peyote/mescaline/morning glory seeds, popped the amyl nitrite, chug-drank three glasses of vodka, then rushed out to the street toward Louise's party.

Sam chuckled to himself as he swallowed the spansule of bitter legendary yohimbine bark (supposedly an import from Africa used by veterinarians at stud farms) just as he danced down the metal steps into the Mindscape Gallery, glancing all directions for his favorite painter.

"Where is she! I love her, I love her! Louise!"

As befitting the world's end, Mindscape was packed. The jittery partisans of Beauty were there, talking too loudly, drinking and smoking too much.

Sam's position was this: Louise Adams just *thought* she was in love with Barton Macintyre. Macintyre was the type that was a compulsive framer, who, if after a hard day turning out major works, had not put at least ten in frames, signed and ready for the checkbook, was unhappy indeed. "He also frames women!" Sam snorted, looking up at the paintings Macintyre was storing at Mindscape.

Sam sometimes went up to Times Square where he

bought old sheet music to popular 1950s songs, underlining key phrases of bliss, and mailed them to Louise, anonymously of course. He had mailed her lots of old 45s also, like "Hearts Made of Stone," "Heartbreak Hotel," and "Mood Indigo," again anonymously. He was hooked.

Sam was bold enough when drunk. But being drunk, and stoned on yohimbine, while attending an End-of-the-Universe teleo-Bacchic dope-grope, this set him on fire. But how could he speak privately to Louise Adams in such a revel? He decided to lie in wait for her in the gloom (he had unscrewed the lightbulb) by her loftbed in the small back storage room, a spot all would have to pass to get to the toilet. He leaned with an arrogant shove against a tied-up packet of Barton's *oeuvres*, chugging down toward the dregs of a small demijohn of vintage Flatbush '62. It seemed like hours before Louise finally walked into the room and nobody else was there.

"Louise," Sam began, "I am tired of sending you phantom plastic!"—thinking this to comprise a firm enough hint that he was the one'd sent the old 45s. "I will confess, Louise, well, I want to touch your boooooooody!"—adding a bit of humor to ease the uncertainty, as he continued blocking the entrance to the bathroom.

"You know, Louise. Barton has spoiled everything with the brutish imperium—it's really a blockade, you know—he has placed on your *soul*, Louise. Maybe if this wasn't the end of Western civilization, ha ha, I wouldn't say it, but, I, I, need you. I swoon, I fail, I. . . ." breaking off into a paraphrase of Sappho.

Suddenly she was against him. She kissed him and cured Sam's schizophrenia in an instant with her tenderness. "I promise," she replied, "if the world doesn't get blown up, I promise to come over one of these nights—

273

and then we'll touch each other's booooooooodies!"—
mimicking but smiling.

Sam melted with happiness. But meanwhile the yohimbine was working him up into a state of panting, bristling
ardor. Sam's family curse (Thou shalt fail, O earth-punk
thou shalt fail) visited him once again as Macintyre had to
return just at that moment from the liquor store, breaking
up Sam's furtive kiss-flash with the woman he felt possibly
the reincarnation of Elizabeth Barrett Browning.

Sam hacked the mini-tented front of his trousers, feeling obliged to push down perforce the evidence of the
apparently permanent hardness. Then he rejoined the
party, now degenerating slowly into a doom-hoot. The
drunken revelers waved back and forth in a circle singing,
"Neow is the howr, when wee muss' say goodbeye. Soon
we'ull be saaaayling. . . ."

All of a sudden Sam was nude, standing with an erection like an ectomorphic herm. He began to sing a Hank
Williams song to which no one—not even Sam—knew the
words. But nothing stopped the sex-maddened young
human who twang-sang onward but found himself suddenly uttering chyme. Difficult 'twas to sing while the
bitter fingers of barf crawled up the throat. He lunged to
the dark pissoir, still singing—

> *I saw the light! I saw the light!*
> *No more darkness, no more night*
> *Then Jesus came like a stranger in the night*
> *Praise the Lord, I saw the . . .*

"Blooey!"—Sam tossed the omelet, the yohimbine, the
vodka, the morning glory seeds, the peyote, into the porcelain vortex. Naked, voiding his stomach, membrum

274

prepared on the nonce to spume scoriaceously, he fell down striking his matted head, heaving again again, holding the bowl, head passing out on the rim, suave and cool, Sam, suave and cool.

He slept there fully for about ten. Refreshed, Sam strode back into the party to claim his attire, which he rapidly donned, and spoke the classic line of a cookie-tossed drunk: "I've got to get something on my stomach."

He caromed from building to building, pausing at the dark stoops, leaning against the railings, as if it were raining, toward The House of Nothingness café. Four cups of coffee and a sandwich later, Sam felt aglow, although the yohimbine and the vodka still had their electrodes in his hypothalamus.

He walked into the chilly courtyard back of Nothingness to sit by the rock garden. He had always loved the raked white sand, the parallel lines that undulated in the raked waves—the autumn moon through the haze. "White! White!"—he shouted. He sprawled down upon the sand, upsetting a section of the perfect raking, his arms spread wide, his legs too, trying to fill up the empty sand in a moment of drunken horror vacui.

He splashed cupped hands of sand upon himself. "Nobody. Nobody. No cause, no hope!"—he whispered. He threshed about wildly in the sand.

"No brain! No brain! I ain't got no brain! No brain." He crawled toward the boulders—three of them closely spaced on the far side, with the sand raked in a neat circle around the triad. The only boulders, the rest just sand. Triad in white. No brain. No brain.

Still on his knees, he began to batter the top of his head into the rocks. "No brain No brain No brain No brain. I ain't got no brain! No brain!" Shouting till he was hoarse and the blood, like wet-weather springs, bubbled beneath his locks. Matted his locks. His head dabbing rough red smudges on the triad. No brain no brain.

He rolled in the white, red blotch here, red splotch there. He grabbed a fistful and jammed it in his mouth, bitter from the chewings of the night, the admixture of smokestack grunge, the incinerators. He tried to spit it out but the granules coated his tongue, teeth, mouth-roof. Some rolled down his throat and he coughed severely. Then he lay still, cried softly.

Several beers had still not rinsed away the white granules. Nelson had joined him at Stanley's Bar. Conflicting reports were tossed along the counter: Russian ships were trying to run the blockade. Or Russian ships had turned back rather than submit to forcible boarding.

It wasn't long before Sam got himself into a near fistfight with some beer-necked philosopher who kept talking about Iwo Jima. "I was there. It's the same. Up and down are one. If we die, so will they. It's a perfect circle."

"The hell it is"—Sam blurted. "Don't give me any of your Iwo jive! You fought for a corpse. Cuba Si! Yankee No!"

The man rose off the stool and made a fist. Sam suddenly remembered the anecdote he'd read about Hemingway and James Joyce who were out drinking in some Paris dive. Joyce was nearly blind and got into a quarrel. The fists were ready to bash and Joyce reached up to try

276

to adjust his glasses, staring into the bleariness, shouting, "Deal with him, Hemingway! Deal with him!"

"Deal with him, Nelson, deal with him!" Sam growled in his most affected voice, a combination of British prison movies and Midwest twang. "Cuba Si!"

That got him a fist in the mouth, hurting his teeth to the roots and splitting his lip-skin. Through an immediate calm-down and through earnest imprecation, Sam managed to avoid getting eighty-sixed from Stanley's. Nelson led him to a back table to sulk.

Nelson had some bad news. "Sam," he said, "I'm going back to Chattanooga. Maybe I'll go to law school. Or perhaps I can get back in at Heidelberg. Something besides this chaos. I've got to get out of the Lower East Side or I'll go nuts"—looking at Sam patting his throbbing head, a curling of coagulated blood down his chin.

"What would Elizabeth Gurley Flynn and Emma Goldman say to you going to law school?"—Sam replied scornfully. That's all Nelson used to talk about, the exploits of those two. Goldman's autobiography was like the *I-Ching* or the *Bhagavad-Gita* to him.

"I should have gone on to Heidelberg," Nelson continued. "By now I'd have my doctorate in theology. And I can just see my book, *The Husserl/Aquinas/Goldman Synapse*, on the presses right now!"

Sam tried to interrupt him with a few atheistic sneers. But he remembered too well Nelson's arrival on the East Side, where he'd planned to visit the *Catholic Worker's* House of Hospitality for a few days, and then it was off to Europe to study. It was perhaps the wonderful lure of hemp, of anarcho-pacifist Catholicism, and the poetry scene, the beautiful bars, the sex, which caused him to cash in his steamer ticket for a pad deposit.

Nelson did soon leave the Lower East Side for law school. Not too long ago he ran as a left-wing Democrat for the Tennessee State Assembly. Little does he know of the syndicate formed by some of us former Eastsiders who hold in a safety deposit vault certain 16-mm films of Nelson and Cynthia Pruitt in a bathtub of kasha varnishkes, which may well make him the first genuine movie-star president, should his *cursus honorum* carry him that far up the ziggurat of power.

"All out! All out!"—Millard shouted, piling the chairs atop the doomed wood. Sam watched Nelson leave with Cynthia, biting his lip.

"Hey Nelson!"—Sam yelled, running out into the street where he handed him the last spansule of yohimbine. Nelson smiled and uttered a silent cackle, and gave Sam a quick slap of five.

Back at the apartment, Sam rolled his final reefer. He counted his candles. There were twenty-four. He placed them in a semicircle around his couch. He crawled half-way into his sleeping bag which smelled like burnt goose feathers from an accident on a peace walk.

He crossed his arms upon his chest, looking pharaonically cool. "This may be the last night. Thank God."

If I die, he thought, I'm gonna continue the struggle. I ain't gonna take nothin' from nobody. He fantasized a hieroglyphic headline: BEATNIK REFUSES TO PICK GRAIN IN YARU FIELDS, OSIRIS UPSET.

Then he lit the circle of candles. He thought about his mother who used to walk him and his brother home after the movies past the graveyard, telling stories of the vengeance of King Tut. "Next galaxy! Next galaxy!"—he mocked.

278

He could hear the woman next door listening to the radio. He prayed to his mother. Forgive me mother that I closed the door. Tears in the young man's eyes beneath his throbbing fontanel.

A Book of Verse

A CARLOAD OF them drove a hundred and fifty miles to the state university for a fraternity weekend during the spring of 1957. They were all graduating seniors at a high school in a small town near the Missouri-Kansas border. Some of them were thinking about attending State U. so they thought, what the hell, why not let themselves be beered and fed free by obliging fraternities.

They left early in the morning in order to arrive in time for the afternoon beer and barbecue party. He wore his forty-five-dollar R. H. Macy flannel suit with the pink and blue flecks he and his mother had bought for the homecoming dance in 1956.

When they arrived at the state university they were early so they killed time by driving around the campus. He spotted the campus bookstore so he said, "Hey, let's stop and check it out." There was a bit of grumbling, but they whipped into the lot and went inside. It was the usual campus bookstore of the time, with heavy emphasis on thick expensive textbooks written by professors cleaning up on sales to captive students. There was a poetry section and a section dealing with what was called then 'the paperback revolution."

They stayed about a half-hour before the urge to guzzle beer tugged them outward. He purchased C. M. Bowra's *Creative Experiment,* plus *Three Ways of Thought in Ancient China* by Arthur Waley, and *Howl* by Allen Ginsberg. That's about all he could afford. Buying *Howl* was a last-minute decision. He had read an article somewhere about a court case and obscenity charges, and he had liked, when glancing at it in the store, the last lines of the William Carlos Williams introduction. And it only cost seventy-five cents so he grabbed it.

The trip visiting the fraternity was otherwise uneventful except that he threw up into the waterfall of a local fancy restaurant when he was drunk. That guaranteed him an invitation to pledge the fraternity. Puking, the symbol of the Fifties.

When he got back home, he read *Howl* and was stunned. Here was a young man whose family had prepared a map of life for him that included two avenues, either a) law school (like his uncle Milton), or b) to work in his father's dry-goods store. *Howl* ripped into his mind like the tornado that had uprooted the cherry tree in his backyard when he was a child. He began to cry. He rolled all over the floor of his bathroom crying. He walked down the stairs in the middle of the night to wake his parents and read it to them. His mother threatened to call the state police. His father went to work an hour early the next morning.

He could not go to school that day, but walked into the field behind his house and strode back and forth all day along a barbed-wire fence shouting and moaning the book in front of a bunch of cows. Over and over he "howled" the poem, till much of it was held in his mind and he'd close his eyes and grab the book, almost tearing it, and shriek passages, stamping the ground. "God! God!" he yelled, "God!" He fell and rolled in the dirt, laughing and shouting, scaring the wet-nosed cows who ran up the hill.

When he returned to school the next day he was a changed person. "Holy holy holy holy holy holy," he must have chanted that word, in long continuous singsong sentences, at least four or five thousand times a day. He felt great. Every care assumed before evaporated. He read the poem to anybody who would listen to him and he got into trouble almost immediately. First it was shop class.

In shop class he had been working for almost the entire school term on a walnut spice cabinet for his mother. It was just about finished after a tortuous slow-motion construction process common to every shop class of the time. In fact, he had finished the project too quickly and was caught having to sand the cabinet for about five straight class days. Then he brought *Howl* to shop class. That day the teacher was called away for a teachers' conference so the students were left on their own, their activities observed by the class snitch.

The bell had barely ended when he began to read the poem to his shopmates, who stood for it for several minutes, staring at him; then right before his eyes they began to go about their business of sawing, soldering, sanding and gluing. He couldn't believe it. Then they started talking loudly as he read, perhaps as a hint. Finally one of them walked over to him and said, "I don't understand what you're howling about"—and poked a bony forearm into his ribs; "Howling, get it? Yar har har!" And a bunch of shopsters joined in to elevate yar har.

He kept on reading the poem, however, and when done, he walked over to his spice cabinet. He pulled a woodburning tool out of the storage shelves and wood-burned a quote upon the door of the spice cabinet:

I saw the best minds
of my Generation
destroyed by madness

which he left on the teacher's desk.

When he arrived in shop class the next day, he found a note taped to the howl cabinet from Mr. Russell the teach: "Take this with you and please go at once to the principal's office. He is expecting you."

"Johnny," the principal paused—"about this spice cabinet"—picking it up. "Now, we know the source of this quote and we feel it inappropriate for a boy of your background to dabble in such filth."

"What do you mean filth?" he replied. "There's nothing filthy about that sentence."

"Let's not kid ourselves, Johnny. What you allude to in this woodburned"—pausing for words, "woodburned stupidity is immoral and suggestive. It's the despicable ravings of a homo. And we both know the implications of that."

The boy couldn't think of anything to match his indignation. "I think it's great. It's going to change the world. There'll be something new come out of this poem. Things will never be the same."

"Nothing new will ever come to *this* town from this obscene filth, believe you me." The principal tugged at the corner of the flag on his desk.

"You just wait," the boy replied.

"Get out of here!" the principal ordered and gave him a light shove. Tears welled in the boy's eyes. "And I'm going to call up your parents. We can't have you polluting our school with filth. Now get on out of here. Do not—you hear me? Look at me! Do not *ever* recite any part of this poem again on school property, do you understand?"

"I'll recite anything I want any time!"

"Get out. You are expelled from school for three days. I'll just call your mother,"—reaching for an index file.

The boy paused at the door and taunted the principal: "I saw the best minds of my generation destroyed by madness starving hysterical *naked!!*" then ran out to the parking lot and drove home in his pickup truck.

He returned to school three days later wearing what he wanted and saying what he pleased. Gone were the days of shoe polish, clean shirts, and paste-on smiles. He began to spend almost all of his time writing poetry. Things went oddly but smoothly until his senior writing class was assigned to write some poems, which were to be read aloud in class. For days he worked on a howling master-piece. He typed various versions and gradually the poem evolved into the rageful shape he desired. It was a rather lengthy twenty-seven pages and there was a language problem. He knew he could never get away with the word *fuck* or other similar words. For a while he thought he could get away with *screw* if he, say, mumbled it during the recitation. Finally he chose the word *planked*— good old Missouri locker-room lingo.

Friday arrived and the teacher made each student walk to the head of the class to read their poems. When it was his turn he shuffled forth, stood, eyed the teacher, and began: "This poem is titled *Springtime Shriek.*" Right at that moment the nervousness overcame him, and there

was a twitch of his hand, and half the poem fluttered to
the floor. Gray dabs of floor-dirt covered his fingers, as he
reached down frantically to grab up the sheets before the
teacher could help him. Then he read:

They dragged their fingers through
their skulls and sang in ambrosia

They lay in the shanks of the night
and screamed for the morn
and dawn was planked atremble on the
couch of the hill

They pulled three aces straight
before they drew the black nine
in the void of cards

They cried for food without profit
They saw in a vision the wheat pour from the
bins enough for the roar of centuries
and drank the champagne of God's eye

They screwed. . . .

"Wait a minute young man!" the teacher roared. "No
one's going to read any filth in *my* classroom! I won't and
never will stand for it! Now you take that nonsense with
you down to the principal's office right now. Scat!"

He didn't even bother to go to the office but instead
drove downtown to play pool at Ernie's Tavern. There
was fifty cents riding on the game near the end, and he
leaned low over the green felt, mumbling, "angelheaded
hipsters burning for the ancient heavenly connection to

285

the starry dynamo in the machinery of night . . ." Clack! The ball bounced back and forth and into the pocket. He grabbed the money eagerly and coaxed Sonny Marsh, who was over twenty-one, into buying a couple of beers with it. He and Sonny chugged it down and then he headed home to write.

A month later he graduated from high school. He went on a last and final drunk with his best friend, the one with whom he'd bunked at scout camp, the one he learned how to get drunk with, sneaking over the Kansas state line to purchase 3.2 beer, the one with whom he had driven countless circles around the county courthouse with a six-pack, gossip, and rock-and-roll on the radio. His friend and he got really loaded and then said goodbye. "I'm going to New York to become a poet."

And his friend replied, "Don't do anything I wouldn't do."

Volume II

Volume 1

I Have a Dream

SOME OF THEM finally fell asleep but most talked excitedly and every few minutes began singing, clapping and stomping their feet through the long A.M. to D.C. Over and over they sang the tunes that aroused them and gave melodies to their philosphical passions. "If I Had a Hammer." "Solidarity Forever." "Ain't Gonna Study War No More." "Dona Nobis Pacem." There was a boisterous contingent who led the bus in "Cuba Si, Yankee No," "We Shall Wear the Red and Black," and "The Internationale," the fine song from the 1870 Paris Commune.

Sam and his friends sat in the back where they passed reefers and alcohol back and forth discretely, till they were deposited in the morning weary and hungry at the edge of the park by the Washington Monument.

Sam had something to do, so he waved to Cynthia, Talbot and Nelson, and ran away. They were all to meet later under a certain elm tree to the right of the Lincoln Memorial.

Though it was ninety degrees, Sam sported double thick snakeproof knee high boots, an orangy herringbone riding jacket flared at the hips, a collarless tattersall shirt, and an Australian campaign hat tied to the side with a NO HOPE WITHOUT DOPE pin. He worried about the pin, and pulled it off, replacing it with an button marked AHIMSA.

He also lugged a 16-mm carmera case and a satchel packed with the new issue of *Dope, Fucking and Social Change: A Journal of the New America,* which he'd stayed up printing till bus boarding time at 2 A.M. That's why he was tired.

He was headed for the Library of Congress, a mile from the bus.

"I'd like to take a look at the Ezra Pound broadcasts," Sam Thomas said. His lungs felt like broken shards in a thermos from running the distance.

They brought him a box of white-on-black copies apparently copied from film negatives of transcripts of Pound's Italian broadcasts from 1941 to '43 as recorded by the Foreign Broadcast Intelligence Service.

Sam was too excited to scan right away. His normal transition time for passing between agitation and calming down enough for scholarship was at least ten minutes. Today he forced it, and his initial notes were wobbly and almost indecipherable.

The research was into what Sam and a few pals called the "Lb Q," short for Pound Question. Not many people that Washington day really thought much about the Lb Q, but to poets in the Beat, Black Mountain, Objectivist or Deep Image traditions, it was a serious problem. If eyes were sandpaper, Sam would have long ago erased the texts in Lb's collected earlier poems, *Personae.* His relentless scholarship, his mixture of tough and tender lyrics, his love of Greek and Latin helped Sam become a poet.

After the war, when Sam was in the first grade, Lb had

290

been indicted for treason, then placed in St. Elizabeth's Hospital in D.C. as bonkers. There'd been a big debate among writers when Pound won the Bollingen Prize for *The Pisan Cantos* while he was in the asylum. Some said he had been a traitor for his wartime broadcasts; others said he was a great poet and his poesy separated him from the broadcasts; others said he was a silly figment of prior times and should be forgotten. In 1963 at the time of the Great March on Washington, Lb had long been deloonybinned, and was back in Italy.

Sam wanted to see for himself and spotted it almost at once—the texts were dotted with "kikes," "councils of kikes" and "kikettes," which was Lb's code for Roosevelt's Cabinet.

"God—this motherfucker really *was* an anti-Sem," Sam blurted out a bit too loudly, causing the desk cat to lift his brows.

A half-hour was enough. Sam stood, dashed with the transcripts to the counter, thanked the librarian, shouldered his camera and the satchel of *Dope, Fucking and Social Change: A Journal of the New America,* and sprinted out of the marble data-center, past the Capitol, the National Gallery of Art, the Smithsonian, the White House, the Washington Monument, toward the Lincoln Memorial reflecting pool.

For some reason he'd stashed a tab of mescaline in his boot—it melted, and seeped through his sweaty socks into a popped blister, so that he was picking up mild colors just as he arrived at the giant throng that crowded around Lincoln.

Sam has never seen 200,000 people before. When he took out the Bell & Howell and started to film, he was aware of a low-pitched, crackly noise that trembled from the multitude. It was Sam's first experience with "mass demo-buzz," which came not only from the crackly roar of the multitude, but also from hundreds at the edges shout-talking for causes and distributing a vastness of leaflets, magazines, pennants, buttons, pamphlets, and broadsides for left, liberal left, civil rights and peace groups.

Sam loved it. It was like a mist of amphetamine hitting his senses. He did not realize that fifteen years of demo-buzzes lay before him.

Nervous with friend-find angst, Sam was zigging and zagging through the bannered contingents looking for his friends. Joan Baez was on the stage just then beginning "We Shall Overcome," which in the summer of 1963, in the freshness of its acceptance as a national anthem, could arouse like no other tune.

He found his friends sharing lemonade by the big elm they called the Peace Tree, which its beautifully serrated leaves. He scooted next to his friend John Barrett, who, like Sam, had brought something he'd just created to the march—a tortoise shell lyre copied from a Greek vase.

"I read some of the Lb broadcasts at the Library of Congress," he said, handing John his notes.

John looked at them:

"No one can qualify as a historian of this half century without having examined the Protocols (of the Elders of Z)." 4–20–43

"Talmudic Jews who want to kill off *all* the other races whom they cannot subjugate." 4–20–42

"American lynch law had its origins in the Jewish ruin of the American South." 6–15–42

"If you don't find a leader, you may have to wait for some kind hearted Bavarian or Hungarian to come free you from the Jews of New York." 3–6–42

292

"I said the Republicans would have all kikeria, all the kike profits out against 'em in 1944." 3–16–43

"For two centuries, ever since the brute Cromwell brought 'em back into England, the kikes have sucked out your vitals." 3–15–42

"The dregs of the ex-ghettoes of Europe, now plastered on the necks of the American people." 3–23–42

"The USA will be no use to itself or to anyone else until it gets rid of the kikes *and* Mr. Roosevelt." 3–11–42

"Hitler, having seen the Jew puke in the Germany democracy, was out for responsibility . . . ." 4–20–42

John stopped reading because the page was shaking.

"These are all quotes from broadcasts?"

Sam nodded.

He and John had thumbed back and forth across America earlier that summer, studying *The Cantos* every morning before hitching, in sessions they humorously referred to as "Round Pounds."

John tore and wadded the sheet, tossing it back to Sam.

"I think he was two people—" Sam said, "at least two people. He was a cracker from the anti-Sem heartland with a trigger temper and a mean streak thick as a heel on a jack boot. *And* he was also a tender cat who could write exquisite Chinese nature poetry." Sam's blister gave him a full color picture of Pound in the broadcast booth, his gnarly beard pressed up against one of those round microphones suspended within a circle of metal, ranting like a crazed hick.

Pound was instantly forgotten when Talbot Jenkins joined the circle of Lower East Siders. Talbot was returning from the speakers' platform at the top of the front steps of the memorial. He was broad shouldered, with a

293

big head of hair, and eyelids that made his eyes seem to curve down at the outer edges; he was known among his friends as Talbot the Great because of years getting bashed, handcuffed and cattle prodded integrating the South.

Talbot the Great had grown up in Harlem where his parents were minister and musical director of a church. He'd been a star fullback till the Freedom Rides of 1961 when the klan had attacked Talbot's bus as it pulled into Birmingham. One of them smashed Talbot's knee with a lead pipe, ending his football career. Even now he limped slightly.

Talbot had intended to avoid Birmingham the rest of his life, but last spring, two years later, the call had gone out to celebrate the hundredth anniversary of the signing of the Emancipation Proclamation with an all-out attempt to integrate Birmingham, where a vicious white power structure had kept the city totally segregated. Blacks were denied any kind of job except mop-up and servitude, and every public place was splattered with insulting signs above drinking fountains and lunch counters, and on the doors of toilets and changing rooms in stores. The Southern Christian Leadership Council, headed by Martin Luther King, was sponsoring it and Talbot answered the call.

The press covered it like a war, and the television and photographic images went everywhere. The world saw children clubbed down by water cannons, arm-biting canines snarling at peaceful faces, and the photo of a policeman's knee on the neck of a woman on the pavement, while the voices of children singing hymns drifted from the windows of jails.

At first Talbot was a walky-talky coordinator on the

streets. He carried a photo in his wallet of the man who had lead-piped his knee in case he ever ran into him again. When organizers learned how quickly and how well he could write, he was assigned to leaflets, press releases and emergency communiques to the Justice Department. They were crazy days. He wrote and wrote and wrote, morn till midnight. He kept a diary and even found time for verse. After thirty-four days of demos and thousands of arrests, Talbot flew back to New York with the manuscript of his first book of poems.

Everybody thought Talbot would be asked to speak at the Great March. He wrote a poem for it and practiced its recitation secretly every day. With the prospect of hundreds of thousands in the audience, the number of people who lunge for the microphone is vast, and there was no space for Talbot's poem. Talbot laughed about it, but his friends were upset.

Talbot returned from the speakers' platform with a tale of censorship. The larger the crowd, the greater the control over text, and he'd been disgusted, watching one of the speakers at a portable typewriter backstage having to rewrite his speech. The speaker had wanted to criticize the Kennedy administration's appointment of racist Federal judges in the South. And he had attacked Kennedy's Civil Rights bill as too weak and too late.

President Kennedy had given a televised speech on June 11 about Civil Rights. The next day, NAACP leader Medgar Evers was murdered in Jackson, Mississippi. On June 19, Kennedy submitted the civil rights bill to Congress. The Kennedy brothers initially opposed the Great March, fearing it would harm the bill's chances. A group of march leaders met at the White House and cooled it out. There was a general agreement that the march would be "creative lobbying," would spare the administration harsh criticism, and Kennedy agreed to support it.

"It was bullshit. Waffling liberal bullshit," Talbot complained. "I have a copy. They didn't want him to say the truth—namely that Kennedy *has* appointed racist Fed judges in the South. And the civil rights bill is TOO WEAK and too late. It's a plate of dry, powdery, undercooked liberal biscuits in a cracked plate."

There was a demo-lull about then, some uninspiring speeches, and Sam handed out his magazine and walked around the Peace Tree shooting a few three-minute rolls with his 16-mm Bell & Howell. When Mahalia Jackson began singing "I've Been 'Buked and I've been Scorned," Talbot came over the Sam, "King's next."

Sam had never heard Martin King speak. He was prepared to sneer, expecting the sort of preacherly pralines he'd heard in church after church in the South on civil rights marches.

He had never considered a voice as an empowering instrument, but never had such a speech been spoken. It was Blake's "Voice of the Bard, that past and present sees." It brought the hot masses there that day into the finest sort of unity. Up above the speakers platform you could see the huge seated statue of Lincoln. And Sam's skin began to tingle, to twinge, to crawl with buzzies.

By the middle of the speech, Sam and his friends were standing in a semicircle beneath the Peace Tree, holding hands—Sam, Rebecca Levy, Cynthia Pruitt, John Barrett, Louise Adams, Claudia Pred, Talbot the Great, Nelson Saite, and pals from the Living Theater, the Committee for a Nonviolent World and the *Catholic Worker*.

Sam looked around, wishing he could touch every hand

in this multitude from the twenty corners of the U.S., and spotted a group of men scampering among the demonstrators. They would stop briefly and bend down above those who were sitting and then make strange quick jerking motions against their own noses with their hands. What was going on? They group came closer and Sam saw the white circles with black swastikas on their armbands.

They passed the Peace Tree. One nazi was making soft spitting sounds and cursing them in a whisper, his hand tracing elongated rhine-lines with two fingers pressed together.

Everybody was listening to King, and no one wanted to be distracted. Sam was angry. He couldn't remain passive when the hellmen of the ovens were cursing those he loved. They had to be confronted. He hoisted his camera upon his shoulder just as King's voice said, "Jews and Gentiles, Protestants and Catholics, will be able to join hands and sing in the words of the old Negro spiritual. Free at last! Free at last! Thank God Almightly we are free at last!!!"

King finished and the roar of a mile wide seashell began as the ovenmen scampered away. Talbot and Nelson rushed after one knot of them, Sam another.

Sam thought of Ezra Pound as he trotted after the ovenmen. Pound who had helped him become a poet. Pound on whom he had once relied for strength and ideas on creative rebellion. Pound who had let him down in the Library of Congress.

"I've learned something very important from you, Ez," Sam said under his breath, pausing to film a fylfot'd armband.

He shouted at the nazis in a mode a bit unmindful of the spirit of Gandhian nonviolence—"Hey, nazi pus! Do

297

you know that you're scum? Come here, I have something for you, you filthy puke!!"

Those words seemed sufficient to cause them to turn around and converge on Sam. His camera caught it all.

"Death to nazi death worms!"

That brought forth the boots. Sam rolled on the ground to protect his guts and his camera. His kidneys unfortunately were exposed and one of the ovenmen got him.

Another raised his boot to break his ribs, so Sam twisted up to his feet. By that time the Park Police were there and the ovenmen rushed to split, with several getting nabbed.

Sam kept shouting at them. He tried to recall the Quaker adage, something like "the spirit of reconciliation is an overwhelming thing," but however much part of him wanted to transform the armbands, part of him clearly wanted to knife them. He couldn't remember the words.

He was separated from his friends when he followed the policemen leading the nazis away. "Nazi barf-gnarls! Nazi garbage!"

He was following too closely. The police warned him, and one of the ovens lunged at the camera, and then Sam too was placed under arrest. His friend Cynthia Pruitt had been keeping watch on him and they let him hand her his camera and satchel, for which he was mightily grateful, not wanting the fresh copies of *Dope, Fucking and Social Change: A Journal of the New America* falling into the files of the fuzz.

To Sam, surrounded by nazis and under arrest, Cynthia was a vision of paradise. She was barefoot, her jeans frayed into dangling white grass at the cuffs, her shirt tied up halterlike in the heat, a canteen hooked upon one of the belt loop of her jeans. Her hair was safely caught up

298

and wrapped around with a bandana, the emergency gas mask of the era. For a moment their wild eyes met. He would never forget her smile and the chipped left edge of her left front tooth she hadn't the scratch to repair. She bent down, and Sam saw for a flash her beautiful nipples as she picked up his light green campaign hat where it had fallen. She donned it and its red and white AHIMSA button seemed to calm him.

Sam went limp, and two cops carried him. He let his head drift back, to a sudden upsidedown view of the Washington Monument. The white-gray obelisk looked like a stark ultra-realistic painting—the outer edges forming a double line of white that bent together at the top against the milky blue of the air like long thin strokes of titanium white made with a palette knife.

While they carried him, he focused on the two dark observation windows at the summit of the monument, which for one startling second looked like the eye holes in a sky-sized klan robe.

Years later he could still vividly recall that startling vision of the giant klan robe, and with the perspective of time, he saw that there *was* actually something like a giant klan robe that tried to blot out the fair weather of America in 1963.

Sam Thomas was wadded up and stuffed into the paddy wagon. Before they shut the door came another startling vision. It was the hovering face of secret policeman J. Edgar Hoover, spread across the sky like a dead carp at the mouth of a sewer. Sam saw a time of crazed peril for America. There was the crackle of insane electricity in the brains of madmen, and planes swooping low over villages with fires that would not stop.

The Shlemiel of Happening Street

HIS NAME WAS Harry Summers, but they called him the Shlemiel of Happening Street. He was a painter, though he flamed into fame with his Happenings. Harry was part of a group of painters who mixed longing for the canvas with a hunger to work a crowd. It was the paint-perf era, for painters with a need to perform, as separate from the perf-po—poets in performance—movement of later decades.

He was the Shlemiel of Happening Street because things always went wrong, wildly wrong, yet in their wrongness almost always twisted the Happening into brilliance and triumph. For the most part the Happening movement was filled with those who fashioned pellucid Apollonian spectacles stitched together with calm, transparent thread. It was the decade they discovered you could paint or draw on sheets of clear, dangling plastic, set chairs in front, hire a cellist on roller skates, play tapes of street noise, and it would cause a stir.

That wasn't enough for Harry. Not for him were these elegant perf-rooms where the silence between activities was like the sipping of wines between courses. "The Hell with this interplay of light and geometric form!" he shouted. "We want sweat!" A sweating audience usually, which came for Harry's special brand of wild-eyed ride. He called it REGA, for Raw Energetic Gestaltic Absolute. He held his Happenings almost exclusively on East 9th between Avenues B and C, and thus the street was known around the Lower East Side as Happening Street.

He was the only one of the Happenists whose performances veered anywhere close to boos and hisses. Marinetti's manifesto, "The Pleasure of Being Booed," had been a great influence on Harry Summers. After a few experiments in paint-perf he found out there was probably nothing to be done to bring back the golden days of "performance scandals," when audiences threw potatoes. But he tried. There was something about the cool, beat audience, rich and poor, that could sit through anything with stitched mouths. Perhaps the ghastly excesses of the century—the wars, the bomb, the outcroppings of evil— had absorbed all the potatoes.

When Harry Summers found how audiences were not prepared in the early 1960s to riot or become agitated, he opened his arms in love and friendship. He relaxed. He felt good about the states of mind of those who walked over to East 9th for REGA. He discovered that when he himself was very visible in these painterly extravaganzas, then there was joy. He inspired the passive and tragicynical. He energized. He made instant actors out of dour bankers and out of the most bitter of the bitter shitters of the art scene.

He was always splattered with paint—clothes, face and hair. It mixed with the sweat of his performances for glowing runnels of color. His pants kept edging downward. He never just walked—it was always rush hour. He

301

strutted like a sorefooted duck, the moon rising with each step as his trousers sank. The sockets were much larger than the eyes, so that his bluegreen glare of joy was like a pair of penlights in darkened recesses, as he cajoled his audiences to join the "spirit of REGA," exploring that fine, embarrassing line between you *can* become part of the Happening and you *will*.

The Happenings were happiness tonics for Harry, raising him to such pinnacles that the later despair was correspondingly low. When Harry was down, which was often, he was in a stupified world of twinkling semidarkness, sort of like a painless migraine. It made him put on shows twice a month, to keep him gliding high.

One of the reasons he became such a visible participant in his Happenings was that he was always pulled into the spectacle as a "stage healer," say, when a scrim was about to heave over on its side, or the pile of canteloupes on a conveyor belt was about to dump into the audience. Then he would dart forward and heal the aberration with a sweating fury of joy.

The art journals covered these events with fascination. One legendary Happening addressed the question, "Why shouldn't you be able to walk on pancakes—giant pancakes—while they cook?" Some of the special shoes Harry designed caught fire mid-walk and the resulting foot-flambé of panicked participants entered history.

In *Dynamite Sonata* he utilized explosives placed beneath a series of heavy metal mats used for blasting at construction sites. Harry affixed paintings upon the mats, and charges were to be set off in sequence by a line of assistants with plungers, in order to provide rhythmic accompaniment to a piece of early electronic music. During the rehearsal, the mats lifted off the ground a couple of feet then subsided in a pleasing expellation of dust around the edges of the paintings. During the actual performance, however, it was different and the resulting drum track of explosions burst a water main and caused a wall to collapse, exposing a tiny Jewish cemetery from the eighteenth century.

In his piece, *Who Is the Puppeteer?*, thick wet threads covered with five-minute glue were spread atop the audience which, as the crowd gave eyes to the action around them and became distracted, dried obnoxiously and in some cases permanently to suit coats, evening throws or upon beat generation leathers and lumberjack shirts. And then there were miracles. The Greeks, who were found of predicting the future through birdwatching, or ornithomancy, would have deemed it a state event if, as happened once in one of Harry's Happenings, virtually all two hundred doves set free above the wide floor of black canvas uttered dooky in simultaneity.

Harry Summers brought something unique to the history of Happenings—the concept of "artistic danger." Word spread and he attracted a peculiar danger-oriented public. You could see them calmly and collectively computing their chances when something was going wrong, each deciding when the point should arrive to shove and scream and grapple for the doors. To Harry's credit, no one was ever hurt.

In spite of these "unplanned events," Harry's paint-perfs were seamless. He was there, roaming the set balletically. The tape player wouldn't work and Harry rushed about handing out phone books among the attendees, and said "sing." Thus the first thirty-voice "phone book simultané" in the history of Happenings, working through the A's of the Manhattan directory. Nudity was good also

303

for stitching together the disparate elements of a Happening. There was plenty of it, men and women, and the nudes didn't just stand around. Harry got them to dance, to dangle from rafters and even to embrace. It was a sure allure in the realm of ticket sales, yet in '63 and '64 it was also a litigious allure—undercover cops or cats from the D.A.'s office came to make sure there were no illegal fondlings, hardons, clit rubs, b.j.s or fornication.

Harry had an assistant named Sweat Brow Bill. He was as tidy as Harry was chaotic, and as tireless. His trademarks were his amber-framed glasses with tiny fossilized bugs and his long light brown hair done in twin pony tails. Sweat Brow Bill was the archivist. He made sure that samples of posters were filed and annotated; that production scripts were saved; that photographs were made and saved; that copies of press releases and articles were neatly glued into scrapbooks; that paintings were repaired.

Sweat Brow was always analyzing the audience for those who would let Harry store props, costumes, scenery and even portable stages and lighting trees in their houses and apartments. It worked. There were many, many stunned people all over New York city who found their pads overloaded with Harry's stuff, all carefully labeled, indexed, crossfiled and boxed. The day of a paint-perf there were hasty cab rides here and there among the boroughs to scoop up needed equipment.

One afternoon Harry was preparing a building for a production called THE BEAUTY OF CREATED THINGS—A HAPPENING ON EAST 9TH. Crew and cast were assembled, including Sweat Brow Bill, Cynthia Pruitt, John Barrett and Sam Thomas. The latter two were going to recite simultaneously, and Harry was fascinated with Cynthia, who had come to watch her lover Sam Thomas perform. Cynthia had come to New York City to live in voluntary ascetic poverty at the *Catholic Worker*. Her base was a building near the Bowery that served food to the homeless and the poor, and where the *Catholic Worker* newspaper was published. She'd proven a bit too randy for the *Worker*, and now was living by herself. Harry Summers was eager to get a clothes fling-off from Cynthia in *The Beauty of Created Things*. She was hesitant, in fact balked.

People often asked Harry about his passion for East 9th, a slum street noted for its smell of poverty and cooked onions. He simply loved it—its buildings, its alleyways, its basements—everywhere he found good angles, posts, walls, interesting window frames, groovy roofs. After picking a building, he convinced the occupants and supers to let him go ahead. He called it "doing a building." Two or three times he went upstate or out on Long Island to "do a barn," "do a mansion," and later on in the decade, to "do a commune."

The new Happening was set in a recessed courtyard between a front apartment building and a smaller back apartment building. In the center of the yard was a semi-circle of standing curtains around a mysterious "Tunnel to Nowhere," which participants were going to be invited to enter by crawling or crouch-walking. Also to the yard Harry had hauled an abandoned wood-ribbed water tower on metal stilts. There was going to be music, pleasing bodies, the simultaneous recitation of verse, and "a secret," Harry promised.

Harry had draped the tunnel entrance with a quilt-like material so that you more or less slid down an incline into the tunnel proper. He persuaded Cynthia Pruitt to do a test crawl with him. They were down there a long time and the rehearsal was delayed. People assumed they were making out. Or maybe not. A naked Cynthia emerged from the tunnel to the great applause of the cast followed by Harry Summers trying to tie the rope around his trousers, where she confronted Sam Thomas, whose eyes she met in a classic beat generation boyfriend stare-down.

Meanwhile, in an apartment on Avenue A not far from the dress rehearsal, the Mother-in-Law had arrived. As always she had glided silently up the four flights to the heavily locked tenement door, carrying an assortment of shopping bags full of largesse for her daughter and the children. These bags the recipients called CARE packages, and today they contained children's clothing from rich Aunt Shifrah, two packets of Streit's brand chocolate-covered matzohs, an assortment of kasha boxes taped shut, many, perhaps too many, cans of pea soup, a camp-sized gallon jar of sugared pears, milk, eggs, fruit, light bulbs, string, magazines and toys.

Most times the Mother-in-Law's visits were brief, and the dirty beatnik—of D.B. as he was known among Marie's family in Queens—would head for the saloons or up to the warm weather writing cabana on the roof, and wait it out. Today, however, the M-i-L was going to stick around till midnight. The Father-in-Law normally waited outside, or patrolled the neighborhood in his Buick, refusing to witness the "beatnick punk with no excuses" who had sucked his daughter into a slum that three generations of greenhorns, those fleeing pogroms, shtetls and war, had managed to escape. Tonight he had business in Manhattan and the Mother-in-Law wanted to spend the time on Avenue A.

There were many temporary tumults associated with a

M-i-L visit. She was always agitated. Today it was the phenomenon of zombie gaze, which alarmed her greatly when handing the twins their new toys. Something was not right. They were listless. Tired. Zombie-eyed. That's wrong here, the poor babies! Had they colds? Shouldn't we take their temperatures?

It was early in the school year and the Mother-in-Law was failing to recognize a condition common among the children of the beat generation. The twins had begun kindergarten and all their lives they had set their biological clocks to the 5 A.M. to 1 P.M. sleep schedule of their parents. Now, hideously, they had to be pulled from the loft bed at 7 or 8 A.M., and for a few weeks would suffer till they had adjusted their sleep cycles.

Marie explained it to the M-i-L as they unloaded the CARE package perishables into the refrigerator, the door of which had taped on it the poster for THE BEAUTY OF CREATED THINGS—A HAPPENING ON EAST 9TH.

The D.B. consulted with Marie. Why not take the M-i-L to the Happening? They had planned to go, had a sitter, and their friends in the cast were expecting them. The Mother-in-Law didn't care as long as she was back by 11:30 to be picked up. They prepared her for bare breasts and genitals, again no care, but not to tell the F-i-L.

The courtyard was packed. The audience was on chairs and lined on the wrought iron steps leading to it from the front and back buildings. Everything was in place—the Tunnel to Nowhere in the center with its curtains and a neon sculpture lighting its entrance. To the right was the poets' platform and just behind the tunnel was the water tower.

And it began. It was pleasant. The Mother-in-Law,

Marie and the D.B. sat next to the action in a row of chairs alongside the most prestigious artists and writers of lower New York. Sam and John Barrett began shouting their poems, and Cynthia Pruitt and several other naked artists began walking in circles around the Tunnel to Nowhere making arabesques with flashlights upon the curtains. Suddenly there was a hiss of sparkling short circuit fireworks in the transformer that led to the circular neon around the Tunnel, and the cloth somehow caught fire.

It seemed like an easy thing to put out. Harry doused it with buckets of water and sand. The event was about to continue when the legs on the water tower began to splay and shift, accompanied by a slight splintering, cracking sound. The tower contained the secret component of the Happening—seven tons of raspberry jello.

The lights went through a final zzzzst, spume, pop and bang, and it was dark. Harry Summers ran into the middle of it all with a flashlight, and the upset, naked Cynthia Pruitt also, and they attempted to calm the crowd just as the seven tons of jello exploded from the wood-ribbed tank.

The sentiment of the entire gathering, to a person, was summed up by one voice, "Let's get the fuck out of here." And the trample began.

The Mother-in-Law became separated from Marie and the D.B. and wound up next to Harry, who grabbed her arm and helped her crouch down into the Tunnel to Nowhere. "It's the only place we'll be safe," he said.

There were screams, and Harry's flashlight strafing wildly about. The Mother-in-Law looked above her at the entrance sign as she started her crawl through the tunnel: ADMISSION $2.00, NUDES FREE.

What Harry and the M-i-L had entered was the legendary and rediscovered "9th Street Tunnel." Harry had heard about it but no one knew where it was till a hundred-year-old building super on Avenue C had hipped him. It led under 9th Street to the corresponding courtyard on the other side, and supposedly had been used by the Underground Railway to help slaves escape the South.

Meanwhile, fire trucks arrived and oodles of police. The street was made eery with flashing lights, the sounds of doors opening and shutting quickly, sirens. It was a zone of desperation. All seven tons of jello it seemed had oozed quickly and dangerously down into the Tunnel to Nowhere. In addition a piece of tunnel ceiling had apparently caved in, and the cement slabs in the courtyard near the mouth had dipped downward.

The firemen were trying to clear the passageway. Only Sweat Brow Bill knew about the tunnel leading under the street. But he didn't know where. He, the D.B. and Marie worked up and down the block, crevice by hallway by basement, searching for Harry Summers and the Mother-in-Law. Where were they? Were they crushed by jello and rock?

Then from the darkness across the street Harry emerged, stepping past a fire engine and across cold wet hoses. Marie wiped away tears of happiness just as the Mother-in-Law said, "We're going to store some things for Harry—some props."

"Way out in Queens?"

"Why not? We've got room in the garage."

Talbot Goes to Birmingham

AT 4 A.M. Sam heard a knock. It was Talbot
Jenkins, who was trembling and stuttering, a tear rolling
slowly down his cheek, shiny in Sam's arrays of nighttime
candles due to no electricity, and which, when it arrived
at the row of beard on his jaw, veered sharply and wettened the hair of his chin. Talbot's well known cool was
gone. He raged in a low voice about something called
"Slage" or perhaps "Slaize," Sam wasn't sure which. Just
before he walked back out the door, his words became
clear and firm. "I'm going to kill someone in the klan," he
said. "Here's a note to my mother if anything goes
wrong."

Sam said nothing at first. His rule was to question the
behavior of his pals as rarely as possible, and so the echo-
ing clicks of Talbot's heels were at the bottom of the stone
and metal staircase before Sam shook his head, this is
insane, and dashed down to the sidewalk. "How are you
getting there? Do you need any money?" He was trying to
think of a cool person's way to slow his friend down.
Talbot did not answer. "Maybe we should go to the House
of Nothingness and tea this out, man. It's probably still
open . . ."

310

Talbot wouldn't slow. "That piece of shit is going to be blasted apart," he said. "Just like they blasted those girls in their robes." Too soon they were at 14th and First Avenue and Talbot vanished into the subway. Sam stood quietly, wondering what to do. There was nothing to do. Talbot was going to Birmingham, and that was it.

Sam walked out to an all night newsstand and bought all the papers—the *Times,* the *Post,* the *Mirror* and the *Daily News*—and went over to House of Nothingness into the raked white sand courtyard in back, where they were putting the chairs on the table tops while he read the horror.

The four children had come out of Ella Demand's Sunday school class where the lesson had been "The Love That Forgives." They had gone to the basement to put on their choir robes and were sitting on a couch in their white satins when it happened.

The horror of those children blown apart in their choir robes! It was particularly horrible to Talbot Jenkins, who himself had practically been raised in a choir robe in Harlem where his parents ran a church. His father was the minister and his mother the choir leader. Even now, Talbot still sometimes put on the satins to sing for Easter or Christmas services.

Hours after talking with Sam, Talbot Jenkins lifted his suitcase onto a wooden barricade and stood staring at the shattered and bomb darkened stain glass of the Fourteenth Street Baptist Church. His anger was total. He squinted his eyes almost shut, thinking of the graffiti that Lower East Side gang members sprayed on walls next to their names, DTK, for Down to Kill. That was Talbot, down in Birmingham, DTK, dynamite for dynamite, death for death.

311

Talbot went inside, where he ran his fingers along the slivers of stained glass in a broken window. He knelt, still keeping his fingers on the slivers, and prayed. The trembling, the grief, the anger commingled with the blood on his hands from clenching the shards.

In his pocket was a piece of paper with a name on it—Ethrom Slage, the head of a klavern outside Birmingham. Slage had wielded a metal pipe in the Trailways depot in Birmingham the day in '61 that Talbot's Freedom Ride bus was attacked. It was Slage who ended Talbot's pro-bound football career with a crushing blow to the knee.

Talbot had learned who Slage was by pestering the Justice Department guys Kennedy had sent down the past spring to monitor the demonstrations. For a long time they had refused to identify the photo Talbot showed them, but he was so insistent that finally one of them wrote Ethrom's name on the piece of paper now in Talbot's pocket.

Talbot had a collection of photos showing Slage assaulting people at rallies. Slage was shaking his pipe all over the South, though Kennedy's Justice Department had threatened to indict him, and he was no longer in '63 as overt as he had been in '61. The way Talbot had it figured, Slage had switched from a lead cylinder to another sort of cylinder. But no more. For Talbot was DTK.

Talbot bought a pistol that couldn't be traced, and a car from someone not connected with any of the civil rights groups in town. If he were caught he didn't want anyone in the movement in trouble.

Talbot broke into a construction site where he shot away the lock on a small shed and carried away a case of dynamite and some caps. He knew what he was doing

312

from working with his uncle in the Bronx blasting buildings to the ground. In his suitcase brought from New York were coils of wire and a battery powered detonator.

Late that morning he drove past Ethrom Slage's farm a few miles outside Birmingham. He'd purchased an auto old enough to fake a breakdown, and he'd pulled a sparkplug wire so that it coughed along on five cylinders. A couple of hundred feet down the road he stopped and raised the hood, memorizing the array of the property as he tinkered.

His visual field was clotted with a distasteful concatenation of dilapidated buildings, including the Slage family farmhouse propped up on one corner with a jack, and a yard cluttered with auto engines on cinder blocks, a row of ice chests riddled with target practice holes, a tin washtub with handcranked squeezer and yellow, pitted rollers, and stacks of wheel hubs, worn down tractor tires, and a few generations of derelict seeders, harrows and rakes. Here and there in the jumble were rooster-sized hot weather crouching pits dug in the dirt.

Next to the house a few speckly gray guinea hens reached their heads hopefully out of a rusty fence yard, the far side of which was comprised of porcelainized kitchen table tops nailed side by side. Leaning against the outhouse, as Talbot later learned, were bundles of out-of-date hate fliers covered with a tarp.

To the left of the house down an incline was a metal roofed barn, whole sections of which had been bent double or torn away by the wind. On the door beneath the hayloft were some pink and freshly salted raccoon hides tacked up to dry.

Talbot couldn't see the area directly behind the barn, but beyond it was a creek, with woods spreading thickly

313

off the far bank up a steep hill for about a hundred yards.

Talbot shook his head very slowly and clamped his teeth so tightly together they hurt his jaw. Something was wrong. He'd expected a fortress, not a failure zone. These messy buildings with their scratched possum chewed entrances *couldn't* be the home of a man who'd done so much organized harm. Maybe it was a front, not the house of Slage, but a cover, maybe there was a bunker beneath the rot. Talbot was sure it was the right place. "Slage" was on the mailbox, and he'd triple checked the location.

The only sign that might indicate klavern was a radio aerial mounted on the roof, which he correctly guessed Slage used to monitor local law enforcement. Talbot saw that the driveway led to the rear of the house and when he moved around to the other end of his auto he spotted a new cinder block garage with a metal roof still shiny and unpainted.

His attention was drawn from the roof to the growling of a thick black dog with an edge of brown fur around its mouth. It looked maybe half doberman, half bloodhound as it paced back and forth along the length of its chain, protecting the front porch and windows. Where it paced was eroded like a creek bed, and its grrr seemed distressingly directed at Talbot. In fact, it strained at its chain, and Talbot expected Slage to burst out the door to confront him. Talbot pictured where exactly in his shoulder satchel he had stashed his pistol, in case he should have to shoot it out with Slage in the front yard.

Talbot's almost threw up when the door actually opened! And a boy of about ten walked from the house to the mailbox, peering toward Talbot as he stacked mail into his hands. His hair was the color of white corn, worn

314

shortly cut except for two curls which curved to the left and to the right down his forehead. He was barefoot and wore jeans cut off in raggedy zigzags at the knees. He gathered the letters and walked back past the pacing dog.

Talbot trudged away as if to go for auto parts or help. Out of sight he turned left and circled through the thick edging of woods to the top of the hill in back of the property. There he could see everything. Where he couldn't see before—between the rear of the barn and the creek, he scanned a pig lot and a small pasture for Slage's cows. He sketched the layout.

That's it! He probably feeds the pigs and lets the cows out to pasture each morning before going to work. He *has* to work somewhere—no one could subsist on such a sub-scratchdirt operation.

Talbot spotted a shed on the hill top where he stood, perfect for an all night vigil. Slage would come to feed them early in the morning. And that would be it. Boom. Blood. Klavern guts spilling from a klavernist.

After dark he returned from Birmingham and stashed his tote bag crammed with flashlight, gun, dynamite, wires, caps, a canteen, gloves and food, including a couple of uppers. He drove the car back to town and then took an eight-mile walk to the shed.

During the A.M. he could tell the dog was unimpressive as a threat. It was always barking, and there were plenty of skunks and possums to confuse it.

Besides, he had a gun, and he was ready to shoot it out.

Just before dawn the kitchen light clicked on. Slage came out on the porch and called his dog. He unhooked it from its chain and walked with it toward the barn. He was carrying a stick-like device which in the gloom Talbot correctly guessed was a rifle.

315

Talbot followed him in the gloom with his binoculars. Slage tied the dog to the outhouse, reached down and pulled some papers from under the tarp, and went inside. He untied the dog when he came out of the outhouse, and went down to the barn and disappeared from Talbot's sight. Five minutes later he emerged through the back door of the barn into the pig yard, pushing a wheel barrow heaped high with something. The pigs meantime had awakened and were jostle-jumping up against the wheel barrow, squealing and grabbing before he could dump the load into the trough. Slage made five trips with the barrow.

He walked back up to the house, chained the dog, then drove away.

Talbot risked all and dashed down to the barn for a look, vaulting the fence, out of view of the house, and slipped through the pig door where he encountered a deep and astonishing concrete pit, about ten feet across, filled with thousands of pastries wrapped in paper—moon pies, twinkies, snow balls, jelly rolls, chocolate covered cupcakes and pecan pielets.

Talbot guessed Slage must have purchased them stale from stores or bakeries. From the slathering and sooey shrieks of the pigs, it was obvious the pigs loved them, and Slage could brag at Christmas about his sugar-cured hams.

The cows were pastured far enough from the barn so as probably not to get blasted, though a few pigs might have to die. He worried about that, whether the pigs would be safe, and the barn swallows too, flitting above the smoke and gloom of a collapsed structure.

Talbot marked the spot for the charge, then went back up to the shed and slept most of the morning and early

316

afternoon. After midnight he carried the sticks wrapped in paraffined paper down the hill, poked a hole for the electrical blasting cap, taped the sticks together, and planted them beneath the great pile of twinkies. He hid the insulated wire under straw and tracked it up the hill to the plunger-box in the shed.

Then he waited.

Dawn was still an hour away when he began to hear sharp tearing sounds, almost inaudibly faint, from down the hill. At first Talbot thought it was the crackles, say, of a campfire. He rotated his head a few degrees at a time, searching for the direction. He stood cautiously and stared out through the shed's broken windows. It was coming from the barn. Crackle. Crackle. Crackle.

He hadn't heard footsteps. The dog hadn't barked. The kitchen windows were dark. It continued.

Should he drop the plunger? His hand trembled, muffling the flashlight lens with one hand and feeling for the plunger with the other. He wasn't sure. He hesitated.

Talbot made his way down the hill to peer through the slits in the gray planks. Inside there was the glow of a lantern, and he could see the tow-headed boy sitting at the edge of the twinkies softness mound, almost directly above the bundle of dynamite. He was opening the cupcakes and tossing the wrappers into a barrel and the cupcakes back into the vat. Talbot pressed his eye up against the dark, dry barn slit just as the boy was sampling a moon pie, a yellow confection comprised of a flopped over circle of dough filled with whitish custard. The kid spat some of it into the gooey pit.

Talbot unlatched the door and entered. The kid's eyes widened in fright to encounter what he'd been taught all his life was the greatest danger, save for the devil, in all

317

of creation—a tall muscular black guy with a gun. Talbot made a shusssh sign. "Don't shout. Nothing's going to happen to you. All I want to know—what's your name?"

"Johnny Ray Slage."

Talbot spoke slowly and insistently. "I don't want you to join the klan when you grow up. Do you hear? You have to get rid of the poison. I'm going to help you. I'll be sending you stuff in the mail. What's the address here? Do you have a box number?"

The boy told him.

"Somebody's got to be your teacher. And I'm it."

Talbot dug into the mound of cakes and snipped the wires to the dynamite. He retrieved the bundle with his gloved fingers, detached the cap, said goodbye and trot-ran across the barn yard toward the hill, wondering if Johnny Ray was going to shout for his dad. There was silence.

He stopped and looked back toward the house. Nothing was happening. Raw nerve took charge. He changed direction and dashed toward the house, got across the fence, dodging the stacks of tires and the farm implements like a broken field runner, his ruined knee reminding him that Slage had once piped it in a bus terminal, to the edge of the outhouse, where he pulled off the tarp and removed a handful of hate fliers to give to Sam Thomas back in the Lower East Side.

Then it was back to the shed in the forest where he was safe. By flashlight Talbot crossed the wooded ridge and down a dry creek bed into the next valley to bury the explosives and the gun where he would be able to retrieve them later if he wanted.

He walked back up to the ridge top, and along it for

about a mile till he veered down from the Alabama hard-
woods to run along the road to Birmingham.

It's Like Living With a Mongol

EVERY MORNING AT TEN in warm weather they met to share stories, a core of six young mothers, expanding some days to ten or twelve, who came leading their children by the hand or pushing strollers and carriages. The older ones played in the sandbox or dangled from nearby climbing rings while the mothers talked.

The place they met was Tompkins Square Park, named after Governor Daniel Tompkins who led the fight to abolish slavery in New York State in 1827. The park is bordered by Avenues A and B on the west and east, and by 10th and 7th Streets on the north and south. There was a sturdy black iron fence around its perimeter that gave it a sort of privacy, with entrances at some of the street mouths. On the Avenue B side near 9th was a spot about as secluded as the place allowed, with the play area in good line of sight from a couple of benches where they bunched together for their talks.

The majority of the women were writers or artists, and all lived with writers, painters or musicians. Some had set aside their own art out of deference to the envies and insecurities of their mates. The women were of varying energies, but on the whole were very spritely, full of vim and idealism. They had not yet been beaten down by the slums and were willing to sort out the rules and to make some new ones if necessary. Most had been raised in, and were rebelling against, the traditions of the postwar forties and the McCarthy fifties—that is, to be bland, blonde and blind. It was difficult in the moil and confusion of quickly shifting lives to articulate completely the issues of liberation that would be fully explicated in another five years. But they sniffed them.

The women's marriages and relationships broke up regularly, but probably not more often than among the squares, though perhaps more vividly since their personalities seemed coded for mating with *homo erectus beatnicus*. Their husbands and boyfriends dipped into an intoxicating tradition—of the lifestyles and madnesses of male writers and artists—such as Charlie Parker, Hemingway, Fitzgerald, Baudelaire, Nerval, Kerouac, Jackson Pollock, Modigliani, Hart Crane, Van Gogh, Vachel Lindsay... There was a mountain of bonkers to climb!

In consequence, a good portion of the men tended to be obsessive, neglectful, drug abusing, pushy, manic-depressive, overly assertive and overerotic yet indecisive and unselfconfident egomaniacs. Most of the women in the park were deeply in love with their guys, but it was a tough love, loving frail, flawed persons and themselves frail and flawed, and all sides trapped in confusion, poverty and conflicting drives. Some of the women were adventuresome and told how when their own mates strayed they tried it themselves. Some liked it, some did not, some were mixed.

They had no name for themselves except one that came about as a joke. Marie Colson had been relating a recent

321

shenanigan pulled by her husband and suddenly exclaimed, "It's like living with a Mongol!"

It's like living with a Mongol—they laughed and slapped their knees. Thereafter they were the Mongol Committee. Of course they were referring to the Mongols of the thirteenth century, and not to the good folk of the Peoples Republic of Mongolia. Marie's husband became the archetype. The Mongol had dishwashing techniques right out of the Pleistocene. He eschewed soap and scouring pads and went to work using his fingernails only, stabbing and scraping at spaghetti bumps on pans like a possum chewing at a gate, a technique he claimed spiritual in nature, and revealed to him as a zen koan by someone named Tony the Beatnik. It helped the Mongol overcome his midwest oleophobia, or fear of having ones actual fingers come into contact with used food or oily surfaces.

The Mongol was archetypally dirty. His genitals were actually gray and sooty. His side of the bed was like a crow's lair, with paper clips, dried pasta, lint balls, snips of paper with writing, and with writing on the bedsheets themselves, spilled coffee, come stains, shreds of pot leaf, magazines, horrible loose staples that cut Marie all the time, *et alia multa*. The Mongol's idea of bedmaking was to toss a madras spread atop the above and scurry thence. Marie tried to give him lessons, but the lumpy, crinkly, all-terrain results always looked like Marcel Duchamp's Dada photo montage, *Dust Breeding*.

The Mongol Committee was useful if only for the value to its members of comparing notes. They could study for example the commonality of excuses that mates would give when they didn't come home:

1. mugged and left unconscious in street

322

2. passed out a Nelson's pad from paralytic Panamanian Red
3. arrested and not allowed to call out
4. passed out at Past Blast's party from yohimbine-mescaline-magic mushroom-tequila punch, no phone.

The Mongol Committee had heard it all.

Their strength came from the power of sharing—for there were almost no support services available to them, no day care, no federal rent assistance, no community outreach facilities from the city. The East Side could have used a settlement house attuned to the mores of the Beat era. There was a clinic of sorts, but it was a good distance away, and of course there was welfare which in those days as now tended to break up families. So they gathered in the mornings, shared their problems, children's sicknesses, the foibles of their mates and the foibles of the times. Some at first were reluctant to reveal all the details of their private lives, especially if they veered to the sordid.

Their first group decision was to seek a total ban on violence and threats of violence in their households. This caused considerable embarrassment and even hostility among the men—there were exclamations like "Who me? What are you talking about? I don't do things like that! That one time you provoked it." And more hostility when they hid out a couple of women whose husbands had rough hands and who then came threatening or whimpering to the various apartments where they thought their wives might be sheltered.

The Committee organized picket lines against particularly creepy landlords, such as against the notorious slum bum named Two Car Louis, who drove a clunker to the Lower East Side to collect rents after parking his Caddie by the 59th Street Bridge, and whose buildings were saved from being called shanties only because those who built them two hundred years ago used brick and stone.

They gave their children traditional Beat Generation names such as Nathaniel, Sebastian, Katherine, Django, and a few African influenced names such as Damjeela and Onghi. Flower Power appellations were a few years in the future. One did not hear shouts like "Sequoia! Get your tie dyes over here!" or "Moon Sorrel, stop throwing sand at Mountain!" There were however a couple of proto-hippie children around the sandbox named Rainbow and Bountiful, and one charming little boy named On the Road Mulligan.

Most of the women did not work, and even if they could have afforded sitters, uptight husbands often would not want them out of the beatific kitchen. Such economic arrangements worked because living expenses were tantalizingly low, so a person could become obsessed with a creative project for a couple of weeks, then surface to scrounge for rent and electricity for a few days, succeed, then dive back to the art.

When a medical crisis came or when the lights and phone were pulled and no quarters remained in the stash bowl for pasta or candles then the full terror of the economics of New York City dropped like Hesiod's anvil into the art, the marriage, the life—and the Committee went into action. They dug into their birthday or Christmas funds and shared it. They passed around phone numbers for quick non-hassle ways to make emergency cash such as modeling for painting classes at Cooper Union and N.Y.U., waitressing on Bleecker Street or at the House of Nothingness, and a multitude of possibilities in the uptown electric forest.

Time went by and the lives of those who gathered mornings in the park moiled forward more happily than before. The writers among them had begun a mimeographed magazine and the painters shared costs for models and group baby sitting.

To celebrate its second anniversary the Committee held a picnic by the sandbox with food, wine and someone even brought a few bennies for those so inclined, wrapped in a silver foil she passed around. Over a dozen women attended, including alumnae who had moved out of the Lower East Side. It was a beautiful morning and both children and mothers were decked out *beatnique splendide*. That temporary phantom known as Happiness had danced into the park.

And the phantom was doing the Morris Dance when Carol Mulligan and her son On the Road arrived. Carol's had been the first and only full blown flip-out to have occurred among them. And now she was back! She had put on some weight, which was good, for she had been alarmingly thin during her distress.

Her husband Bart was an "Apocalyptic Bop Prose Spontaneity Avatar," i.e., a post-Kerouacean novelist and poet who wrote quickly and quantitatively in the First Thought=Best Thought mode. Bart had hitched to a poetry conference in California a while back and returned with a woman named Ocea the Other, or just plain Other. Ocea the Other had a intense career on the Lower East Side for a couple of years before she went back to Berkeley to pick up her Ph.D. She was determined to join the New York School of verse, so like someone nodding her head just before running beneath the Double Dutch skip rope, she filled her backpack with all the right and current books and measured the gamut of themes so she could join the game.

The Mulligan family had been on the tightrope of welfare prior to the flight to California. When Bart returned, the city insisted he look for work, any kind of work, and though he had taken the vow to Live Off Words, when they threatened a cutoff he surrendered and the welfare folk gave him money for a suit, button down shirt and tie with which he was supposed to seek work in the uptown office buildings.

Bart Mulligan took the money over the West Side and found an actual zoot suit with sharp wide lapels and a shirt with duck wing collar wherein he strutted with Ocea the Other along the L.E.S. cobbles from cafe to cafe, man, Apocalyptic Bop Prose Spontaneity like clicking the cobbles with the next Edna St. Vincent Millay, like dig it.

He saw less and less of Carol and On the Road, and gave less and less money. Finally, welfare cut them off and he was in the end trying to live with two women in two apartments in equal circumstances of poverty.

Carol Mulligan's philosophy had been instant vengeance—an eye for an eye, a fuck for a fuck. When she had learned of one of his escapades, she picked up someone at Stanley's or House of Nothingness and balled him. Now was different. She became demolished. Carol's trademark attire was long black T-shirts upon which her straight light blonde hair fell in sheaves. She had cheeks that were ruddy 365 a year, and light gray eyes that seemed watery and which fluttered when she was upset. She took to wandering around the L.E.S. with On the Road in tow. They had dinners with the alcoholics in the *Catholic Worker* soup room.

326

Though the Mongol Committee helped when they could, Carol had to sell almost everything, all the way to the humiliating depth of putting a box of stuff for sale, silverware and saltshakers, in the hallway at the bottom of the stairs hoping some of the tenants would buy.

Finally it was too much—her eyes were ringed a Fauvist fierce red and she had wept herself into a daze. One night Bart had promised to bring food and money, but by midnight had not shown. That was it. Carol Mulligan opened the closet door, scrooched down, planted her back against the cold closet wall, gave out a slow sign of bye bye, and inch by inch sank to the jumble of sandals, shoe trees, books and rubber hookah tubing of the Dust Breeding floor. There she resided, with the door shut and On the Road bringing her bread and water for several days till Bart by accident opened the closet and there she was.

Bart was not amused, nor was Ocea the Other, over the closet situation. Carol kept her eyes tightly closed and seemed unconscious. The husband finally called Bellevue and a flip-out squad was sent. The Committee contacted her family in Idaho and she flew home. On the Road remained with Marie Colson.

The night before the picnic Carol was reunited with On the Road, and now came triumphantly into the playground to actual applause.

On the Road, the brightest of the children, was carrying an armful of publications—a novella he'd written called *The Decline of My Parents' Marriage*, which contained some of the better descriptions of beatnik marital discord. While his mom was resting in Idaho, On the Road demanded Marie Colson bring him to Peace Eye Bookstore with the manuscript. Marie and I typed the stencils and we mimeographed it, with a cover drawing he filched from his mother's folios, and On the Road Mulligan at age six was off the press.

He was a very precocious child. If you had said, "Come here On the Road, we're going to learn some Akkadian," he would have been writing cuneiform on wet clay with a stylus in a couple of days.

Later he arranged to sell his book at the Eighth Street Bookshop and the Gotham Book Mart and On the Road became something of a sensation. The *Village Voice* ran an article on the literary marvel and there were inquiries from uptown presses, much to the chagrin and anxiety of his father.

During the picnic, On the Road sold the book to passersby. His pitch was tactful—"My daddy hitchhiked all the way to California, and I wrote a book about it! Only fifty cents!" He sold about twenty five copies in a half hour. On the Road was going to go a long way.

The atmosphere in the park approached that morning what Samuel Pepys termed "a glut of mirth." The glut was seasoned however by the arrival of Marianne Bonfiglie, up all night searching for her boyfriend Llaso who had disappeared without a note, taking her TV, stereo, jewelry and money, plus her prize buffalo-hide drum. She told her story, laughed, and said, "My mother said he would." Someone a bit too tipsy on a bennie and wine mentioned to Marie that Llaso's most well known poem sequence, *I Am a Sociopath*, perhaps should have tipped Marianne off.

Marianne was most upset over the loss of her drum, for she was that strange combination of poet, actress and drummer. Women drummers in the first pentad of the sixties were not plentiful—Marianne Bonfiglie was known

328

later on for trying out for the Velvet Underground and almost making it. For rent money she acted in soft-core nudity movies. She and Llaso sometimes modeled for the Mongol Committee sketch sessions. They had matching purplish birth marks, he on his penis, she above her right breast. During the hot months of their time they viewed them as their wedding marks.

Marianne left the part to continue her search and a few minutes later On the Road Mulligan ran up to announce Llaso was unloading stuff from a cab and carrying it into Fence Lady's store at 10th and B. Fence Lady ran one of those antique/jewelry/household goods places where junkies could deal their rip. She also took orders—one could request an IBM typewriter, say, and Llaso or Andrew Kliver would raid N.Y.U. or an office and get one. The place was known for the scent of the belladonna-based asthma cigarettes she puffed to mask the pot the boys from the neighborhood sometimes smoked in the store.

One of the women stayed with the children and the other eleven ran out of the park to confront Llaso who was dressed in the attire he was known to sport whenever on official business—a large silver cross on a ribbon and a pseudo-clerical collar, tight black Levis worn about two inches too short so that his shiny pointy-toed tight black boots could star, and a Bowery giveaway black jacket. Llaso was tall with a narrow face and Finno-Ugaritic eyes fronted by thick Coke bottle lenses. He had headed for England where he could become a legal junkie.

Llaso tended to be the secret kind of addict, as opposed to his friend Andrew Kliver, who had once shot up in the middle of an art opening. Llaso was both proud of his addiction, and ashamed of it. Sometimes he announced he had kicked when he had not. Sometimes he wrote poetry promoting heroin as a purveyor of pacificsm. England or not, Llaso was soon to get the needle hep that twenty years later would kill him with liver cancer.

His notebooks held an occasional poem dreading his cruelty to his lovers, and when his Coke bottle eyes spotted the swarm of the Mongol Committee he turned toward them, still clutching Marianne's television, and began to tremble. Fence Lady analyzed the situation and clicked the lock.

The women surrounded him. On the Road knew a good story and flipped open his notepad and wrote furiously. "Get his bags!" shouted Carol Mulligan. Someone reached into the cab and grabbed the satchel containing his passport. During this, the author of the *I Am a Sociopath* poem sequence began kicking at the crime screen on Fence Lady's door with a pointed black boot, and then like a good 'path surrendered to the inevitable. He handed over the television, and made the sign of the cross, no doubt recalling all the times he'd spent hanging out at the offices of the *Catholic Worker* newspaper.

"Please tell Marianne I'm sorry," he said, shut the door of the cab, and sped up Avenue B toward lotus in London. Carol arranged with Fence Lady to store the stuff until Marianne could be located. Then everybody went back to the park for the rest of the picnic in a full glut of mirth. Carol remained with On the Road a few more minutes in front of Fence Lady's till he had blocked out his next story.

The Van Job

ENID BAUMBACH had a date to blow Talbot the Great over at his place. Just that, and no more. It was her idea, she set it up, and she was on her way.

Enid was a tireless fighter for social justice. She worked for SANE, for the Congress of Racial Equality, for the voter registration drives. She was perfect for the maddening plentitudes of small pieces piling up all at once that have to fit together on the spot when you organize effective demonstrations. Her specialty was getting *New York Times* reporters to show. It was a miracle talent. Enid could have gotten a *Times* guy to arrive at midnight in an empty tunnel. Later on she was an ace printer of draft cards for the Vietnam railroad.

In her recreational moments she loved to fuck. She lived for it, and expected hours of it, striving where possible to avoid neurasthenic, passive beatnik boys with invisible mirrors grafted in front of their faces. She was in her early twenties and bony skinny. She was from Arkansas and claimed to be part Cherokee, part Rumanian Jewish. There was a hint of the Ozarks in her drawl/twang that stretched the vowels alluringly when she told someone she wanted to fuck him very badly, right then, right there. She had long fingers like in an Egyptian painting that could soothe out your soul, so adroitly they could pass over your skin.

She was extremely well groomed. She was so clean you could have done surgery using her stomach as an operating table—her stomach, that flat, long surface, tanned around the year, with just the tiniest roll of skin near the beltline. She wore African necklaces and accessories which set off the luster of her long black hair that dangled in raven mingles. When possible her lovers were black civil rights activists, and her favorite routine was two a night, each unwitting of the other.

She was unfathomable to some. It was difficult to tell how intelligent she was, she was such a loner. She used few words, except she could articulate for hours her positions on issues. She cooked the most elaborate meals for herself, with candles, crystalware and napkins under the silver, which she would munch in the tiniest bites, with the most finicky of manners, for hours, until the first of her dates would arrive.

As for money, no one knew or bothered to find out how she survived. Sometimes she worked for ad agencies. She had quick fingers on the keys, and was good on the phone. In later years she was a coke mule. She sometimes clerked at African boutiques. Or she would split for months and come back to the Lower East Side bragging about living in a shack on the west coast of Mexico with a youth recruited from a local town who could fuck all night without stopping.

She helped writers. She had just typed Talbot's book of poems he had written during the Birmingham integration campaign the previous spring. She helped Sam Thomas with mimeo stencils for *Dope, Fucking and Social Change: A Journal of the New America*. Once in a while she made it with some of the poets who hung out at the Peace Eye Bookstore, but reluctantly, and the bards were astonished, when comparing notes, to know she always wept as they began to fuck.

Enid wore some of the stranger sunglasses. They were the coolest e'er to appear in the beatnik-hippie era. They were her trademark. One lens would be in the shape of a heart, say, and the other shaped like a clover; or both were shaped like atomic mushrooms. It was a late summer day, and Enid was in her wildest glasses. She was walking north on Broadway just about to turn right at St. Mark's Place and head over toward Talbot's pad. She was wearing leotard-like tight tigerskin-patterned pedalpushers and a halter. It was just about the last day in the season you could do that.

An electric supply company van passed by, with one of the guys leaning out to whistle and bang gently on the outside of the door. The van stopped for a light. So did Enid, who turned toward them with her heart and clover glasses, put her hands on her low-slung tiger 'tards, and said softly, "Let's go."

It was an occasional caper of desire. She called it a van job. One guy looked at the other, shrugged, and opened the door. Enid stepped up and in. It was one of those vans without windows and it was dark in back. She felt some thick coils of electrical wire and piled them together.

"Right here," she said. She left on her sunglasses, tied the 'tards around her shoulders and peeled her panties into a neat roll which she stuffed into her sunglass case.

One guy drove around while Enid fucked the other;

then it was the second guy's turn. She was out of the van in twenty minutes. She asked to be dropped off near Talbot's.

Where she was right on time. She excused herself to wash in the bathroom, and then went into Talbot's bedroom, sank to her knees, unzipped his trousers, and made her peace.

Sappho on East Seventh
a sho-sto-po
(short story poem)

POET JOHN BARRETT was a graduate student in classics at New York University. His obsession was Sappho—there were drawings of her on the walls of his apartment, as well as stats of fragments of her poems found in papier-mâché coffins in Oxyrhynchus, Egypt. Barrett's translations of her poems were taped above his desk, and the living room was converted into a workshop for the construction of a four-string lyre with a sounding box fashioned from the carapace of a European tortoise. John had collected about a dozen shells. They were in all the rooms—tortoise shells on milk crate book shelves used by his friends as ash trays. He ate his morning oatmeal out of a shell. The time was late summer. The place East 7th Street near Avenue A.

He had an obsession for Sappho
He lived inside her meters
like a trout in running mirth

He was building a four-string lyre
to sing Sappho down
Sappho come down

He copied lyres
from the Parthenon frieze
looking for the perfect shape

There were tortoise shells
                hanging by nails
                        on the wall
Another lay on his desk
near scraping tools, a saw,
                    a pot of glue,
        some whittling knives
                from H.L. Wild.
Goat horns
        were hard to get
                on the Lower East Side

So he carved the arms
        from the legs
            of an armchair.
                    found in the street

and a thin rounded sounding board
cut he   (from a spruce-wood shingle)
            to fit
                    on the shell

The crossbar from arm to arm
had tuning pegs from
        an antique broken banjo
                found in the trash
                        of a burned-out store

A bridge he
        shaped & notched
                from an ebony comb

        and when he had built one
        with which he could sing
        he scribed it with Sappho's
        Ἄγε δια χέλυννα μοι
        Φωνάεσσά τε γίγνεο
    "Come my sacred lyre
        make yourself sing"

The Lyre
        transformed him—
                in the mode of the

Dada masks
transforming the shy young poets
in the Zurich cabaret.*

Barrett became Some Other Bard
striding through his rooms
holding his lyre
singing with all the passion to summon:

"There is a river
in Mitylene
where Sappho
used to swim
with a friend

dropping their sandals
with ivory inlay
at the water's bank

I saw Sappho
bending in the foam
peplos-less and chiton free
on a summer's day

singing a song
that is lost

They later lay
in the
creekside glade

soothing each other's
skin
with oil & caresses

---

*Referring to the Cabaret Voltaire of 1915 and the spontaneous poem and dance performances inspired by the donning of Marcel Janco's famous masks.

singing a song
that is lost

O Sappho come down
Sappho come down."

A friend from school,
Consuela,
lived next door

and heard John Barrett's prayer
through the tenement wall

She listened each night
to dig what it was
and finally understood

when Barrett sang:

"as a glider
sweeps down
from the cliffs

over the birchen hills

swoop thou down oh
Sapph' swoop down"

She lay in bed
with her ear
to the wall

spiss-hissing with held-back laughs.

She mocked him:
"as a cornflake
through the
subway grate

                into the
                        bubble-gum
                                muck

                        settle thou down
                        Sapph' settle down"

The next day   she told her Greek class
Together they plotted a trick

One night she would
appear on the fire escape
she shared with Barrett
—attired in chiton and peplos*
and sing/chant some Sappho

as if she were Sappho's *geist*

She bought a bolt of white linen
on Orchard Street
and brocade for the edges
of Ukrainian symbology
                at Surma on 7th
                & sewed herself Sapphic attire

She memorized the Hymn to Aphrodite,
Consuela,
                to sing Sappho down
                Sappho come down

It was late afternoon when she
came from the shower, donned the chiton
and peplos overgarment,
crawled upon the windowsill, shoved
aside her boxes of flowers

---

*The basic attire of ancient Greece, both garments being fashioned
from oblong pieces of cloth. The chiton was a tunic of linen or wool
worn next to the skin, doubling around the body. It was pinned
over each shoulder and held at the waist by belt or cincture. The
peplos was a heavier cloaklike overgarment.

—she knew it was the hour that
                    Barrett would sing—

and crouched upon the gritty
black ironwork
                    blistered and pitted
            from 20 coats in 90 years.

When she heard Barrett's loud
prayer begin and the strings
of his lyre resound, she

stood to sing—Consuela
saw the air above the fire escape
come apart—as if some giant hand
had scissored a line
in reality's tarp

There was a chirping of birds
and dim dots clouding the view.
Through the pointillist gray
an arm was thrust,
            holding a lyre,
then another arm—
            the fist of it clenched

then opened, and tiny kernels
fell upon the grate
of the fire escape
to rain on the courtyard below

Conseula sank in awe,
the rungs of the fire escape
streaking her knees with grit-gray stripes

while Sappho's body
seemed to float
            through the tarp-warp gap

the very second Barrett's
edge-of-frenzy voice

sang

       "Sappho come down
            come down Sapph'!"

At first John Barrett
    tried to
gaze at the apparition
with an it's-about-time expression

        Then, "Sappho!" he gasped,
    for actually

        Barrett had little trust
        in the summoning power

of a lyre with arms
        from a scrScaroungèd chair
and a tremulous voice
        more like a dare

He glanced about his di-
sheveled beatnik apartment
and wished he had cleaned away
the bottles from the night before

Sappho picked up his lyre
    from the desk
        setting her own aside
           and started to sing

He could *see*
    the words she sang
above her
    with a throbbing life of their own

Words of Water

342

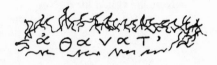

Words of Fire

Words of Broken Oars

When the song was over
        Barrett stood stunned
                tears on his cheek

sinuses cloggy, vision blurred,
ache of love in his stomach.

Then she walked to the wall
        where he'd pinned
                his translations

He tried not to glance
                at her breasts
just as he did not look
                in Stanley's Bar
                on a midriff summer night

The bosom
        of a ghost
                is not for the kisses
                        of eyes.

Barrett was horrified
                to see Sappho stand
                        reading her verses' versions

It was hard to keep from
                        ripping them down.
Finally, she turned away, & laughed,
                        "Better than Byron's—
                                at least."

343

Next she visited his shelves
                              "Let me gaze upon your
                                    Book Boat," she said

SAPPH'

Oh, no!
        though John Barrett,
worrying about the many marginal tomes
                            in his Book Boat

The gibberish of friends,
                    the smut, the
                              malmarked scholarship.

                Sang then Sapph':

                "There is a boat
                      for every bard
                bobbing in the waves
                        a Boat of Books

                Some will say
                    to build a boat of death

                Others will sing
                    a trimaran of green

                But a bard
                    had better build
                        a Boat of Books

                for the troublesome
                    flow.

And you shall find
      a Muse for your age
            in the Book Boat prow:

      Retentia
     Muse of the Retained Image.

The pan pipes
      the seven-string lyre
            the arsis & thesis—
    The muses
        with which I sang

     but yours is the era
        of captured sunlight
          & oxide-dappled tape

     Retentia
catches the beauteous flow
swifter than a cricket's foot

The photos taped to your wall
of my poems' shreds
        were wrought by
    Retentia

She rushes to the aid of groaning Clio
whose scrolls lie thickened & black
She helps you to sort
       to soothe
          to winnow

      as well as to keep
         to save
         to shape

The Image is safe
       with Retentia
           for a million years
     till the pulsing fires
     which scorch all lyres

                  O

Once on an
incurved hillock
      near Mitylene
a circle of maidens sang
       —Alcaeus was there

      if only
      if only
   I could hear
      their image again!"

Sappho stopped singing
      There was a near-sob tremble
            in her voice

"Pray to Retentia, John Barrett,
for each muse aids
        in her measure
and the task
     is to know
the mix of the muses' gifts
         in your lines."

She moved her hand to the wall
     to touch the photostated papyrus
       The wall cleaved apart
         and forth stepped Retentia
     in a blue-black gown
crackling on its surface with
      tiny jiggle-jaggles of lightning
which seemed to form
      almost a lightning lace
        above the blue-black weave

Barrett was wondering
    what sort of prayer
        was proper to utter

in praise of a new muse
        standing in his room
            from the Book Boat prow

He was foolishly thinking
        of scooping the floor
            to kiss Retentia's hem

when Sappho walked to the kitchen cupboard
            and opened the doors

"What does she want?" Barrett asked himself.
        "I don't have any Methu," he said,
    inwardly praising himself for his wit.

(Methu was a famous
            wine produced
                in ancient Lesbos)

"Have you no herb-scented oils?"
            she spoke in complaint,
        shutting the cupboard doors—

    "How frailly you fail
    in matters of love
    & longing," she said

    "How can you think
    a woman like Louise
            would love you,
    knowing what you know?"

She entered Barrett's bedroom,
            a tawdry chamber
                with its mattress
                    on the floor
                        'mid candle spatters

and a blue print of Sappho's
face, large as the wall,
above the bed

"Now you shall learn
the Rubbing of Oils
& Glossa Didacta."

Retentia
appeared at the door
bearing a tray of
tiny canopic jars

—oils & unguents
with which Sapph'
could ply her hands

as she slid the
clothing from shy John Barrett's
skinny frame
& rubbed him thrillsomely
from jar upon jar

                each oil having
        a different thrill
                —a mild sting here
                        and a tremble there—

        & sweet smells
            mixing with
        smells piquant

"There is much you do not
know,"
            spoke she,
neatly hanging her peplos
upon a nail on the door
after she had shut it

She drew Barrett down
O Barrett come down

"We have called it
                the Glossa Didacta
and every bard must have
                its perfect knowledge"

        Down sank they
                upon J. Barrett's mattress

        She pulled his poorly combed
                badly washed curls
        down upon the only thing substantial

            It was like a softened rosehip
            The rest of her was ghost-mist

            "Your head is the rudder
            & I shall steer it over
                    the rapids,"

this way
        that way

steering with fondly grabbed ears
steering the rose bud
steering the bard boy's brow

showing him pressures
                    motions
                            patterns

            "That's it
            That's the way
            That's perfect"

        clitoris bifurcated
                    like
                    a
                    lithops
(left side to the right brain
right side to the left brain?

                    twain
                    bundle
                    of come-nerves?)

Lithops bella

She came in words arcane,
Sapph'-sighs writhing above her
in jumbles of
            hieroglyphic neon,
        as when she had sung—

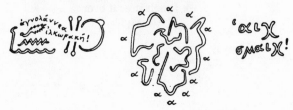

She spoke to him in Latin,
"Now I have taught you
           the Lingus Didacticus
and those you coax
           into its trembly thrall
shall know a dance more lightly tapped
then the meters of Euripides."

Then she bade him
           come inside her

"Don't you make it only with, uh, *gunaikes?*"
           he replied, breaking into Greek.

She'd arranged Chianti bottles
           around the bed
                      with flickering candles within

Barrett looked up
           to see the shadow
                  of the ghost
against her blue print image
                  on the wall
as she tugged him gently
           but insistently
till they lay
           face to face
           & she guided him up & within—

an hour
           to make him
                  believe anew in the
                          thought of the Numen

or an hour
           as a catalpa blossom
                  floating in the River Thrill.

                  Ahh, côte à côte
                  he longed to lie
                  with her
                  upon the dawn—

351

"Stand up," she said instead,
"We're going on a journey."

"If so," replied John Barrett,
"give me satyr legs!
yes, sturdy hairy legs
            & hircine hooves
to spring and leap!"

Sappho smiled, but
could not comply.

She held his hand
& floated
from the room on East 7th

above the green copse of
            Tompkins Park

dizzily dizzily
whirling a further era back—

to 1911
where Emma Hardy sat alone
on a spring morn
        at Max Gate*
her husband downstairs
correcting
    proofs
        with his mistress.

They entered Emma's bedroom
through the dormer windows
There was a feeding station
        by the sill
           for the birds

---

*Max Gate: Thomas & Emma Hardy's house in East Dorset, Dorchester. In 1908 Emma had ordered dormer windows built in her attic boudoir, outside of which the birds at the feeding table would flock to eat from her hands.

Sappho felt pity
        for bitter Emma Hardy
                whose husband's hands

were ever poised
        to trace the
                curves of youth.

She was trying
        to ready herself
                for the day

but her face
                was twisted in pain
                        from a torturing back

The pain was too consuming
                        for her to lite
                                a plate of crusts
                                        to the birds

        She rang for her helper, Dolly Gale
        to brush her hair
        Dolly stood behind her
                unbraiding untangling uncoiling
                        the sleep-jammed tresses

        The slightest tug
                of the bristles
                        brought agony's gasp

        till Sappho reached out
                to place a soothing palm
                        on Emma's spine

                to ease away
                the axing ache

"The oil, John, the oil," Sapph' urged
and John Barrett parted the robe
                from the painèd shoulders

and began to caress
    with Mytilene's finest
        from a thin-necked jar.

The peace in her back
    brought the first smile
        in months

"Call the birds for us, please Emma?"
Sappho asked, and Emma Hardy
    walked to the sill
        and raised her hands

        Emma was 68
        Emma in pain
        Emma threw open the dormer
        to feed them her wedding train

There must have been a hundred birds
in a wild gustation of feathery blurs
above the feeding station
        pecking the breakfast crumbs

"This house Hardy built," Sappho said to
John, with a tone of disgust,

    "without a hot-
    water tub!"

She took his hand again—"Prepare for a trip
to A.D. 642"

There was a further whirling
after which
        they alighted
at a site of steam & fire

Barrett thought for a moment
they might have followed
Dante and Vergil
        into a bolge of hell

There was a hairless man
with a shiny skull
& a missing tooth in front

throwing bundles of papyrus
scrolls
        into the word-eating mouth
        of an open-hearthed ceramic furnace

Water boils above it
                in a large copper basin,
feeding through ducts to a
                        series of copper tanks
        of varying stages of heat
        so that a bather in
        the pool can tug a string
        for the heat of her choice.

        Stacks of scrolls
                jut this way and that.
        Barrett cranes his head
                to read the names
                        upon the next thatch
                        to be tossed

                Oh, no! It takes a few seconds
                        reading the run-on script
                                for John to recognize
                                        the plays of Aeschylus!

                They are heating the baths of
                Alexandria
                with the last of the ancient
                libraries

        "Look!" she cried, "do you know what that is?"
        The attendant had an armload of volumes*
        with projecting knobs. "He's just about to burn
        the final set of my collected works."

---

*Volume: from *volumen*, papyrus rolled around a stick or sticks, the
text written in narrow columns.

The fireman
tossed them two by two in the fameless flame

Barrett tried to grab them
but his hands brushed through
like mist into a redwood bough

      "Some of my poems were
      torched by Caesar

      burning the ships in
      Alexandria's bay
          & the fire reached ashore

      Some were chopped into
      papier-mâché for the
      middle-class coffins of Thebes

      Some were destroyed
      when surly Christians
      sacked the Serapeum*
      in 391

      And now it is time
      for ashes and chars
      to come to the
          mixolydian mode

      Some poets' words
      are written on water
      Others make flame
          to make it moil."

Just then
    the voices of women
        & the clack of clogs
        were heard

---

*One of the two ancient archives in Alexandria.

The daughters of General Amrou†
                had come to soak
                        in the steam-topped pool

& to smooth
                with pumice bars and strigils‡
                        their steam-soft skin

The women
                passed their towels
                        to their servants

and the high-doomed room
                was soon resounding
                        with laughter and aqueous splash

All of a sudden Sapph' shoved past
                        the sweaty man by the furnace
and gathered the final rolls,
                        to Barrett's gasp,
                        and flicked them into the rage

She turned, disrobed,
handed her chiton to
                        Barrett

and slid into the water
to sit on a marble plank
                        with the damozels
                        in the moil pool's midst

---

†Amrou seized Alexandria for the caliph Omar in 642. The latter, it
is said, ordered the remaining books in the ancient library destroyed
on the grounds that now that the Koran had been written, they were
no longer needed.
‡Curved scrapers for removing bath-softened skin.

"Hotter, hotter," she urged
the attendant, tugging on the rope
to empty a torrid tank
        upon them

    while out of the furnace
    a burning fragment fluttered

just a corner of paper,

    curling & burning

with Sappho's last word

βρενθείω
flaming
βρενθείω

It fell at Barrett's feet
He tried to stamp
        at the fire

to no avail

A silver knob
    from the end of a scroll stick,
worked in a pattern of porpoises,
        rolled out of the furnace
    all that remained
  of the works
of Sappho of Mitylene

Barrett reached down to seize it

He slipped
         & smashed to the floor.

He came awake
         in his pad on East 7th
and saw a foot on
         the fire escape.

"Sappho!" he half-screamed
         and rushed to the window

but it was Consuela
         in her Orchard St. chiton and peplos

She seemed asleep
         but opened her eyes at once
                when he touched her
         She told him her tale
         He told her his

         showed her
         the silver knob

         and the smell of the top of his wrist
                still thrillsome
         with Sappho's oil.

         Afraid, yet
             unable not, to
                talk about
         it

         Barrett told portions
         to some, &
         the whole event
to a few

         with the silver knob
         as carefully shown
         as a saint's bone.

To some
         he was
                 Crazy John

("You sure this wasn't
         the head from your
                 grandfather's cane"
                         Sam Thomas sneered)

To others
         he was
                 Lucky Bard

(to carve the proper lyre
         to sing Sappho down
                 Sappho come down)

Though he sang her each eve
he saw her no more
till later that year
on a snowy night

John saw Sappho
her neck laden
with heavy
Russian crosses

praying in the deep drift snow
on Avenue A

before it was disturbed
by salt & sweep

outside the redbrick
St. Nicholas
         Carpatho Russian
church

Icons were
melting in
her hands

& rubies
dropped
from her
crusted neck
into the snow

(though later
      they vanished)

He ran to see her
She was weeping

            "You'll cry too"
            was all that she said

& she walked
away into the blizzard
weeping & wailing

& Barrett
never saw her again.

Wild Women of East Tenth

BLONDE DEBBIE HARNIGAN was lounging in bed that afternoon waiting for the sperm to dry on her ass in shiny patterms like egg white brushed on challah bread, reading Jane Austen. Debbie was one of a trio everyone called the Wild Women of East Tenth, who lived in an apartment across from the Peace Eye Bookstore. They came in and out of Peace Eye all the time—that's how I got to know them. They *were* wild, even by the tunes of the times, and I kept a diary of their wildness for a couple of years.

Debbie Harnigan was a musician. Tuli and I had just formed The Fugs and we held rehearsals every afternoon at Peace Eye, to which sometimes Debbie would bring her guitar and sit in. We had just finished an album and we had signed probably the worst contract since Leadbelly's. Too late I did crash research into the theory of contracts, knowledge I shared with Debbie Harnigan. She learned quickly, and soon knew more than I, though that didn't prevent her from signing management deals with a succession of "I will make you a star" droolers, on her way ultimately to one nighters at Madison Square

Garden, but that was a decade and a half ahead.

Debbie was beautiful. They say skin, as an organ, has almost a life of its own. So it was with Debbie Harnigan. Nothing seemed to blemish its Giotto perfection—neither nuclear fallout, household chemicals, cuts, pesticides, pecker tracks, ultraviolet radiation—nothing. And her body was as beautiful as the Winged Victory at Samothrace at the Louvre. All the beatniks and painters at Stanley's wanted to get drunk and high with her.

Even with her stunning beauty, Debbie had a proclivity for saying yes to odd looking guys, many of them the aforementioned "I will make you a star" skags she met in the West Village. Her roommates would laugh at the oddments Debbie would invite into her bedroom on East Tenth. It took her a few years to learn the crucial differences between managers, dog leashes and boy-friends.

She spent years on the Greenwich Village folk scene, singing on open mike nights at clubs, and hanging for hundreds of long nights at the Gaslight, Gerde's Folk City, the Kettle of Fish, Izzy Young's Folklore Center, the Village Gate, Cafe Figaro, Rienzi's, the Tin Angel, Cafe Reggio, The Wha, the Night Owl, San Remo, the Bizarre, the Derby, Mills Tavern, Minetta Tavern, the Borgia, the Other End, a number of which places are blitzed now, but then they were hot.

The other Wild Women of East Tenth were Enid Baum-bach and Mary Heath. Enid worked for civil rights and peace organizations, and Mary was a painter who earned her bread by waitressing at the House of Nothingness cafe on Tompkins Square North. As much as Debbie was curvy, Enid Baumbach was starkly and erotically skinny; Mary Heath was short and stocky with remarkable shiny black hair that, when unwound, reached all the way down to the occasionally lustrous challah.

They had the coolest pad, large for the East Side, with three separate bedrooms. Everything was haphazard yet carefully chosen. They collected art. Somehow, without paying one dime, they packed the walls of that one slum living room/kitchen with a Joe Brainard, a Rauschenberg, a Mike Goldberg, a Louise Adams, a Larry Rivers, an Oldenberg, a Marisol, a Schneeman, *et alia moochifica.*

One of the pieces comprised the most famous stash of the beat era—a tall, finely painted mannequin with a spring-wound moveable arm. The pot and pills were placed within the outstretched hand. If fuzz should raid, the window would automatically open, and the spring would cause the hand to fling the dope out into the littery courtyard four stories below.

It was the era of rebel pharmaceuticals. Even birth control pills had not long ago been difficult to get—the tendency of doctors had been to reserve them for married women. But by the time Enid, Mary and Debbie shared their apartment, birth control pills were everywhere, and however they were later perceived as potential health harmers, then they were the magna carta of freedom to fuck, and the Wild Women of East Tenth could make out anytime, anywhere, with anyone.

They drank too much, and refrained from few rebel pharmaceuticals except downers or skag. For a while they were fond of the strange new substance known as LSD-25. Most of all it was the living rebel pharmaceutical known as the beatnik male—guys who came, came, and went and the Wild Women of East Tenth laughed them on their ways. Guys tended to show up unannounced around dinner time and of course the Wild Women refused to cook for oafs, and tacked a sign on the outer door, THIS IS NOT A CAFE. They were determined to remain unattached, and so forgave one another when by accident they made it with each other's boyfriends. What everybody noticed was that they laughed all the time. And Debbie's guitar was always there leading them in song.

The Wild Women of East Tenth taught me a valuable lesson that carried me all the way through the rest of the decade. I tended to be morose and always worried about things. Events, projects and decisions swirled around me in terrible turbulence. Nobody had any time to sleep. Everybody had about five careers. What I learned from them was the Dickens Principle—it was the best of times, it was the worst of times, but it was *our* times, and we owned them with our youth, our energy, our good will, our edginess. So let's party. Under the Dickens Principle everything was a party. Poetry was a party. Work was a party. When I put out a new issue of *Fuck You/A Magazine of the Arts* and there was a night long collating session at Peace Eye, sitting lotus posture in front of stacks of pages with Peter and Julius Orlovsky and Barbara Rubin—that was a party. Fugs rehearsals were a party. Even demonstrations and long meetings planning the revolution.

Speaking of parties, the afternoon Debbie Harnigan was reading Jane Austen, Andy Warhol invited me to a party that night at his loft up on 47th Street. Warhol had done the cover for a recent issue of *Fuck You/A Magazine of the Arts*, and he had created some silkscreened cloth banners of his famous flowers that I hung on the walls for the grand opening of the Peace Eye Bookstore. His parties had a kind of weird energy into which everybody wanted to dip at least once, twice or thrice.

365

I asked if I could bring Enid, Mary and Debbie. He said fine. It gave me an excuse to go over to their pad. They were excited. Mary Heath would meet rich collectors, museum directors and gallery owners. Debbie might meet record executives. Sam Thomas would be there, he'd been in one of Warhol's movies. Enid Baumbach volunteered to get them all complete sets of party clothes—dresses, accessories, shoes, even bras and underwear.

"Get" was a key word, for Enid Baumbach could be said to have been a practitioner of the art of astro-grab, that is, of shoplifting by the stars. She had horary charts for her major targets: Macy's, Gimbels, Lord and Taylor, Saks, Henri Bendel, Alexander's, Bloomie's, and Gucci, which worked out for her the best hours, the best days, the best stores for astro-grab. She was very fast, very efficient, and had never been caught. She was an expert at confusion—she would affix a Bendel tag, say, to an garment from Saks, then dispose of the Saks tags with a twist of the wrist quicker than a pit stop at a Grand Prix.

The afternoon of the Warhol party seemed particularly propitious for astro-grabbing some Warholian fifteen minutes-of-fame party duds, so she rushed about taking notes on their sizes and generally what they wanted. Enid Baumbach was a very empathetic shoplifter, whose taste was to be trusted, and usually brought back stuff that was groovy. She flattened fresh shopping bags from the best department stores, and hid them rolled or pressed here and there in her clothing.

After Enid left for the astro-grab, Mary Heath took her usual afternoon walk around the Lower East Side. She went over to the Mindscape Gallery, where she was going to have an opening soon, and then up to the A&P on 14th to shop. Unknown to her, Sam Thomas followed a block behind.

He had learned about one of Mary Heath's secret passions and he was determined to film her—film her that very afternoon. He wanted to take the footage with him to Warhol's party. Sam had an arrangement whereby Andy sent Sam's footage out with his own to be developed, a sort of long-term loan never to be paid back.

Mary's secret passion was that she became sexually aroused when standing near the meat counter at a grocery store. Very sexually aroused. Swoonishly aroused. There had been a Happening titled *Meat Joy* at the Judson Memorial Church over on Washington Square South. Mary Heath had been on the front row as naked bodies rolled around smeared with bovine blood.

Mary's teeth began clicking together nervously. She hyperventilated, seemed close to fainting, and was mumbling beneath her breath. The Happening Movement had almost seen its first instance of the charismatic swoon-moaning of a snake church or tent revival. Nelson Saite was sitting on the same row and told Sam, who did some research, and learned Mary had confided to one of her roommates about her erotic sensations in the steak department of A&P. Hence Sam skulked behind Mary as she pulled her shiny two wheeled shopping cart to the store, and then peeped around the corners of aisles which she purchased vegetables, cereal, etc., and best for last, paused lovingly at the meat section. She gazed at it all. And gazed and gazed. Sam touched her shoulder and said hello.

Sam could get just about anybody to film. He was terribly ingratiating. He'd come up to you in Stanley's and say, "Why don't you come over tonight and let me film your left testicle, man," and like someone in a trance, an

hour later you were letting him. There is a whole generation of men and women, wild beatniks and weirdos then,
and doctors, deans, wheat futures brokers, congressmen,
ministers, CIA officers, and heads of corporations now,
who sweat Sam's footage, saved only by its probably
graininess and by the difficulty of matching twenty-year-
old naked body footage with fully clothed mid-life crisis
faces.

So he went to work on Mary Heath. He picked up a
particularly redly rheumy piece of steak and rested it on
Mary's forearm. She seemed stunned. He cooed like a sales
person selling the Hope diamond. "I'd like to shoot some
footage. Nothing much. Maybe you could pretend like
you're cooking the steak. It'll be a short. We'll call it Meat
Fit."

Mary balked.

"Okay, okay, we won't call it Meat Fit. We'll just call it
Meat." Mary still balked.

Sam pretended to forget his plan, and chatted about
this and that while Mary chose some steak, a hunk of
roast beef on a bone, and a pound of hamburger, foods
she would have purchased anyway. They walked out
together. Sam pulled Mary's shopping cart, and somehow
steered them down Avenue A past the hallway leading to
his little twenty-three-dollars-a-month film studio in a
back building. He invited her in for some grass. Mary
Heath rarely refused a toke, true to the principles of the
Wild Women of East Tenth, and so went back through
the tiny dark courtyard with its crisscrossings above them
in the damp, dank air, of gray clotheslines extending like
a spider web through four floors, and into the back building with its leaning walls known as the Leaning Tower of
Avenue A.

Grass and alcohol were Sam's loosening agents. They pulled on some mild Buck's County Mauve in a little cherrywood pipe. And Sam timidly began. Mary Heath had wide eyes to begin with—and wider they grew while Sam slowly unwrapped the packets of meat and laid them on the white porcelainized bathtub cover next to the kitchen sink. Mary seemed unable to move. He placed his hand on her upper chest and her heart was beating like the bass drum in a marching band at a state championship.

Sam was a vegetarian, and really did not want to handle raw meat, but hey, we're speaking of art, so he lifted the chunks of cow onto plates, then hastened to wash his hands. He loaded his 16-mm Bell and Howell, screwed it into the tripod, walked around the room switching on the well placed clip-on fixtures of photofloods, and began filming.

Meanwhile, Enid Baumbach came back to Tenth Street weighted down with fifteen packages, and she was also wearing three or four layers of purloined finery. She was the only beat era shoplifter who would also get things giftwrapped.

She lay the three party dresses onto the divan. Debbie jumped out of her clothes, and donned the black Henri Bendel gown that plunged down the back all the way to challah land, and in front showed plenty of the Giotto perfection of her breasts. Debbie had wanted a backless pushup bra for some reason, and Enid had gotten a size much too small. So Enid went back to Gimbels to "exchange" the bra.

Debbie retired to the bathroom where she was wont in the afternoons to become very attentive to her crotch. She was one of the few of her generation who douched with Bulgarian yogurt, to improve its pH, and so soon she was

369

smooshing the yogurt into her crotch, and thereafter she drew her bath.

It was time then for the exercise known as the Golden Waters of Danae. Debbie slid down into the bathtub, till she was flat on her back, with her legs extending up onto the drain board of the kitchen sink. She positioned her crotch so that it lay directly beneath the faucet and then turned on the stream, the water rinsing away the milky Buglariana, then shifting her crotch slightly, feeling the weight of the jet until it began to feel good, then adjusting the heat, slowly making it hotter, rotating herself in circles so that the water circled around her mons, and then around her clitoris, and since the nerve bundles on the left side of it seemed more sharply thrilled by the stream, she tended to swerve the water there, and the stream streaming until she was moaning and almost screaming beneath the Golden Waters of Danae. She took the waters often.

Then she shampooed her hair, and was toweling when there was a knock at the door. She scanned through the peep hole and saw two men, one of whom she recognized as a friend of the dealer next door.

They wanted her help. They had the key to next door, they said, and they wanted her to take it and let someone into the apartment in a half hour. One of the guys, in a blue raincoat, had a fresh hundred dollar bill in his hand. It was hers.

"Why don't you stick around and let whoever it is in yourselves?"

"We have to leave. Someone is coming."

"Where's Ray?" Debbie asked.

Blue raincoat looked at the other guy. "He's sick. The doctor is coming to take care of Ray. We have to leave."

Debbie was suspicious. Not wanting to get caught in the midst of a drug deal, and more than that not wanting to get into a pattern of helping dealers, she asked, "What do you mean, he's sick?" She didn't say it, but she knew he'd probably o.d.'d in the apartment next door; he might even be dead.

"Look, take the key and the money. Ray's sick. The doctor will come and take him to the hospital. He'll be okay. We have to leave." There was a scraping sound as they slid the hundred beneath the door and then the trumpling of feet fleeing down steps.

At the very moment the guy in the blue raincoat was crouched down poking the c-note beneath Debbie Harnigan's door, Sam Thomas and Mary Heath were fucking beneath the photofloods in the back building off Avenue A. Mary had a steak clenched tightly in each hand, whereupon she reached up and pounded Sam's back with them, the droplets of red spraying the flower patterned curtains lining the walls.

From his location on the mattress Sam was running the camera equipment through remote devices he had invented. He operated the zoom lens with his foot through a series of levers, pulleys and strings leading to a ring on his left toe. Camera angle was controlled by a similar apparatus affixed to his left hand.

Sam glanced to the side at his stained walls and felt a vegetarian belch of nausea well in his guts. Sam told me how once when he was a kid he'd found a dog skull on a rock outcropping, and he'd decided to make a necklace of the teeth, so he couched there like a savage pounding teeth out with a rock, until a full Jean-Paul Sartre nausea attack had engulfed him in the midday midwest sun, and he had vomited. That was the nausea Sam was starting to

371

feel that afternoon from footage he was probably not going to take anywhere to have developed. A little bit of nausea never kept a beatnik from coming. He felt its incipience, and he whispered to Mary, "Should I stop?" "No, don't stop, come in me, come in me, don't stop." Mary began swoonmoaning like at the Judson Church performance of *Meat Joy*.

Sam heard a crash at the door, and suddenly three policemen were in the room. They saw the blood and immediately drew their revolvers.

Sam was naked except for a blood-drenched shirt. "It's just a movie!" he shouted. "It's just a movie! Look, these are steaks!"

He asked for a search warrant, and finding there was none, Sam was confident he was going to win in court. That confidence however did not prevent the police from grabbing his cherished rolls of film from the shelf above his editing table—the raw footage for many of his "studies," as he called them.

"I am a responsible American filmmaker," Sam confidently intoned, pulling on his trousers. The cop chuckled and pulled Sam's hands behind his back, handcuffed them, and hustled Mary and Sam out to the squad car and off to the Ninth Precinct, where they were booked for meat fuck.

Back on East Tenth, another two men came up the stairs and knocked on Debbie's door for the key to Ray's pad. She kept the door chained, and handed it over, whereupon they clicked open Ray's door. Debbie's door was at right angles to Ray's and by staring through the peep hole she could see inside for a moment when they entered. Ray was slumped over the kitchen table. He looked wounded.

372

She was terrified. Apparently they then wrapped him in a rug, and were trying to leave, when they dropped the bundle, so that it wedged in the doorway. One of them knocked on Debbie's door. "You have to hold the door open and lock up when we leave. Please." Debbie was trapped—afraid to help, and afraid if she refused. So she opened the door, and held Ray's open while they lugged their bundle free and began trundling down the stone-on-metal steps. Just then there was a siren, a slamming of doors, and a line of blue coming up from below.

Soon Debbie too was led away to the Ninth Precinct, but not before she triggered the mannequin stash fling, and an assortment of mescaline tabs, yohimbine bark, ibogaine, pot, yage, meth, peyote and I Ching coins were flung into the air of the courtyard.

Meanwhile, Enid was at Gimbels exchanging the bra. Gimbels was the absolute best source for clippable undies during the best era. Greater caution naturally had to be expended on an exchange of shoplifted merchandise. The store was rather empty so Enid went to the exchange counter, but for some reason the line was slow, so she shook her head in impatience and headed for the bra dept to make the exchange herself. Her curious behavior triggered the attention of a security guard, and they cuffed her.

She protested. "How dare you. I purchased this yesterday. And I'm going to a party, so I was in a hurry and exchanged it myself."

"Sure, mam, sure. May we see it?" Enid forked it over and the security guard held up Debbie's 36D bra against her skinning 32A torso.

Back on East Tenth three lovely party dresses lay forlornly on the living room divan.

They all called me at the Peace Eye Bookstore about the same time—Sam and Mary from the Ninth Precinct, Enid from the precinct near Gimbels, and from another room at the Ninth, unwitting of the plight of Sam and Mary, a weeping Debbie Harnigan. Weeping in frustration over the endangered evening.

I laughed and laughed. They all wanted to be sprung in time for Warhol's party.

Farbrente Rose

THERE WAS A SOUND somewhere between a hiss and "snerk!" perhaps more like "sthufffthuh!" as Talbot the Great brought the joint to his lips then fashioned a wall of his pinky, ring and index fingers pressed tightly together, behind which he lowered the rough circle comprised of thumb, roach and forefinger, twisting his wrist so that the burning end was not to be seen from the front, in case it was fuzz that was whacking the door. With the other hand he slid away the police lock, pulled aside the dead bolt, clicked open the key lock and answered the knock.

The caller was a nervous looking woman in her fifties or sixties, dressed very squarely in a matched wool skirt and jacket, a new raincoat and shiny black purse with small gold initials on its upper edge. Talbot thought she might be somebody's mother. Moms were always raiding the slums to monitor errant offspring. Talbot's eyes were drawn to the visitor's striking red hair, for she was very short and he could see the top of her head very clearly, rippling with red, and the groovy wisps of very curly white near the temples, above dark thick eyebrows.

375

"Good afternoon," the woman said. "I'm Rose Snyder. I used to live here."

"Come on in," said Talbot. "Did you leave something?"

Rose Snyder laughed. "Not quite. The last time I was here was forty-one years ago, but I was born in this very room in 1894."

Talbot was startled. "Hey listen," he shouted to those sitting in the kitchen. "Rose was born here in 1894. She hasn't been in the pad for forty-one years!"

There was a scurry at the kitchen table. One of them helped Andrew Kliver scoop up his scag, works and glassine envelopes in one hand and a spoon he was just about to cook over the stove with the other. Kliver scrambled toward a bedroom where he could work the dope into his arm without the attention of outsiders.

"We're having a pre-demonstration, uh, get-together," Talbot explained to Rose. He did not want to use the word *party*, though that's what it was. "Some of us are going to commit C.D., Civil Disobedience, at the U.S. and Russian missions to the U.N."

Talbot introduced Rose Snyder to Nelson Saite, John Barrett and, when he returned from shooting up, to Andrew Kliver. Sam Thomas and Cynthia Pruitt were also in the apartment, but Sam had hauled her into the second bedroom for nervous, pre-demo make-out. Sam had left the door an inch ajar, so Cynthia arched her pelvis to the side, shifting the hyperventilating bard atop her out of the way enough for her to stretch out her toes to shove it shut when she spotted the stranger in the kitchen.

Talbot continued, "Usually we meet before a sit-in. It's sort of a party, I guess, but it helps calm us down. Sometimes there are last-minute picket signs to be painted, or

376

statements for the press to be typed. Just before we leave we form a circle and sing."

Cynthia and Sam came out of the bedroom and were introduced to Rose Snyder. Sam opened two quarts of Rheingold and handed one to Rose as an introductory gift.

No one in the room yet noticed how upset the older red-haired woman was who, with some difficulty, was standing in their midst holding a thick wet quart of beer. She was only beginning to decipher what sort of den of mishuganas she has invaded and also trying to think of an excuse for not drinking from a bottle offered her by a possible drifter. On all sides of Rose Snyder were agitated youth striding then sitting, then jumping up and striding, laughing, sighing and talking too quickly. They were like convicts in a prison yard trying to keep the guards from getting a count during a breakout. The motivity in the room obscured the stranger's disturbance.

Rose was accepted among them without question. They thought she was probably there to take part in the demonstration, that it was just a weird coincidence she had been born in Nelson Saite's pad at 56 Ludlow Street.

"Are you from the Quaker Action Committee?" someone asked.

"No, I'm not. I was born here, she repeated. I haven't seen it in years. I thought, before... I thought I'd see what it was like now."

"I bet things haven't changed that much," said Nelson Saite in his mid-South baritone. "It's still a poverty-stricken hole but we love it! Do you recall if Stoltzburg's Dairy Restaurant at Ludlow and Grand was there in your time? Sam and I practically *live* there, writing leaflets over borscht or blintzes. The owner lets us spread our papers out on those nice big tables after the breakfast rush."

Rose remembered the exact locations of all the stores from her youth. "It was a clothing store when I lived here," she said, her spirits beginning to rise, if only partially to mimic the ebullience of the room, though it was a long way to ebullience from the murk of soul she'd suffered when just five minutes ago she had slowly ascended the narrow flights, her heart pounding from the climb, pausing to calm her breath at the landings, toward a pad that had been crumbling and dismal since at least 1850, and was still crumbling and dismal.

The venture had been made even more uncertain by the battered array of mail boxes in the foyer. Some had their name cards in the slots, others could have had no name cards because their box doors had been torn away, while a few hung loose and open, twisted and angular, the victims of robbers with pry bars. She had planned to jot the name of the occupant of her childhood home then call to make an appointment. However, as best she could tell, a nameless, bent box with a nuclear disarmament sticker was the one that corresponded to hers.

They brought Rose Snyder into the living room where she sank rather alarmingly into the collapsing engulfment of a weak-springed grimy green street couch with pockets of extruded stuffing the color of griseous caramel dangling from the arms and sides.

Unknown to any of the firebrands in the apartment, Rose Snyder had been one if the leading socialist and union activists in New York City during the early decades of the century. When she was in her early twenties, around 1915, she had been one of the *farbrente meydelekh*, the burning young women who arose from the

378

sweat shops and tenements to lead a movement that, had World War I not intervened, might have brought democratic socialist economics at least to New York City. In those days Rose Snyder's nickname had been Farbrente Rose.

Much had happened to her in the forty years gone by to fill her with doubts and regrets, a situation compounded now, in her sixty-ninth year, with frightening mood swings. It's a problem with those who have spent years or decades in the struggle for a better world—the tendency to feel guilt. For Rose it meant that her mood swings corresponded with cycles of less guilt, more guilt and most guilt.

She tended to dwell on obscure moments in the history of American radicalism. It was as if she could get to the past in a time machine to alter some botched event then the rippling effects of its improvement would forge a corresponding improvement in the present. The events which taunted Rose Snyder's mind were those only a scholar of the American Left would understand. "If only I'd signed the May 22 proclamation . . ." or "We could have picked up more votes for Debs in the 6th Ward if only I had . . ."

The hand-wringing unhappiness and the Matthew Arnold/William Cowper anvil of sadness she felt pulling her down came upon a woman with no energy. She who had once run fifteen projects at a time now could barely get to the store. So unhappy was Rose Snyder she would have welcomed a heart attack as it beat her ribs from the strain of the stairs at 56 Ludlow.

Rose Snyder's face looked in all directions around the living room of Nelson Saite's little four-room pad, for it was in this very room at century's turn that Rose and her

379

family had worked fifteen hours a day for a "sweater," sewing pockets into trousers and linings into caps.

Talbot Jenkins plopped down next to her in the grimy green engulfment and introduced himself. She was interested in what sort of demonstration they were planning.

"We're against the testing of atomic bombs," Talbot told her. "This afternoon there's going to be two demonstrations at the same time at both the Russian and the U.S. missions to the U.N. Kennedy's about to sign a test-ban treaty, but we don't think it solves the problem. Like, what about *underground* tests. Both the Soviets and the U.S. are going to continue, for God knows how many more decades, to test underground bombs. This stuff stays down there—molten, lethal, poisonous, with deadly radioactivity—for centuries! We want *all* tests stopped, not surface tests only, and *now*, in 1963!"

"And cancer!"—Talbot was angry by now—"nobody wants to talk about cancer, but these military industrial surrealists are going to force all of us to die of it because they are poisoning the world with their filthy tests. So that's why some of us are going to sit down in front of both missions. If there's enough we'll block the streets too. Those who don't want to get arrested will hold a support picket up the street. You ought to join us."

Talbot pointed to the posters resting face-out and side-by-side on the wall opposite Rose. Cynthia Pruitt was on her knees next to them with paint and brushes sketching some nuclear mushrooms and bombs on oak tag. Rose was fascinated by the posters. She wiggled to the edge of the sofa to see more clearly. She couldn't stop staring. Something was wrong.

All at once the wallpaper changed color. The lighting dimmed. The light sockets were different. There were brass gas-lamp fixtures, though no longer used, still in place above the bulbs. No longer was it poster array '63, but poster array '13!! Rose saw the same wall, with a row of signs in the same place from fifty years ago!

"Now I remember!" she exclaimed. "I was wondering if my mind was playing tricks on me, but I'm *sure* we used to make posters in this very room for strikes and Labor Day parades. My mother and I would line them up *just* as you have them!"

Rose gave them a brief account of her work with the Women's Trade Union League and later with the New York branch of the Socialist Party. Nelson broke in to ask if she'd known Emma Goldman. Yes, she said, Goldman and she had worked on a magazine. Nelson was thrilled. To have met someone who had known his goddess, Emma! He wanted to find out more so Saite asked Rose to tour the apartment with him.

The pad Rose now inspected was much more dirty and shabby than the spotless rooms her mother and she used to keep. Nelson apologized for the disarray and for the unseemly glut of Rheingold bottles teeming the floor, tables, shelves and sills. One thing was the same as in Rose's day—the place was packed with posters and bundles of literature. Nelson was a pack rat, and spoke of opening a Museum of Ahimsa some day. Thus relics of sit-ins and civil disobedience were carefully stored—a burned suitcase from a torched Freedom Ride bus, photos of pacifists swimming out to confront nuclear submarines, montages of news articles against the A-tests.

Rose found evidence of her family everywhere she looked. In her day, the only heat for the bedrooms came from running the stovepipe from the coal stove in the kitchen through the bedrooms before venting through a metal sleeve in the back window. Rose pointed out to Nelson the round metal plates, crusted beneath decades of paint, tacked over the pipe holes.

Rose recognized the bathtub as the same one her parents had fought the landlord for years to obtain. How many letters and visits to the Health Department it had taken to get in-pad plumbing! Up to then, she told Nelson, the only source had been an ever-trickling common faucet above a rusted basin in the hallway, which neighbors left clogged with potato skins, hair, soapy skin and sock skuz.

Rose began staring intently at the linoleum. "Where did you get it," she asked.

"When I moved in, we peeled about seven layers off the floor, until we came to this one which seemed groovy and unworn. It was like an archaeological dig—this was Ludlow Street, level 7-A, like it was Troy or Mycenae."

Rose kept blinking her eyes to improve her gaze. The pattern was unmistakable.

She recognized the border of murex-purple stars or

diamonds from 1922. The stars had always reminded her of the line from the song, "the stars shine down on the workers' hands." Rose had saved for months to buy the linoleum. She was so busy with union work she only had had a part-time job. She remembered the afternoons after work at the linoleum store on Delancey Street agonizing over which pattern to choose. It was just before she was married and moved to her own apartment, so it was a going away present to her parents who were determined to spend the rest of their time on Ludlow Street.

It was too much for Rose. The memory of that happy day installing and cutting the linoleum with her parents brought cascades of grief, rivulets of grief, chunks of grief breaking off, grief rolling in chasms of grief. Her poor mother and father, so soon to pass away after her marriage and move-out. Maybe they would have lived longer had she stayed behind? Her father too blind finally to write for the *Daily Forward*. Her mother crippled from arthritis and heart disease. And now the dour mousetrap of infinity was ready to crunch her also, just as it had them.

Rose made a sudden gahk! sound and began to sob. She felt for a chair and dropped down with her whole weight, so that the leg of it buckled, tossing her to the floor. She rolled upon the patterns given so lovingly so long ago, covering her legs with one hand and wiping her eyes with the other.

Talbot, Nelson and Cynthia sprang to lift her to her feet and brought her back to the green couch where Talbot and Cynthia sat on each side of her, stroking her back, offering to make her tea and trying through conversation to soothe her. Sam Thomas wedged himself next to Cynthia and he was sliding his hand beneath Cynthia's

383

slightly elevated left ass-half while she leaned to the right consoling Rose, when Becky Levy and Louise Adams arrived in the kitchen. As quick as a cockroach diving off a table top, Sam removed his hand from the quadratic curve and met the eyes of Becky Levy, the woman with whom so recently he had wanted to spend his life—had talked about children and how and where to live.

They had broken up over Andrew Kliver's theory of the "Wiggling Apexes." Kliver's theory had been wrought from his remarkable skill even for the Beat era in maintaining triangles. But a mere static triangle was insufficiently imbued with Gandhian openness and truth, Kliver reasoned, so he made sure the "wiggling apexes" of his triangles came into contact as often as possible. Sam followed that theory into disaster, and Becky Levy tossed him from her life.

Sam struggled to his feet from the engulfing divan, careful not to use Cynthia's leg as a push-off, and talked with Becky, who had her short dark hair tied up in a bandana as a protection against the rough hands of the police. Becky saw Rose with her head bent upon her arms. "What's wrong," she asked. "Who is she?" "She just came here," Sam replied. "She's a Yiddish-speaking socialist. From the old days. She apparently was born in this very apartment. She decided to come back and check it out."

Just then Rose Snyder said she was leaving. She was embarrassed and out of place. The others said, please stay. Tell us more about what it was like here forty years ago.

"I'm not sure what's up," Sam continued to Becky. "She's somehow weeping about the past. She lived here. When I helped Nelson rip up the linoleum, we exposed the pattern she had once purchased for her parents. She

384

saw it and began to cry and somehow she fell. She's very upset."

Becky went to the green couch and introduced herself in Yiddish. Rose was surprised, not having spoken it in years, but replied in kind and a brisk conversation began. Becky was about to look at an empty apartment next door, and did Rose want to come also. It turned out that Rose and her husband had considered the very same apartment in 1922. Becky's gaze scorched Sam as she and Rose passed out the doorway.

Nelson and Andrew Kliver also left. They loaded up some boxes with empty Rheingold quarts, worth five cents each, enough to get a couple of quarts to bring back. "Just what we need for a barricade buzz," said Nelson, thinking of the line of policemen with clubs they were going to face.

"See if the new issue of *I.F. Stone's Weekly* is there," shouted Sam Thomas. I.F. Stone, the premier data sheet of the era, was good jail reading. It was easy to hide if the jailer wanted to seize it as contraband and it was the sort of writing you could read over and over.

Nelson came back with the beer just about the same time as Becky came back from looking at the pad.

Sam asked her if she were going to take it. She didn't think so. It was too small, she said, though the real reason was having to live next door to testosterone-crazed drunks and dopers. Plus Sam would always be scrounging around monitoring her love life and begging for attention. She was one of those poets who are *very serious*, and live verse around the clock. She was both obsessed with and critical of Sam and his lout pals who also lived it around the clock, but the clock hands trembled with erotomania, dope, lines shouted above a sax solo, quickly stapled

385

manifestos and insanity. Hence her affair with Sam Thomas was not the love/hate first delineated by Catullus, but fascination/flabbergastedness.

Rose Snyder seemed calmer, so Nelson wanted to ask more about her years in the union movement. "We don't have to leave for a few minutes," he said. "Why don't you tell us what it was like here fifty years ago? Tell us more about Emma Goldman. Eugene O'Neill. Paul Robeson. In fact, why don't you tell us your whole life story?"

Everybody was excited and spoke at once. Had she known Scott Nearing? John Reed? Elizabeth Gurley Flynn? Eugene Debs? Morris Hillquit?

"Who in the fuck was Morris Hillquit?" Sam Thomas interjected.

Barrett looked sourly his way. "You mean, Sam, you've never read Hillquit's *History of Socialism in America?* He ran for New York City mayor as a socialist in 1917. Picked up something like twenty-two percent of the vote—isn't that right, Rose?"

Rose nodded. It required some coaxing, but Rose told her tale. In speaking she gave out the sparks that had once made her one of the *farbrente*. Shy at first, she dropped her grandmotherly reserve and opened wide the folios of the early century. Everybody in the room, nervous as they were about the sit-in, became attentive. There was silence except for the splisst! splissht! whenever Nelson placed church key on Rheingolds and passed them around, during the story of Rose Snyder of Ludlow Street, which we relate below, filling in some of the details she was reluctant to relate to her new-found friends:

386

1

The cossack reined in his stallion cruelly
by the hut on the edge of the shtetl,
snapping the bit so neck-twisting tight
that a slobberflip from the horse's mouth
wetted the doorstep where Rose's grandmother stood.

The cossack raised his wrist
for a whaap! of his iron-tipped whip which
wounded her face before she could turn away.
The whip whapped down again, and more, till
she fell to the mud, protecting her face and chest.

The raids wouldn't cease
nor the Czar's decrees
nor the peasants, rotgut mean,
with fleas' feet meshed in
embroidered beds of flowers
on their holiday shirts,
attacking at Easter with
        scythes and dirk-tined rakes,

so her grandparents moved
from the Russian Pale to Warsaw.

Her mother and father
        were married there.
They published a Yiddish paper
        The Socialist Dawn

which tried to put into practice
        the spirit of
                "*In di gasn
                        tsu di masn*"
                Into the streets,
                        to the Masses.

Even in the city the raids continued.
The Socialist Dawn was crushed
& Rose's parents went underground
putting out pamphlets and fliers
                    to spread
                    in the factories

                    In di gasn
                         tsu di masn

                              2.

The courtyard was aflock with dashing children
and men with pails of water and milk.
Someone was beating a rug on a rack
with a curlicued wire on a stick.

In the middle was the toilet house,
afflicted with rats, destructive to the nose.
The windows facing the courtyard were
opened outward

and there was a faint "clack clack clack"
of a printing press on the top floor,
inking the fliers, "*In di gasn*
                    tsu di masn"

They came into the yard, not bothering to be quiet—
pails were dropped, children ran for the doors
windows grumped shut.

They ran up the stairs, kicked open the doors
and rifle-butted those within,
smashed the printing press,

carried the leaflets down upon the polished stone
of the yard, doused them with kerosene,
left them burning, shoving the prisoners
to the street

Dirty Jews! one of the police detachment shouted
at the empty courtyard, whapping his whip
among the piles of flambent fliers

and sparks of burning word
flew up past the frightened faces.

3.

Not many months thereafter
the couple gave it up,
fled Warsaw, its incessant hostility,
passing first to Antwerp,
and then to London. From there, in 1891,
to 56 Ludlow Street, in the Lower East Side.

Rose was born in 1894, and a sister in '96,
in the midst of one of those incomprehensible
economic collapses New York gives to its poor.

Her father wrote for the socialist paper,
            Arbeiter Tseitung
            but that was not enough
        they set up a shop in their home
took in boarders
            to pay the exorbitant rent—

the rents in the slums were often higher
than cleaner neighborhoods. The East Side
had been slums
            since the overcrowding
                after the War of 1812—
two-thirds of the tenements owned by speculators
getting 15 to 30 percent (or more) on their money.

She remembered the battle against dirt—
the fear of smallpox and typhus—
the rats that scurried in cribs—
the milk always sour—
coal lamps on dirty tables—

the laundry tubs on the firescapes
and so many shredded sheets on crisscrossed lines
from building to building
for five flights down
she could barely see the boys
playing stickball in the court.

In the winter, her heart went out to the tramps
in a row at night
on the roof of the bakery, just down the street,
their feet in packing crates.

4.

In 1897, when Rose was three,
        she sat on her mother's knee
                in the Bowery's Thalia Theater
for the night of "The Spoken Newspaper"
        when a huge audience paid 10 cents to hear
                a group of authors & editors
                        read aloud
                                some articles and editorials

raising the cash
to start the *Jewish Daily Forward*,
for which her father wrote the rest of his life.

In 1905,
        when Rose was eleven,
                there was a revolution in Russia

which spread to Warsaw
                and then was crushed.
Soon there were uncles and aunts and cousins
                fleeing the violence
sleeping on the floor
                by the swatches of tweed
                        and the claw-foot stove.

When she was 16,
        she joined the Women's Trade Union League
             and led a strike in 1910
at the place where she stitched linings in caps.

She was beaten and jailed.
        Her mother sold some furniture
            to pay the bail.

5.

There were bells and sirens on Broadway
near Astor Place, where Rose was stitching
a hundred caps in a fourth floor loft,
on a March day in 1911.

People were screaming in the street about a fire.
Rose shoved aside her boss and ran down the steps.
She rushed to the scene of 18 minutes of hell
on the edge of Washington Square.

Just as she was rounding the corner of Washington Place
Rose heard the rushing sounds of airfilled garments,
pla-thock! pla-thock! the last to leap from
the fiery windows of the Triangle Shirtwaist Factory,
its workers locked in by the boss, unable to escape.

No other
symbol of evil
until
the camps of Hitler
so seized the
mind

as when Rose saw her friends among the women dead upon the
pavement.

It changed her life. She spoke at rallies
after the fire with overwhelming power.

It was then she became one of the *"farbrente meydelekh"*
with a voice newly found
to unify the Yiddish-speaking socialists

> *In di gasn*
> *tsu di masn*
> Into the streets,
> to the masses.

Sam Thomas was much too excited to hold his voice in
check any longer. "Wow, what a couplet! *In di gasm/tsu
di masn!*"

Rose heard the error but was silent. "Thou art truly
maddened in the gonads, Sam Thomas," said Nelson Saite
with a laugh. "It's not *gasm*, man, it's *GASN.*" The other
smiled but Sam went ahead. "*In di gasn/tsu di masn, In
di gasn/tsu di masn.* That's exactly what we have to do
with nonviolent direct action. Into the streets with it! To
the masses!"

6.

For twenty years the
East Side socialists grew
(in spite of the problem of voters
not wanting to "waste" votes
on a socialist
when a reformer
ran against the corrupt machine).

They filled the arenas
and packed the streets.

The night in 1914
that Meyer London
was elected a socialist

392

to the House of Representatives
            from the Lower East Side
They gathered in Rutgers Square by the 1,000's
and partied till the sun blushed the color of communes
above the docks.

In 1917 the Socialist Party of N.Y.C.
sent ten assemblymen to Albany
and seven to the N.Y.C. board of aldermen
and even elected a municipal judge

while Morris Hillquit
pulled 22% of the vote for mayor—

Throughout these campaigns
Rose wrote pamphlets, gave speeches—
it looked
as if the socialist dawn
might move as a spill of thrills
out through the state.

7.

But a surge of bellicosity
retarded the socialist dawn,
and not just in the Lower East Side.

Rose beamed her powers of oration
against the gradual drift to war.
Some were sympathetic
to the strong socialist and
union movements in Germany

in a struggle
            against
                    Czarist barbarism—

others felt it
            was just a distracting disturbance
                    between Russian and German militaries.

The Lower East Side was split.
The pressure to support
their new country
                        was great.

In February of 1917
the Czar was stomped down.
In October
        the Bolsheviks seized power—

The Revolution
        gave the American left
                        such hope!

No more rich!
        No more poor!
                No more pogroms!

Oh, that it would spread!
                even to Ludlow Street.

The socialists met in
                St. Louis
                        in April of '17.

It was Rose's first trip
                to the smug interior

She stopped in Terre Haute
                for a conference with Debs—

And then on April the 6th the U.S. Congress
voted for war
                and the next day
the socialists issued what was known as
the St. Louis Resolution,

"We call upon the
        workers of all countries

to refuse support
to their governments
in their wars."

The Wilson administration
generated war hysteria.
Rose spoke at street rallies
with toughs breaking banners
and shoving at the edges

Scott Nearing, Eugene Debs
went to jail.
The government threatened the mailing rights
of the *Daily Forward*
and other socialist publications
opposing the war

and Debs when he was sentenced
on September 12, 1918, said

"While there is a lower class
I am in it; while there
is a criminal element,
I am of it; while there is
a soul in prison, I am
not free."

*In di gasn
tsu di masn*

8.

In 1919 in Seattle, a strong union town,
60,000 shipyard workers struck,
calling for nationalization of key industries.

Federal troops
invaded
Seattle
at the Mayor's request.

395

> Military Intelligence ops
> snooped and manipulated
> Martial law was threatened
> The strike was squashed

> In April 36 bombs were
> mailed to prominent public officials
> who were "notorious anti-radicals."

> Then there were May Day riots
> when cops and vigilantes
> bashed legal rallies
> in Boston, N.Y., Cleve, Chi, Detroit, L.A., et al.

> In Cleveland the police & soldiers drove
> tanks & trucks
> into crowds.

Then in June 1919, Rose told the room, someone tried to dynamite the home of Attorney General A. Mitchell Palmer, and Palmer went into action. What are known as the Palmer Raids ensued. (In August of '20 Palmer created the General Intelligence Division to be headed by a 24-year-old law school grad named J. Edgar Hoover, who began at once to work the media to spread the Red Scare.)

Meanwhile there were race riots in the summer of '19, in the fall the Boston Police Strike, and a giant steel strike. Military Intelligence units were positioned in all major cities, and the steel workers repressed with wholesale clubbing and shooting.

9.

> They were having a meeting at 56 Ludlow.
> There were Rose, her parents,
> and a number of others,
> crowded within.

396

They paused below,
comparing notes to a fluttering match
that they had the correct
apartment

then trample-ran loudly up the stairs
and kicked in both doors to Rose's pad—
the agents of U.S. Attorney General
A. Mitchell Palmer.

It was January 2, 1920,
and Rose's house was only one among many.
Palmer's agents crashed into
"radical hangouts" in over 30 cities
looking for what Palmer labeled
           "alien filth."

Though only aliens were supposed to be arrested,
1,000's of Americans were caught in the Net,
and they seized from Rose's apartment,
as criminal evidence,
a packet of Joe Hill's ashes.

Now it was Nelson Saite's turn to interrupt Rose
Snyder's story. He was outraged. "You mean Palmer's
sleazy sludge actually attacked this apartment!?" He
looked about him angrily as if they were still there to be
shoved out the door.

Rose spoke of how after the war there had been hideous
inflation, and F.O.B.—fear of Bolsheviks, like the fear set
off by the French Rev and the Paris Commune.

All of it mainly a
false promulgation
to crush the union movement.

Laboriously constructed
labor organizations
were decimated

397

Small town/small city socialists
in places like Kansas and Oklahoma
were scared back to bi-party blandness.

In New York City the police raided the
Chinese branch of the I.W.W.
Public school teachers were fired.
The Lusk Committee of N.Y. State
            Legislature
        conducted raids on the Rand School
            and other radical orgs.

There was a campaign to expel socialists
from the Assembly. Rose's powers of oration
beamed against it, but five were banned.
The socialist Victor Berger (from Milwaukee)
barred from taking his seat in the House of Rep.

By December of '20, Emma Goldman and Alexander Berkman
            and 240 others
                deported.

Meanwhile the Socialist Party was rent
with the birth of the Communist Party
and the Communist Labor Party
and some spent the next 30 years
bewailing th' bewaning of socialist strength

while others clawed aftward
much more fevered
        for factional advantage
            than relief of suffering.

By the end of '21
Rose had lost all faith in the Bolsheviks—
She didn't feel
        the dictatorship
            was transitional.
It was obvious that the Czarist repression

had been spat forward
          into the revolution
before it could heal.

                    10.

Farbrente Rose
          met her husband Sam
                    on a picket line in '21

Their wedding night they
wrote an appeal to President Harding
for the release of Eugene Debs from prison

and the next day they left
for a train and hitchhiking tour
of the States.

The newlyweds looked at the
apartment next to the one where Nelson
now lived, but Rose wanted off
of Ludlow Street
so they moved "uptown" to 9th and 2nd Ave.

For years it was paradise
balanced between the rough world
of the trade unions
and life among the playwrights
and poets and places like the
Provincetown Playhouse
plus work for the Socialist Party,
enticing the unconvinced as best they could
through lectures, leaflets and rallies.

Music was never far away—
Rose on accordion Sam on flute
playing in socialist stomp bands
          in the summertime.

Children were born in '22, '24, '25,
after which they joined the
line of radical moving vans
to the Bronx, to Brownsville, and
in their case to Long Island,

where Sam became a college professor
and Rose formed a publishing company.
Her next twenty years were
                a Hymn to Pamphleteering—

        O Paine! O Defoe!
        O Spirit of Pamphlets!
        There is no
        orchestration of sounds and smells
        like the clack of the printer
        the squnch! of the stapler
        the squish of the binder's glue
        and the urge, immediately upon mailing
        it out, to begin another at once!

                A beautiful era
                skiing into a volcano

                happiness of motherhood
                and pamphleteering
                while so many friends collapsed
                in
                the lure of money
                and middle class ooze

                while the country
                through the '20's—
                with unemployment
                at 10% —
                sneaked drinks
                and danced the Charleston
                in raccoon coats
                on the way to
                        Depression.

11

Roosevelt's initiatives
        soaked up much of the right's rage
but also
        weakened the left.

It was hard to
      be a democratic socialist
        in the 1930's
wedged in pain between
        the sharp tongued Moscow leftists
         and bitter shitter rightists.

Rose worked ceaselessly
        for a chaos of causes
raising money for
        the Southern Tenant Farmers Union
campaigning to save
        the more radical
         among Roosevelt's programs—
pamphleteering for child labor laws—
tedious train rides to Albany
        to jostle the governor's mind.

At home Rose had the plight
of so many leftist parents.
There was not to be a socialist correlative
of the Zen concept of "Transmission of Mind"

as they found, with the backs of their hands
to their mouths in shock,
the cause had not been passed to their kids.

Rose blamed herself
She hadn't enough time to oversee their
educations, didn't bring them enough
into meetings and actions
(or perhaps it was the opposite).

It was then her guilt began.
That and the strife from
what her friend Emma Goldman called
"affairs of the heart."

She took an occasional lover
while Sam sought solace
in their home where
outsiders were barred.

Hitler seized power in '33
and fascists murdered Spain

while she watched with sadness
how the Socialist cause couldn't lure old friends
from the Communist party
as they swung to the right
after the '36 Moscow show trials

Watching the earth grow evil again
with the reign of war

12.

Their son was killed in W.W. II
and one daughter married a psychiatrist
and became a history professor,
embarrassed over her mother's past.
The other married a Republican banker
and settled for softness and safety.

Rose was an abrasive as ever
with "shirkers and shrinkers"

and when, after the death of Roosevelt,
it had become clear that the State Department,
through Breckenridge Long,
          prevented the refugees from Hitler
                    from flowing to the U.S.A.

Rose went back to pamphleteering.

There was a surge of union militancy
in '47 and '48 but then the right
made its move,
and Rose stood trembling age 54
no longer sure of herself.

She and Sam talked about emigrating
to Israel but the bloodshed halted them

Rose decided at last to rest
She had done her work
She had enjoyed her moment
& now she would be still

but the '50s
        made the pillow
            a fevered place—

        McCarthy and the snarls of the War Caste
        The decision to build the H Bomb
        The Rosenbergs The Korean War
        The SACB (Subversive Activities Control Board)
        The House Unamerican Activities Committee—

        When Einstein called for defiance in '53 of
        congressional committees inquiring into
        political beliefs, Rose went back to
        pamphlets and ink.

        The repression of the '50s somehow
        crushed Sam and Rose
        as the repression of the Palmer Raid era
        had not.

        '53–'54: Red hunts in the schools,
        the Cotton Mather
        of it being
            police state Eddie Hoov'

Sam Snyder was threatened with
loss of tenure
and went into early retirement.

They were so crude as to ask questions
about "Negroes in your home"
and that he had shown his students
issues of the *New Masses*
in class

They brought
up lectures in 1954 Sam Snyder
had given at the Rand School
in 1924!

In retirement
they summered in the Catskills
and wintered in Long Island
There was solace in rurality
Rose played the accordion
          for the first time in decades
They formed clubs with other radicals
to talk about the times

while the rest of the '50s whizzed past
the deployment of ICBMs in '57
Marines into Lebanon '58
and then the shriek that
bounced through her skull the rest of her life
the day Sam Snyder returned
          with the dooming hospital tests.

She nursed him through
          a long course of cancer
                    till he died in 1961.

13.

Though she painted a brighter picture
than the paints of her depression
those in the room knew her plight—

The black lists and
          her husband's dread death
The bitter burden
          of a world barely changed

The Bay of Pigs
          atmospheric tests
                    repression in the South

There was nowhere to move
for even the briefest kiss of peace
          forward
                    backward
                              sideways

and nothing inside
but a passion for justice
          that never fades away
and heartbreak
          to know she had failed
to build a New World
                    inside the New World

and then that day in late September
she took the train to Manhattan
and a cab to Ludlow Street
and climbed
          the iron steps,
pausing, thinking to flee,
till she saw the door where she had lived
with a sticker by the peephole:

**WORLD WIDE
GENERAL STRIKE
FOR PEACE**

JAN. 29 - FEB. 4, 1962

---

and knocked.

405

Rose finished and the group applauded. "Beautiful!" exclaimed Nelson Saite. Everybody wanted to throw their arms around her. Rose's story calmed the room, because it was so obvious that their single sit-down was like a speck of pine pollen in the decades of upheaval which lay before them, with struggle flowing into struggle without a lapse.

"Rose, why don't you come with us today," Sam said. "You don't have to sit down. You can be in the support picket." The others urged her also.

At first she shook her head. Her daughter, she answered, the history professor without one single sheet of paper in her F.B.I. file, and her shrink son-in-law, were expecting her, the depressed and crushed down radical mother, for dinner by early evening. They would be very worried should she be late. But the demo was uptown not far from where she was going, so why not lift a picket sign one more time? "All right," she said, and they applauded her one more time.

As good as Rose had made them feel, the trepidation surged again in the room as they prepared to leave. Several rather belatedly called their bosses and said they'd be late for work—like two weeks late. They'd chosen not to pay bail or fines.

Sam Thomas lifted off the bathtub cover and took a quick bath. He always wanted to be as clean as a priest of Apollo for civil disobedience. You never could tell when cops would strip search you and you wanted to be clean.

It was Louise Adams' first civil disobedience and she was very nervous. She was worried about leaving Mindscape Gallery untended during the time she would be in jail. And she was afraid of being hurt. Sam shouted from the bathtub about "opening ourselves to the stomp-out," words which did not soothe Louise.

Becky Levy was on the phone with the sergeant who would be overseeing the arrests, working out the final details. Gandhian openness required detailed notification prior to civil disobedience.

There was a moment of sadness just before leaving when they said goodbye to Andrew Kliver, who for the first time wasn't joining them because now that he was hooked on junk couldn't risk the prospect of being drenched in sweat bashing his head against cell bars doing cold turkey in the Tombs. Trying to blend a junkie into a circle of friends was always difficult because of the need to steal. "Breaking and Entering is breaking up that old gang of mine" was the name of the tune.

Petty dealing no longer fed Kliver's jones so he had gone to petty theft, then when that wasn't enough the crowbars went after the police locks. That night he was due to roam Long Island with an auto team. Andrew heard Louise Adams worry that Mindscape Gallery was going to be unguarded and grim thoughts of stealing her kiln made him look away and down.

They formed a circle, held hands, and sang "We Shall Not Be Moved," then left the apartment and headed for the train. *"In di gasn! Tsu di masn!"* shouted Sam Thomas.

An hour later Rose Snyder was carried away by the police, her first arrest since a rally for the Southern Tenant Farmers Union in 1934. On the perforated metal seats of the paddy wagon, she sat between Sam Thomas and Talbot the Great, their feet rocking and stomping the floor with a medley that included "God Bless America,"

"Solidarity Forever" and "We Shall Not Be Moved."

When Becky Levy was tossed among them, Farbrente Rose told her she was going to take the apartment. Later Rose telephoned her daughter from the precinct house and told her the same thing.

"You mean you're going to *move* back to Ludlow Street after fifty years?" her daughter asked.

"In di gasn, tsu di masn," replied Rose Snyder.

Cynthia

CYNTHIA PRUITT awoke on a day in late 1963
and spent the early morning translating the fourteenth
century political poem titled "The Evil Times of Edward
II," the one beginning

> Why werre and wrake in londe   and manslaught in y-come
> Why honger and derthe on erthe   the poor hath overnome,
> Wy bestes beth i-storve   and why corne is so dere

The eery rise and fall of the vowels and the subtle alli-
terations were qualities she hoped to bring to her own
poetry, now that she had decided to write a book in her
new apartment on Eldridge Street.

Her roommate was Rose Snyder. Rose had left early
that morning for a demonstration against U.S. con-
tinuance of underground atomic tests. A treaty had just
been signed between the U.S. and Russia to ban the
leukemia producing above ground tests, but the war caste
insisted on continuing to poison Nevada.

Cynthia and Rose were holding a housewarming party
later that night. Cynthia set aside the poem, bathed, put

in her diaphragm and went up to Sam Thomas' apartment on Avenue A. She and Sam had to meet in secrecy because Sam was *non grata* at the *Catholic Worker*, where Cynthia was on the staff.

After college, Cynthia had been drawn to the *Catholic Worker* movement, its life of voluntary poverty, its insistence on doing good, its antiwar efforts and its direct action support of the impoverished and the weak. She was given a CW staff position where first she helped paste up and distribute the *Worker* newspaper. Later she wrote articles and also worked on the soup kitchen the *Worker* operated, and at least once a week went out on picket lines. She needed almost no money and for the first year lived free in a *Catholic Worker* apartment near the House of Hospitality, the name for CW headquarters which then were located on Chrystie Street south of Houston.

Celibacy was expected of unmarried CW staffers, but there was a laxness of enforcement, and Cynthia loved to fuck. Many on the staff were devoted celibates, but there were others who mixed fervent radical Catholicism with eroticisms wide of wedlock.

Along came Sam Thomas, who sometimes confused Dionysus with Christus. Sam had friends on the CW staff and edited the early issues of *Dope, Fucking and Social Change: A Journal of the New America*, at the *Worker*, had typed his mimeograph stencils on *Worker* typewriters, and even borrowed four or five packets of leaflet quality paper from the *Worker* with which to print his first issue. Cynthia had allowed a couple of her randier poems to be published in D.F.S., and a several other staffers also. These transgressions came to light and Sam was banned from the CW typewriter, and CW staffers were forbidden publication in D.F.S.

410

Talbot the Great lived upstairs from Sam in a back building on Avenue A. Talbot was coming out of the building when Cynthia was entering. He was on the way to the post office with his weekly package of records and books for Johnny Ray Slage, the kid whose father was the head of the klan chapter outside Birmingham, and whom Talbot was secretly "educating."

She paused to chat with Talbot, and admire his great football mashed nose. He had been a football star before he became active integrating the South. Why don't we hang out together sometime, Talbot suggested, and Cynthia gave an eager yes. Her first black lover. She couldn't wait.

By the time Talbot arrived at Stuyvesant Station on 14th Street taxis were beginning to stop in the middle of the street. People stepped from the sidewalks to crowd around them, demanding the drivers turn up their radios. Pay phone circuits went dead. There was shouting, there was weeping, there was anger, there was disbelief.

Talbot ran back to his building to tell Sam. Sam and Cynthia were already naked on the pallet. Sam was reaching up to adjust a hot photoflood when Talbot knocked. "Hey, man, the President's been shot. I think he's dead."

Near Cooper Union was an old garage outfitted as the Luminous Animal Theater. Its founder, dancer/singer Claudia Pred, was heading a rehearsal that morning of John Barrett's musical drama—*Bomb Calf*, which traced the invention and construction of the A-bomb and its seizure from the scientists by the military-political apparatus for Hiroshima and Nagasaki. Barrett was nervously watching. The door at the rear banged open and there was an hysterical shout from the street.

411

Difficult as it may be for those who read this in later decades, in 1963 very few on the set had a television. Televisions were derided as "plastic," as time wasters, and as the electric opium of squares. Claudia Pred cancelled the rehearsal at Luminous Animal and she and John Barrett trotted to Stanley's Bar where there was a TV. Talbot Jenkins, Uncle Thrills, Becky Levy, Cynthia Pruitt and Sam Thomas were already there. Rose Snyder and Past Blast arrived too. They crowded around the fuzzy little screen behind the bar top. It was the first time some of them had been in tears since childhood.

Even Sam wept. "You could not escape the feeling," he said, "standing by the reflecting pool last August that things were about to change. Kennedy was coming around."

Only Uncle Thrills, who had gone to Harvard at the same time as Kennedy, seemed unaffected. "Another dead punk," he said. The others glared at him and ssshed him to silence. There had been virtually a moment before/ moment after change in the radicals—all the anger at Kennedy for slowfooting on civil rights, for not going ahead and banning underground tests, the sneers about warmongering at the Bay of Pigs and Cuban missile crisis, had ended and a pain whose duration, bounds and qualities could not be predicted had begun.

The young man known as Past Blast also seemed not so concerned about the President's death. He was cheerful and ordered drinks. To him it was the first day of the redemption of the world through anarcho-chaos. "He tried to blow up the world," Past Blast said. "Now the world has retaliated."

Sam snapped, "Shut the fuck up, man."

Thrills was more prescient. "You guys ought to weep

412

not for Kennedy, but for the soon-to-die. You have to understand that the war creeps are in full control now. The rest of the decade is going to bleed."

Eighteen years later Past Blast was sitting in Cynthia Pruitt-Abrahamson's kitchen in Vermont. At first she was reluctant to believe that it was Past Blast, companion of her youth, sitting in her house. Past Blast, now a respectable journalist whose weekly columns were published in about eighty-five newspapers, and of course no longer writing manifestoes under the name Past Blast, but rather inking the past instead of blasting it.

Cynthia could not resist asking, "Do you still have your tattoo?"

Past Blast removed his jacket, pulled open his shirt, and revealed the words on his left shoulder: HISTORY'S NO MYSTERY/BLAST THE PAST!! A message seldom shown to his editors now that he was a famous inkist clicking the keys of his laptop on flights around the globe.

His purpose in visiting Cynthia was an article on what the rebels of the early sixties Lower East Side were doing on November 22. He'd already spoken to Sam Thomas, John Barrett, Becky Levy, Talbot the Great, and just before he succumbed to leukemia, to Uncle Thrills.

Cynthia made some Almond Sunset tea, wondering whether to trust Past Blast not to trash the truth. She decided to tell most of what happened. He probably had much of it anyway from Sam Thomas, and Barrett had let P.B. read his diaries from those months. All she asked from Past Blast was that he change her name in the story.

"Ok," said Cynthia Pruitt, "November 22 was supposed to be Rose Snyder's and my housewarming party. Of course we cancelled it. Everybody was naturally upset.

413

Rose went uptown to spend the night with her daughter and son-in-law. I tried to go to bed early but couldn't sleep. I went out at midnight to see Sam. I'd never seen him so morose. He was watching his footage from the Great Washington March over and over. When he switched off the projector he had the saddest expression. He looked like he'd fallen against an electric fence. He said he was thinking of giving it all up and going to law school.

"I felt the same. I wanted a change desperately. Our affair was wonderful. It was great to make it with Sam now and then and talk through the night. I'm sure he felt the same. I was tempted to fall in love with him, but everybody knew he was still gone for Becky Levy.

"That night, like Sam, I was in a stupor of misery. I had brought the handmade rosary, fashioned from tight balls of rose petals, that my grandmother had given me when I came to New York.

"I had already made some decisions about changing my behavior. First of all I was going to attend Mass again. It had been drilled into me it was a mortal sin not to go to Mass. I was nervous and twisting my grandmother's rosary around my fingers. Sam spotted that and tried to unwind it. All this stuff about humility and going to law school was swept aside. Sam said, 'A god-grovel is dope for dopes.'

"It's hard to change. We started to fight."

"I also wanted to have a baby. I thought about that every day. But with Sam? I wasn't sure. Molecular biology was not so advanced then and we did not yet have the term 'chromosome damage.' But Sam was a bit nuts. And of course Sam didn't want a baby. My thinking was the same as a lot of the girls on the L.E.S.—why settle down with a beatnik boy to have him treat me badly and run off in a few years? All of them were quitters. I was not about to become a whiny, clingy square, but I did not want to raise a child alone on welfare on Eldridge Street.

"Sam would have listened to a creep like Uncle Thrills and he'd have been long gone. Do you remember him? Thrills had this disgusting rap about poets and wives. He'd say, 'Here's what you do, Sammy, you're a poet. A poet can always fill his house with women. The uglier and scroungier the poet the better. You can insult the typewriter with the worst mimeographed gibberish and you'll still be able to sucker seven generations of wives. Here's how you do it. You marry the first one when you're young and you dump her in your mid-twenties; then you get another one until you're in your early thirties and when she wises up get another, only make sure the new one is at least ten years younger than you; by the end of your thirties dump number three and troll for number four, who should be very young and very rich. Keep four until your mid-forties, or at least till you get a big divorce settlement out of her. Then go for five in your early fifties; number six is a gamble—you might keep her all the way or you can get number seven in your mid or late sixties and go with her all the way! But remember, this last one will dump *you*!! Dump you in the grave.' And then he would laugh and shout, 'ImGrat! ImGrat!,' which I'm sure you remember, and stupid Sam would be nodding and taking it in as if he were reading a Herman Hesse novel."

Past Blast told Cynthia that Thrills had just passed away from cancer.

"I'm sorry he's dead, but he was a horrible person. To him women were something you cleaned with a fingernail file. Forget about madonna—Thrills had a prostitute-dirt complex."

415

"What else happened the night of the assassination?" asked Past Blast.

"We kept fighting. I accused him of using me to make Becky Levy jealous. Sam was upset that I was going to stay on at the *Catholic Worker*. If I did, it was going to be difficult to keep seeing each other. I had a secret concern in all this, and that's what was fueling the fight. It took a while to get the nerve to bring it up. It was the footage. I was determined to get ahold of that footage. Did Sam tell you about it?"

"You mean the *Spontaneous History* footage?" Past Blast replied. He was being polite. The full title was *Spontaneous History of the American Blow Job*.

"Yes."

Past Blast laughed. "We never see it listed in Sam's catalog of credits now that he's the head of a film school."

"Well, I'll tell you why you never see it listed. I was sitting there twisting my rosary so tightly the beads should have scattered on the floor. There was the genuine heat of shame on my cheeks, thinking of my 'role,' if you can call it that, in *Spontaneous History of the American B.J.* Sam had this thing—you'd be making love and all of a sudden the film was rolling. I was convinced it would ruin my life somehow. Sam would show it at the Bleecker Street Cinema and put my name on the marquee. My grandmother would read about it in an article. Finally I got enough nerve to bring it up.

"'Unfair!' he yelled. 'This will be regarded in future generations as *religious* footage! This will be a sacred videotext viewed in the pageants of the New Church!'

"I want it back,' I said. 'I want it destroyed.' He was as shocked by that as by anything I had ever said to him.

The thought of throwing away something that was to him an art project was completely unacceptable.

"I was determined to walk out of there with my section of that film. Sam had his apartment designed like a harem. The walls were completely covered with silky floral cloths that hung from wires at the ceiling. I knew that behind one of these cloths were the shelves where he stored his films—a shiny black cloth with large gold metallic flowers. I went over and shoved it aside and I began flinging film cans to the floor. Some fell open and film was exposed. He had an editing desk where he had a lot of strips hanging by clips from horizontal strings. These too I grabbed and flung to the floor. His filing system was not the best, and I was scrambling all the footage from his various projects—*Amphetamine Head,* his Washington March film, and *Spontaneous History.*

"Sam went crazy. He began waving his hands in the air, shouting 'Okay! Okay!' He isolated the footage I wanted by putting the reel up on the editing machine and cutting it out. I held it to the light to make sure he wasn't fooling me. There I was—kneeling in front of Sam and blowing him. I expected lightning to strike me down, I was so embarrassed.

"I pulled it off the spool Sam had wound it on and made a big wad of it and was holding it in both hands, with loops and spirals dangling down toward the floor. Sam got into it. He started to do the same.

"'You're right!' he shouted. 'It's all gush. It's a flowin' ooze! Everything oozes! It's mush. It's gush. It's skush!' He went into a fury of abnegation. I knew he absolutely loved his films but he began hacking at them with scissors. I couldn't bear to watch him destroy his art so I started screaming at him to stop. He screamed also. We were the

417

scream twins. I went for the door. He was still sane enough to ask if he could film me holding the wad of *Spontaneous History*. I turned around and let him. He switched on the floodlights and caught me with the wad, then I ran into the hallway and out into the streets.

"Down on Avenue A, I still had all this film in my hands. I didn't know what to do with it. I didn't want anyone retrieving it so I crumpled it best I could, crushing it on the stones of the gutter, and tearing it into pieces. Some I pushed through a sewer slit and some I deposited in garbage cans.

"I was totally out of it. I wandered about not really paying attention to where I was. Some streets as you know were more dangerous at 2 A.M. than others. On some you could get killed, but I didn't care. I just kept walking."

Cynthia found herself outside a red brick church at 10th and A, across from Tompkins Square Park. The sign read THE ST. NICHOLAS CARPATHO RUSSIAN ORTHODOX GREEK CATHOLIC CHURCH. It was a building she'd walked past hundreds of times without really letting it register in her consciousness.

Cynthia stood beneath the tall dark bricks which were surrounded by a black iron fence topped with spikes, straight spikes alternating with wavy. The church was not an architectural master work, and it had no history on the set as a power zone. Yet that night Cynthia felt its power. Carpatho power. The awesomeness of the Carpathian Mountains, the keening of the wide Carpathian culture for the Deity. Cynthia had tied her scarf like a shawl over her hair. She grasped the spikes of the fence with both hands and closed her eyes in prayer.

Then she sank to the pavement, resting her head against the space between the two fence bars directly in front of her, the cross on her rosary clanking the metal.

On the Avenue A side of the St. Nicholas Carpatho Russian Orthodox Greek Catholic Church, where Cynthia crouched, there was a one-story dropoff that left a gap of about eight feet between the edge of the sidewalk and the wall of the church, which in the daytime is clearly visible as a lower floor. That November night it looked to Cynthia like a moat or a pit. There seemed to be a chill coming from it and there was an uncontrollable shuddering that seized her shoulders and arms.

"For years it bothered me to remember it," she told Past Blast. She laughed—"At the time I was afraid to tell anyone. They only people that knew were Sam, Talbot and John Barrett. John, as you know, had a similar experience outside the same church. If you had this experience twenty years later you could go on TV talk shows and run expensive weekend seminars describing it, but then you kept quiet.

"I could see a tunnel. It was like the entranceway to one of those underground parking lots where you twist down ramp after ramp. My ears began to roar. There were sparkly dots in the tunnel. To me they were hell flecks. The only thing I'd ever experienced that was similar was sometimes you wake from a dream and there's a throbbing pulse in your temple veins and a kind of rushing sound in the ears, and till you wake up, even though your eyes are open, you see sparkles, kind of two dimensional fireflies that make a kind of crackling noise. That's what it was like.

"I couldn't stop this wild trembling. I was jerking like a puppet. I felt blasted with a power that was rushing

419

inside me with the pepper of a desert storm in the face. I made a decision on the spot. Whoah! I thought, I don't want any part of this. You have to turn your back on the pit. I could always see hell later."

Cynthia pulled herself up by grabbing the spikes at the fence top and walked around the corner to the church's front entrance on 10th where she knelt on the steps beneath the door and prayed. Something distracted her. She heard what sounded like the chirps of birds, impossible for a late November night. She looked down the street toward Avenue B. It was as if there was a six-foot vertical slice in the field of view, and a figure stopped out of it, to the side, and forward. It was a woman.

At the same moment there was a waft of petals drifting from Cynthia's seventy-year-old rosary. The woman was barefoot and wearing a long loose robelike wrap, with part of it seeming to be draped back around over her shoulder so that an edge of it dangled diagonally down the front. There was a cap, or perhaps a scarf on her head, with a jeweled band holding it in place around the forehead. Her hair was gathered in long, thin bunches arrayed like tines of a fork across the front of her shoulders.

Even from a distance Cynthia could clearly see the woman's face, for it seemed very lightly to glow. It was round, with cheek bones close beneath the apparition's startling, gleaming eyes, and the lower eyelids stretching in almost a straight line from corner to corner. Her lips curved every so slightly downward, yet the pout of the lower lip made the mouth seem a smile.

The vision came near and handed Cynthia a set of beads. They were the same as her grandmother's except they were affixed with a silver medallion embossed with a

420

lyre and a bee instead of a cross. They melted into her grandmother's beads, and became them. There was the neighing of horses yet no horses were anywhere on the dark street. The apparition opened her robes and Cynthia could see above her breasts the tattoo of a heart wrapped in green thorns.

There was snow on the street around the vision's feet and here and there in the snow were piles of jewels, crowns, ikons and chalices crusted with ornamentations of ivory, ruby and sapphire.

Cynthia could see that the figure was sobbing. Cynthia knelt in front of what she always later called the Carpathian mother, and reached out to touch the hem of her robe.

And then the vision was gone, and the scents fading also, and the snow gone, the jewels gone, the weeping mother gone. All gone. Gone gone gone.

"I probably prayed at that spot for at least an hour," said Cynthia Pruitt. "I began to feel all this joy and energy rooted in mercy. Right then, as I still knelt on St. Nicholas's steps, I remembered how Dorothy Day had quoted in her autobiography from the preamble to the International Workers of the World constitution, about a 'society in which it is easier to be good.'

"That did it. Never before had I felt such a lifting away of burdens. There was only one vow I could make—to do more—to serve—to spend years in prison against the war machine. I was willing to stay poor my whole life—I *wanted* to be poor—and, yes, chaste. But that would always be a problem. As for the Catholic church, I vowed both to challenge its injustices and to live within it.

"I stood and suddenly I was very cold. I pulled the coat close to me. I felt a piece of something sharp on my neck.

I touched it. It was long and thin. I was so out of it I didn't realize for a while what it was. It was a strip of *Spontaneous History* that had necklaced itself on my coat. I rolled it up and kept it."

"Do you ever look at it again," Past Blast asked.

"I did. I still have it. Now, rebel that I still am, I wish I had all of it."

"What did you do next?"

"I returned home to Eldridge Street at 6 A.M., took a cold, chaste bath, then went over to the *Catholic Worker*. I had the key. Let myself in, cut potatoes, and helped serve breakfast to the Bowery guys. I was praying constantly. I recall the hot air pressing through swollen membranes in my nostrils onto my upper lip which was red and sore from all that crying."

Cynthia trembled in her Vermont kitchen. She was reliving those minutes in the *Catholic Worker* soup kitchen: "I was praying for myself, and I was praying for another Catholic, John Kennedy, and I was praying for whatever it was I saw outside the Carpatho Russian church. I prayed for Sam, for Uncle Thrills, for all my pals on the East Side and on the picket lines. I prayed for my mother and grandmother, for my father and brothers. And then the poem from the morning came back. I was ladling oatmeal for the alkies, and found myself singing it:

"Why werre and wrake in londe and manslaught is y-come
Why honger and derthe on erthe the poor hath overnome
Wy bestes beth i-storve and why corne is so dere...

The Muffins of Sebek

As the gluons
bind the neutrons
within the atom's core—
so too Rent Control
binds us to the Perfect City.

O Rent Control!
You are the root,
the bast, the base
of any decent way of life
in a land where food is abundant!

Rent Control!

Sam Thomas spent the morning working on his "Hymn to Rent Control." It was difficult searching for fresh images to sustain an ancient concern. It couldn't be just doggerel or the empty shuffle of a bundle of placards dropped resignedly behind the sofa after the demonstration.

But, man, he loved rent control! That most powerful of

decencies, the right to live cheaply in good housing even if your country or city is convulsed in spasms of greed and landboomers.

Speaking of rent control, Sam's morning ebullience began to wane toward noon, as he began to worry about his fifty-one-dollar rent-controlled rent. His normal practice was not to think about it till the 20th, after which it usually was an easy project to raise the cash.

But not this month, when he faced the phenomenon of poverty-within-poverty, a grim condition subsumed within the concept of long-term poverty. Sam and his beatnik pals had long ago acquired a tolerance for long-term pov—the sudden shut-offs of heat in midwinter, water pouring from ceilings onto paintings, junkies stealing the few shiny objects from your junk. But there was somehow always a surplus for art. If you could scrounge the rent, then money for food, thrills and art supplies somehow always arrived. But not this month. Sam Thomas was down, busted, without a cent, with no job, no prospect, and without a single friend from whom he could borrow some bread.

The only food he had was a fifty-pound bag of oatmeal with which he made his daily banquet of Yum—soy sauce, raw eggs, Hellman's mayonnaise and raw oats glopped together in a wooden bowl. In times of drought he did without the Hellman's and the eggs.

Sam stood from his desk and began to pace the room, instructing his mind to come up with ten or fifteen instant formulae for cash. He felt the same nervous twinge in the stomach as just before a sit-in at the Atomic Energy Commission. His close friends were similarly afflicted with sudden poverty. Nelson Saite, Becky Levy, Talbot the Great, Cynthia Pruitt, Louise Adams—dimeless. All were in their respective pads worried, plotting, making lists, consulting the phone numbers of relatives in address books, lining up hockable items on kitchen drainboards, stirring pots of coffee and biting lips.

Not many blocks from where Sam Thomas was pacing his bamboo floor mat, Uncle Thrills was beginning what he railingly described as a "three-day penury whack." Thrills too had the iron hobs of pov in his face and had vowed to remain at home till he'd solved the problem. Home for Thrills was a tiny pad in a decrepit back building that actually leaned to the side so much that it was known on the set as the "leaning pad of Thrill Street." Only by resting against the building to its left did Thrill's back place manage to stand. There were long rod irons impaled through it and into the next building that kept it from wobbling. Its bricks were heavily charred from what must have been a great fire sometime in its two-hundred-year existence. There were zigzags of cracks leading up to marble window plinths through mortar so crumbly that many bricks could be plucked out at will. The place had been an instant slum when speculators had quick-built it in the eighteenth century on top of the kitchen garden of the house in front, and it was still a slum.

Thrills allowed no one, except an occasional woman, to visit him. He always tried to fling aloft the legend that his apartment was a luxurious citadel of genius, hidden in the slums like the lair of Balzac, a place where he could work the tribulations of his calling. The truth was that he lived in a chaos of lonerhood. Not that Thrills lacked lovers, for he always attracted those surprisingly numerous women who are drawn to wizened, beaten-down and fatally flawed creative types. He was a master at plying the Love-a-Loser Factor, his ravaged and pitted face defying the vicious, stupid world and his head trying not to shake with oppression as he handed the sheaf of verse to the damozel in the cafe, just minutes after meeting her. In an hour or two, they would be quick-stripping by the bed in her apartment.

He always stalled bringing them to his pad, for the Love-a-Loser Factor, strong as it was, usually could not hold up under the horror of encountering Thrill's rooms, which in the fifteen years he'd lived there had never been dusted or swept except for the table where he ate and wrote, and in the sense that the paths from toilet to bed to table to bookcase were broomed by the scuffle of sock and slipper.

Neat stacks of books, newspapers, underwear, socks, notepapers, etc., six feet high or more lined the walls. Now and then one would topple in an ozymandian jumble, and if it wedged in an out of the way place it would just lie there for eight or nine years while long gray skuz grew upon it like the tufty remains of an animal long deceased on the forest floor.

In spite of the hispid forest floor of it—I mean, just *walking through* his pad wearing clean clothes and not getting dirty was a big project—Thrills would always emerge in the clean, pressed, perfumed and colorful clothes of a dandy or boulevardier, his bountiful black hair with two wide streaks in front like perfectly combed marble curlings, and his shoes as shiny as an oily East Side gutter puddle. There were hints of the struggle here and there in his pad—a box of spotting cloths and the smell of carbon tetrachloride, a suitcase full of twelve-year-old shoe polishes, cracked and dried, most with only tiny chunks still wet enough to be used, and a jumble of former shirts, now blotched polishing rags.

There was no thought of fophood this afternoon as Thrills sat at his desk in black and white checked flannel pajamas, torn at the crotch, that were down and out in grimesville, man, grimesville. Taped to his typewriter's housing was an odd notation—"3 for 5"—which meant he had three days to make the five hundred dollars a porn publisher was offering for a completed manuscript. The publisher was one of those who take sadistic pleasure in setting unrealistic deadlines. In this case, if Thrills did not submit it in three days the deal was off.

"Another Dharma Bum Whack," muttered Thrills. He was referring to Jack Kerouac, a friend from long nights at the San Remo bar on MacDougal in the fifties. Thrills had always marveled at Kerouac's ability to click out books quickly. The 1953 *The Subterraneans* had been written in three days and the '57 *Dharma Bums* hadn't taken much longer. Thrills knew he could stay awake three straight days before swerving into coma—the problem was to stay creative. As in Kerouac's case, the speed of the key-click was to be augmented by amphetamine. A needle was boiling in a pan on the stove. Thrills had also devised a methedrine vaporizer to switch on at crucial times for billowing an energizing though possibly corrosive methedrinous fog on his mucous membranes and lungs.

Thrills always had trouble with his opening sentence. The first thirty-five words were almost as much of a toil as the 50,000 that followed. This afternoon he was already up to his 47th:

The bat dick slid into the left nostril of the Countess while Count Cornflower stroked its wings with a stalk of celery.

427

"Owl quim!" he cursed, x-ing it through and searching for another way to begin his tale of interspecies love.

> Dr. Whitney held the enema bag in triumph as he walked toward the zebra.

No again.

> Her jissom-drenched lips slid across the sea lion's flipper along a trail of chocolate-covered ants toward Count Blithecomb's pecker . . .

"That's it!" he exclaimed, and went forward without a pause into a long and twisted tale of towers, enemas, frottage, celery stalks, oil-dipped corsets and cravings for zebras in castles.

The very moment Uncle Thrills had found his opening sentence, Talbot Jenkins was giving the signal at Andrew Kliver's pad—four raps, a pause, then a single rap. Cynthia Pruitt was at his side, wearing a dress for the first time since the sit-in at the U.N. two months ago. She could only stay a few minutes—she was beginning a job waiting tables at the House of Nothingness and they were making her flash gams as part of the gig.

Kliver opened the door. He was bent over, standing in longsleeved cream-colored long johns and socks, with a stiff white clerical collar around his neck and a five-inch silver cross suspended on his chest from a thin black ribbon.

Kliver was a minister in a beatnik Catholic sect called "The Gnostic Rite of Old Glastonbury." His lips were drooping; he'd just shot up. He was holding a kitten in one arm.

428

Talk about sudden poverty! Both Talbot the Great and Cynthia Pruitt were glum with it. Christmas was just ten days away and Talbot was down to six dollars while Cynthia had only a subway token and the *Catholic Worker* soup line. As tough and revolutionary as their chatter was, there were elements in their attitudes similar to the silent, self-doubting depression of broke Americans at Christmas, the sort who feel like zeroes as they walk by the bell-ringing Santas in front of department stores they feel unworthy to enter.

Talbot especially was gloomy. Christmas presents were impossible, since he had used his savings for the trip to Birmingham after the bombing of the 16th Street Church. His mother and father—chief singer and minister at a Harlem church—made a big deal out of Christmas. There was already the tradition of Talbot showing up on Christmas eve with a stack of gifts for parents, sisters, cousins, uncles and aunts. He also wanted to get some books for Johnny Ray Slage, the klan kid he had met in Alabama, and to whom he had been sending weekly educational packets. Cynthia wasn't worried about not having presents when she showed up in her annual holiday trek home. Her problem was the bus ticket. For some reason her mother thought that hitchhiking was the signal of total depravity. Cynthia was determined to avoid the strained, horrified "Ha! I predicted it!" expression on the mommie brow when she unlocked the kitchen door, having thumbed through winter storms, her room kept perfect with the dolls and teddies of her childhood, door closed against dust, blinds drawn, waiting like a museum exhibit.

Cynthia's usual procedure for cash-scrounge was to band together with friends from the *Catholic Worker* and sell its newspaper at night on crowded streets. The cover price was a penny, but people would often give a dime or a quarter, and they would divide the extra money between themselves and the *Worker*. Thus she could come home with up to seven or eight dollars, enough for a week's diet of grains and pasta. She hadn't been able to do anything since the assassination except suffer and pray; in fact, she had come out of her depression only a couple of days ago, and had gone against a long standing vow never to become a waitress to avoid the humility of home-hitch.

Kliver chided them over their "yule mewl." It was just an ignorant game, he said. "Why do you want to show up falsely prosperous and hand out stupidities wrapped in overpriced paper for hostile relatives who, whatever you brought them, would accept them with the barely inaudible snickers of squares!"

Cynthia and Talbot sat down on Kliver's mattress and smoked a reefer to the background track of jazz from the smashed guts of a radio in a shoe box, while Kliver entertained them with a stream of quick wild tales culled from the life he lived at the intersection of anarcho-pacifist Catholic poetry and the world of small-time heroin users.

There was a succession of coded knocks as they talked, mostly trey bag and nickel bag customers. Among them was an N.Y.U. student from the suburbs named Sandy, who arrived in a blue boater's coat with gold buttons and penny loafers polished in oxblood to an antique gloss. His blond hair, already thinning at twenty, was cut crewcut short, yet he'd managed to part it and plaster it against his noggin in what was known as the Princeton style.

His cheeks spoke of pink health and his notebooks from chemistry and physics lay beside him on the mattress. It was obvious Sandy hadn't done that much smack. He bought $250 of nickel bags, presents he said for his pals on the Island. Kliver was very happy, and as soon as Sandy left peeled off five tens and handed them to Talbot.

Talbot the Great at first refused them, but Kliver insisted. "Get some presents. Wrap them well. Be an American!"

Meanwhile, back in his pad Sam had decided it was premature to worry about poverty till his oat level dropped to around 20 or 25 pounds. Instead he was working on an editorial for the next issue of *Dope, Fucking and Social Change: A Journal of the New America*. He was addressing his enemies. "And remember," he typed, "the Egyptian word for asshole is ⳝⳠ — *pekhewet!*—and so beginning with this issue each D.F.S. shall bestow Golden ⳝⳠ Awards." He typed a list of bestowees, among them J. Edgar Hoover of the FBI, new president Lyndon Johnson, Governor Wallace of Alabama, Bull Connor of the Birmingham police, and Morty Kemp, the latter being a theater operator on Second Avenue who had attacked Sam in the crowded lobby after a poetry benefit the other night.

He hated making enemies! Yet Sam always found them rising against him. Morty Kemp detested the mix of pacifism, reefer, eleutherarchy, nonviolent direct action and democratic socialism promulgated by Thomas in D.F.S. It was one of those cases where the offended party overreacts, foaming at the bicuspid—"You try to mollify the masses with sex, drugs and pseudo-politics! You know you don't give a damn about the poor! And you're insensitive to the class struggle!"

Sam said nothing at the time, but he was bothered by the charges. One of his secret obsessions in his early years

431

on the East Side was to make lists of friends and enemies. Not that Morty Kemp was such a perfect revolutionary worker, and Sam should lose sleep over his deprecation. The sneers of peers were part of Sam's introduction to the sweet-sour spoon of renown—signing his first autographs, gluing his first book reviews in a scrapbook, kvelling over ads for screenings of his films, learning about the strange sub-world of book and relic collectors, people rushing up with praise in the street to get the latest issue of D.F.S., which he always gave away free, and women offering ImGrat, Uncle Thrill's acronym for immediate gratification.

Sam typed the list of recipients onto the stencil. Then he untied a canvas roll with fobs containing his styluses and engraving tools and began etching the ⌁𝕵ⓒ𝟜𝟜 ⸆ —hieroglyphs next to each name on the blue film. It gave him such pleasure to calligraph the glyph, say, for *"pekh,"* ⌁𝕵𝕵, the hindquarters of a lion. He was beginning to worry, however, about the spelling for asshole. Was it correct? He didn't want his Egyptian professor, to whom he always send D.F.S., grinning over a goof, so he turned to the stacks of milk crates against the wall containing his Eyptology books, and pulled out a dictionary of Middle Egyptian.

His joy in his Egyptian collection was unbounded! He patted the books, feeling the electric thrill on his fingertips bumping from binder to binder! How he loved the lore of the Nile—the sky above the narrow flood plains along its banks swarming with a vast assortment of deities, and the underground cities of its dead packed with wondrous ceremonies! And the art of the hieroglyph, was there anything more beautiful!

After he'd checked the spelling, Sam tarried at the

crates, skimming through old crumbly-edged issues of the Journal of Egyptian Archaeology. He hefted the huge Alan Gardiner *Egyptian Grammar,* and the marvelous books of Wallis Budge, such as *The Papyrus of Ani* and the two-volume Medici Edition of *Osiris and the Egyptian Resurrection.* All of them had a mustiness and dustiness and chippédness that hinted, in themselves, of ancient amulets on natron-packed bones and dusty chambers under the lid of the earth.

He sat in the lotus position on the bamboo mat, the faint December sun beaming upon him past a crisscrossing of clotheslines and wet sheets in the courtyard. He was feeling a paradise *pro tempore.* "This is surely the Three V's!" he shouted, as he pulled forth more books from the crates. By the Three V's he meant *Voluntas, Voluptuas* and *Vastitudo*—will, thrill and vastness. It gave him a pacing peace, the sort of energized *pax* that he guessed monks must feel who pace while meditating. At random he opened a facsimile edition of the Ebers Papyrus, a long medical treatise on Egyptian medicine that includes some 811 prescriptions and formulae for treatment of disorders.

By accident Sam's eyes came upon the section on cosmetics—cures for baldness, formulae for wrinkles and outbreaks on the face. Sam read intently—it was intriguing what the Eqyptians used! One remedy for wrinkles consisted of "incense cake," whatever that was, wax, olive oil, something called cyperus and fresh milk. Another had bulls-bile in it. Yet another featured "whipped ostrich egg," and runoff of dongwash, that is, water used to wash the genital.

Sam was particularly fascinated by a wrinkle cream consisting of sea-salt, honey, oil, meal-of-alabaster and crocodile shit. It must be noted that dung of every origin

433

was utilized in Egyptian pharmacology. They even had a medicinal use for fly spots.

He stared at the formula for several minutes. Finally his mouth formed two words in silence—"Christmas rush." Sam saw upon the screen of his visual cortex a jar emblazoned like a photo slide. A jar of Egyptian face cream. It was resting on a shelf in a Greenwich Village store. "Yazzah!" Sam Thomas shouted, jumping to his feet, still carrying the Ebers Papyrus, dancing around his pad, hopping first on one foot, then the other, trying to click his heels togther. "I've solved my money problem! Thank you, O Sebek!" Sebek was the Egyptian crocodile deity.

Sam waited impatiently till his heart rate lowered enough that he could sit back down and start sketching ideas for label text, the shapes of jars and so forth on smooth, hard sheets of the paper they call Bristol board. He executed a fine likeness of a crocodile beneath which he lettered his product's temporary title, "The Muffins of Sebek Ancient Egyptian Face Cream & Miracle Toner."

"What do you do with the crocodile dooky?" Sam asked suddenly. He'd gone to the Bronx Zoo and was standing next to the pool where an attendant was cleaning away the crocodilian detritus. Sam looked longingly at the poolside depositions. "I need about twenty-five pounds. How much?"

At that, the attendant turned to Sam, wondering what sort of vagabond from bonkersville had shown up at the acrid edge of his enclosure. The young man he encountered was wearing a pith helmet and knee-high snake boots. Sam had planned to pose as an expert on African fauna with a legitimate scholarly need for croc-offal, but had quailed.

Sam had watched the keeper for some time before

addressing him. There was something balletically hip about the way he was cleaning the enclosure, so Sam gambled. "You see, I'm an inventor. I need it. I'll give you a nickel bag of Panamanian Red. I can come back whenever you want."

The attendant kept cleaning the enclosure, acting as if he hadn't heard. Then he turned to Sam, "It's a deal. Better come back in two or three days. I'll gather them into some cans. They'll have a chance to dry."

The next step was walking all over the Lower East Side on jar patrol. He needed at least a hundred, and they had to be cheap—preferably free. He browsed in the junk shops on Houston near the Bowery; he smirched his sleeve cuffs on the edges of supermarket waste bins and dove armpit deep into those huge retangular debris boxes at construction sites.

There were several containers that came close to what he wanted, among them Skippy peanut butter jars, abandoned for their inelegance, and the jars that had once contained the milky rolls of Vita brand herring, which were too small. Also abandoned were blue glass Noxema jars. He needed something with a wide mouth so that a hand could easily scoop for the facesaving Sebekian ooze and which was large enough so that he could charge bountifully for it. As primitive as his business sense was, Sam knew that on this project the object was to deal a few at macro rather than many at micro.

He found what he wanted while walking past a car wash on Houston Street, eyes darting like an experienced can diver to any and all garbage locations. There they were! Hundreds of wide-mouthed metal-lidded jars that had once contained auto wax—perfect for an ancient Egyptian cosmetic! All he had to do was scrape off the

435

labels and add his own. Sam returned with gunny sacks and loaded up as many as he could carry and trotted back to 11th Street.

The plan called for Sam to pick up the muffins early in the morning before the zoo was open. Sam arrived with newspapers, cord, tape, surgical gloves, oodles of shopping bags and some paralytic grass on credit from Nelson Saite.

Before the keeper's astonished gaze, Sam tamped the chunks into shot-put-sized accretions and wrapped each one in newspapers, sprinkling a few drops of attar of roses upon them before sealing the edges with tape. He began filling the shopping bags with the packets till he had twelve, which he tied together into two six-bag bundles, one for each hand. Thus he could walk out of the zoo quite comfortably, if slowly, enjoying the stroll along Fordham Road past Fordham University toward the subway at the Grand Concourse.

It was the rush hour when Sam Thomas shoved himself aboard the D train. The car was packed, yet you'd be surprised how much space can be found when someone presses forward with twelve bags of lizard shit. The train took him to 14th Street where he switched to the crosstown subway to First Avenue, then walked up the steps toward home.

Sam didn't look behind him, as he usually did, before entering his building. As soon as the door began to swing inward, someone shoved his shoulder from behind so that he lurch-stumbled upon the ▆ -patterned tile floor common to hallways all of the East Side. He turned around, expecting to be robbed, and recognized a famous team of narcs known as Mutt and Jeff that specialized in busting beatniks.

One was short and chubby, with a high blood pressure face and his pants cuffs rolled almost to his sock tops. The other was tall with the pits of pox on sunken cheeks and a knife scar cutting upward from his left eyelid through his eyebrow. Mutt and Jeff kept their collar count high by interdicting beatnik pot traffic, but they were extremely weak on heroin. Not long afterwards they would be busted for peddling dope from the evidence lockers. For now, however, they were knotting their ties high upon the arm of power, breathing hard and cackling with pleasure at cornering the overburdened Sam Thomas.

"Okay, Thomas, let's have a talk in the hallway."

Sam looked carefully at them. He hated being alone in hallways with plainclothes cops. He'd heard stories. One of them had his hand on his hip near his holster, so Sam went into a yes-sir grovel, thinking they might shoot him. It was like being mugged as they shoved and jostled him to the wall, patting his legs and pockets for weapons.

He was preparing to collapse to the floor, as he would have at a peace demonstration, when the shorter one with the muffin'd cuffs said, "We saw you leaving Saite's pad a couple of hours ago. What's in the bags? You delivering?"

Sam abandoned the floor-collapse. Instead he fought back the urge to smile, and replied, "It's some stuff for face cream."

"Sure it is," Mutt answered. "Open them up, Thomas. You'd better not ever lie to us. We know where you live."

Sam untied one of the six-shopping bag bundles and tore away the coverings to expose the muffins. The unmistakable waft of perfumed crocodile dooky crowded the hallway.

Jeff became excited. "Look at those bricks of hash, huh, Thomas? Looks like you and Saite were going to start a little business."

437

Mutt stepped back about five feet and pulled his revolver, "Check it out, Jeff."

Jeff picked one up. "This smells like perfume or spice. Maybe they added stuff to cut it."

Sam was beginning to relax. He said, "I guess you should do something to make sure, huh, officer?"

"Don't get wise with me, beatnik creep!" Jeff snorted. He brought the chunk to his lips and took a small nibble. Words cannot adequately depict the ensuing facial grimace as he spat it out and hurled the rest to the floor. "What is this shit!?"

It became one of those legendary moments—the day Sam Thomas got the muffin of Sebek in the narc's mouth. Sam could no longer keep from laughing. He pinched himself to keep from guffawing to the floor. He didn't want them beating him up. He spoke in a half cough, half laugh. "You heard—harf! harf!—of the Egyptian god Sebek? Well—harf! harf!—it's a gift from Sebek—harf! harf! harf!

That confused them. It reminded the officers that after all they were dealing with an imbalanced space cadet. Without speaking, they left Sam Thomas in the hallway and Sam walked elated up the steps to prepare for the Christmas rush.

Sam had already soaked the labels for the auto wax jars and had put them on the fire escape to dry. He'd cadged a piece of alabaster from a sculpture supply house and began hammering it into a meal-of-alabaster, an ingredient of the cream, on his porcelainized bathtub cover. The Ebers Papyrus was silent on relative proportions so he had to experiment, using one of his Yum bowls, which, as the crocodile skuz began to work into the cracks, he decided to retire from food service. He realized that it had to resemble actual American facial products or no one would buy it.

He lit a row of candles along the kitchen drainboard and taped a flashlight on the underside of the cabinet above the tub so that it beamed down upon the tub cover and the wooden bowl. He added some meal-of-alabaster, oil, some honey, the sea-salt, a chunk of muff', plus, for fragrance, myrrh-gum and oils of hyacinth and columbine. To his distress, the mixture lacked body. Oats were the answer. A toss of raw oats fluffed it up nicely and gave it consistency. By increasing the oats he found he could decrease the crocodility. He mashed and whipped the improvements into a proper puffy elation. Its color, however, was a most unappealing tanny gray, so he added blue food coloring. And there it was.

The sink was too small for the entire batch so he lifted away the covering and sacrificed his tub. He unwrapped the remaining depositions of Sebek and dropped them within. He added the alabaster frag's, the oil, a gallon of honey, the myrrh, hyacinth and columbine, the dye, and most of his remaining oatmeal. The ingredients did not automatically fall into commixture. He had to exert considerable downward vectoring in order to mash it all into the proper glopitude. This was accomplished by using his galoshes. He rested on his knees at tub's edge and thrust his arms down into his galoshes, using his hands as feet, and then performed a sort of plodding dance, working it slowly into a shiny blue mass.

His speed increased, passing "Twist, baby, twist," on the way to "Tutti Fruiti," when Sam heard a knock at the door and left the galoshes in place, withdrawing his arms, and lumbered over to answer. It was a very upset Talbot

439

the Great, carrying a stack of yule-trimmed presents which he tossed clunkingly upon Sam's bamboo floor mat.

Sam clicked on the flashlight above the tub and urged Talbot, "Look at my ancient Egyptian face cream!"

Talbot stood dejectedly in the gloom-flicker of the row of candles and was too distracted to give anything but a quick glance at the boots in the blue. "Sandy's dead," he said.

"Who's Sandy?"

"A cat I met—an NYU student—who bought a few c's worth of skag the other day from Kliver. I happened to be there at the time of the deal. I was broke and Kliver just walked over and gave me fifty dollars from Sandy's money. I used it all on Christmas presents.

"I'm going through horrible changes over it, man, because I just visited Kliver and he said the cat died yesterday of an o.d. out in Great Neck."

Sam tried to change the subject. "What'd you get for Johnny Ray Slage?"

Talbot pointed at some packages. "The Bob Dylan album, a subscription to *Liberation* magazine and Martin King's *Letter from the Birmingham Jail.*

Sam was excited. "Terrific presents to help shape a klan boy's mind!"

"But I can't give them to him," Talbot said.

"Why not?"

"Because I just bought a bunch of Christmas presents with Sandy's death. It would be disgraceful to give them out."

"What are you going to do with them?"

"Two things. Either I'm going to throw them in the East River or into the garbage pail. I also thought of leaving them anonymously in the hall for the kids in the

440

building. In any case, I can't have them in my pad. They're driving me crazy."

All Sam could think of saying was, "The lily grows from the burro's bones," hardly a sentence of consolation. Talbot split, telling Sam at the door, "We're going to have to force Kliver to give up junk. Tie him down to his bed. Get him into a hospital. Something."

Sam agreed. "Right! We'll lock him into a human Kick Grid! We'll draw up a list and guard him around the clock till he turkeys out of it!"

Sam jotted a reminder in his notebook to deliver the presents to Talbot's parents in Harlem, and to send the klan kid's presents to Alabama. Then he went back to the cream.

He was almost finished packing and sealing the jars when Cynthia Pruitt arrived after her shift at the House of Nothingness. One minute she was grumpy, the next depressed, and she was singularly under-enthused when Sam shined the light upon the wavy surface of blue pharmaceutical in the tub.

She hated the job! Each hour of toil had lowered her natural idealism. It was spoiling the surge of religion she'd felt in the days after JFK's assassination. She'd always loved the House of Nothingness, loved to read poetry there, loved to treat it as an all night scrounge-lounge for fun and play. It was humiliating to have to wait on the same people with whom she had sported at table, her knuckles wet with spilled coffee and table grit, watching them in their roles as careless louts.

And the grunge of it! "Did you ever try to clean up a plate of brown rice and seaweed someone has dropped into a sea of white sand?" she asked. One of her duties was wiping and mopping the men's room. The hair, the

441

dirt, the incontinence! It wasn't just the derelicts that stumbled in from Tompkins Square Park! Your ordinary run-of-the-reefer beatnik would spray the rim and floor with urine as if he were having a seizure at the same time! Cynthia was disgusted.

And the tip-clips! You couldn't leave a tip amidst the clutter on the oak more than ten seconds. She had caught a poet with seven mimeographed books in print walking sneakily among empty tables making mongoose-quick tip-goniff scooping gestures. "I'm going to quit this fucking job the minute I raise my half of the rent and the ticket to Vermont," she said.

Sam believed one of the few things lighting the path from the downer trough was eros, so he helped Cynthia off with her coat, and led her to the divan. He opened her blouse to rub some of the cream into the cavity between the tops of her breasts. "Try it," he said. "It's the oldest beauty formula in civilization. Not that you need a whit of improvement. For you, St. Cynthia, are be-uuuuu-ti-fullll." That was one of the love names Sam had given during her month of prayer.

Cynthia lowered her chin to stare at the shiny blue grease. "What's in it?"

Sam recited the ingredients.

She tried to stay calm. "You mean I've got crocodile shit on my tits?"

Sam nodded.

Her anger was sudden, like a glaze of gas on a flat rock. She ripped the flashlight from where it was taped above the tub and stood with it at the sink, running water, rubbing the saurian sludge from her chest till it blushed an abraded red.

Cynthia's reaction was a surprise to Sam. It had not

442

occurred to him that anyone would hesitate to apply the pomade from an Egyptian papyrus to her body. For a few moments Sam pondered the ethicality of the project. Was it fully in tune with the concept of Gandhian nonviolence to foist upon the public a product, a component of which had come from the rear of a lizard?

The moment of doubt was brief. Sam felt a surge of *faith* in the Ebers Papyrus. These formulae represented compilations of folk remedies tested through the centuries. He thought of the well known women of Egypt who might have used the Muffins of Sebek Ancient Egyptian Face Cream & Miracle Toner. Hatshepsut! Nefertiti! Queen Tiy!

Cynthia stood in a silent rage, refusing to face him. Sam walked to the tub and scooped up mighty handfuls and pressed them to his face so that it looked like a deflated blue soccer ball. "Here!" he shouted. "This is an efficacious ancient formula! The Egyptians built up their medical knowledge slowly and carefully over the course of thousands of years! This is good stuff!"

Then he did what he did so well. He fell to his knees on the bamboo mat and apologized with molten words.

They went to Stanley's where they spent some of her bus ticket money on calming vodka, then Sam walked her home to Ludlow Street and hurried back to finish the face cream.

Her hostile reaction to the contents made Sam meditate on the name, The Muffins of Sebek Ancient Egyptian Face Cream & Miracle Toner. Perhaps he should lessen the emphasis on muffins. The title did seem somewhat ponderous and quackish, like one of those blue glass bottles of Dr. Fromkin's Mandrake Bitters from the nineteenth century.

443

It was time to publish the labels. One of the finest stylus-on-stencil artists anywhere, Sam bent down over the stencil, carefully scratching its surface, but not so deeply as to pierce it, using his assortment of very thin round-tipped styluses and icepick-sharp engravers tools.

The Ancient Egyptian
MIRACLE COMPLEXION
CREAM

"What a label!" Sam exclaimed as he executed the final tiny Eye of Horus, his flashlight wedged between his knees and protruding upward to form a small round light table.

He smoothed the stencil upon the drum of his Speed-o-Print mimeo, poured ink into the portal, and had labels in ten minutes. He was up till dawn, hand coloring each label, and gluing them neatly onto the jars.

Next he printed cards which explained how the formula rested upon an ancient papyrus, a formula proven effective over 3,000 years ago due to the powerful effect of oils, grains and what Sam delicately described as "essence of Sebek." He punched holes in the cards, threaded them with loops of Christmas ribbon and suspended one from each jar's neck.

It was ready. The rest of the project was push and shove, and shove Sam did, wheedling, beseeching, begging his wares aboard the shelves of Village stores right at the time when trembly-fingered shoppers, determined to

444

spend, were jammed as tightly as lambs around a bale of hay.

Within a week, all one-hundred jars were sold, giving him enough for the rent, to turn his lights on and to buy some paper for the next D.F.S. Lie quiet, o Sebek.

Southey Came Back From Portugal

WHAT A BEAUTIFUL THING it was when the people tossed the Bastille stone by stone into a vast plaza of rubble. It was beautiful and its beauty still shines in our century. The expectation of the people for freedom of expression and a fair system of economics to end poverty arose everywhere.

In England five years later a group of young people organized by poets Robert Southey and Samuel Coleridge wanted to set up an intentional community. They called it Pantisocracy. A possible location was in America on the Susquehanna River. There were to be twelve couples in the Pantisocracy and the plan was to work maybe two or three hours a day, to share the produce of the commune equally, to have a good library, to spend great time, both sexes, in liberal discussions, and great time in the education of their children. This was 1794.

There was a pool of idealistic, energetic, intelligent and adventuresome young people willing to go, including the famous Fricker Sisters—Mary, Edith and Sarah—all of whom married guys planning the Pantisocracy. The commune was to begin in April of 1795. The problem was

446

money. Each couple had to come up with 125 pounds.

The world might have changed for the better if Coleridge and Southey had been able to obtain funding or a line of credit from a decent state bank in Europe or a decent common purse of a decent economic system. It was a dream that a People's Bank for Experimentation and Improvement should have funded instantly.

Southey and Coleridge went to the private sector for cash, placing hope in the formula, ink = $. The hope was Writing, Publishing and Lecturing. Money was held in common, though Southey later groused, in a classic commune common kitty complaint, that he outgarnered Coleridge four to one. In a few days time, Coleridge and Southey spewed together a three-act Dramatic Poem, "The Fall of Robespierre," which Coleridge tried to peddle around London for the Pantisocracy. The fall of '94, Southey's rich aunt heard about Pantisocracy and about his engagement to one of the unacceptable Fricker sisters and threw him out on a wet night, wanting never to encounter his communardal visage again.

Coleridge was always a bit of a flake, and dropped out of sight for a few months from a broken heart. Southey retrieved him in early 1795, and the quest for Pantisocracy start-up money, through the formula ink = $, began again. There was hostility between England and the United States, so the Susquehanna was abandoned and the new target was a farm in Wales.

Writing, Publishing and Lecturing, as often, proved a cruel fiscal triad. The two bards, who were sharing a pad in London, not only ran out of cash, but went into debt and Southey had to go live with his mother. The family put great pressure on him. He refused to "prepare for the Church," but like a creek bank caving under a spring

447

flood, suddenly agreed, okay, okay, I'll study law.

Then they isolated him from the Pantisocrats by getting him to accompany his Uncle Hill on a six-month trip to Portugal. He did defy his family in one respect, by secretly marrying Edith Fricker a few days before leaving. He also informed a pissed-off Coleridge that he was giving up Pantisocracy.

The communard, who had hungered for Europe to become a new, equal state without war and with freedom and sharing, came back from Portugal a changed person. Revolutionary Fever, hereafter known as rev-fev, was gone, gone like a Nothing Matters mantra, gone.

In place was a person comfortable with the Church, with current economics, with empire, with the War Machine. Better to be a gentle person stabilizing the Tory system (with cash in ones pockets) than an impoverished ineffectual spore of rev-fev. It was the old story of Toryization, as common in the twentieth as it was in Southey's century. "Heh, heh," goeth the writer undergoing Toryization, "I guess I didn't understand human nature." Now Southey could focus his righteous energies on a small circle of friends, and on generalized sympathies along the lines of "We must make things better for the poor, we really must, oh must, but nothing too specific or controversial."

From most accounts, Southey was an affable, rather than a gory Tory. He tried to study law, but found his calling in the adjusted formula, haphazard flood of ink = $. Great, ghastly gobs of writing. No one apparently has ever added up Southey's scriptive ooze-out: reviews, anthologies, poems, translations, editing jobs, weekend-penned epics, plays. What they did count totaled ten volumes of poetry and 40 of prose. He was one of the main lights of the Tory *Quarterly Review*. He was poet laureate at age 39 and Byron attacked him as a "balladmonger," but his inky pen inked onward for 69 years.

From 1795 we turn to 1964 and the case of Eric Balin, one of the fiercest and most active nonviolent revolutionary workers of his era. Hassles and hirdumdirdum were his milieu. Every hour was a string of crises to be overcome. In the parlance of later decades, he was "wired." His hair was like that, tightly curled, springy, intense. He was a little bit too convex in the eyes, perhaps from exophthalmic goiter, which gave him a look of great watery vorticity, especially when his ringlets were black with toily sweat. He was known as Get It Done Balin, Not Much Patience Balin—a pain to his more relaxed coworkers, but he made it happen.

They say Jack Kerouac with his great athletic ability and stormy mind could produce a novel that was really a novel in a week. Eric Balin had a similar physique. He could hurdle, jump, putt, slam, toss a football 80 yards in a smooth spiral, pole vault 16 feet, and run the half-mile in a minute and a half. He brought this prowess to the peace movement where he was the Ajax of ahimsa. Instead of novels, he produced great rhapsodies of leaflets, sit-ins, articles, conferences of peace people, and other complicated structures of action.

The groups for which Eric Balin did volunteer work included The Committee for a Nonviolent World, Congress of Racial Equality, SANE, the War Resisters League, Greenwich Village Peace Center, *Catholic Worker*, Fellowship of Reconciliation, Fair Play for Cuba, the Committee to Abolish the House UnAmerican Activities Committee, *et*—impossible to consider—*cetera*. If we had to measure his dilution we would speak of parts per

449

million. It was maddening. They *all* wanted him. They left messages under his door. They phoned. They cajoled. They begged for this handsome intense peace-athlete, and he raced back and forth like a Wilt Chamberlain to comply.

He was the volunteer they all drool for—someone who will work twenty hours without complaint, and when a staff position opens will take it for subsistence. After a couple of years nonstop, with only two weekends off, Balin was one of those perma-tired peace workers, his scorched, overused, Grave's disease eyes enmeshed in crinkle-circles. He trained himself for microsleep, to be alert and instantly responsive when the phone rang at 4 A.M. with problems. Often he spent the night atop his coat on piles of flyers by the mimeo machine so as to beat the dawn. He had an ulcer and bowel problems by 24. He awoke from microsleep stunned like an opossum in a sudden light, but slapped himself and dashed to the action.

Some compulsive peace workers are ultraplacid on the outside but seething on the inside. This was Eric Balin. His main money source was a 35 dollar a week staff job at the Committee for a Nonviolent World where he seetheslaved 15 hours a day. He began to resent the work shoveled at him by co-workers. Could he please do this, do that. They'd ring him at midnight. There's a light on at the office; could you go down and turn it off, check to see things are okay. Could you pick up my laundry? He secretly smouldered.

He withheld pleasures. He ate beans and rice. No movies. No pot. No jazz. Just books and a few beers now and then at Stanley's Bar with the neighborhood poets. Balin wrote poetry himself and was eager to be *in* on the scene. He drank at Stanley's with a group known as the

450

"mean poets of Avenue B." There were John Barrett, famous for summoning the ghost of Sappho with his tortoise shell lyre; Sam Thomas, poet and publisher of *Dope, Fucking and Social Change: A Journal of the New America*; Nelson Saite, coiner of the phrase, "Strength and Intelligence Through Nonviolent Hatred"; Talbot Jenkins, poet and hero of the Freedom Rides; and Andrew Kliver, poet, second story man, methedrine dealer and junkie.

Eric could only meet with the mean poets every week or so, but they were there every night. He resented the free chatty time they enjoyed, the pointed pointlessness of their unharried examinations. The luxury to pursue, without the slightest toke of guilt, a "fine verisimilitude," as Keats would have said, or hundreds of verisimilitudes, similitudes piled upon versimilitudes, for hours over beers and bu around a milk crate on somebody's bamboo mat. Didn't they realize the danger of wasting time!? Couldn't they see the *enormous crisis and pressure?* The world was in a bucket of slime and they were talking verisimilitude!

Nevertheless, he wanted In with the Best Minds of My Generation crowd. *In* with the mean guys of Avenue B. He wanted to be *known* as a writer, not just Eric the Mad Activist Who Slaved Twenty Hours a Day for the Revolution. He felt guilty if he didn't write every day, and when he did, he felt guilt over neglecting important peace work. Among the mean poets of Avenue B he was viewed as a kind of slow learner. He felt like Maupassant among the Impressionists. They hated his poetry. Thomas would not publish him in D.F.S., and Sam took joy in printing gibberish alongside works of genius.

And then there was the resentment of poverty. The Committee for a Nonviolent World could pay only 35 dollars a week, not enough to live even in the era of the 35 cent breakfast and the 25 dollar pad. His family helped, but with the alternate chilliness and encouragement of disapproval. He asked for fifty for rent and utilities, they sent 35.

His Uncle Earl was assigned to work on him. It was incessant. "You have a future," Earl told him. "You're educated. Look at human nature. They're all crooks. Protect yourself. Once you learn to protect yourself you'll know how the country has to be protected. You'll wind up old, broke and crushed. You'll get to be forty and you'll run out of energy—believe me, *out of energy*. Unless you set up your financial future by age forty, you're finished. You're through. You'll die broke with no conveniences. You'll waste away on a bed in a poor house with no painkillers. These people are just using you. Among them are dupes and agents of Russia."

Uncle Earl tended to stay away from the agents of Russia one-liners, because then Eric would get mad, hang up or flash him an anarcho-Marxist, Kerouacian/Kierkegaardian glare and walk out.

That spring Eric fell in love with a sister of one of the mean poets of Avenue B, who was visiting from the Midwest. She was going back home to settle her affairs then come back to live with Eric on the Lower East Side. She looked around the slum and spoke of plush divans and pleated floor-length curtains. Eric gulped, with not enough cash to purchase the chairs he'd wanted from the second hand store across the street so they would not have had to eat their love meals off the linoleum.

She would return in four months, and Eric began to think about money. His family disliked her. She was a hick. She was not what they wanted for dear, darling Eric. They wouldn't help.

He'd been learning about printing. The Committee had put him in charge of it. He was a good designer, could paste-up perfectly. He didn't need rulers, guides and grids. He had goshawk sharp eyes and an artist's sense of a perfect flow of type fonts for a poster, brochure or leaflet. He knew about burning plates. The regimens of good binding. He was always inked up. His nails and cuticles flew the blues and blacks and reds of the revolution.

His plan was to forge a Pantisocracy—a Guild of Revolutionary Printers. From that would evolve the solution to his marriage, family, money and career problems. In a Kerouac-like four day round-the-clocker, Balin wrote a 300 page commune Operation and Maintenance Manual for the Guild of Revolutionary Printers. It had everything worked out—a fifty year plan—a Pantisocracy for the twentieth century. There were sections on kitchen chores, interpersonal relations, decision making, exact rules on the distribution and saving of money, plans for pensions and even a section on garbage collection. Textbooks! the most powerful social tool, and giganticallly remunerative. They would publish the textbooks to forge the new age!

He found people willing to commit to the Guild. A good brochure designer, a machine repair guy, Cynthia Pruitt for the paste-up and art department, a young actionist named Past Blast, and others. A full house. There were eleven of them, all of whom were believing in and counting on Eric. He had them convinced it would start as early as next month. Some went so far as to give notice to their landlords.

They searched for a building. The print shop would be on the first floor, if possible, and living spaces and a common kitchen on the other floor. It was ironic that the

Lower East Side had so many supporters of the concept of a commune and so few suitable locations. There was something about the configuration of the slum tenements that was cell-like and uncommunal. Perhaps a front and back building could have been sought, with the courtyard as a common space, say, to be turned into a garden. But there was no place they could find that would give them the communality they needed—a common library, a common kitchen, a common laundry, a business office and a large room for printing.

They found a building, a former rooming house, on West 24th that was perfect. It had wide winding stairways, large windows and rooms that invited communal life. They needed twenty thousand dollars cash or somebody with believable assets to co-sign a loan. They dropped the name Revolutionary and went to a Rockefeller bank but were turned down. Eric's Uncle Earl, with all his liberal beliefs, also said no. Eric roused all eleven Pantisocrats to call all their relatives, even distant uncles and aunts, the sort who only surface in one's life with gifts of cuff links on graduation days. But there was nothing; a total paralysis of the co-signing fingers.

Nevertheless, Eric went ahead and ordered equipment. He purchased a printing press at an auction, and lighting boards, cutters, tables. He began lining up customers—art galleries, the Luminous Animal Theater, peace groups. He had a thousand dollars worth of orders from SANE, the Quaker Action Group, and CORE.

The destiny of the Guild of Revolutionary Printers finally rested with Joyce Merlpin, one of the main financial backers of the Committee for a Nonviolent World. Eric learned about her from parties and office gossip. Joyce Merlpin was angry with America for going ahead and developing the H-bomb. She gave money, oodles of it, to the peace movement. She funded things like the sailing of boats to try to block the American nuclear tests in the Pacific. She financed blockades of the launchings of boats bearing nuclear tipped rockets. She gave hundreds of thousands of dollars to the Committee for a Nonviolent World.

Joyce had also learned of Eric. She was among those who prevailed on him for favors. When she was out of town, Eric fed her goldfish and checked the apartment. She had a fascination for this beautiful young man and his perfect pole vaulter's body, his charisma, his Zeus-like ringlets, his love of change. A couple of times Eric had gone to her place for dinner, and then to bed, where he was started to find a quart jug of Mazola corn oil by the vase of fresh flowers on her bed stand.

Joyce Merlpin was 40someodd, very voluptuous, and one whose beauty increased with passion. Soon they were rubbing oil upon one another. It was more than rubbing. Joyce liked to fling it like a robin in a bird bath. His curly chest hairs were soon stirring on her breasts with frantic scouring. They were pouring it over each other, ruining some expensive sheets edged with Rotterdam lace. "Don't worry about it," she said, i.e., the oil-gray mattress. "I'll get another delivered tomorrow." He had a feeling the bed store man would chuckle at another call from the Mazola lady.

Eric let it slip among the mean poets of Avenue B, and Joyce became known instantly as Mazola. Sam Thomas published a scandalous account of it in D.F.S.

Thankfully Sam had changed her name, so there was a certain hope of victory when Eric went to Joyce Merlpin to finance the Guild of Revolutionary Printers. Again she invited him to her apartment for dinner.

He shared with her the plans. She seemed cold. He was afraid of turn-down, so held off the formal request. There was one more dinner and one more ruined mattress before he asked her.

"I can't give you the money," she said.

He was overwhelmed by the rejection. "But you're a radical. You believe in universal disarmament. The Guild of Printers will be the greatest asset to the revolution ever!"

"That's war and peace," she replied, with a tone of irritation. "This you propose is economics."

"This will be a whole new economics!"

"It's been tried. My grandfather tried it back in the 1880s." She wouldn't say more.

He was puzzled. "You think it's a straight nineteenth century anarchist venture!?"

They talked for several hours. She wouldn't budge.

"But I have four tons of printing equipment literally on the sidewalk!"

"I'm so sorry. Perhaps you could store some of it in the basement at the Committee Office."

"You'll outfit a whole yacht to try to block an H-bomb blast! *You* are a radical. What I'm proposing is the most radical of all! A long term, working, sharing, genuine, freedom-based Communist guild—to last for the next fifty years! Or as long as America. My God, can't you *see?*"

"We are constrained. My family has given *so* much, that there's very little more remaining to give. Certainly not 20,000 dollars."

Eric knew that was a lie. She'd just given the Committee $30,000 to sponsor a blockade of one of the naval weapons depots. She was living on the interest on her interest.

456

"You think I can't be trusted? That I'm a freak?" He reached into his satchel and handed her a copy of the operations manual for the Guild of Revolutionary Printers. "Here—look at this. This is a fifty year plan! It's real. It's now. It's everything the future needs."

She was silent. Eric saw the bottle of Mazola oil on the kitchen counter. It looked lower than the other night. He could never get from Joyce Merlpin the real reason for the turn-down. But he knew the Guild was doomed. Another eleven Pantisocrats were destined again to be unable to explore it.

The failure was overwhelming. Eric hated Joyce Merlpin so much as to hate her beliefs. He was trembling. Dog-like groans flipped from his lips on her stairwell. His ulcer slashed like a knife. He wept for the second time in his life walking the two miles of blocks from Joyce's pad to Stanley's Bar, where he joined a table of the mean poets and began to gulp the drinks.

Everybody was boisterous and celebratory, especially the triumphant Sam Thomas handing out just-printed copies of D.F.S.

"What's wrong, Eric baby?" he asked. He told them and the incident was tossed off with "Balin got turned down by Mazola." At which everybody laughed. So what, who cares, it doesn't matter, it's a fly speck. Or that's the way it seemed to an enraged Eric. Their jollity nearly gave him convulsions. He hated them all, these punks with their sick lives and third-rate art.

Many of his most fiercely held positions on civil rights, peace, unilateral disarmament, test bans and civil disobedience he reversed and reviled that night in one shocking, surprising change of philosophy.

457

"Suppose what we've done is all wrong. Listen to me," he said. "Suppose we're endangering our culture. Our freedom. Our country. Suppose we're a monster at the throat of our civilization."

The mean guys let him have his say, though Sam spoke up, "Suppose we are?"

"Don't you see what you are? You're assholes in the death of the planet!" shouted Eric Balin and headed for the bathroom. The urinals at Stanley's were these giant porcelain things. They were big, wide and tall. You could pass out in them. The mean guys called them the porcelain phone booths. Eric threw up and fell into one of them, his shoulders, face and hands having the cold, smelly and unpleasant experience of shuffling and sliding in the urine of '64. He collapsed unconscious, his head resting on a metal drain by the floor shaped like a tiny crown. His enemy Sam Thomas found him and helped him back to a table filled with poet rivals, bearing the humiliating wet hair of a urine crown pass-out.

When he took his chair someone made a crack about "strength and intelligence through nonviolent puking."

"I'll show you the value of nonviolent direct action!" shouted Eric, and punched Sam Thomas in the mouth.

Getting violent was a serious transgression among the pacifists. It was also serious in Stanley's Bar. Stanley walked slowly toward the fray, first wiping the counter, then the table nearest Eric's. Stanley 86'd someone in a slow and wherever possible zen get-out-here maneuver. At one time or other most of the mean poets of Avenue B had been 86'd from there.

Fortunately Stanley had a forgiving formula for being un86'd. But this was a legendary night. Eric Balin easily won the 86'd from Stanley's contest of the 1960s. First he performed one of the more talked-about feats of prowess. He leaped from a standing position to the top of the cigarette machine where he continued his lecture on war and peace.

Stanley let him speak a few seconds, until the alcohol whittled his delivery. "Fuck Russia! Fuck peace! Fuck all these poets!" And gave forth one more gag-out that dribbled bile on the cigarette machine. He began stomping the machine out of embarrassment and Stanley grabbed a leg, slid Eric down and out the door.

At home all he could think of was suicide. If this is what life is, I want out. His head was swirling so rapidly the tears should have been flung to the sides.

The best thing about defeat is you wipe up the puke and trudge onward. So the next morning Eric recovered and was thinking maybe everything was normal. He was due at the Committee for a Nonviolent World for his regular day, had put a few inches of lukewarm tap into his spider-web-dappled kitchen tub and was soaking the hatred from his bones.

The phone rang. It was Uncle Earl. "Get your bags packed. We're going to Europe for a few months. I have business. But not so much that we can't see all the museums. And have some fun. Get you out of here. Then we're going to the Far East. Ever been to Singapore? It'll take about six months. We can even give you—I checked with the company—checked, hell, since I own it—a salary. Not much. But you can save most of it. What do you say!"

Eric stood up in the tub and leaned over against the dish drain.

"I'll do it."

Kick Grid Time for Kliver

ANDREW KLIVER answered the angry door bash in itchy-scratchy bent-over soporific happiness— falling into micro-sleep right as he stood in the doorway, jerking his head back and trying to locate Sam with his foggy eyes.

"Why did you boost from one of your best friends?!!!" Sam Thomas shouted. "Give me my archives back, you worm-eating gunge!"

Kliver answered with a dope drawl three feet thick: "When ah steals from muh friends, ah kin only make amends by get tis twice as kucked up on the proceeds."

"Okay, motherfucker, it's kick time!" cried Sam Thomas. He was furious with Kliver for breaking into his studio and stealing his 16-mm editing machine and some boxes of manuscripts and archives for *Dope, Fucking and Social Change: A Journal of the New America*. Kliver had tried to peddle the latter at the Lantern of Knowledge Bookstore on the West Side, and Jack Barnes, the owner, had called Sam.

This and other events had led Kliver's friends to band together at last to force him off junk. Last week a kid named Sandy, a biology student at N.Y.U. who wore blue boater jackets with gold buttons and shiny oxblood-hued penny loafers, had died from an overdose Kliver had sold

460

him. Everyone had been shocked and Kliver wavered between remorse and defiance, claiming to have argued with Sandy for hours not to try skag. And then the other day Sam had listened glumly to Kliver's animated description of his first stickup. The victim's son, a junkie pal of Kliver's, had set him up, but Kliver had done the sticking. The victim was so nervous his eyes bulged and the tiny ball on the end of his sleeping cap had bounced on the shoulders of his pajamas while he let out a low frequency scream that knocked the cheap .32 out of Kliver's twitching hand.

It was affecting Kliver's poetry, which more and more was saturated with the egomaniacal world of stealing, dealing and sick, sweaty sun-ups. Heroin was the Grand Metaphor, the Big Question, the Equation, and the plight of the junkie was woven with capital I's.

Andrew Kliver had moved to the L.E.S. in late '61. He had been in the army and had picketed his own base in uniform as part of a General Strike for Peace organized by Judith Malina and Julian Beck of the Living Theater. Kliver was dismissed from the army and moved to East 9th where he began an amphetamine business. "Now I can afford to be a junkie," he told Sam Thomas. It was pre-planned and very exhibitionistic. Kliver liked to shoot up in crowds, at gallery openings and even at poetry readings as part of a poem. No one minded at first. The rule was don't level anyone's high, a rule which underwent change when its adherents had to buy police locks against Kliver's raids.

Sam Thomas had read Kliver's notebooks and poems and was convinced he had found an American genius. He published him as often as he could in D.F.S. and helped spread the Kliver legend. Kliver had a hunger for religion and joined a tiny Catholic sect called the Gnostic Rite of Old Glastonbury, whose members sported white clerical

461

collars, each one calling himself reverend. They were an odd assortment of poets, libertines and pacifists who signed their correspondence, Yours in Christ the Sexual Lamb.

Kliver was drawn to trouble. He stared his clear green eyes into the shiny eyes of trouble and begged for attention. Women loved him, however much junk disengaged him from dongal puissance. He was fond of triangles, and then of bringing the apexes into contact. Let there be turmoil! Since he was a lotophage, and skag was his lotoboat, then turmoil was the wounded river for his voyage. In his floating closed system on the River Turmoil he could banish the anguish that had driven him to the needle. He swore it had qualities of priestly asceticism—he liked that sense of not having eaten for three days because of not having noticed he was hungry, and when he finally noticed he still didn't care.

Sam Thomas organized a Kick Grid to save Kliver, to be staffed around the clock by close friends so that during withdrawal he would never be alone. It looked like this:

	12-3	3-6	6-9	9-12
DAY ONE	TALBOT	SAM	ROSE	CYNTHIA
	12-3	3-6	6-9	9-12
	LOUISE	P. BLAST	THRILLS	CLAUDIA
DAY TWO	JOHN	BECKY	LLASO	MONGOL
	SAM	TALBOT	P. BLAST	HARNIGAN
DAY THREE	SAITE	LLASO	BECKY	BECKY
	TALBOT	SAM	SAM	MARIE
DAY FOUR	LOUISE	P. BLAST	ROSE	BECKY
	THRILLS	CYNTHIA	CLAUDIA	BECKY
DAY FIVE	TALBOT	SAM	SAM	ROSE
	SAITE	TALBOT	TALBOT	SAM

The Kick Grid began three days before New Year's Eve. Sam mimeoed the chart so everyone would know exactly

when they were to sit it out with Kliver. For the first
three days Kliver would gradually reduce his intake of
heroin, then it was to be total withdrawal. The flaw in
this scheme was that the doper controlled the dope. Kliver
angrily claimed that of course he had the discipline to
shoot himself up with punier and punier amounts. He
made a big display of bagging up the incrementally
decreasing skag shots. He showed Sam the flap of kitchen
linoleum under which he was stashing them.

The Kick Grid went smoothly for the first few shoot-
ups. As the shots weakened, he began to get junksick
sooner. New Year's Eve came at the most crucial phase of
the Grid, with Kliver on the verge of total withdrawal,
only one more shot, and he was a miserable sight, lying
on the bed shivering in long johns beneath a Mexican
blanket, oozy with sweat, his eyes hurting from the light
so the pad was in gloom.

"Sam *had* to complicate this Grid by beginning it just
before Louise's party!" Nelson Saite complained, blowing
hot air onto his cold clenched hands as he and Becky Levy
walked toward Kliver's columned porchway for the nine
to midnight sit. Kliver lived in one of the better East Side
buildings—at 604 East 9th, between B and C, a building
known for its long fire escapes of flowered black grillwork
across the front side, and thin elegant metal corinthian
columns at the entranceway. The poet Charles Olson,
according to the legend on the block, had lived in the
building in the late Forties, and in Kliver's day, Frank
O'Hara lived just down the street across from the Cantina
of the Revolutions, an anarcho-Maoist soup kitchen poetry
cafe.

Over on East 12th at the Mindscape Gallery the New
Year's party was just beginning. On the walls were some
new paintings by Louise Adams. It was a great night!

Everybody seemed to be up! The normally down and depressed among them could look at one another in bewilderment and say, "What's wrong, I'm happy!"

From behind curtains in the back of the gallery where Louise had her illegal kitchen and loft bed came the rrr-rrr rrr-rrr of a hand saw. "I bet no one has built a Scythian sauna for a thousand years!" Sam Thomas exclaimed to John Barrett as they drilled holes at the top of a yurt-like frame of one-by-twos, lashing them together through the holes with wire.

In Book 4 of his *Histories*, Herodotus describes a bathing practice of the ancient Scythians, nomadic peoples that roamed the steppe from the Carpathian Mountains to the River Don in what is now the Ukrainian S.S.R. The Scythians stretched wool cloth around a tripod of poles to make a tent, and dropped hemp seeds on a dish of red hot stones. According to Herodotus the Scythians "howled with pleasure" at the engulfment of the cleansing cannabinous steam. Tonight Mindscape would have its own Scythian sauna.

The onomatopoetic verb for *howl* Herodotus used was ὠρύομαι; Sam used it also, *oh-rooh!-o-my!*, over and over while he and Barrett tacked layers of sheets, shirts, towels and blankets to the yurt frame to make an impervious hemp steam seal.

They were more than eager to try it out. Trays of fire bricks were heating white hot in Louise's kiln. "Coming through! Coming through!" intoned Nelson Saite, quilted gloves on a deadly tray, moving placidly toward the sauna.

Sam did not hesitate to walk naked through the party, but Barrett was not about to dingle-dangle among diarists, and so held back as Sam rounded up a few friends and helped them strip. Inside the yurt Nelson opened a

464

bag of pot seeds mixed with lemon oil and hissed them upon the tray of bricks.

There was coughing at first, but the pot billows energized them and they too, like the Scythians, howled with pleasure. For fifteen minutes they howled, while John brought them trays of hot bricks, and one by one they exited into Louise's shower stall for a cold water dousing.

Then Louise appeared in a blue robe and went into the Scythian sauna alone. Sam had finished his shower by then and pointed to the sauna, encouraging John to go in there with her. Barrett was hesitant, but Sam shoved him against the entranceway, and John entered fully clothed.

Soon he was passing his trousers, sweater and shirt out to Sam. Man, was it hot. There was a faint glow of red from the gallery lights filtering through a thin red plaid shirt that was part of the walls of the tent. Louise opened her robe to show John where she first began to sweat in a sauna, on the upper chest between her breasts.

Touching the tops of her breasts made John gasp. It gave him courage, but not enough to keep from biting blood from his lip on the "v" as he told her he loved her. It had taken him months to gather the nerve.

Even in such heat they began kissing. Fucking seemed out of the question. After all, it *was* a gallery opening and there were around 75 people standing with drinks close at hand. All John had to do was think of the fresh sweat he had touched beading on her breasts and the heart beating beneath his hand, and he became as hard as a hickory stick.

It was the first time either had made love on a milk crate. John tied the yurt flap shut from the inside and Louise tossed her underwear to the side. She sat on the crate, where John urged her with his prying hands to spread her legs.

465

John walked on his knees up against the crate between Louise's spread legs and began to nuzzle her breasts with his lips, then he bent down to her crotch where he licked the lithops, exploring with Louise the secrets taught him by Sappho.

Louise soon howled with pleasure, and then John lay on his back on the floor with Louise straddled atop him, hot hands on his shoulders, rocking back and forth upon his cock deep inside her, and it was John's turn to howl with pleasure. Howl, Herodotus, howl.

Sam realized what was going on and guarded the entrance flap, chugging vodka and papaya juice, smoking as many j's as he could yell his way, clad in a towel and a pair of borrowed shoes. Sam lifted his doper eyes upon a guy who was staring at Sam's lower legs. "Why are you wearing *my* shoes, man?" the guy wanted to know.

It was Louise's off and on boyfriend, the painter Barton Macintyre. "Yeah," replied Sam, "I got some of your shoes down from the loft to use as Scythian sauna slippers."

"Take them off!" ordered Barton Macintyre, who was known to treasure his many many shoes almost as much as his many many paintings. Although he and Louise had split up months ago, his enormous collection of shoes still edged much of the mattress in the loft. It had been his way of marking his territory, and Louise now used them as convenient pouches for things like socks, bobby pins, extra panties, cookies, kleenex, cold cream and her diaphragm.

Barton looked about with horror and saw many of his treasures on nearby feet—his engineer boots, his Wellingtons, his tassel-fronted ultrashiny low cuts for when he had to dance, his blue suede shoes all the way from high school, his white bucks from his days as a Kappa Alpha rush, and even his get-a-job specials, those

466

black boats impressive to employers, with half inch ledges around the edges.

Sam tried to keep the conversation at a high enough volume to distract Barton from the moans of Louise and John. "Louise!" Barton shouted, his voice a gravel of jealousy. Macintyre began to strike against the tent cloths, apparently aiming for Barrett's head. There was a crunching of wood, and the tent collapsed. Louise and John collapsed also, struggling mightily to avoid smearing raw skin on hot bricks and flaming pot hulls.

Four or five of them pulled Barton Macintyre into the other room where the sight of his remaining shoes lining the loftbed platform seemed to calm him and he carried boxes up the ladder and carefully packed his shoes. When he split, Louise stacked the last of his canvases on top of the boxes of shoes he was carrying.

By that time it was nearly midnight and Barton's bonk-bonk was forgotten, especially in the uproar and hurrahs and applause greeting the arrival of Talbot the Great and Rose Snyder. Talbot read them a letter he'd just received from Johnny Ray Slage, the boy he'd met last fall near Birmingham whose father ran a klan chapter. Talbot had been secretly corresponding with the boy, and regularly sent packages of books and records. Johnny Ray Slage was the first Bob Dylan fan among the children of klavernoids. The boy had an aunt at whose address it was arranged for Talbot to send the packets.

Rose Snyder was also hopping happy. It was difficult to believe that she was the same person who, old and worn down, had come one afternoon to Ludlow Street, where by accident she had run into a group of protestors about to stage a sit-down at the U.N. How different she was just a few months later! She was putting in fifteen-hour days working for peace and civil rights groups. Her thick eye-

467

brows and long wavy red hair were already known everywhere on the East Side. Rose Snyder had been a legendary socialist activist in her youth, one of the "*fabrente meydelekh*," or burning young women, who had led the drive for the eight-hour day, decent wages, safety and health care. In 1914 she had helped elect Meyer London, the only socialist Congressman in the history of the Lower East Side, or of New York State for that matter. She had arrived back in the Lower East Side after forty years in a deadly depression, but now she was full of vim. At age seventy she was again Farbrente Rose.

Talbot the Great had to go over to Kliver's at midnight to take his shift in the Kick Grid. He had a bottle of champagne in the icebox. He opened it and looked for Rose Snyder. He found her by the bookcase with the two volume autobiography of Emma Goldman on her lap.

"I have to split," he said. "I wanted to wish you happy new year." He handed her the glass and leaned down to kiss her. They stood up while their lips stayed together in a long rolling smooch, their surfaces pressing and pulling, section by section, those of the red haired firebrand and those of the veteran of the Freedom Rides. She felt his pocket swelling against her leg and her heart was like a bird buffed up against an alleyway in a squall.

At midnight, Talbot arrived at Andrew Kliver's to find Becky Levy reading from a biography of Coleridge to the unhappy poet. "Man," Kliver said in a voice as watery as oatmeal gruel, "I don't want to hear about Coleridge, I want some smack!"

Becky's reading focused on Coleridge's long and unhappy struggle against laudanum addiction. It had sapped his chops, she argued. He had not been able to finish some of his finest poems because of it.

Kliver was not so watery that he could not raise a rebuttal. "Kubla Khan," he reminded her, had not been

468

a poem ruined by dope, but rather had fructified in a dope inspired dream, only part of which he'd been able to write down before being interrupted by the legendary "gentleman from Porlock." But that was the gentleman from Porlock's fault, not dope. Hence, laudanum aided art. "Bullshit," replied Becky Levy.

Becky had been reading from the life of the author of "Christabel" for an hour. It he hadn't been so sick Kliver would have dug it. He and Coleridge were brothers, two Christian dope fiends, a minister on laudanum and a Free Catholic Priest of Old Glastonbury sweating it out on East 9th.

During the midnight to three shift, Talbot and Becky talked in the kitchen while Kliver lay with foggy glasses on his mattress, his respiration rate arisen and his nose running as if it were being spritzed with ragweed or pine pollen. Friends kept dropping in. Talbot barred those who seemed to be junkies. One dealer threatened to return with henchmen to "rescue our man."

Talbot had always thought it was an hallucination from the writings of William S. Burroughs that junkies have a time of intense sexual need during withdrawal. One of the apexes of Kliver's series of interrelated triangles, a banjo player named Buck's County Josie, arrived. Josie wiped Kliver's face with a towel and was cleaning his glasses. Kliver's liquid voice could be heard beseeching her for something. Talbot was afraid it was drugs he was a-beseeching and stood in the doorway only to watch Kliver's watery voice, like a slightly sped-up James Stewart, but not as boingy and twangy, work its wonders.

Buck's County hoisted her dress and straddled Kliver, pulling aside her panties while Kliver tugged the Mexican blanket upon Josie's shoulders. It was only a few seconds before his sick genital frothed and Kliver whispered many aqueous thank yous.

Kliver went back to sleep and Josie left. Talbot and Becky were both tired and they were dozing in their chairs when they were startled by a thudding bonk bonk bonk bonk bonking sound.

They thought it might be someone knocking on the radiator for heat. It continued. Both of them realized at the same time what it was and rushed to the bedroom to find Andrew Kliver clunking his head against the wall. He begged them for a shot. Becky had to endure Kliver kissing her hand, his runny nose dampening her knuckles with hot mush-gush. "It'll only take another few hours, Andrew," they told him, "and then you'll be free."

Kliver rolled over and appeared to fall asleep. Talbot and Becky tiptoed to the other room, hoping he'd sleep through the final agony.

A few minutes later something was obviously very wrong. Kliver who was supposed to be in agony walked into their room smiling and relaxed. Talbot sizzled apart. "Kliver! you cheating little fake!"

"It wasn't very much man. Just a. A tase" He was scratching himself, his arm sleeve sliding up and down beneath his scratching nails, his lids drooping like someone on a morgue slab.

Talbot began ripping up the edges of the linoleum around the room. He skirred the ragged chunks to the center of the room, their sharp edges drawing lines in the dust as they slid. It worked. He found some cheat-stashes and flushed them down the toilet.

Talbot was merciless. He slammed Kliver down and twisted him onto his stomach amidst the chunks of linoleum, pressing him with a reverse figure-four wrestling hold while Becky tied his hands and feet with rope.

"If it has to be a rope kick, motherfuck, then it's a rope kick," Talbot snarled.

470

Sam Thomas arrived at 3 A.M. for a crucial double slot in the Kick Grid. His skin was still ultrasensitive from the last howl in the Scythian yurt. Sam was hoping Becky Levy would still be there. Maybe she'd stay with him till nine.

He could sense something had happened. The apartment was empty, the front door unlocked. There were linoleum chunks everywhere, a jumble of blankets on the kitchen floor, and a snarl of ropes on Kliver's bed. He picked up a coil of the rope—it seemed wet, as if it had done duty in the Mindscape yurt.

On the counter next to the sink lay S.T. Coleridge, opened to "Kubla Khan." A splash of Kliver's blood in the rough shape of a circle was bisected almost exactly by the line "Weave a circle around his thrice," like a ring around a planet.

A match, a spoon, a blob of blood and wet ropes.

Auden Buys Some Diapers

W. H. Auden

W. H. Auden

W. H. Auden

W. H. Auden

W. H. Auden

W. H Auden

HE WAS SITTING in the rock garden in the courtyard section of the House of Nothingness cafe on Tompkins Square North on a late summer afternoon. His friend Nelson Saite was raking the white sand of the garden in pleasing Kyotoesque parallel furrows around clusters of small boulders, pausing now and then to pick up a cigarette butt someone had thrown into the whiteness the previous night.

472

The writer was concentrating on the "W"—perfecting the peculiarly overextended upward flourish Auden gave to the left-most bar of it—with the slight inward bending of the line beginning to curve again to the left at its upmost termination.

W. W. W. W. W. W. W. W. W. W. W

For an hour he polished the signature, his eyes darting back and forth from his own endeavors to the Auden exemplars he'd traced from the library of a friend—till he had it!

But it was one thing to have it, another to transplant it. One mistake and it might be impossible to correct it. The signature had to be fluid and without mar or erasure. He felt like a sumi painter whose badger hair brush was about to sweep down a scroll of thin rice paper with a stroke that could never be changed. Talk about living in the Now! It was the only place to be—Now Alley, Now Polis, Now Kiva, Nowsville. Let's go!

The book was in his canvas bag, a mint condition first edition of *The Age of Anxiety*, its dust jacket free of chip, crease or stain. The House of Nothingness cafe was a place where any sort of instant accident could occur, so he wanted the book safe in his bag until the final moment. He pulled the treasure forth, opened it to the title page and laid it extremely carefully upon a bed of napkins.

473

Then he went into last minute training. W.H. Auden... W.H. Auden... W.H. Auden—ten times he wrote it and then, just as if he were Wystan Hugh himself at a publication party, he positioned the pen just above the spot beneath Auden's printed name, paused, lowered the point to page and dashed it off.

He looked at it. Ahh, it was perfect! Diaper money and spaghetti sauce, here I come!

There was one thing remaining—and that was the line through the type. Auden usually autographed directly beneath his printed name and then drew a horizontal line through the typography immediately above. In the exemplars the forger had examined the line curved slightly upward then sank, so that the chord subtending the curve was more or less parallel with the bottom of the page.

For some reason the young man thought the line through Auden's printed name would be the one place he'd most likely fuck up. His line might miss the typeface altogether or veer weirdly into an un-Auden upward curvature. He chastised himself, remember the badger hair brush, then tightened his lips and drew the line. It was perfect. He wrapped the book carefully and put it back into the canvas bag.

Next he turned to the matter of William Seward Burroughs, which was going to be a cinch compared to W.H., since Burroughs often signed books with a felt tipped pen. Magic markers were not so common in 1964 nor were their points nearly as narrow as in later decades. The signature "William S. Burroughs" was delivered in a horizontally wide but vertically narrow formation, a joy to forge because the vertical compression precluded adornments and curlicues of execution. Therefore the practice session prior to signing the Olympia Press edition

474

of *Naked Lunch* was brief. Its brevity was ever more enforced by the fact the pen was going dry and he hadn't the time nor the fifty cents to purchase a new one.

The mallet of poverty was pummeling and the pleasant give and take of normal family discourse had been replaced by bitter pecunialalia. The lights had been turned off now for almost two weeks. The gas meter was on the inside of the apartment so it had been spared. No doubt Con Ed would soon get a court order and come crashing in to get it. They'd run a cord to the kitchen from the toilet in the hallway. There was no way to hide the lightlessness from friends, so they joked about it, but they were already weary of burning thin white candles from the corner bodega, and Clara was less than eager to continue scraping away the sloppy runnels where he'd knocked over candles on the floor, the table, the hallway mirror trying to shave, the dictionary looking up a word, her row of dresses in the closet trying to select a shirt.

He had long ago taken the Poet's Vow, placing one's hand on a first edition *Howl* and swearing to live on the proceeds of poetry, which thankfully included the selling of one's books and archives. But where were the books? Just last year their bookcases had teemed with rarity, but slowly he'd sold them till even their books from college were gone. At the parties of older friends it was always a pleasure to be able to locate in some obscure section of their shelves a tidy row of odd-colored, faded tomes left over from studies—*Elementary Psychology, Calculus II, Advanced Portugese, New Theories of Cognition (Vol. III), Studies in the Modern Scandinavian Novel, Microbiology, William Cowper's Agony, et alia milia.* Now they would never get to have their own college nostalgia section.

He missed his books and more than that the letters of his pals, some of whom were well known enough that there was actually a market for their more intimate out-pourings. The poet regretted selling his archives. It made him feel as if he were erasing his own history while he lived it.

Nevertheless, he cherished the fame of his friends because their books, letters, notebooks and manuscripts would then assume a zoom configuration on the Best Minds graph:

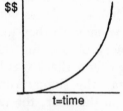

The Best Minds Graph

The book dealers stood to profit most in promotion of the Best Minds curve. There were those who sneered at the dealers, calling them jackals in the cemetery of verse with armbones in their teeth. They sneered that books bought cheaply in most cases were then treated like displays of diamonds on velvet cards while poets ate Velveeta.

A poet with two hungry children stopped sneering when the only books left to them on the Best Minds graph were the Burroughs and the Auden. They were down to a day's worth of candles. They were out of diapers. The phone was going to click dead soon and their strained connection with those relatives still willing to help would be severed.

He pondered purchasing a nickel bag of grass, rolling

476

ten or fifteen joints, maybe mixing in a little oregano, and working the edges of the park, but he lackéd the capital. He hated to deal—it lent a hustler's overply to his career as bard, it violated the Poet's Vow and selling a J in those days could get you a few years up the river.

Much as he hated to deal, he hated more the possibility of Clara disrobing again, as she had earlier that week when she'd left him with the children and modeled for a figure class at Cooper Union. He'd never admit it to anyone—except as a hint or a sulk to Clara herself, and certainly not in words, that he did not want her to pose. He told himself it was not any lowly concern about the eyes of others on his wife's beauteous curves, but it was lofty, man, lofty. Like what? Like, what about the formula: Cooper Union today/Sam Thomas tomorrow.

Sam had been shooting 16-mm films all summer, recruiting his stars from among the poets and painters. He'd asked Clara. The poet shuddered contemplating his wife being recruited for a cameo in *Spontaneous History of the American Blow Job.* Clara's husband held the beat generation version of the double standard. He wanted to fuck around, blaming it on alcohol and the wings of genius, but would have been as miserable as Catullus for some other poet's saliva to drop upon Clara's tiny naked shoulders from above.

Nelson had finished raking the zen sand at House of Nothingness when the bard finished wrapping *Naked Lunch* as neatly as he had *The Age of Anxiety.* He found book dealers gave better prices if he arrived neatly dressed bearing well wrapped treasures. He was not quite famous enough to utilize the "I am a genius" factor in selling rare books.

That morning he'd applied model airplane cement to

477

reattach his shoe sole to its upper. Now, as he left House of Nothingness, it separated again, causing an embarrassing flap-flop as the foot smote the pave. He was extremely casual in his attire but there are standards of appearance even among those sleeping in vomit in an alley. He'd felt a jolt of humiliation sitting in the park wrapping masking tape around the end of his shoe. It was an emblem of his poverty which no boastful words, no brillant poetry in magazines "published in eternity" or brilliant badinage in saloons could enshroud.

He walked to the West Side to the Lantern of Knowledge bookshop where Jack Barnes, the owner, was packing and mailing out orders to the customers of his catalogs, mostly rare book curators at university libraries and collectors in the hinterlands hooked on *rari libri*. He unwrapped first one, then the other for Mr. Barnes and they discussed rather crisply for several minutes the question of prices.

The young man had been pleased the shop was empty. There were seldom more than two or three customers at any one time in Lantern of Knowledge. He glanced to the front when the door bell jangled. He couldn't believe it. Here come the Fates! Clotho, Lachesis and Atropos themselves had converged on the store to snip the threads of his scam!!

It was Auden. It had to be he. The person approaching the desk bore the well known fleshy nose, angling very slightly to the right, and the unmistakable thatch of hair which curved down over the right side of the forehead. And the famous hyperwrinkled face, shy and sensuous, which caused the young man to think of sprinting into the back room, kicking open the alleyside door and fleeing in shame.

478

"Just in time," Jack Barnes said, and he extended the copy of *The Age of Anxiety* toward its perpetrator.

"Just in time for what?" Auden replied, an enormous smile settling briefly upon his face. It was enormous because he did not smile with the lower portions of his face alone, but the entirety of his head seemed to become involved. The crinkles in his eye corners carried part of it as did the furrows of his cheeks on the left and right of his nose. Even his eye bags—and there were many of them, made mirth. The deepest lines projecting perpendicularly from between his brows up to his hair line reddened slightly when the smile pushed the left and right planes together.

Auden pulled his reading glasses from his rather rumpled suit jacket and briefly examined the signature. He handed it back to Jack, glancing at the young writer. "Where did you get this?" he asked.

"At a rummage sale at the Greenwich Village Peace Center," the young man lied. "It was hidden at the bottom of a box of science fiction soft covers."

"It appears to be genuine," the older poet said to Jack Barnes. Perhaps the seller was being overly fearful but he thought he detected a tone of doubt in Auden's confirmation.

Having Auden himself in the store boosted the sales price back to he young man's original request. Jack also bought the signed *Naked Lunch*. "I suppose you want cash," Barnes said, and without waiting for an answer added, "sign this and I'll cash it," speedwriting a check for twenty-five dollars.

The young poet handed Auden a magazine with some of his verse, shook his hand and departed. All the way through Washington Square he felt wonderful. The mallet

479

of poverty had been banished! The rent, $37.50, was not due for a couple of weeks, so he wouldn't have to begin fundraising for that for days yet.

When his taped foot began splatting along St. Mark's Place the guilt hit him. Splat splat, he vowed, splat splat, never to forge, splat splat, another name, nor, splat splat, to steal another single expensive art book, splat splat, or to sell any more letters, splat, splat, splat.

With cash in pocket he grew afflicted with the condition known as "beatifique riche." The symptom of this malady was a barely controllable urge to spend. While still at the Lantern of Knowledge bookstore, he'd felt the temptation to buy a nice three-volume edition of Ben Jonson. On St. Mark's the spend frenzy increased. I need some film. Wow, look at that cherry cheese cake in the window—maybe I should get a few pounds of it. How about copping some Panamanian Red over at Nelson's? Some toys on 9th Street for the kids. Some diapers. Wine for dinner. Some canvas shoes at Hudson's Army and Navy. A coal oil lamp.

An aura of beatifique riche must have emanated from him because beggars ran from across the street to follow him. A friend asked if he could loan him five or ten. A drug merchant with trembly hands waved from a third story window while shouting in code, "I got some cheap lasagna in the oven. Come up and try it!!!"

He spent nothing until he passed Gem Spa at St. Mark's and Second Avenue where he plunked down fifteen cents for a chocolate egg cream and ten cents for the *Village Voice*.

Cynthia Pruitt and some people from the *Catholic Worker* were on the corner selling the *Worker* and passing out leaflets against the escalation of the bloodshed in

Vietnam. Vietnam—he still wasn't quite sure where it was on the map in relation to Burma, Laos and Cambodia. He continued on the way to Tompkins Square memorizing the details of the flyer, and nearly knocked Sam Thomas off his feet when they collided. Thomas too was reading while walking.

The two friendly antagonists said hello. Sam announced he was publishing an "instant anthology" that very day. The deadline was fifteen minutes away, did he have anything for it?

"Give me five minutes."

Sam said he'd wait at his "editorial offices," meaning a cool stone and metal stoop with floral grillwork on the hand rails, near First Avenue where on warm days he spread his papers and poems and edited his magazine.

The poet went to a bench in Tompkins Square Park. He did not have to wait for the images. They were like the pounding, pulsing, relentless flood in his forehead vein. They were torrid, tornadoey, antlered, angry, lemon-yellow, arotolalic, crimson, antlered, convulsive, serpentine, ghostly, antlered, rhapsodic, resinous and antlered. He had only to pluck a few of them for today's bardic brain song and fork them over to Sam Thomas.

The title came at once: "W.H. Auden Buys Some Diapers."

Yes, that's good. Then the text:

W.H. AUDEN BUYS SOME DIAPERS

> I had angst because
> you were
> the coffee
>
> on the 9th day

```
    I am in bed                     I feel like
with                                      infinity—
        the cormorant         what's wrong with that?
    by the ditch of wine


                    That's why
                    The Turbaned Buffalo
                    calls out
                        "No Regrets"
                    this silly summer day

                The Age of Anxiety
                pulls us all into the cucumber

                        The ditch of wine
                            is talking to me
                    "No Regrets"
                        Tell the truth
                        like a Babe Ruth
```

"Genius!" he exclaimed, then signed it, dated it, and walked over to Sam's stoop to hand it in. "I want a page one or two slot, Sammy my man," he said.

Sam said nothing. He held the poem in one hand while in the other were the gathered pages of the anthology. He glanced at the lines, then inserted it in an honored spot at the beginning. That was good, because an instant anthology on a hot day might tire one's eyes by around page nine or ten.

Just then Zack Thayer, an artist, opened up the garbage cans at the edge of Sam's stairrail. His rummaging techniques were sloppy—old shoes and malodorous mounds of decay fell to the sidewalk. No one would say anything, except perhaps the super who was not around, because Zack had a nasty temper and surely a razor blade was hidden somewhere near his hand. He asked them if they wanted to purchase any bennies.

"How much?" the poet asked. Two for fifty cents. He said goodbye to Sam Thomas and walked away with Thayer.

"I'll have some copies at Stanley's later on," Sam shouted.

Zack Thayer had some of the dirtiest hands in the history of American art. He would drip India ink on them and smear them across panels of canvas. These same hands would dive into garbage cans searching for objects suitable to glue into clustered statuary. Soap rarely touched these hands. Zack did not want to disturb their fields of genius.

He loved amphetamine. That obsession had made him one of the A-Head Artists, a school of art with practitioners throughout the 1960s but about whom no textbooks have yet been published. Zack shook two bennies upon a dirty hand from his stash, an army surplus canteen he wore on his hip. The "obvious" stash was often as successful as the hidden, although Zack had to be careful about sudden moves causing his canteen to rattle like a dried gourd.

They walked up First Avenue concluding the deal, and parted at 12th Street. The poet pulled one pill from the foil and flipped it into his mouth, saving the other for later. The faces in the clock shop on Avenue A said 6 P.M. Uh oh. Clara was going to be miffed, since he'd assured her he'd be back early in the afternoon with cash.

"I sold some books!" he exclaimed from the hallway,

483

dropping a twenty on the table. There were hours of light left, so they walked out for food, brought it back for a quick summer meal of borscht, boiled eggs and potatoes, and then to the park where the twins rode the swings, after which the mood of beatifique riche carried them across the street to the Tompkins Square Sweet Shoppe, an institution now gone but then a treasure, for sundaes.

Clara shuddered when he recounted the sound of the bell tinkling in the bookstore when Auden arrived in the middle of the book deal. Walking home, one child already asleep in her arms, she sang for them in her soft clear voice some verses from the song she'd been writing. He praised her when she'd finished, and read her the poem he'd written for Sam Thomas' anthology, the one with the lines

I feel like
infinity
what's wrong with that?

A Night at the Cafe Perf-Po

THE BLIZZARDY WIND made the banner flap over sidewalks so thick with snow that pants legs were whitened to the middle of the shins. It was sieving downward on East 10th near Avenue B, obliterating footprints in a few seconds, and one's attention was turned from the mystery *of* the city to the mystery *above* the city. Nevertheless, there was no room for any more people inside the Cafe Perf-Po and at least fifty waited outside in case someone should leave.

A giant banner, SPECULATORS STAY OUT! was stretched from the roof of the Cafe Perf-Po across the street to the top of the high fence of the Tompkins Square Park handball courts. The event was a fundraising marathon put on by the Live Cheap or Die Anti-Gentrification Coalition in February of 1984.

The Cafe Perf-Po was assuming the same role for its generation as the Cabaret Voltaire in Zurich had for the Dadaists. The perf-po generation was spreading and the Cafe Perf-Po was coordinating it carefully through a steady flow of manifestoes, cassettes, videotapes, posters and pamphlets outlining the latest advances in the strange

485

confluence of poetry, music, dance, mime, acting, lighting, dada multi-track simultaneity, electronics, visual imaging, and in general, the theory of Working a Crowd under the muses of perf-po.

The walls of the club were a peculiar quilt of idealistic flags and banners, such as the cloth painting:

MONEY FOR JOBS

NO VIETNAM WAR IN CENTRAL AMERICA AND THE CARIBBEAN

Here and there among the idealistic visuals were a few carefully chosen perf-posters advertising the appearances of such well-known groups as The Ghost of Keats, The Four Great Poets, Word Stream, the Goof City Ramblers, Metem, State Smash, Write Me Up!, and The 6th Street Mouths. It was considered a great honor to have one's poster on the wall, for it guaranteed the rarest perf-po pearls, i.e., out-of-town engagements. There was already a perf-po star system, and a few managers had evolved, striving to make perf-po economically viable. There were even one or two perf-po moguls, whose goal was to tour hockey arenas with the milky way of perf. There was talk of an International Perf-Po Festival next summer in Central Park.

Tonight some of the finest performers in perf-po land had assembled to speak out against the forces of upscalism, luxury co-oping, money grovel and rat race. In

486

between performers there were speakers demanding the return of cheap rents, urging commercial rent control, and demanding greatly expanded programs granting low interest loans for the modestly moolah'd to fix up and to own rundown buildings.

The dressing room groaned with perf, and the overfill sat at tables on each side of the stage, jitterly attentive to the performances, for one always wanted to check out the cutting edge of perf, both to steal and to mutate ideas, and to avoid being left in the rear guard of the movement.

All in all, the perf tables looked like a casting call for a Dali/Buñuel/Cocteau production of *A Midsummer Night's Dream*. Some were in costume; others wore white mime's makeup; some sported unusual haircuts; others held next to them the accoutrements of perf-po: hand-held synthesizers, masks, finger cymbals, washboards, claves, tape loops, roller skate cases, suction cups, toothpicks, bags of persimmons, *et alia multa*.

However nervous they were, most nevertheless were deeply satisfied, out of obedience to the adage, "Perf-request is the perf-quest"—that is, there is no greater honor than being asked to perform. It could have been otherwise. All over N.Y. that night there were perf poets staring glumly at their performance charts, their perf-Casios clicked to the OFF position, humiliated that there had been no phone calls inviting them to the stage for the Live Cheap or Die Anti-Gentrification Marathon.

The noise level of perf-po will normally prevent all but the most strident tableside talk, so that by the first intermission, the audience was starved for chatter and the conversation from the tables almost matched the decibels of the perf. Tables were pressed so tightly together that a set of ears could hear the conversations of five or six clusters by slowly rotating the head. Ten or fifteen sets of ears at least were turned to the table talk of Saunter Sally, one of the stars of perf-po the moguls mentioned when they talked about working hockey arenas. Her hair was permed into the style known as Nouveau I-yi-yi, its many angular spikes waxed and twisted in apparent imitation of Viking runes, so that the crown was a hemisphere of runic tridents, bent L's, 7's and lambdas.

Saunter Sally was speaking with her backup band. "Wait till you hear my new piece," she exclaimed. "Just in time for the new album. I've decided to call it 'Perf-Po Debt Retirement.'" One of them asked what that meant and she explained. "I used to hate it that all my sculptor and painter friends were paying off their dentists and doctors with artworks. What could I pay with, a yodel? So, when I went in to have my crown done, I told Reuben I wanted to pay for it with a performance piece. He was absolutely flabbergasted. I half-expected him to say no, but he went along with it!"

There was a spontaneous burst of applause, for it was truly an historic moment—the first instance in North America of payment through perf-po. She continued, "He sat there bleary, red-eyed and squelched in his office chair—you know how they always complain of being overworked—while I performed a fifteen minute piece. The next visit I dangled from a tree in his courtyard and wrote poems with a smoke gun while he videotaped it."

Sally was so enthused from her recitation she rose from her table and whirled spontaneously across the floor, singing, "I'd like to pay all my bills with perf-po!" The tables surrounding her responded as if at a tent revival, shouting "Here! Here!" and "Saints be saved!" and "Hallelujah!"

My attention, I must say, was beginning to be torn between the interesting spectacle of Saunter Sally and the chatter of a table next to hers containing a group of weighty theoreticians of the perf-po movement. These five gentlemen edited the magazine *Perfpometry,* which had published the initial historic manifesto of the generation, "The Time of Perf-Po Is Now!" *Perfpometry* had helped spread the movement around the world. There were already perf-po centers in Cologne, Berlin, Sarajevo and a cassette perf samisdat in the U.S.S.R.

The editors of *Perfpometry* all sported giant craggy heads and unfashionably lengthy locks. Wags called them Mt. Perfmore. Throughout the evening Mt. Perfmore would bend among themselves, nodding gravely, daring to laugh whenever they wanted, sucking in gigabytes of perf-data to be sorted, ranked and tucked in their proper spots on the paradigms of perf theory.

Cheese and crackers! There was such excitement that night on Mt. Perfmore! They were in the midst of that opportunity of opportunities—the chance to grab off an entire generation! There would be perf text books to write, and perf symposia, and NEA-funded perf fests! And then, as the clack of time's chariot clacked forward, there would certainly be graduate students approaching Mt. Perfmore someday in the Golden Perf-Po Retirement Colony to ask about the birth of perf-po. "And who first thought of the name, 'perf-po'?" one of them will ask. "I did!" a theoretician will exclaim, "it came to me in the shower!" "No! No!" a second will exclaim, "I was the one—in a dream!" "Not at all, perf-creep!" a third, and so forth. They were living examples of the truism that the theoreticians of a movement can make a better living out of it than the practitioners. By 11 P.M. the second set

489

began and the room noise sank to a mumbly hush. Up to the glory stepped the group known as Metem. "It's not psychosis!" one of them shouted into the Shure. "It's not metempsychosis! It's just Metem!"—an opening so familiar that the room shouted along in synch. Metem's set was a string of *poèmes simultanés* above the amplified heart beats and gurgles of the endocrine systems of the performers. I thought it was wonderful, giving us a hint of what it might have been like in Zurich in 1916 when Marcel Janco, Tristan Tzara and the others had perf'd the first simultaneous po's.

Metem was followed by the Perf-Poes, an ensemble specializing in terrifying ghost poems. They worked through an eery "Ulalume" and a very satisfying rap version of "The Fall of the House of Usher." I could feel the excitement buzzing about me as the Perf-Poes howled their final haint from the haunted castle, and the word was spread that Saunter Sally was next.

When a great performer walks into spots from darkness there's always that joyful crowd-gasp followed by thunder palms. That's what it was like as Saunter Sally mounted the stage, her runic spikes looking like an exhibition of bent X-acto knives in a dazzle of blue lights. She was one of those who appear all to all—she was both tall and short, frail yet sturdy, a camelia wrapped around barbed wire. And what respect she commanded! Even Mt. Perfmore was silent.

Saunter Sally sang with a calm, clear voice that always astounded her devotees. What perf-pipes! The thrill trilled through the audience with a sweet ache of vowels. For hook-lines and choruses she ran her voice through a block of pitch-transposers so that she could sing four-part harmony with herself.

Sally had written an anti-gentrification anthem for the evening. The room responded with a fervor that went beyond the revivalist's tent. There was the type of applause that abrades the skin from palms.

> There's no greater ease
>   to a poet's soul
> than a yearly grant
>   . . . .and rent control

Sam Thomas was in the room, at a table between Mt. Perfmore and Saunter Sally's. He'd not been in this building for almost exactly twenty years, since February of 1964 when it had been, not the Cafe Perf-Po, but the House of Nothingness, a zen-inspired poetry center/ restaurant that had served the first tofu and brown rice casseroles in the history of the Lower East Side.

Sam was in New York for a retrospective showing of his films and to puff some life into his literary career. He'd seen the notice for the Anti-Gentrification benefit in the *Village Voice*, not realizing at first it was in the same building as the House of N. He wondered if anyone in the room recalled the House, his eyes searching among the tables as if he were looking for lost relatives.

Her song on rent control brought a rush of emotions. He recalled his own "Hymn to Rent Control," over which he had slaved in late 1963, and which he had not long ago left out of his collected poems. He felt a pang of remorse he'd not been able in the end to leave behind an ever-enduring ozymandian fragment.

Earlier that day, before the snow had begun, Sam toured the East Side for the first time in over ten years. He watched them stretch the SPECULATORS STAY OUT! banner

491

across Tenth Street. He walked by the creaky old back building which Uncle Thrills had rented for $38 a month twenty years ago. By chance Sam ran into the super who told him it now rented for $1300! All that for a paint job and an entrance light that now worked?

He was shocked to find a gourmet cheese shop on Ave. A across the street from the site of the Total Assault Cantina, a rebel lounge of 1961, now boarded up and forgotten. But the biggest jolt came when he had driven his rented car past the building on East 7th where John Barrett had seen the ghost of Sappho. There had apparently been a fire, for the entire five floors in front were sealed by cement blocks, with a single hole about three feet high leading into the basement. Sam paused, letting his engine run as he jotted down a description in his notebook and clicked some photos. A boy of about ten came out of the hole carrying a clipboard and walked up to Sam's car to take down his skag or coke order, then spat on the windshield as Sam shook his head and drove away.

The applause for Sally only faded with the beseeching of the M.C. that there were 23 perf acts still to come, after which there was a faint clattering sound from the other side of the dressing room door. "Here comes the Brainotron!" someone shouted.

"Wow, the Brainotron!"

An excited murmur swept wind-over-wheatfieldishly across the Cafe Perf-Po once again. The door thumped open. A gasp. An explosion of whacked palms, and forth tremble-walked the Brainotron. It was a tremble walk, because the object appearing before us was a slender young man in tan trousers, with his head and upper torso encased in a heavy red and yellow apparatus that, had it been topped with a few feathers, would have given the overall look of a huge Hopi Kachina.

492

His arms were free and he pushed in front of him a wheeled tea cart teeming with electronics. He walked gingerly so as not to run over or step upon a rainbow bundle of color-coded computer cables looping down from the top of his head and attaching here and there to the console atop the cart.

The Brainotron's face was hidden behind a smoky window in the helmet and no one knew his name. It was said that the 'Tron, its fans' fond name for it, was an electronic genius, developing microminiaturized brain-monitoring equipment able to be fit on a tea cart, the same devices normally requiring an entire room. Beneath the encasement and above the noggin, a multitude of electrodes fitted against the scalp to pick up and to isolate electrical waves from specific parts of the brain.

There were two "keyboards" to produce music from the 'Tron. The first required external stimuli. The 'Tron would flash images on a screen in front of him and the music would respond. That is, the apparatus would pick up the specific brain waves created by the images as they worked through the neural brain paths, and turn them into music—a chord, a flurry of notes, a melody frag or just a rush of interesting sound. Music could also come from somato-sensory stimuli. The stroking of the 'Tron's chest hair with an asparagus fern produced an enormously satisfying musical sigh.

His own voice triggered music. "Grief! Grief! Grief!" spake the 'Tron, and a dire Moan of Moans came forth from the speakers.

"Joy! Joy! Joy!" intoned the Brainotron, and the music of a peaceful sea-slap on a pier was heard.

The second "keyboard" to produce 'Tronic music was

493

through self-induced brain activity. The crowd went wild. Especially pleasurable was the piece called "Joyce Juice," in which music was made from brain waves beneath the Silvian fissure (located above his left ear), the home of the stream of consciousness.

Finally the audience was encouraged to shout lines of verse at the Brainotron. "Out of the cradle endlessly rocking!" someone shouted, and the 'Tron gave forth an orchestration. "So much depends/upon/a red wheel/barrow/glazed with rain/water/beside the white/chickens!" another person offered. Sam Thomas yelled lines also: "Beatific Spirits welded together!" and then "Appropriate Technology!" and "Topos/Typos/Tropos!" After that the 'Tron slowly pushed his tea cart toward the door, across the snow, and into a waiting van.

A perf-po marathon will always have a few dud acts—someone will stand on his head intoning gibberish in front of an inappropriate tray of slides; or the whipped cream machine will break down; or the synth-drum built from a converted toaster will short circuit and cause a seizure *petit mal* in the performer. Everyone expects it, but no one in the Cafe was expecting the Death Beam. Nor could one have expected it viewing the well-dressed young man with just the proper minimum amount of cowlicky angularity to his hair that could be quickly trained in the morning mirror to lie quietly before returning to work at the bank. He was lugging a long T-shaped frame of wood that appeared to have been part of an easel. Stretching about five feet from the right edge of the T down to the lowest point of it was a spring of the type used to shut screen doors. There was a foot bar near the floor allowing the tension of the spring to be increased or decreased.

An electronic pickup on the spring was attached via

494

cable to a long S-shaped array on the floor of the sort they call in musical circles an "effects chain." The effects chain, which altered the sound fed through it, consisted of a stereo chorus, a phaser, a digital delay, an Eventide harmonizer, a reverb unit, a fuzz box, a Mutron octave divider, and a high-tech microchipped echo chamber built inside an empty RC Cola bottle lying on its side.

It was innocent at first, the artist foot-punching various components of his chain so that the little red diodes glowed in the ON position. More ominously, however, he reached over to his Peavey amp and twisted the volume knob to 10. He bent down about the frame like a jazz bassist and began to sprong the spring. The resulting beam of boing boing was as loud a noise as any in the audience had ever encountered.

One of the unspoken rules of perf-po is never to let anything phase you. This was different. Everywhere the auditory cortexes were interpreting what was happening as Death Beam. Activity at the Cafe Perf-Po halted. Waiters stood frozen in place unable to deliver their trays of perf-po fizzes. People slumped down upon their tables as if they were school children during an air raid drill in the fifties, casting perf-propriety aside in order to save their ears, covering them with napkins, hands, kerchiefs, winter coat sleeves and pages torn from *Perfpometry*.

There was one human in the room, however, who did not view the boing-boing as death, and that was his fiancée. She stood at stage edge with outstretched hand holding a tape recorder as far as possible in her beloved's direction. You could see by her stare of adoration and the moisture on her lips she was not thinking "dud," but rather "Thou, o Chopin! Thou, o Schiller! Thou, o Britten!"

Suddenly it stopped and a blessed zone of silence whacked the room like a mallet. There was no applause. The only sound was the faint click of the tape recorder being turned off. People were suspicious and remained bent down in howl-pain position at their tables, unwilling to risk uncovering their ears in case it was just a trick and the Death Beam would start up again.

To Sam Thomas the silence was a miracle, not because it was freedom from the Beam, but because the Beam had somehow served as his personal Brainotron. It had liberated his experiential record, and he was recalling in minute detail, as in a dream or trance, a party held twenty years ago, in the very same room, when it was the House of Nothingness. It wasn't the first time Sam had experienced a "past trance." It happened now and then, an example being his first peyote trip when he had relived the "bio tapes"of a junior high roller skating party from years ago.

It was a sad occasion Sam was seeing—the final night at House of Nothingness before it closed its doors. The place was jammed with its friends. There was a table laden with food and Stanley Tolkin of Stanley's Bar had given some kegs of bock at cost. The House of N had been a cooperative, with the profits split among the employees. An unjust rent increase, throughout its history one of New York's greatest evils, was killing the House. The new lease proposed such a jump in rent that brown rice, poesy and bean curd could not sustain.

There was a tradition at House of Nothingness that each Friday night at midnight poets would gather to clean and rake the white sand of the courtyard garden after which there would be a poetry reading. The final night the poets sadly performed the rake, then read. Every few minutes someone went out to sweep the snow from the sand and boulders. They left the lights shining in the courtyard, so that the zen sand should cast its final dazzle.

As he sat in the Cafe Perf-Po, he could see the clearly drawn faces of his friends that night in '64—Nelson Saite, Cynthia Pruitt, Andrew Kliver, Past Blast, Becky Levy, Louise Adams, Talbot Jenkins, Claudia Pred—as they were. He listened to their poems line by line again. What a feat! Try to remember someone's poems from fifteen minutes ago, much less twenty years! He watched himself read his own "Hymn to Rent Control" and the response was nearly as noisy as the one just minutes ago for Saunter Sally.

Only John Barrett was absent. He was supposed to be there hours ago. He had left his apartment on East 7th for the House of N in a topcoat so thick and obdurate to the touch it seemed more like three layers of horse blankets stacked in a shed. The snow gathered on its shoulders as on any steep slope, that is, it built up for a while then slid to the pavement in tiny avalanches.

For hours John walked the snow, crisscrossing all the streets from Houston to 12th and First Avenue to C. He who never felt down was feeling a rare gulch of total depression. He didn't realize it, but he was having a "fame fit." He couldn't tell if he were happy, unhappy, on top of it, or sorely beneath. The success of *Bomb Calf* at the Luminous Animal Theater had made Barrett, within weeks, the most famous literary figure on the set. He was in demand. Offers for his next play were arriving by registered mail, by telegram, by messenger. He'd received his very first overseas cablegram. He was as hot as you could be in '64. Yet he was depressed. He who had so long resided in what Balzac called "the obscure mud,"

497

in a world that addressed him, "Hey, Mac!" and "Hey, bub!" had gone in a few days to "Hello, Mr. Barrett, I read about your wonderful play in *Newsweek*!" Fame always carries its own towel. It was the first moment Barrett realized you could be delivering your Nobel Prize acceptance speech while feeling like a pinworm.

John loved the fresh snow, for it covered the slush of prior weeks. Words fail East Side snow slush. Brown rivulets of frosty-freeze surge over the curbs, wherefrom strange bubbles slowly rise amidst a floatage of straws, dog dook, can lids, wrappers, plus, sunken as in quicksand, a slashed chair of wettened plaid, its stuffing the color of a dirty old football, covered with sooty white, and at the curb's edge: rows of dingy tan tire tracks like zippers on a vast spattered cloth.

John was walking up the middle of Avenue A to avoid the hidden filth. He looked upward, sensing something rising above him, and saw he was at the edge of the red brick Carpatho Russian Orthodox Greek Catholic Church at 10th. He squinted his eyes to try to see the Lion of St. Mark high upon its third floor chimney, but the flakes made wet tickles on his eyes and brows and he couldn't keep them open.

He was startled, turning his attention back to the street, to see a figure in purple robes kneeling at the steps. It was unmistakable. He breathed inwardly so swiftly a twist of snowflakes hooted up his nostril.

"Sapph'!" John Barrett whispered.

It was the same woman, vision, apparition, dream or ghost he had seen that crazy evening last summer. Sappho of Mitylene. Tonight her neck was laden with heavy Russian crosses and her knees were obscured by the drift that covered the lower steps of the church. She was holding

498

ikons in her hands and John was blinking his eyes as rapidly as he could to knock off the snowflakes as he approached her, for the ikons seemed to soften, to melt and drop in blobs from her fingers.

He could see that she was weeping. There were streaks of kohl down her cheeks. "You'll cry too," was all that Sappho said. She turned away from Barrett, pulling the purple cowl upon her hair, and walked away into the blizzard weeping and wailing. John Barrett would never see her again.

John's despair left him almost instantly. It was as if Sappho had carried it away with her. He waited a few minutes in case she should return. He patted the drifts on the steps for rubies and ikons but of course there were none, and soon even her tracks were filled smooth. At last he walked down 10th Street to the House of Nothingness where his arrival brought applause and shouts of "John's here!" They clapped for him to read from *Bomb Calf*, but John shook his head, seemed dazed and sat next to Sam Thomas. "I've seen her again," he said.

"The Big S?"

Barrett nodded and recounted what had happened. Except for his experiments in calling down Sappho, John was otherwise an agnostic with absolutely no proclivity toward Deus-flashes, soul travel, spiritism or the like, but now having seen her twice he was sure he was going into the bonk zone. Besides that, Sappho in role as Carpathian weeper had stunned and baffled him.

Sam was puzzled also, for he was the only one to whom Cynthia had confided her religious vision of last fall, which had occurred at the same location in front of St. Nicholas Carpatho Russian. Sam could sense his friend was worried about the chariot from Flip-Out City.

499

"You're not going bonk-bonk," soothed Sam. "Maybe you *wanted* to see Sapph', and the cosmos merely obliged, as a friendly gift."

The shouts for John to read from *Bomb Calf* continued. There were minutes of excitement as he read, but after that the plummet toward glumness was swift. The energy waned. The food was gone and the kegs were hissing air. Tomorrow the sign HOUSE OF NOTHINGNESS would be pried from its niche above the door and the adornments of the antique store that would replace it would be hauled aboard.

Sam walked from table to table trying to enliven the scene. "Party while suffering!" he urged, or just "P.W.S.!" After that he moved to the walls, carefully putting the accumulated posters and flyers of the past three years and placing them in manilla folders for his archives. He'd done the same thing when the Total Assault Cantina closed down. He was only twenty-three and already the beat bistros of his youth were becoming footnotes and bones. People began recounting their favorite moments at the House—specific poetry readings, the frenzy of preparing for protests, of posters being painted on tables, of waiting for the bus to pick them up on the way to the great D.C. March last August.

Rose Snyder, Talbot the Great and a friend of Rose's named Wolf Lesker sat together at a table. Lesker had been a famous anarcho-Communist activist early in the century, when the appellation "syndicalist" meant that the battle with capitalism was total. His cane was hooked upon the table's edge and he was drinking his tea out of a glass with a spoon in it. He'd removed sugar cubes from his breast pocket and held one clenched between his teeth as he drank. He must have been in his late eighties; his

skin was stretched like a translucent tissue over the pinkness of his bones, but his hand did not tremble and he
spoke with as much quick energy as Talbot and Rose.

Rose and the old man were talking excitedly. She was
urging him to do something. "Go on, Wolf, go on. Do it!
Speak!" She was pushing with one hand and tugging with
the other. In protest he fluttered his hands and knocked
over the tea. "I can't. It's been so long. No one would be
interested."

"Are you kidding?" Rose almost shouted. She stood and
asked for silence, and a few seconds of shhhshes swept the
room. "We have in this room tonight someone who has a
very special story to tell. His name is Wolf Lesker, a man
whom I've known since 1910 at least—for over fifty years.
You should hear what he has to say, before the doors of
this peace center close for good."

The old man unhooked his cane from the chair's back
and used it to stand, shoving upward with his other hand
on the top of the bentwood chair, then steadied himself
with both and took a few steps forward.

"It's obvious you are upset by the closing of your
activist cafe," he began. "Some of you may weep for the
closing, but don't weep! You may not know how many
things have happened in this very room, before most of
you were even born. In fact, I would like to tell you a
story that took place in this room when I was a very
young man, even younger than most of you are now, in
1894.

"I was an anarchist. In the 1890s, many of us were
attracted to the philosophy of anarchy. It wasn't the sort
of mindless violent chaos the newspapers published, but it
was well thought out and it presented us with a consistent
economic and social view. We wanted to establish an

501

economic system based on what we called 'free contracts between autonomous independent communes and associations.' We were also solidly behind the trade unions and marched in the big May Day parades to Union Square. This is not the time for a lecture on anarchist history, so I'll get back to my story.

"There was a terrible depression in New York in 1893, and the winter of '94 was so severe that people were found frozen in their flats when they ran out of money for coal, coal oil or even wood. Naturally the capitalists raised the price of coal. Coal, you understand, was a principal source of heat. Everybody had a stove in the kitchen. And that's all there was. Sometimes the stove pipe would run through the bedrooms and that would be the heat for everything.

"Poor people would go out and look for packing crates in the streets, but with coal prices up in the sky, so was everybody else! That's when we started the Anarchist Coal Collective. Right here! In this very room. And out in back where you have your rock garden—that's were we stacked our coal. All of us—artisans, workers, even a few writers and poets, we joined in the dirty work of delivering coal. We were glad to do it. It was part of our doctrine of 'esthetic individualism.'

"We used to have meetings in this room just like you have them. The floors were often black with footprints. There was a shed in back next to the coal where we had a printing press. We published leaflets and posters. Between ink and coal dust the place was pretty dirty, but we'd sweep away the dust and have parties anyway. We served refreshments—we'd sing and dance and recite verses.

"The winter of '94 was so cold! We had a big stove in the middle of this room and families from the neighborhood would huddle around it all night.

"We knew, of course, it wasn't enough just to supply cheap coal! The prices kept going up! The capitalists were murdering us! So, we took action. We wanted to attack! We held rallies. We demanded worker control. We threatened them with coal riots and food riots.

"Then, in February, some women were arrested for cutting limbs from trees in the park. When your children were paralyzed with cold you burned everything but the Holy Word. They were treated like bank robbers; kept overnight without food or water.

"There was an outcry. We printed a poster for a mass gathering in the park. We couldn't let it go unprotested. It was still very cold, but it was warmer than it had been. The snow had melted. It was Sunday afternoon, February 26, 1894. I can always recall the date. We met in the park just across the street from here. We started a coal fire to keep warm.

"That's when they attacked. There was a line of policemen, some of whom were on horses. They marched into us. The horses trampled us while the police clubbed us. People fled into hallways. I recall one cop raising his revolver and firing into the air.

"They chased some of us into our store front. That's when it happened. A police horse tripped at the curb or perhaps it slipped on something loose in the street. It fell into the front glass window and shattered it. The policeman was thrown unconscious, but his injury turned out not to be serious. The horse, on the other hand, was badly wounded. There was a large cut in its chest in between its front legs. It kept rearing up, and a long sliver of glass fell from the wound, giving off a tinkling crash.

"They carried the cop away but left the horse there

with blood pouring out. We didn't know if it was the heart or what. The horse trotted down 10th Street to the corner of Avenue B. One of our associates—he was well known all over the East Side as Noiak the Anarchist—grabbed the reins and calmed the horse down.

"It was weak. We half-led, half-carried the horse into an alley on 11th Street that connected with the back courtyard—the spot where you have your garden. Noiak had once worked as a veterinarian for the czar's cavalry. He wadded his shirt and stuffed it into the wound to stop the bleeding. We made a bed of straw from mattresses and the horse lay down upon it. He didn't move for a few days. We thought he was going to die.

"Meanwhile, the newspapers made a big deal out of it. How someone had stolen a horse from the police. There was a big search, so we moved the horse in a closed wagon up to 20th Street by the river. That's where Noiak nursed it.

"In a few weeks the horse was healthy again. It was a fine animal—we named it Anarch! We dyed the fur a little bit to confuse the authorities, and soon we were using it to pull our little coal wagon from the coal boats at the docks to the storefront!

"Anarch led our contingent in the May Day parade of 1894. We put a red and black banner on her that read, ANARCHIST COAL COLLECTIVE! Meanwhile, the authorities were putting enormous pressure on our landlord. They searched us over and over looking for subversive literature. They threatened the landlord so much he asked us to move out.

"Some of us felt beaten down. I said to them, 'We won! We gave away many tons of coal to the people. That's what counts. We helped hundreds survive the winter!'

"You'll never know how sad we were to carry our

504

possessions out of this room. But there's a truth here I can swear to you as sure as I'm eighty-seven years old—we'll have to keep opening and closing our storefronts, our collectives, our social action centers till the capitalists and totalitarians are beaten back forever!"

Wolf Lesker leaned on his cane and started back to his chair.

"Anarch!" someone shouted. "What happened to Anarch?"

He turned, his face flushed with happiness. "You want to know about Anarch? I'll tell you. We were able to send her to a farm in Staten Island where she lived the rest of her life.

"As long as I still have your attention, I might as well say one more thing. Just as the Anarchist Coal Collective once shut its doors, your House of Nothingness will shut its also. But the spirit! The spirit lives here. I feel something about this room. It's the same place, whether it's the Coal Collective or the House of Nothingness! And believe me, in the future there will have to be many other places, but they shall always have the spirit of the Rebel Cafe! That spirit will open these doors again and again! Long live the Rebel Cafe!"

There was a wild ovation and trampling of feet as Wolf Lesker sat back down to sip his tea.

1894 The Anarchist Coal Collective

1964 The House of Nothingness

1984 Cafe Perf-Po

same flow
same glow

505

Freedom Summer

FOUR OF THEM crossed the Mississippi state
line through cotton and soybean country in an old yellow
Studebaker that only worked in second and third gears.
The air was Touch of Evil hot and tar-scented steam arose
from the buckling slabs of the highway. Nothing seemed
to cool them, not even wet towels pressed upon their arms
and necks from a bucket of ice, and itchy runnels of sweat
tickled unpleasantly down their backs so that, whenever
they shifted slightly, their shirts slid squishly on the hot
seat covers like sponges over the wet, rice-speckled table-
cloths of the House of Nothingness cafe.

Talbot the Great had driven during the night, but now
that they were in klan country. Cynthia Pruitt was working the wheel, Past Blast was sleeping and Rose Snyder
sipped coffee from a thermos while jotting down a plan of
action.

Without much sleep, frazzled, low on energy, and deep
inside the tar-scented land of the lynch mob, the four
were about to toss themselves into a difficult and even
dangerous campaign to free Sam Thomas, who was
trapped in the Bixden County jail on charges of assaulting

506

a police officer, inciting to riot and, after a vacuum cleaner had sucked his pockets at the jail, for possession of pot shreds. The sheriff was trying to bump the assault to attempted murder.

Sam had gone down to Mississippi for Freedom Summer, a campaign to register voters, to crush segregation, to help set up what were known as Freedom Centers, and to challenge the all-white Mississippi delegation to the Democratic National Convention in Atlantic City, New Jersey. Thomas had been sleeping in a kitchen shed next to a Freedom Center located in a church in Dorville, about ten miles from Bixden. Three nights ago, the klan had burned down the church, and the next day church members and staff from the Freedom Center gathered by the ruins for a meeting.

There were prayers, there were angry words and then songs that spoke of triumph and eased the pain. From a mile distant the dust of approaching klan cars could be seen, and soon the clunk clunk clunk of pickup doors was followed by the thunk thunk thunk of pipes and bats.

The Bixden County sheriff just stood there with his jaw muscles pulsing, so Sam jumped onto the dark green hood of the Sheriff's new squad car and shouted at the deputies to intervene. The klannies were loath to nick the fresh paint with their clubs, and therefore left Sam alone on the hood, where eftsoon the sight of blood on his friends' faces made him snap. Sam screamed, threw up his arms, and jogged up and down on the green metal, calling the klan men grunge, shit, filth, motherfuckers and nazis. This was the basis of the incitement-to-riot charge.

Sheriff Harme himself yanked Sam Thomas down upon a jumble of charred boards. Sam continued shouting until a deputy's boot heel and a flexed leg pressed down into his

507

face and twisted his mouth so that his lower lip protruded grotesquely beneath the Cat's Paw rubber like a piece of tomato from a sandwich. "Hoee dah reyew let the se klah n nazisa taack us!" were Sam's final words before the pressure cracked his jaw. They backed Bixden County's sole paddy wagon, a rusty pickup truck with a wire mesh cage bolted to the bed, so close to Sam's boot-pressed face that black grit from the exhaust pipe sprinkled upon his neck.

Harme told *The New York Times* that Sam tried to escape on the way to the county jail—that he punched an officer in the face, that he hopped, wormed and hobbled his way into the woods in shackles and cuffs for a hundred yards before they caught him. It was his word vs. the two deputies.

Sam was sure they were going to kill him, and so he violated several key pacifist principles, including the one that urged him to speak to the redeeming qualities in opponents. While not violent physically, Sam summoned all his skills in quick jibes and wounding phrases, honed to perfection from years hanging out in bars with the New York poets, and taunted his captors to take his blood. It was a calling contest. He assured them they were mongoose puke. They beat his head again and called him a dirty Communist beatnik. He called them racist devil-scum. It hurt to shout after they kicked in his ribs, so he whispered and worked words up through his nose to get a little more volume: "Come and get me you putrid rubes. Hey, you chaw-chewing angus, guys like you are the laugh of the west! Did any of you phlegm kill Chaney, Schwerner and Goodman? I bet you did, and someday you'll get caught and your brains will fry in the chair. Listen to me, gunge, do you know what the klan is? It's the shit that's smeared on your birth certificates!!"

Finally he was alone in a cell with throbbing jaw and a rib cage that felt like it had been ice-picked. Calmness brought a desperate feeling of grief. He had violated the spirit of Freedom Summer. Instead of speaking truth to power, and instead of offering love to the hate, he had spewed out razor words and raillery.

He felt like a maggot on the slab of beef in "Potemkin." He could see the newspaper headlines—how the dangerous and psychopathic editor of *Dope, Fucking and Social Change: A Journal of the New America* had flipped out in the South. There was nothing to do but weep and do the maggot.

At midnight, they gave him a phone call and he reached Past Blast at the Total Assault Cantina on Avenue A and begged for help, any kind of help. "Please do something," he pleaded. "They may kill me. Evil is eating my eyes! Apopis the Egyptian Monster is wrapping its oily coils around me!"

Past Blast spread the word, and the next noon the Studebaker with the grimly grinding gear box edged away from Tompkins Square Park toward Bixden County, Mississippi.

II
The Inflaming Potency of Beatnik

Acronyms sometimes take on a temporary power to inspire or to inflame, and so it was with the word COFO, for Council of Federated Organizations, the nationwide coalition of civil rights groups that sponsored Freedom Summer. In Mississippi of 1964, COFO was the sound of empowerment to the opponents of racism, but at the same time the whisper of it into the ear of a klansman could kick his impulsivity to violence to nightrider status.

The word "beatnik" had a similar, though weaker, power to inflame. In Bixden County they often derided the thousand volunteers who had come from around the USA as "beatnik college kids," and "beatnik race mixers," and, in a nod to science fiction, "beatnik invaders." The word even had powers of hortatory pejoration on the level of a mother scolding a son returning besmirched from a mudball fight, as in, "Billie Bob, *where* have you been? You smell like a room full of wet beatniks!"

All summer long Sam Thomas had been happy to set aside his wild beatnik proclivities, drop all his projects in New York, and submerge himself in a mass movement, just one of a thousand others. He tried not to stand out, and strove mightily to subsume himself beneath the perfection of a "Beloved Community" in a total nonviolent confrontation with evil.

And what a summer! Sixty thousand black voters were registered, but thirty-seven churches were burned, and another 30 black homes or businesses burned or bombed, and there were 35 shootings, four murders, and 1,000 arrests. A Beloved Community did get built, *pro tempore*, but every member of that community had moments of Total Fear, and moved within a majority population that, however much it would change in just a few years, during Freedom Summer wanted to spit acid on them.

The klan metastasized through the state that year organizing the bitter poor and those otherwise well-settled humans with a wild hair of racial hatred in their psyches. Thus, when the white hoods with the eyeslits burned the crosses on church lawns, the shoes protruding beneath the white hems were not only the scuffed and worn down

510

boots of psychopaths with blood caked tire irons, but also the shiny saddlesoap of the lawman, and the perfect black gloss of the church deacon and the storekeeper—few in number, but enough to provide the inside knowledge of the workings of local law enforcement that a violent secret society has to have.

And Bixden County was as violent as there was. A black and a white chatting on a porch swing getting a friendship started were targets for bullets. There were some residents of Bixden County who killed blacks at will, or on a speck of slight, and dumped them in the river. The rest of the population made sure they did not learn about it, or if they knew, went along out of fear, indolence, cruel resignation, or out of a kind of spiteful "Please don't tell me" cracker anti-gnosticism that's one of the great barriers to social progress.

III
Swamp Time

"They've found them!" Rose shouted, rousing the sleepers to listen to the broadcast that froze August 4, 1964, into each of their brains. The three missing COFO organizers—James Chaney, Andrew Goodman and Michael Schwerner—had been found beneath a cattle pond dam outside Philadelphia, Mississippi, after being missing for six weeks. The Studebaker trembled with the horror of it—the image of backhoes and bulldozers, the cruel glare of sudden terror, of bodies dragged dripping with swamp slime by hostile men on a hot day.

There was no thought of napping after that. Everybody felt the sharp blade of fright. Each pickup truck that passed them was death. Every police car was a slave ship.

They glanced for long metal objects in every window, and every sudden noise was a portent of violence till the auditory cortex could sort it to innocence.

Rose phoned COFO headquarters and they told her to call and give their location every few minutes the rest of the way to Bixden.

They drove straight to the county courthouse and were just sliding into place along wooden benches like church pews when Sam was brought into court. He was in chains, his forehead was wound around with bandages and his broken jaw made his voice sound like he had a mouth full of hot scrambled eggs.

Sam turned around, raising his handcuffs over his head till the nerves in his broken ribs stilettoed his brain, and he sucked air through his teeth. He spotted his friends from New York, and the sudden succor made tears roll out of his eye corners, which the pain of raising his cuffs and chains again would not allow him to brush away.

The prosecutor opened his satchel and shook onto the table a clutch of opened-up cigarette packs with writing on the insides. "Your honor, this morning we confiscated the filth this young man has been writing in our county jail." He held it up before the judge and turned his head away from it as if it were the rotting entrails of a carp.

The judge nodded with his chin toward the wastebasket by his clerk's desk, whereupon the prosecutor lunged forward, tore it and tossed it.

"That's my poetry!" Sam shouted.

"Furthermore, your honor, this agitator has vowed to put out an illegal prison newspaper."

Sam smiled.

"He's smiling, judge, because we've already caught a piece of sedition he passed on to other felons."

Sam had told his jailors he would have *The Bixden Bullshitter* published within forty-eight hours, and kept his word, samisdatting it handwritten from cell to cell on the back of prison forms.

From the rear of the courtroom there was a clack and a stumbling sound. Everyone turned around to observe a young man in full priestly regalia—a clean white clerical collar, a fresh haircut, new jeans with the little white dabs of thread still in place on the upper back, the Scuffcote barely dry on his black engineer boots, and a red International Workers of the World pin with white stars on the lapel of his winter weight jacket, rather out of place in a room where it was about ninety degrees beneath the lazily turning ceiling fan.

Those from New York groaned, "Oh, no, Kliver!"

Andrew Kliver, poet and pal of Sam Thomas, clattered to the front row pew and sat down, sniffing and snerfing a little too much like a junkie, although he swore he had just gone cold turkey at Rikers Island. That claim was met with universal disbelief among those who had just arrived in the yellow Stude. The truth was that he'd stashed his works, a spoon, a tie, and some skag in a red metal Prince Albert tobacco can in a soy field outside Bixden.

Kliver always insisted that being a junkie did not preclude having a social conscience, nor did it forbid direct action and sit-ins, and no motherfucking set of circumstances was going to keep him from coming to Mississippi to help his main man Sam.

Sam looked out at Kliver and shook his head in disapproval. Kliver nodded furiously, his eyes gleaming like a deer above sweet summer flowers. Seeing Kliver made Sam's thoughts drift north a thousand miles to his pad on Avenue A, to his projects and all that he had dropped and

513

left behind.

He wondered if he'd ever see New York again. He had been in the middle of printing a new issue of D.F.S. when he had decided to come to Mississippi, and there were still piles of uncollated pages all over his pad. Ah God, his pad—it bloomed in every detail in his mind even as his attorney was beseeching the judge to set bail—his untended pad, with its groovy collection of jazz, its record player, its Wollensak tape recorder, its film equipment, its books and manuscripts, all up for grabs to whomever should axe his door, such as Kliver.

He missed New York so badly—missed the cafeterias of midtown Broadway which still, in '64, were haunted by legendary ghostly beatniks; he missed Stanley's Bar, Tompkins Square Park, the art galleries, the bookstores, missed the vodka, the grass and the wild sighs of left wing damozels in his lucky arms. He even experienced, shackled and broken-jawed in a klan courtroom, what is possibly the most abstract hunger in all of Western culture— the longing for an evening inside the four-dimensional gestalt field created by the reassuring and confident cadences of a New York beatnik cafe poetry reading!

It was over. His life was wrecked. His pad would be robbed. Kliver would boost his Wollensak and his Bell and Howell. His mimeo. Sell his books. Scatter his fine library. Kill his archives and fine collection of jazz. There was nothing but vomit now, and the vomit was vomiting in the vomit.

Sam's attorney from the National Lawyers Guild argued with all the eloquence of Freedom Summer, but the judge ordered him held without bail until the grand jury should vote its findings. Meanwhile, he was going to be sent out on a chain gang, like some swamp movie from the Thirties, to clear the ditches of Bixden. He was look-ing foward to it. "This person has splashed out of the slop bucket of foreignborn dissension and violence our State has had to endure, and it must stop," the judge droned, and gaveled Sam Thomas out to the gang.

After court, Rose went down the hallway to introduce herself to Sheriff Harme. In a place where a black could get murdered for tone of voice, Harme had a reputation as a moderate. He could at least keep his anger in check talking with voter registration workers.

Harme was not some Holstein in overalls with lips bebrowned from exspumations of Red Man chewing tobacco, but he was tall and skinny, and known for his oyster eyes, that is, red rimmed watery glares kept rube-ous through decades of staph infections from rubbing them with emunctively besmirched fingers. Sheriff Harme was a man of affairs; he owned a restaurant, several farms, a sorghum mill, and he had discovered that good farmland could be covered with subdivisions and sold to guys on the GI Bill. His pride and joy, built atop his father's best bottom land, was the development known as Paw Paw Flats, which, even though the land was thoroughly perpendicular to the midday sun, aped the era and brought to Bixden its first split levels.

Harme kept his tendency to cheat, steal and bully under control through daily recitations in his bedroom mirror from *Genesis*, *Exodus* and *Leviticus*. They called him the preaching Sheriff, and Sundays found him standing at the pulpit begging for Bixden County not to allow the values of rural Mississippi to fall to the devil's bog of whiskey, cards, loose music, trailer camps (he wanted folk in his split levels) and godless tampering with the will of

515

America (i.e., voter registration).

Harme was a typical small-town "line" man. He had a line on everybody. In Bixden, once they had a line on you, you were lined forever. If you were the guy who tossed his cookies at the 1956 homecoming dance, that was it. You could have later walked on water, but the line stayed. The line on Rose was Jew granny race-mixer from New York.

Rose said she didn't believe there was any evidence against Sam. She challenged Harme to list a single shred.

"His very own words that afternoon," replied the Sheriff, lifting his lips into a sneer beneath his oystery eyes at having to discipline himself not to toss this Communist hag from his office. "And his actions, too, against my deputies. Now Sam Thomas, you say he's a friend of yours, he tried to kill one of my best men. And he reviled him with curses right out of the mouth of Absalom!"

Rose asked him what it would take to free Sam.

"Free?" replied Harme. "Sam Thomas will be breaking rocks in Bixden County till he's an old, old man."

Rose's cheeks blanched as white as the white curls at her temple. She was white with determination, white with fear, and white with hatred of this staph-lidded geek. "Sam will be freed," said Farbrente Rose, and strode out to go into action.

Her first stop was just down the hallway at the tax assessor's office where she posed as real estate dealer and acquired a road map of Bixden County. From the county clerk, she cadged a telephone directory. Next was the hardware/dry goods store for flashlights, rope, paper, pencils and a first aid kit.

516

IV
Liquid Gum on Hot Shoes

They parked the Studebaker behind the Freedom
Center in Bixden and brought their luggage inside where
they met Sam's friend, Reverend Charles Pickens. Pickens
arranged for them to borrow a car with Mississippi plates.

Pickens and Sam had become close friends in the moil
of Freedom Summer. Each discovered in the other a love
of poetry. They shouted their favorite lines back and forth
at the most dangerous demonstrations. Dogs, waterhoses
and singing children thus were mixed with shouted fragments of Whitman, Poe, and especially Charles Baude-
laire, of whom both Sam and Pickens knew whole poems
by heart.

Charles Pickens was the leader of a small group of
young left-wing Black ministers who were ready for a vast
shift in the economics of America—they dared to speak of
cradle to grave state-sponsored health care centers even
when voting wasn't yet allowed.

Pickens loved his home state of Mississippi fiercely. That
is, he loved the land beneath the culture. He defended its
rivers, its soils, its rich farmlands and orchards. He was a
ruralist and an environmentalist twenty years before that
word edged into the frightened American dream.

"This state could be such a paradise," said Reverend
Pickens. "There is *such* abundance. We could have farms
for every single family, fishing cooperatives in the gulf,
community orchards! The whole state could be this perfect system of small towns. This could be the America you
dream about—cotton, soy, cattle, sweet potatoes, white
potatoes, onion fields, community forests and endless

517

groves of fruit trees as far as you can see! Enough for every single person—black, brown, yellow, white or red—to prosper! This place can be redeemed!"

You could tell the heartbreak looming for Reverend Pickens, with the white people around him bursting with guilt and hate, and the liberals not able to face the underlying injustice in the economic system. More than anyone, Pickens knew how the sharecropper was bossed by a plantation manager, who was employed by the local bank to run the land it owned; this bank was controlled by a bank in Memphis, which was largely owned by a bank in New York, Cleveland or Chicago, or the land was owned by a life insurance company.

Pickens was a restorer of antique automobiles, and he and Sam were known to putt off to a roadhouse late at night in one of his roadsters. They were thrown together in a death zone, and it made them close friends overnight.

"Sam got off the bus in Jackson," Pickens told them. "He was wearing knee high riding boots, an Australian campaign hat, sunglasses, a goatee, and a T-shirt on which he had spray-painted OUTSIDE AGITATOR.

"You don't joke about things like that around here. Plus he had some issues of his magazine. He wanted to know if he could leave them at the Freedom Center. I got him to mail them right back to the Lower East Side.

"Then he calmed down and he was the best organizer we had, till the other day when they burned Dorville. Sam had a bookstore mail a bunch of poetry books down here and he taught a poetry class at the Freedom School. He had a group of fifteen kids chanting Shakespeare and William Carlos Williams as if they were some sort of ancient choir. He was very, very upset when they burned the church. I was there.

"As you know, we had a rally at Dorville the first thing the following morning. Then the klan came to visit. First, Sam just shouted at the cops to stop them, but the sheriff did absolutely nothing, absolutely nothing. Sam began yelling something which nobody could understand. It took a while for me even to catch it. He was reciting Baude-laire! You would have enjoyed watching Sam perform "La Beauté" from atop Sheriff Harme's car!!! If he'd just stuck with Baudelaire and not called the deputies motherfuckers and nazis, they might have let him be."

Everybody laughed.

While the quartet from New York was at the Freedom Center with Reverend Pickens, Andrew Kliver visited Sheriff Harme posing as Father Aloysius Mughateen, Sam's Catholic priest from childhood, who'd come all the way from Manhattan to save Sam's soul. Kliver wept for Sam in an Irish brogue, brandishing a Bible and mumbling ersatz Latin prayers, and then placed a rosary upon the ink blotter of the horrified sheriff's desk. "You've got ta let me see me boy Sammy! The fires of perdition are at hand for him, if ye don't."

They were so anti-Catholic in Bixden County that even an Andrew Kliver, nodding out and sporting a Wobbly button, looked like an okay priest to them! Therefore, Sheriff Harme, whose piety at least matched the good Father Mughateen's, personally escorted Kliver to Sam's solitary confinement tank.

When they were alone, Sam told Kliver that during the time the deputies had stopped and beaten him on the Farm-to-Market to Dorville, someone had slowed down and possibly stopped—he couldn't see clearly—but that it was right at the moment the cops were beating him, and whoever it was could testify that he had offered absolutely no resistance.

519

Sam smuggled out a note to his friends through Kliver, along with a new issue of *The Bixden Bullshitter*, this one published on pieces of freezer paper. Kliver caught up with Rose and the others as they were leaving Pickens' house. It was quite a memorable experience to watch Frater Mughateen dashing toward them, beads of sweat the size of baby pill bugs on his forehead, and his heavy silver cross jiggle-jangling back and forth on his chest and striking his red Wobbly button with a metallic drumming sound.

Sam's note kicked off the investigation. They had to find whoever it was that had seen him being whacked. Pickens traced on the map the route the deputies took in taking Sam to the slams. Sam's attorney gave them the two deputies' names, and Rose called them trying to get the exact location of the putative violence from Sam. They refused to speak with her.

Rose asked Pickens for a second automobile. She wanted to send out two teams to stop at each house along the ten-mile road from the burned Dorville Church to the Bixden jail. Past Blast and Cynthia Pruitt would begin from Bixden, and Rose and Talbot would drive to Dorville and work their way back and meet Cynthia and Past Blast somewhere in the middle.

Pickens loaned Cynthia and Past Blast one of his prize restored automobiles, a showroom perfect shiny white 1949 Dodge Coronet with Fluid Drive and a wide white chrome-edged sun visor above the outside of the front window.

It was a beautiful car, old even in 1964, and as far as Pickens was concerned it belonged in the Museum of Modern Art along with the Calders, the Giacomettis and the shapes of Kandinsky.

"Just *look* at the curve on the left edge of that rear door!" Pickens exclaimed. "As beautiful as any in Brancusi or Arp. Just look at it!"

Past Blast and Cynthia soon were alone on a loony backwoods road where they did not want Blacks even to smile. Past Blast stayed in the Dodge while Cynthia walked from house to house when houses were close, or drove her onward to the next one. It was very unpleasant. One woman sicced her dogs on Cynthia, another told her she'd be dead in just a couple of days, so why not go back to the Jews where she belonged. Finally there was someone who had heard something, but just then her husband appeared, and she forgot at once. While they were at one home, a deputy arrived and pulled his revolver on them, "Don't you be bothering these people." No one would give them water, and it was so hot that the matches in the pocket of Past Blast's jeans were too wet to light.

Talbot and Rose were quiet on the way to the church in Dorville. No one had to remind them that the three murdered COFO men had gone to a burned church when they were seized and killed back in June.

Dorville's black section had a general store, a garage, some houses, a one-room elementary school built by setting aside some of the cotton crop each fall, and the church. The matriarch of the congregation was Retha Hubb, a woman about sixty-five whose own house, where Rose and Talbot were to stay the night, was just a few hundred feet from the chars.

Trouble was an old acquaintance of Retha Hubb. Already she was raising money to rebuild the church where she'd met her husband, where she had been married, and where some day she wanted her coffin to be carried up against the altar. Her grandfather had been lynched back before World War I for refusing to sell a choice piece of land to a white farmer. Her husband, Wilson Hubb, had been one of the founders of the local NAACP chapter, and was beaten every year for showing up to pay his poll tax and register.

Last year, Retha and Wilson had helped CORE in a "Freedom Vote" for the governor's race. Those not allowed to register voted in the Freedom Vote. At that point they were the wealthiest black family in Dorville, but then their store was bombed and no bank would give them credit to rebuild. They had trouble selling their cotton. An application for a federal crop loan was torn up in their faces, so that it took just a few months for a fragile prosperity built up over forty-five years to be stomped in the muck, and Retha Hubb had to take work tending the children and cleaning the houses of whites.

Last fall, the sheriff had arrested Wilson Hubb on a pretext and hauled him away in the wire cage paddy wagon. He slipped while placing his knee at the edge of the cage door so as to pull himself up and inside. He fell backwards, his legs inside, but his body hanging towards the ground and his head almost in the roadway. The deputy kicked him and Mr. Hubb raised his hands and arms to protect his face. The deputy's blackjack whacked downward onto the stomach and skull. He was never well and five months later he was dead.

Retha had her doubts about words such as "We Shall Overcome." Like many of her own generation and generations before, she was beginning to look forward to fluffing up her pillows and gliding to the Beyond. It gave her a tremble to look out her kitchen window to see the stone markers in the graveyard where she hoped to find her rest charred now like an examination of ravens.

Before Talbot the Great and Rose began their door to door canvassing on the road to Bixden, they wanted to sift through the wreckage. They half expected to find clues as they lifted aside sharp pieces of tin from the roof and half burned wooden beams whose sides had charred in odd chunklike shapes like rows of small black bricks in a Dantean mortar. There was nothing in the ruins. They searched the grounds for dynamite wires or a gas can. Nothing.

Talbot, whose own parents and grandparents were ministers, knew what a tragedy he was viewing—that the church had not just sprung to life in an Amish-type weekend church raising. It had taken generations of anguished work and scraping together of resources by enslaved and impoverished people to build the Dorville church. There was a personal sacrifice invisibly inscribed upon every single beam and board.

The first version of Dorville had been built just after the Civil War, a frame of pine poles with a roof of brush and pine straw. That church was called the "Brush Arbor." The Brush Arbor was followed by a log church, with its cracks packed with pine pitch. Next was a "Box church" with rough-hewn timbers, and finally, about 1900, they raised enough through church suppers and the tithing of crops to build a well-joisted fane with marble steps, a small bell tower and some stained glass windows in the hallway.

Now there was nothing but the 1870 foundation posts of the Brush Arbor. Talbot spotted jutting from the pile of scalded posts the tiny claw of a sparrow. Talbot pulled away the timbers, and freed it. He and Rose buried it on the edge of the cemetery. He knew it was his own sanity down with the wings and feathers in the dirt.

Then they went slowly door to door, receiving the same hostility as Past Blast and Cynthia. People sometimes hid in their living rooms and refused to answer the door, or menaced them with shotguns; threw slops at them. They learned nothing and came back late in the afternoon to Retha Hubb's house to wash and have supper.

Retha showed them a klan flyer left on her porch last night. DON'T PUT UP RACEMIXERS OR YOU TOO WILL BURN, it said.

"It was the same engine sound," Retha said, "with tappets clicking like they were going out, same sound as when they put out the leaflets before the burning." The klan had been dropping hate notes on her porch all summer long.

Retha was defiant. Her pearl earrings shook so violently that they could have flung rain drops off them, but Talbot and Rose insisted they sleep somewhere else. They decided that Rose would stay in a building behind the church where they stored tables and chairs for church socials. Other Freedom Summer people had stayed there, and it wasn't likely the klan would come back just to burn a shed. Talbot would sleep in the field far enough from the road so that a flashlight could not find him.

Talbot hid the automobile while Retha and Rose carried bedding to the shed and masked with dish cloths any hole where lantern light could escape. Retha came back with a pitcher of lemonade and a pail of water, and then walked home across the field as Talbot carried his sleeping bag to the orchard, afraid to use the flashlight. When an auto slowed on the road, he flattened to the ground.

In a few minutes Talbot returned to the shed to get some water to brush his teeth. They washed their arms side by side in matching white porcelainized bowls. Then

Talbot peeled off his T-shirt and washed his shoulders and chest. Rose had gotten ashes on her blouse and removed it also to rinse it. Cleanliness and sleuthery march together, especially in the sticks, so it was important to stay as neat as possible. Talbot started to leave while Rose washed her blouse, but she motioned him to stay. She put it on semi-wet to dry in the heat.

After that, they walked out to the orchard where they could safely talk.

All afternoon Past Blast and Cynthia worked the Farm-to-Market Road looking for witnesses, and when it became dark and therefore dangerous they returned to Reverend Pickens' house by the Bixden Freedom Center. Past Blast was exhausted and fell asleep.

Sam had told Pickens hours of anecdotes about Cynthia Pruitt, and Pickens was eager to meet her. There was a cafe down the street where Freedom Summer went into a different mode late at night. Blacks and whites could mingle without worrying about the police and society's sneers. There was beer, greens, grits, chicken, and dancing to a juke box.

Talbot and Cynthia went there for dinner and a couple of beers. Then they returned to Pickens' pad. By then Cynthia was standing close to him and reaching out to touch his arm now and then as each talked about their lives.

Pickens kept staring at the spot just above her breasts where Sam had once rubbed his Ancient Egyptian Skin Cream. "Sam told me the story about his famous lotion," he said and reached out to touch her throat just above it. Cynthia looked down at the spot. The button on her blouse had somehow come undone. She pulled it open a couple of inches more, and said, "Right here." Pickens slid his hand down and touched the now reddening spot where Sam had rubbed the myrrh-sweetened Muffins of Sebek. Then, he reached further down into her cutaway denim, and ran his fingers across the buds of her breasts, which were as electric and hand-buzzing as the bees of lyric poetry.

Cynthia was hesitant. She felt guilt, and Reverend Pickens too felt the natural qualms of a minister in whose mind the faint strictures of the Seventh Commandment, not to mention the Tenth, were drumming. He also felt the guilt of a birddog, since he knew of Sam's on-and-off affair with Cynthia.

Pickens' wife and children were staying with her mother in North Carolina during the violence, which made his own guilt as thick as the rough black binding on a family Bible. Baptist guilt commixed with Catholic guilt, however, has a lot of nervous energy attached to it, and so the lonely Catholic girl who hungered for justice and the minister who hungered for freedom combined hungers and combined guilts and lay down in front of a rattling floor fan. Pickens was loath to take off his clothes in the event a sprint to avoid the klan should become necessary.

As guilty and already repentant as she was, Cynthia showed Reverend Pickens, during a five or six second period, her greatest athletic skill. Had there been world records for undressing, Cynthia could have been on the Olympic team. That is, she blessed the bedrooms of her lovers with ecdysiastical microtime. As soon as she was convinced a fuck was underway, she became naked in a white blurr of rapidity, and her shirt, jeans and underwear seemed to float down together into a pile by the bed. In fact, her underwear was still parachuting upon the pile as she began to kiss Pickens with the wild abandon only a danger zone like Freedom Summer could engender.

If there was guilt at Reverend Pickens' place in Bixden, there was no guilt at all out beneath the stars by the ruins of the Dorville church where Talbot and Rose sat talking side by side on Talbot's sleeping bag.

Talbot went back to the shed and brought back the lemonade. They rubbed insect repellent on each other's arms and faces. Rose leaned into Talbot's chest while he soothed her back with his hand. He thought of the time they'd kissed at Louise's New Year's party. So did she.

He swallowed, took nerve, and bent close to kiss. First they were shy and tentative, and then, in the spirit of Freedom Summer, threw into kissing the same passion they threw into urging the vote. There were many minutes of carezza. She soothed his wide back and arms, he her frail shoulders, gulped, hesitated, then slid his hands upon her voluptuous breasts, the nipples of which sprang up beautifully as did their rings of satellitic pinkness hungering to be kissed.

Talbot worried about the klan strafing the field with flashlights, but Rose pointed out that if they moved the bag a few feet, then a patch weeds would shield them. That accomplished, she pulled him prone for weed shielded smooching.

Rose sat up and unbuttoned her dress, setting it aside on the crickety grass. Like Charles Pickens back in Bixden, Talbot was reluctant to remove his trousers totally, in case he had to sprint thence on the nonce. "Get them off," ordered Farbrente Rose.

She slid his hand over his stomach, asking him to let her touch the scars on his knee from the Freedom Ride. She

527

traced them, with his hand guiding her wrist, then she broke her wildly pulsing hand away, and traced up his thigh to his stomach hair, till white knuckles slid over his cock, white over dark beneath the hot gray-dark of the Mississippi sky.

She grasped her skinny sharp-angled knees on both sides of his wide back and guided him inside her. Talbot was afraid she would break or be bruised. After all, she was seventy years old. "Don't worry about me," whispered Farbrente, wiggling from side to side with a dexterity that nearly made Talbot come as quickly as a schoolboy.

Crickets by the thousands were rubbing their legs together in the barrens and the tuned throats of the frogs in the pond the next field over were going "doanh! doanh!" Above them were beautiful crackling webs of heat lightning, and there was strange synchronicity in the flash of countless fireflies in the Mississippi meadow, plus a couple of clicks, far distant, of the night time telephoto lens taking in the event for the files.

Back in Bixden, Pickens and Cynthia were fucking as if their energy could lift the world to a better place.

Pickens, whose ears were normally supernally tuned to the slightest sound outside the Freedom Center, did not hear the door slam, nor the hollow sound of the can lid being unscrewed, nor the splash of gasoline down the Brancusi lines of his perfect '49 Dodge, nor the roar of sudden conflagration, and the crackling sound of hot white paint and catabolic seat cushions.

v

A Phone Call From Alabama

The next morning Pickens somehow got his torched

Dodge started, and, using a wooden milk crate as a front seat, drove it to Dorville with an important message for Talbot the Great from the Meridian COFO office.

The speedometer had melted into a misshapen oval that looked like a cracked Duchamp piece. The sunvisor was rippled and the windshield was thoroughly shattered, with the rubberized edging flapping in Pickens' face as he raced to Dorville.

Talbot was to call Johnny Ray Slage in Alabama. It was life or death. Talbot, though very, very suspicious, nevertheless went with Pickens to Bixden and called him. "How'd you get this number?" he asked.

"You sent me those articles you wrote. It said in the *Village Voice* you were going to be in Mississippi. In the one in *Liberation,* you told about your mother and father's church in New York. Till you sent those last articles I didn't even know your last name."

Talbot had used as return address only his first name and his box number at Stuyvesant Station. One took care when sending radical publications into a Klan house.

"I called a bunch of Jenkins in New York. Finally I got your mom. She gave me a number in Jackson. I called Jackson and they told me the Bixden number. Mr. Talbot," he continued, "they planning to do in another church, in fact a bunch of them. I heard it myself."

"Wait a minute. Let's go back to the start. Where am I calling? Is this your house or what?"

"Nah. My Aunt Mattie's house." Talbot knew what that was. After returning from Birmingham last September, he'd begun the Freedom Packets to Slage. After a couple of mailings, he'd received a letter asking future packets to be sent in care of a Mattie Farlo.

He asked if Johnny had read Martin King's book. "Not

529

yet, but I been listening to that Bob Dylan record all the time. I like 'Masters of War' and 'Hard Rain's A-Gonna Fall,' but my favorite is 'Blowin' in the Wind.' I been playing the guitar too."

Talbot had mailed him an old acoustic guitar that once belonged to Bob Dylan. Dylan had given it to someone in the Lower East Side, from whom Talbot had bought it. Johnny Ray had already taught himself most of Dylan's tunes on the guitar and was combing his hair in a pre-hippie rockabilly swirl.

"My daddy caught me listening to Dylan. I thought he was gonna tack me up on the side of the garage with the coon skins. 'What blowin'? What wind!?' daddy said, 'The only wind blowin' around here is on your hide!' He went out back and pulled down a willow switch and almost tore off the back of my legs.

"When he was out back cutting the switch, I fooled him. I hid the records up in some of mom's church records. Daddy tore and stomped the records, but he got mom's instead."

It was the only time in the conversation that Johnny Ray Slage laughed.

"My daddy shaved my haid when he caught me with the guitar. That's when I got my Aunt Mattie to get the stuff you send. I wrote you her address."

"And you called my mother?"

"Yes sir, it's important. They're planning another one—this one has been moved to Mississippi, with dynamite and everything. But they gon' run it from here."

"To kill people?"

"Nah. They told my dad be sure and only get empty churches. The government gets too excited otherwise."

"Dynamite?"

530

"They had a meeting at our place. They came from all over Alabama and Mississippi. They told my daddy Mississippi was being invaded by Jews and Communists and they needed help. My daddy's group decided to ride in from Alabama. They gon' burn out a whole list here of Nig—Negro churches."

"What churches?"

The boy read slowly from a notepad. "They's in Atherbee, St. Lo, Challis, Slayton Creek and Starkdale. The one called Atherbee Zion is gon' get fired up first, because that's where the Communists are trying to take over. They said that one's tonight."

"And Mr. Talbot," Johnny ended, "If my dad ever finds out someone told him out, that person's dead. I've seen it happen."

"I promise your name will never be mentioned to anybody. When can we talk again?"

"I guess tomorrow, around the same time."

That morning Retha Hubb had done house cleaning in Bixden. While Talbot was talking to Johnny Ray Slage, Retha returned and told Rose Snyder about something she had heard.

"You ought to go see Doc Ferry. I think he saw something."

"Who?"

"Doc Ferry. He's the mailman. I clean his house. He was out on the route near Corlew's pecan grove when he saw the paddy truck. Doc Ferry watched it all. He said they pulled Sam out, and he just slumped down on the ground and they were pounding on him."

"No resistance?"

"Doc said he was just in a pile doing nothing."

531

Quicksand

Talbot, Cynthia, Past Blast and Pickens drove back to Dorville after the call to Slage. There was still a few minutes left of morning cool, so they met with Rose in the field in back of the kitchen shed, where they were sure no one could hear them.

Everyone was too nervous to eat the breakfast they needed for a day dodging death. Cynthia broke open a packet of sweet buns but the first bite was like dry hay in her mouth. Past Blast poured Wheaties out of a small box into his hand and chewed with his eyes closed. Talbot snacked on his cuticles, and Rose spilled half the coffee she'd made at Retha's for everyone when her thermos kept trembling above the cups.

Cynthia had dreamt every night since coming to Mississippi of being raped and chopped up by nightriders. Last night, after Pickens' Dodge had burned, she couldn't sleep till 5 A.M., at which time the lynch mob entered her mind and stayed till she screamed herself awake at seven.

Past Blast had been inflicting five or ten minute rages on his friends, but this morning he had slipped into a kind of passivity glaze-out. For all his bombast and methedrine nihilism, his hipness and coolness, Past Blast, the guy who felt that America was a comic opera of psychopaths, that the flag was fluttering above something soon to pass beneath the boots of rubble, Past Blast, whose eyes only looked out at things to picture them smoldering and burning in the shriek of revolution, Past Blast, who lived for the tornadoes of tear-down, for the anarcho-tanks blasting down Broadway to grab up City Hall for the Tomorrows—Past Blast was not reacting well to chaos. Past Blast could *conceive* a good chaos, but *actual* chaos, with its blood, guts and flames, drained his vim.

Rose forced enough coffee into him, combined with sharp words, to dezombie him enough at least to drive.

Reverend Pickens was the only one among them who had to remain in Mississippi when Freedom Summer ended, and he too was rattled and distracted because he was worried about his house and his family. Would his wife and kids be burned to death? And the Freedom Center next to his house—was it too destined for a jumble of chars?

So the five of them gathered in various states of fright, enervation, catatonia, pyrophobia, anger and Yankee stubbornness in the field behind Retha Hubb's church. They needed to freeze time, but time that morning seemed to accelerate and they had to make decisions in a few minutes that should have taken a couple of days.

Here's what they decided to do. They knew there was no protection for them, not from the sheriff, not from the FBI, not from the 1,000 Freedom Summer volunteers, and certainly not from the people of Bixden County. The only answer was to play the WHOLE WORLD IS WATCHING card, and to get warning letters to the wire services and to the reporters who had come to Mississippi to cover the violence.

Talbot lugged to the field his portable typewriter, set it on a clump of tall bent-over grass, rolled a mimeograph stencil into the carriage, and began typing a press release.

"Should I use Ethrom Slage's actual name?" he asked his friends.

There was silence. Talbot swallowed, and began typing:

533

A group of Ku Klux Klanners operating out of Tattersall, Alabama, located near Birmingham, and led by Ethrom Slage of Box 93, Tattersall, Alabama, will enter Mississippi tonight as part of a plot to burn and destroy the following churches...

Talbot listed tonight's target as Atherbee Zion and called for the police, the newspapers, *The New York Times* and the FBI to protect the church.

Cynthia proofread the stencil just before Talbot was to take it to Bixden and mimeo it at the Freedom Center. It gave her an idea.

"I think I know how to save the church," she said. "Let's go there tonight and hold an all night vigil. We'll surround the church with lights. We'll get kerosene lanterns, smudge pots, flashlights, whatever we can find. Maybe we can rent a gasoline generator somewhere."

Everybody agreed.

"We'll invite the sheriff, the FBI, the newspapers, the Justice Department, anybody who will help ward off the klan."

They looked at one another, grasped hands in a circle, and sang.

Cynthia and Past Blast drove away to Jackson to rent a truck and the electric generator, and to locate some lights.

Rose and Pickens drove to Doc Ferry's house. Doc and his wife May were the town liberals, that is, they read widely and subscribed to magazines such as *The Nation* and *The Progressive*. May ordered weird books on taboo subjects such as Freud and psychodrama from New York publishers that enraged Nell and Harry Harme, the sheriff's brother and sister-in-law, who ran the post office.

Doc Ferry was a pleasant, round faced, high blood

pressure sort of chap, with fine, blond hair "slicked down like an onion" as they said in Bixden. He had just returned from his mail route and he and May were arranging pecks of tomatoes for their roadside produce stand, when Rose Snyder and Charles Pickens arrived.

Doc's very nickname showed how "lined" he was. They called him that because he had once attended a medical school which had a fancy new dissection lab where the cadaver would rise up out of a refrigerated vault in the floor, doors swinging upward and outward, accompanied by a whirring sound like an automobile lift. The dread of hearing the whirr was almost enough to cause Ferry to i-yi-yi out of there, but when one afternoon a couple of classmates did Double Dutch with intestines to a roar of laughter from other pre-meds eating their lunch on the edge of the slab, Doc dropped out of school and was viewed as a coward in Bixden ever after. His father retired as a rural deliveryman and the job was handed to Doc just as it had been handed from grandfather to father.

Doc was afraid even to speak to Rose. He invited her with an almost inaudible set of whispers out of the side of his mouth to meet him down the road, where he denied seeing Sam beaten.

He was lying. "How can you remain silent?" Rose asked. "You people have to start standing up to defend your town. A whole army of sheets is coming to kill people in this county. *How can you* remain silent?"

"If I were to testify in court, how long do you think I could live here before my house would be just a pile of two-by-fours? I just can't do it."

A very discouraged Rose Snyder was dropped off by Reverend Pickens in Bixden where she tracked down the deputies. They were very hostile and threatened to arrest her for tampering with witnesses. Late in the afternoon, she and Pickens drove dejectedly to join the vigil at Atherbee Zion church.

At the end of the morning, Talbot Jenkins had drawn a Triangle of Evil on a map of Mississippi—eighty miles to a leg, from Bixden to Jackson to Laurel and back to Bixden—a 240 mile triangle he had to cover in time to get to Atherbee before nightfall.

After he mimeographed the press release, Talbot brought a copy to Sheriff Harme, who was busy sketching next Sunday's sermon and hated to be wrested from this task by a Communist COFO spook. Talbot was brief. "We *know* that at least two more churches are going to be fired by the klan. The first one's tonight. It's in Bixden County, and what are you going to do to protect it?"

Harme did not believe him. "Many of us in law enforcement know otherwise. These colored folks are so beguiled and riled up by outsiders that they are burning their own churches!"

Talbot resisted the impulse to haul the sheriff's pistol from the holster and slap him across the face with it. "You *have* to take action. Surely you don't condone murder," he said.

"You can't eggspeck me to believe the word of a bunch of, of, Freedom Riders!"

Talbot decided to stay another minute. "My source is from inside the klan itself. The Justice Department knows about it. And the FBI. Surely, you don't want the FBI all over your county, so why don't you take charge."

The sheriff exploded, looking around to see if his secretary was listening. "That's a pitchfork of pig shit if I ever heard a word from an idiot. How could someone like

536

you—a godless outsider almost as dark as an innertube—know anything about anything?"

Talbot the Great called D.C. and spoke with his pal in the Justice Department, the one who had told him it was Ethrom Slage who had crushed his knee during the Freedom Ride. Talbot ran down the information from Johnny Ray, then asked, "Bart, is there anyway you could check to see if Sheriff Jim Harme of Bixden County—that's where I'm working, and see if he's in the klan? After what happened to Chaney, Goodman and Schwerner, you must be compiling some sort of list."

Bart told Talbot he couldn't promise anything, but to wait by the phone. A few minutes later there was a ring, that, although he expected it, made Talbot jump with surprise. "I called the Meridian office," said Bart. "Told them the A.G. himself wanted the information. They bullshitted me that it had to be fed through Hoover, but finally they relented. They tell me your man Harme is the freshly inaugurated Exalted Cyclops of the Bixden klavern. I'd stay away from the Bixden County jail if I were you."

Talbot drove out of Bixden along Tallahaga Creek through the system of small towns that Reverend Pickens wanted to transform into a democratic socialist zone of abundance. First in Jackson, and then in Laurel, Talbot begged the FBI to bring into Bixden County some of their black cars with long antennae which so enraged and intimidated the racists.

"We'll look into it."

"What do you mean, 'we'll look into it'?"

"Just that."

Talbot dropped off statements with the wire services, and found a motel in Jackson where some of the reporters were staying. He slid flyers under their doors and used a pay phone to call the *Times* office in N.Y.C. His mother agreed to pester the *N.Y. Post* till they paid attention to the story, and to tell the *Village Voice*.

He did what he could, and felt that he had failed. Around dusk Talbot sped toward Atherbee Zion, praying that his friends were safe. He had hoped he would be returning with a squadron of dark FBI guard cars, but the only thing he brought was a migraine, an empty stomach and bloody cuticles.

VII
When the Bats Flapped Awake

There was a moment just before darkness when the bats flapped awake at Atherbee Zion church. They hopped to the horizontal slats of the attic vent, according to an order of dominance, and one by one began to squeeze through the narrow slits till their wings dangled free, then down they dropped, freefalling for two or three feet, followed by a floggle floggle floggle sound of wings lifting them high over the church and off for a night of moths, gnats, mosquitoes and fireflies.

A mile from Atherbee he saw the flames. Everybody thought the slime would attack at the coward's hour of 4 A.M., but instead they had struck right after sunset. "Harme!" Talbot shouted, slugging the steering wheel and almost veering by mistake into the ditch.

The grounds of the burning church were deserted. He leaped from the car and ran as close to the heat as he could, losing his eyebrows and eyelashes as he screamed for his friends. "Rose! Cynthia! Past Blast! Pickens!"

He thought they might be trapped inside, perhaps

wounded and bleeding, so he pulled his shirt across his face and crawled even closer to the whistling crackles, thinking maybe he could haul someone out.

The bats that had so recently lifted out of the attic were diving at sharp angles above him, turning back and forth every few feet to snip moth bodies free from their wings with their razory teeth—with the wings tumbling and fluttering downward like pieces of paper into the red spectra.

Talbot was ready to die. He lay unthinking of his own safety on the ground, screaming and pummeling the dark Mississippi soil, cursing the FBI, the sheriff, himself, the klan, his fate, America, and even the burning church.

He heard an engine start and the squealing of wheels, followed by what sounded like shots and curses, and, if he could believe his ears, wild laughter.

Andrew Kliver's wild laughter.

Kliver had wreaked revenge on Ethrom Slage. Unknown to any of his friends, Kliver had sneaked into a nearby woods and lay in wait. Kliver was not a pacifist, and brought with him a gun. His vantage spot was on the opposite side of the church from where the klan men did their work, but when Slage's truck with kraft paper covering the Alabama license plates careened past Kliver, Kliver shot out the wheels so that the floggle floggle of Slage's tires matched the floggle floggle of the bats above the fire. Slage abandoned his truck, ran to another one and disappeared.

Kliver tossed his revolver into a drainage ditch and jumped up and down in exultation by the dead pickup truck. He trotted over to the edge of the fire, and seared his hands pulling out a flaming rafter which he carried back to the pickup and jammed against the seat covers to

539

torch them. Piles of klan flyers on the floor seemed to explode with smoke and roily red. Kliver stood dancing by the roar—with his red Wobbly pin agleam, and his watery eyes wild with triumph.

Then Talbot heard other voices. He sprang to his feet and dashed forward as when he was a football star—head low, back parallel to the ground, and knees high—to his car. If the noises were from the klan, he wanted to be able to run over a few of them. But it was his friends! He motioned for them to keep low, and to crawl. He loaded them aboard, then picked up jubilant Andrew Kliver by Slage's pickup and fled to the Freedom Center in Bixden, just as the sheriff, the FBI and a station wagon full of reporters arrived.

"It took till almost sundown to get stuff organized," Cynthia told them. "Charles had to spend all day getting the congregation to agree to the vigil. The okay came about six and we began setting up. We had a generator from Jackson, and borrowed some spotlights and light trees from the Freedom Summer Theater. We were stringing the lights around the church when the two trucks without license plates drove up."

"They told us to lie down and not to look at them. One guy planted the charge against the foundation, lit the fuse and ran. We all crawled away as fast as we could. It was a terrible explosion. I think it might have perforated my eardrums. They had pulled their T-shirts over their faces as masks, leaving their beer bellies exposed. They looked like fools. The place was already totally wrecked. The only thing standing was the front wall and the bell tower. They splashed it with gas, threw a match on it, and left. Right then you came. You don't know how close you were to them."

The next morning Doc and May Ferry learned about Atherbee Zion, and Doc went over to the Freedom Center after his mail to speak with Rose. He was willing to tell the grand jury what he had seen. Rose brought Ferry to Sam's attorneys, which now numbered three, including the future mayor of a major Eastern city.

Sam's team threatened to go into federal court if Doc Ferry were not called before the jury.

The morning of his testimony, Doc and May stopped first at their church to pray, but the minister had locked it against them. He was sketching the layout for an invitation to a Christian Endeavor Cake Walk and had no time for praying with peace-creeps and liberals.

From there it was five minutes to the courthouse, where the nearby Clovis Cafe emptied out, with a line of crackers loping toward the side door of the court house, and Dale, Cecil, Spake, Clyde, Roman, Jed and Hongo—the boys of '64, began spraying Doc's hood with hockers—katooh! katooh! katooh! Inside the court there was a long wait while Doc Ferry chainsmoked in the corridor, smoothing out his onion-colored hair about every forty-five seconds, and visiting the bathroom on the quarter hour escorted by a deputy, till at last he had his say before the jury.

As a result, Sam's charges were lowered from assault to refusing to obey an officer and resisting arrest. A lab analysis of the putative pot frags found in Sam's pockets revealed them to have been from a Bull Durham pouch, probably planted by one of the deputies.

Rose put up the bail money and Sam was set free that night. Sam was no longer in any mood to compromise his beliefs. His poetry workshop at the Freedom School was set for the next day. He announced the topic: the erotic poetry of Theophile Gautier.

541

Pickens was not about to risk the Bixden Freedom Center for such a flame-producing topic. Instead, Sam's friends urged him to leave the state. He was too hot. Too dangerous. Too controversial. His presence alone could insure the Center was torched. People could get killed because of Sam and Gautier.

They offered him an airplane ticket, but, defiantly, he opted for the sputtering Studebaker, which he insisted parade through Bixden the next morning so he could wave to the boys outside the Clovis Cafe. The Stude then clanked out of town up a long red clay slope to the North, with Past Blast at the wheel. Talbot and Cynthia remained behind to work on final plans to attend the Democratic Convention in Atlantic City with the Mississippi Freedom Delegation.

Reverend Pickens, Cynthia and Talbot followed them for a few miles in the burned white Dodge, which he had already sanded and made gray with primer paint.

The churches and the sheriff's subdivision at Paw Paw Flats could be seen in the rearview mirror. Sam asked Past Blast to pull over by the Bixden cemetery at the summit of the hill. They walked among the stones, and stood beneath a pecan tree, staring down at the village.

Sam thanked his friends for coming to save him. "I would have been on the chain gang till I was fifty if it weren't for you," he said, and brushed tears to the sides of his eyes.

He raised his canteen as high above his shoulders as his broken rib would allow, and saluted the jail, the church, the courthouse. "Bixden! This is the 1960s talking to you. We are the scissors of Matisse, the bugle of Joshua, the sax of Coltrane, the wail of Ginsberg, the orations of Emma

Goldman, and the illumination of Blake! Love, Energy and Righteousness are sloshing on your shores, Bixden!"

Sam took a long drink from his canteen, then threw his arm around Rose Snyder, and the Studebaker went back to New York. "Come, o sixties!" Sam shouted to his friends who were waving goodbye. "Come and take us on thy thrilling ride!"

CITADEL UNDERGROUND provides a voice
to writers whose ideas and styles veer
from convention. The series is
dedicated to bringing back into print
lost classics and to publishing new
works that explore pathbreaking and
iconoclastic personal, social, literary,
musical, consciousness, political,
dramatic and rhetorical styles.

For more information, please write to:

CITADEL UNDERGROUND
Carol Publishing Group
600 Madison Avenue
New York, New York 10022